A Dance of Shadow

A REIGN OF SHADOW NOVEL

ML WISSING

ISBN Paperback 978-1-961078-63-5
ISBN Hardback 978-1-961078-62-8
ISBN e-Book   978-1-961078-64-2

Printed in the United States of America.

Springer Literary House LLC
6260 Lavender Cloud Place
Las Vegas, Nevada 89122, USA

www.springerliteraryhouse.com

DEDICATION

My loving family, your support makes everything possible. I love you so much! Thanks for listening to my rambling of ideas, reading the manuscript aloud to find errors, and helping me find solutions when I am lost in the shadows.

To my Flightline family, your role in this journey cannot be overlooked. You've been my creative partners, sounding board, and inspiration. Thank you for your unwavering support and belief.

To my publishing and marketing teams, you've helped me achieve something I never thought I could accomplish. I've soared higher and further than I thought my wings could carry me. I look forward to continuing this journey and sharing it with the world.

To Marcus Ranum, for permission to use your photography in the book cover.

Thank you to my amazing readers who do so much to keep me going!

Your feedback, excited conversations, questions, theories, and comments inspire me daily.

Welcome back to Hinestra!

For Roger 'Chief' Roop.

You will never be forgotten. Fly high.

'Til Vahalla, brother.

ALSO BY ML WISSING

MILITARY POETRY

Fragments

STANDALONE BOOKS

The Game

THE WORLD OF HINESTRA

Lost in Shadow (a *Reign of Shadow* novel)

A Dance of Shadow (a *Reign of Shadow* novel)

THE DARKNESS CALLS

with Amber N.P. Mays

To Hell and Back

ANTHOLOGY

Healing Words: A Journey Through the Ladder UPP

PRAISES FOR LOST IN SHADOW
(A REIGN OF SHADOW NOVEL)

"From the first page, I was hooked by its unique world-building and the layers of intrigue woven into the story. It's the kind of book that keeps you turning the pages late into the night, and trust me, it's worth every second. The highlight I loved about this book is how it seamlessly mixes action with emotional depth. The storyline is fast-paced, yet you still feel the weight of the characters' choices and the world they live in. The author has done a masterful job of creating a world that feels alive, despite being overshadowed by darkness. The way the characters grow and evolve throughout the story is particularly impressive. This book is a fantastic read for anyone who enjoys immersive fantasy worlds, gripping tension, and a dash of emotional struggle. I found this book to be an experience, not just a story one that lingers long after you finish reading. The writing is sharp, vivid, and keeps you grounded in a world of shadows and light. I can't wait to read more from this author. Overall, an immersive and thrilling read! Get your copy today and dive into the captivating world of *Lost in Shadow* (a *Reign of Shadow* novel) by ML Wissing. Happy Reading!"

— newbooksreviewer.com

"I wasn't sure what to expect. Quite often I find certain tropes leaned on too much or stories reaching predictable conclusions. While I respect that it's more about the journey, some journeys just don't break into something original. *Lost in Shadow* is truly unique, breaking free from tropes and ordinary story plots with unique ways of forming both interesting and believable character arcs but the story arc itself never revealed too much of itself until it was the right time. The pacing is beautifully done, not forced. The characters naturally play their part in the story and reflect accurately upon what's happening. It's all so incredibly believable and immersive. This is helped by the author's deliberate and precise method of describing things, and overall the story being genuinely an interesting one to get into. I cannot wait for book two!"

— poet Nate New-Castle

"I am really enjoying the story! It takes fantasy and helps interject enough realism that I find myself really getting pulled into the character stories and world! Hoping the next book comes sooner rather than later!"

— reader review

"I am an avid reader, but fantasy has never been a genre that has interested me. I did not expect to really get into this book; even put off starting it. I was especially leery, knowing that it involved a society that had its own lexicon, and thought that would overwhelm and confuse me. But once I started it, I did not want to put it down! Great characters and storyline. I am very much looking forward to the next book!"

— reader review

"This book is a coming-of-age fantasy that features 4 POVs (points of view)! This is a first in a new fantasy series. I overall loved the book. The beginning was a tad "slow" for my usual reads, but it did not take long for it to pick up. This book very much gives me *Eragon* and LotR (*Lord of the Ring*) vibes in terms writing and fantasy. There are interesting creatures and a unique society within this book. The front of the book contains pages of information to help understand the language and the society!"

— reader review

"Very enjoyable read. The words flow so easily you'll look up and find yourself several chapters in before you know it."

— reader review

"I loved reading this book! It's a fantasy world but feels so real. She's built an entire world with language, culture, and traditions. As a veteran, I appreciated the amount of training and education that happens for some of the characters, and I felt a connection through that. I can't wait for the next book! Congratulations, ML Wissing!"

— reader review

"This book is amazing! It has wonderful characters that are totally relatable, especially if you are a veteran or current military member. The world may be fantasy but it feels very real. I'm so excited to read the next installment!"

— reader review

"ML Wissing put me behind the eyes of the characters I was reading. She was able to get inside the minds of her characters, bring to mind the terrors that they see, the emotions that they feel, in such a vivid fashion that you feel that you are the one experiencing the story. Few authors, even the greats, are able to do that to that degree. She is not Tolkien or R.A. Salvadore, but I believe she will get to that level."

— reader review

"My favorite part? The whole damn book: it kept me on my toes! It is like the *Shannara Chronicles* and *Game of Thrones* had a baby."

— reader review

"My favorite part is the *Glimpse into The World of Hinestra* in the front; with all the languages and rankings, it makes the world come alive!

— reader review

A Glimpse into the World of Hinestra

ESELUND
DRAGONLANDS (UAK'HANI)
Blood Temple
N'TYNGAH
NAR'SHADA
Waride
Thraxxian Crater
SHADOWGULF MOUNTAINS
AERUKATAN OCEAN
ATERMIR
MERIDIAH
D'LCEE
CENTURA
EXONESIS
Akima Bay
IRONFALL MOUNTAINS
CASTET
The Grove
IKNARAS
SHATTERED LANDS
SOLANTRAS
THE WORLD OF HINESTRA

SERIES TIMELINE

THE DRAGONIAN ERA
WAR OF THE TURNING LEAVES
BYRONIAN ERA
SCOURGE WAR
REIGN OF SHADOW
 - *Lost in Shadow*
 - *A Dance of Shadow*

NAME PRONUNCIATION

HUMANS

Apollo	AH·poh·loh
Clep	klep
Dulcea	DUL·see·ah
Eratas	er·AH·tas
Siral	si·RAHL
Ratsbayne	RATS·bay·ne

SHADON

Lukras	Luk·ras
Mykel	MY·kel
Wilihem	WILI·hem

BELVASH

Desira	de·SI·ra
Narisa	NA·ri·sa

DAWNWARRIORS

Lenaka	LEH·na·ka
Draven	DRAH·ven
*Rhan'*Ashanna	ra·HAN AH·shah·na
*Rhan'*Kahan	ra·HAN KAH·han
Koani	KOH·ah·nee
Kiko	KEE·koh

ELVES

Mari'anath	mah·ri·AH·ath
Mari'aida	mah·ri·AI·dah

HESTA'KAN RANKING

*Ro'*Shadon society is spread into different *Hesta,* starting with the 12 *Hesta'kan.*

Numbers attached to a *Hasta'kan'*s family name signify their house ranking, which grants several privileges, including personal audiences with the *Kolotor'ix,* marriages, alliances, land, and more. Many lords will add their order in front of their *Hasta* when speaking. These rankings are subject to change due to duels, deaths, and falling in or out of the *Kolotor'ix'*s favor.

The following list is the rankings of the *Hesta'kan,* before the *kalidesh ik'kolotor.*

One/First	**hon**	*Hon-Hasta'kan ik' Blagdon*
Two/Second	**kon**	*Kon-Hasta'kan ik'Halidesh*
Three/Third	**kun**	*Kun-Hasta'kan ik'Blackmont*
Four/Fourth	**kik**	*Kik-Hasta'kan ik'Branial*
Five/Fifth	**ero**	*Ero-Hasta'kan ik'Remhold*
Six/Sixth	**eri**	*Eri-Hasta'kan ik'Shealbri*
Seven/Seventh	**eshi**	*Eshi-Hasta'kan ik'Armtomb*
Eight/Eighth	**yako**	*Yako-Hasta'kan ik'Rutherrene*
Nine/Ninth	**tira**	*Tira-Hasta'kan ik'Caulmer*
Ten/Tenth	**takir**	*Takir-Hasta'kan ik'Nicholnor*
Eleven/Eleventh	**treya**	*Treya-Hasta'kan ik'Carrait*
Twelve/Twelfth	**tribya**	*Tribya-Hasta'kan ik'Livingnor*

SHADESE LANGUAGE

Shadese has 6 vowel sounds: **a** |ah|, **e** |eh|, **i** |ee|, **o** |oh|, **u** |oo|, **yr** |yeer|.

Some words in the Common language do not exist in the Shadese Language, as the *ro'*Shadon deem them unnecessary, such as **a, the, is, are**.

Shadese has two forms: formal and informal. Formal speech is used by those of social standing, such as lords, ladies, *belvash*, and the *Kolotor'ix*.

Informal does not use the words **I** and **you**, for it is understood by whom the speaker is speaking to.

- Formal example: *"Shiresh kotu jakeitra khar,"* he said, gesturing to the other Lord he spoke with. ("I will see you tomorrow.") [lit. "tomorrow I will see you"]

- Informal example: *"Shiresh jakeitra,"* he said, gesturing to his friend. ("I will see you tomorrow.") [lit. "tomorrow will see."]

In Common, nouns have two Grammatical Numbers: Singular and Plural. In Shadese, there are Singular, Plural, and All.

- The plural of most Shadese words is denoted by taking the first vowel and turning it into an e. There are a few exceptions to this rule, including the word Shadon, which is used for both singular and plural.

  - Example: *hasta* (house), *hesta* (houses).

- "All" is denoted with the prefix *ro'*.

  - ***Ro'*** is attached to the plural form of the noun.

- Example: *ro'hesta* (all of the houses).

Verbs have three tenses: Past, Present, and Future.

- Past tense is denoted with **-*as*** at the end of the word, which replaces the last vowel of the word.

  - Example: *natshi* (attack), *natashas* (attacked)

- The future tense is denoted with ***ja-*** at the beginning of the word.

  - Example: *ja'natshi* (will attack)

LEXICON - SHADESE

This list is composed of the Shadese which appears in the book, in alphabetical order.

-kyr	"Death of", "end of". It is also attached at the end of the name of someone who has passed away.
-nyta	Attached to a verb or noun to make it negative.
-on	"People of" [Example: Nar'Shadon, "People of Nar'Shada", Shadon "People of1 Ash"]
'ix	"leader of". This follows the noun in which the person is the leader of. Examples: *kolotor'ix, hesta'ix, balvash'ix.*
asta	"after"
balutrae	"honored foe", rival. Plural is *belutrae.*
balvash	"blood sister", a female who bears the Sigil of Blood. Plural is *belvash.*
balvash'ix	"Leader of the blood sisters", also known as Blood Matrons, leaders of the Blood Temple. Plural is *belvash'ix*
brak'ha	"Father". Plural is *brek'ha*
drika	"name". Plural is *dreka.*
ero	"Five," "Fifth"
et-	"at". Goes before a place
Et-kiv	"here". Literally "at this"
Et-kivnyta	"not here", "nowhere". literally "not at this"
fyr	"Fury", "Rage"
hasta	"House". Shadon society is based upon Houses. Plural is *hesta.*
hasta'heh	"medium house", Minor House. These fall under the Hesta'kan and act as buffers between those lower than them and the *Hesta'kan.* Plural is *Hesta'kan.*
Hasta'kan	"House large", Major House. This is the only instance of *Hasta* that is capitalized. Plural is *Hesta'kan.*
hasta'yo	"small house", Lesser House. These are the lowest of nobility and answer to the higher *hesta'heh'ix* and *Hesta'kan'ix.* Plural is *hesta'yo.*

hin	"Son". Plural is hen
hin ik'san	"son of mine", "my son"
hon	"one", "first"
ik'	"of" For example, *hasta ik'Blagdon* (house of Blagdon), *ik'san* (of me/mine)
kava	go
kavasta	"follow", literally "go after"
kavasha	"improve", "going well". Literally "go good"
khan	"brother". Plural is *"khen"*
khar	"you"
kishtu	"honor"
kiv	"This". Plural is *kev* (these)
kiv-kyr	"This ends", "the end of this"
Kokolar	"black", a combination of "shadow" and "color"
kolar	"color"
koldraka	"shadowsteel", a rare metal that few have seen, and even fewer have items created from it.
Kolosae-ro'ja'aritas	"The Shadow who has eaten, eats, and will eat all things". *Ro'Shadon* revere it as a deity that lends them their power in the form of Sigils of Shadow.
kolotor	"shadow"
Kolotor'ix	"Leader of the Shadow"; This is the title of the *ro'*Shadon leader, it is always capitalized.
kolvorkav	a carnivorous horse-like creature hailing from Nar'Shada bred for speed. Plural is *kelvorkav*.
kolvorvik	a predatory horse-like creature from Nar'Shada bred for riding into combat. Plural is *kelvorvik*.
kotu	"I"
korrati	"commander". Plural is *kerrati*
kreva	"consort" Plural is *kreve*.
kriss'ix	"soldier leader"; "captain." Plural is *kress'ix*.
krushku	" to fornicate without honor", commonly used as a swear.
na'	"from"

nar' "from", used for places.

Nar'Shada "from ash", the homeland of the Shadon, is also the name of the capital. The name refers to the legend of Thraxxis.

Nar'shadon "people from ash", often used for those from Nar'Shada who do not have the Sigil of Shadow upon their bodies. Like Shadon, this word has no plural form. Also spelled *narshadon*

natshi "attack"

nogut "fool". Plural is *negut.*

nyr "lie", "false"

ro- the Shadese grammatical number for "all". It is used with the plural form of the verb. Example: *ro'*Shadon "all of the Shadon," or "the Shadon race as a whole"

roje "heart". Plural is *reje.*

rolto "order" Plural is *relto.*

sae- "one who", placed in front of the verb

san "me", "mine"

scavyr "power"

sesha "mother" Plural is *Seshe.*

shada "ash." Plural is *sheda.*

Shira "daughter"

shakolar "white", a combination of "ash" and "color"

sholta're A greeting used after midday, but before twilight

sri' "old, older, elder"

sri'balvash "elder blood sister", a *belvash* of the second rank. Plural is sri-*belvash*.

yok "that"

DAWNESE LANGUAGE

Because of their social and religious closeness with the Dragons, dawnwarriors use both Dawnese and Dragonic words in their language.

Dawnese has five vowels, each with a long and short sound. **a** |ah|, **e** |eh|, **i** |ee|, **o** |oh|, **u** |oo|

The long vowel sound is denoted with a line over the vowel. This sound is held a little longer than normal. ā |aah|, ē |eeh|, ī |eee|, ō |ooh|, ū |ooo|.

A symbol that looks like an apostrophe comes before a sound with a guttural stop, similar to the Common word "uh-oh."

Example: *to'ki* (male)

Many words in Dawnese mean several things.

Example: *Hela* "to trade, market, or sell"

LEXICON- DAWNESE

-na'a	"all", placed after noun
Aila	"Sadness"
Api'koa ma'liko	Greeting for the morning
Haka'nou'u	"Thanks to you", "Thank you"
hela	"to trade, market, or sell" Plural is *hela'lo*
hela'ko	"one who trades, markets, or sells". Plural is *hela'ko'lo*
helaono	"marketplace," a combination of "market" and "place"
Hepa	"gone"
Ikanu	"day"
Kahena	a dawnwarrior soldier who protects the Exonesis border. Plural is *kanena'lo*
Kōnu	"fade"
Lakoni	A dawnwarrior soldier who patrols inside Exonesis, protecting the people. Plural s *lakoni'lo*
Maipo	"dance"
Nela	"light"
Niapa	A dawnwarrior spy for the Rhani. Plural is *niapa'lo*
Noko'alo	"done", "finished", "no more"
Nopu	"pain"
Nuikanu	"tomorrow", a combination of "future" and "day"
O'anu'po	priestess and priests as a collective
O'anu'tale	"priestess". Plural is *O'anu'tale'lo*
O'anu'toki	"priest". Plural is *O'anu'toki'lo*
o'o	*"of"*
Paikanu	*"yesterday", a combination of "past" and "day"*
Pari	"parent". Plural is *Pari'lo*
Pu'uni	"foolish"
Pu'tri	"uncle". Plural is *Pu'tri'lo*
Ukanu	"Fear"
Un'nui	"tear" (as in crying). Plural is *un'nui'lo*
Wan	"left", "remain"

LEXICON- DRAGONIC

Pu'fu	"nonsense", "nothing"
Rhan	"Leader, king". Plural is *Rhani*
K'han	"Dragon". Plural is *K'hani*
Uak'hani	"Land of the Dragons," shortened over time from *Uaka o' o k'hani*

PROLOGUE

140 YEARS AGO

He shivered, standing on the *Starcaller's* bow as it rocked violently, water soaking his dark brown skin and grey-speckled feathers. *Dawnwarriors are not sea-faring folk,* he moaned mentally, the rocking and pitching making his stomach turn. *If we were meant to be on boats, the K'hani would not have given us wings, but alas, this storm and the distance restrict our travel. They are either teaching us humility, or we have bad luck.* He longed to see the sun and blue skies again, but they hadn't been seen in a week, souring any hope for ending this misery. The lurching of the ship made Draven grab the railing, his knuckles whitening as he prayed to *K'han'Exonia* that he wouldn't fall overboard.

A blue-skinned elf grinning as he checked ropes that held the sails tight, moving across the wooden deck as if it were the easiest thing in Hinestra.

How do the Benstafi elves do this? "How much longer until the storm passes?" Draven shouted against the wind and rain, wings tucked tightly around him, short black hair dripping with salty water. *I should have brought a real cloak; my feathers are soaked. It will take hours for them to dry once we get to shore, which means more time without flying.*

The elf laughed at him, facing the wind and rain fully with bare arms open as if to embrace the elements, the swirling design of his Sigil of Water dark across the lighter blue hue of his skin. "Ya call this ah storm? This is but ah little rain, my dark-skinned friend! How do ya dawnwarriors fly in the sky so close to the clouds if ya afraid of a little rain?"

"It's not the rain; it's the world rocking under me! The ground is supposed to be solid!"

As Draven clung to the railing, his wings helping him balance while threatening to turn him into a kite, the Benstafi elf went to him, pointing into the distance. "Do ya see that darker spot near the horizon?"

Draven squinted, trying to see past the rain. "No!"

"That be ya destination, the forbidden isle o' the dragons! Are ye and yer kin sure ya want ta go there?"

"Well, we were supposed to meet their envoy to trade, like we do every fifty years, but then they never showed up, and so we came to see if they are a—"

"Oi, feathered friend, a simple yes or no would have sufficed, not a damned bard's tale."

"But I *am* a bard!" Draven exclaimed, but the elf was already walking across the deck, uninterested. Sighing, Draven headed below deck to gather his things.

The other dawnwarriors looked up as he came from above deck. Asoo, one of the *kahena'lo*, spoke up as he sharpened the spear; his red and black beaded braids hung down his back between his black wings. "Are we almost there yet?"

Draven nodded. "Supposedly, but I swear when he pointed at where he said the island was, I saw nothing."

"We are lucky if you can see anything past your quill and notebook," Taboh, Asoo's brother, spoke up from his slingbed, turning his knife over in his fingers aimlessly. Like his brother, he had two lines of white paint adorning his nose and forehead. Standing side by side, the two were unmistakable as siblings, though Asoo used his spear more than his younger brother, who favored throwing knives.

"I see a lot more than you think," defended Draven, frowning, "bards have to see a lot of things and chronicle them, which is why *Rh*—"

"*Rhan*'Kahan entrusted you with this mission, to record why the envoys didn't show up." Uk'aka spoke up, running her red wings over a wide-toothed comb made of black polished wood, "You've only said it a hundred times in the last three weeks."

Draven frowned as he sat on his slingbed, pulling out his quill and parchment, and began writing, trying to think about anything but the rocking of the ship beneath them. The slingbed helped and he listened to the other dawnwarriors laugh while he wrote about the storm. Even though he'd been a part of this group for months, he still felt like an outsider. *I wish I were back in Meridiah with the group I had traveled with before it was outlawed to be outside the mountains. At least they had more fitting tales to tell and would let me ask questions so I could write them down.*

He wasn't sure how much time had passed before a shout came from above deck, and the dawnwarriors hurried up to see what was happening. When Draven stepped out into the open air, he found the rain had stopped and so had the *Starcaller*.

"This is as far as we take you." The captain spoke up, his Sigil of water dominating the side of his neck. "You will have to go the rest of the way by rowboat. We dare not anger the dragons with our presence too close to their sacred shores."

I cannot blame them, for their birthing grounds are on this island. If I were they, having strangers near my hatchlings would upset me.

O'anu'tale Kiko stood at the bow, her hands toward her companions as if her palms were directing their deity's protection and closed her eyes as she spoke in their native Dawnese, leading the dawnwarriors in prayer. "*K'han'Exonia*, keep us safe and guide us all. This hour is blessed, and we have been guided through the storm to our destination, for your bright right eye shines upon us and warms our skin and wings! We will step onto the shores of *Uak'hani* and commence our trading in time to begin our journey home toward Exonesis before your left eye is in the night sky! Praise to the *K'hani!*"

The dawnwarriors repeated the phrase, and the *O'anu'tale* looked at Draven.

"Come, let us get into the boat and do our sacred duty." She did not wait for him to answer, walking to the railing and stepping carefully into the rowboat.

Draven followed and almost fell into the smaller vessel as the Benstafi elves lowered it into the water. "Why could we not simply fly there? We are close enough, which is not a long distance."

The *O'anu'tale* sighed. "We have been over this. They may see us as large birds if we fly into their lands. Do you want to be eaten?"

No, but I can maneuver better in the air than sitting on a boat like a target, he thought grumpily as he set his bag between his feet.

"It is just us two heading over first to speak with the *K'hani* envoy. If we brought more—"

"They may see it as a threat. I understand, *O'anu'tale.*"

"The others will wait on the Starcaller and if something goes wrong, you use one of the two enchanted tubes to signal for help. You have them, correct?"

"Yes, I do." Draven patted his bag. His sole job was to record the transactions and meetings so that future records could be kept in the Exonesis library. *If everything goes according to plan, one day, all of Meridiah will know my name as the greatest bard ever to write!* "You don't think the noble dragons will object to my presence, do you?"

O'anu'tale Kiko shook her head, her white robes contrasting against her warm brown skin, beads of golden Dawnsteel in her hair and jewelry, catching the light with its small sparkling surface. Long white feathers with black tips adorned her back, folded behind her. "I do not believe so. We are here to trade goods for dawnsteel. Their envoy missed our meeting for the first time in centuries. It would insult history not to allow you to chronicle this." She picked up an oar and began pushing away from the *Starcaller,* Draven doing the same.

As they neared the island, Draven frowned slightly. "I thought the island would be greener," he said, looking upon the mountains in the distance and seeing they were dark, almost foreboding. *This isn't what I had imagined it to look like.*

"There are many types of Dragons. Perhaps live in the darker volcanic mountains, similar to the Shadowgulf Mountains north of Meridiah," the *O'anu'tale* answered, turning slightly to look at the island. "It is thought that *Uak'hani* has habitats for each of the Dragons, for each color has its favorite environments to live."

He frowned, looking around. "Blue dragons live in the ocean, but I've not seen one since we've set sail." He glanced into the water, wondering if a dragon was following them under its surface. "Do you think--"

"Let us keep our questions and comments to a minimum once we arrive, Kil'lik'Draven. Remember--"

"I am to write and observe, not speak," he finished for her. *I am just curious about the world around me. Why is that so bad?*

The clouds were darker over the water, yet the sky was cloudless toward the island's center as if it were the center of yet another storm. *I hope it doesn't start raining; I'm just getting dry.*

The boat skimmed over a sandbar protecting the bay. It moved across the shallower waters to shore until the front of the rowboat slid onto black sand. The two dawnwarriors dismounted and pulled the vessel onto the sand to prevent it from drifting back to the ocean.

"Now," said *O'anu'ta'le* Kiko, brushing the sand off her hands, "let us see to the *K'hani.*"

Turning from the boat, the two dawnwarriors blinked at the strange sight before them; crystalized forms rose from the ground, and dozens of branches reached upward.

The *O'anu'tale* touched one, finding it brittle at the surface, with flecks coming off her palm. "I had thought these were trees. What is this?"

"When lightning hits the sand, it turns to glass-like crystals," Draven said, looking at a structure much taller than he was but three times as wide with his wings outstretched. "I've read about similar formations being created along the coastlines of the Shattered Lands. Do you think it could be from an ampithere's lightning attack?" he asked, referencing a cousin of the dragon with a long serpent-like body with wings but no legs. *K'hani'Aka'asha* was one such creature. As the *K'hani* of storms, her breath ripped across the skies on cloudy days to pour rain upon the world below.

"I am not sure," admitted the other dawnwarrior, looking at multiple structures in a line, "Was a *K'hani* chasing something? Why would they use its lightning breath on the sand? Surely, they could catch a creature to eat with teeth or tail strike instead of risking it being trapped within these structures." She frowned, making the white painted line down the center of her bottom lip pucker slightly before walking further inland, the beach growing denser with trees and foliage.

Engrossed in his surroundings, Draven stumbled over a hard object, his wings flapping wildly as he fell. He ducked his head slightly when he heard the disappointed sigh of the other dawnwarrior. Slowly, he sat back on his knees, looking at the plant life around him. *There's something similar to ash on the ground.* He adjusted his sandal and looked to see what he had fallen over.

A line of sizeable half-buried vertebrae was at his feet, and he followed them to see a colossal ribcage stuck from the ground. Trees had begun growing between the bones, creating a blend of life and death. His foot touched an object, and he looked down to see something metallic half-buried in the soil. Draven brushed off the dirt, finding an exquisite dagger, its hilt made of twisting bands of silver around a glass-like container filled with a swirling bluish liquid.

It is quite a decorative piece. He hissed in pain as he touched the tip of the dagger's blade, a drop of blood welling on his skin. *It's also still sharp.* He slipped the dagger carefully into his bag and hurried to catch up to his companion, sucking on the tip of his finger to stop the bleeding.

He was so busy wondering who would have owned such a beautiful weapon that he hadn't realized that the other dawnwarrior had stopped walking, and he collided with her. He quickly backed up, apologizing, but *O'anu'tale* Kiko had not responded or even snapped at him for not paying attention to his surroundings. Wondering what was wrong, he stepped out from behind her wings.

The ground was gone, dropping in a crater with what looked like the remains of a skeletal formation of rocks that barely held their shape, chunks of land and debris suspended in the air around it.

Was that once a mountain that exploded from the inside?

Remnants of trees were leaning away from the epicenter, stripped bare of branches. Hundreds of different-sized skeletons littered the area, some floating in the air as if trying to flee the scene.

Draven felt his stomach drop as he saw the scattered bones of what could only be a hatchling floating beside broken eggs. *There are too many to count. What in the world happened here?*

The *O'anu'tale* collapsed to her knees, a high-keening sound escaping her as she clutched her chest, rocking back and forth. "Dead," she whispered in Dawnese, "they're all dead. The *K'hani* are dead! What do we do? They're all dead! The *K'hani* are dead!" She began repeating the words over and over, like a mantra.

Draven looked at the land around them helplessly, unsure how to help her, stepping away to give her privacy.

O'anu'tale Kiko's words bled together as she began wailing wordlessly, breaking the heavy silence of the area.

Draven glanced over and froze.

The *O'anu'tale's* face was a mask of red, blood covering her skin, her hands on her cheeks, coated to her wrists, her hands in front of her. It had begun dripping onto her white robes, staining them.

Draven rushed over, falling to his knees, reaching for her and looking around for a creature that may have harmed her, but everything around them was dead. "What is it? What happened? Did something bite you? I have some bandages; facial wounds bleed a lot— " His voice trailed off, and his blood ran cold as he looked upon her as she held out her bloody hands toward him, something in her palms. *Her eyes. She clawed out her eyes.*

He placed his wing between her left hand and her face while he held her right wrist, stopping her from prevent her from further harming herself. Using his free hand to rummage through his bag, he retrieved an enchanted tube from his bag, aimed it skyward, and tugged its string with his teeth. A lightweight ball launched high into the air, trailing red powder. He carried two such tubes— one red and one blue, to signal those back on the *Starcaller* if they were in danger or on their way back. Red powder meant trouble, and even though he wasn't sure if they were in danger, it seemed the right thing to have the others here.

He glanced worriedly at the *O'anu'tale*, who fell on her side, hugging herself while sobbing loudly. No words of comfort came to mind. *I cannot blame her;* he thought numbly as he pulled out parchment and the enchanted quill, beginning to record the scene, *for how can you have faith when our gods, the K'hani, are dead?*

BLAGDON

PRESENT DAY

The sun started covering the land, casting warm tones beside shadows that stretched lazily between the buildings within the stone walls surrounding Stormhold. Though it was early, the grounds were full of movement, from the creatures leaving their stables as the stablehands entered them to the maids already busy with their daily chores inside the keep. The *kelvorkav* growled at the neighboring *kelvorvik*, who snorted at them as they ran along the fences separating their paddocks. The Meridian horses began walking along their pasture to graze safely away from the carnivorous creatures. Wilihem, the *Hon-Hasta'kan'ix ik'Blagdon*, watched from his window. *It looks to be a beautiful morning.*

He turned from the window to his large bed where a blonde woman still slept, blankets gathered around her and a hand under her pillow. A soft smile played across her lips, and he was unsure if it was due to the late night the two engaged in or if she was dreaming of bleeding someone dry. *One could never be too sure when one's wife was a Sri'balvash.* He gently adjusted the blankets on her shoulder, mindful of the arm near the dagger she kept under her pillow. He carefully kissed Narisa's forehead to avoid rousing her, as being stabbed the first thing in the morning was not a pleasant experience. Instead of steel, he was awarded with the smallest of sounds, possibly a murmuring of affection, which he accepted as such. *I will never tell her that she makes them or that I find them cute. She would deny making them entirely, but they are a small thing I cherish about her.*

He dressed and walked outside, nodding at the Dark Army soldiers who greeted him as they patrolled the grounds atop their *kelvorvik*. The hired hands were already loading and unloading fresh meat and hay carts, and Blagdon watched them for a moment before letting them continue to work in peace. These were the hardest workers in Stormhold, and he dared anyone else to say otherwise. Blagdon ensured they had everything needed to keep his territory running efficiently. To do anything else was beneath him.

Blagon whistled as he stood beside the fence of the *kelvorvik* paddock. Forty-six pairs of ears turned toward the sound as *kelvorvik* and *kelvorkav* turned their heads to look at him. Blagdon watched as the largest *kolvorvik* began trotting forward, red eyes fixed upon him. Once the creature stopped at the fence, Blagdon reached into the enchanted pouch on his belt and threw a piece of fresh meat into the air. The *kolvorvik*'s nostrils flared once and immediately snapped up the meat with its sharp teeth, chewing a moment before snorting. Blagdon reached out and patted the black muzzle of the stallion, careful to avoid his mouth. As a colt, Ruin had bitten off two fingers on Blagdon's left hand, forcing the Shadon to wear a glove with stuffed fingers to prevent letting others know about his weakness. Blagdon had no intention of repeating the mistake.

"Ruin, we will ride again soon," Blagdon promised his mount before nudging him away to be with the pack again. The other *kelvorvik* watched as they came closer, eyeing the treat bag, waiting for him to toss them pieces of meat. After tossing some pieces to the others, he stepped back from the fence, careful not to turn away until out of reach. As tame as they seemed, *kelvorvik* could just as quickly eat him as they would allow him to ride upon their backs.

As he watched Ruin lead the rest of the pack away from the fence, Blagdon focused his thoughts, attempting to reach the alpha mentally. *Ruin; hear me and return.*

The great *kolvorvik* gave no indication it had heard him, snorting as he nipped at a mare's hindquarters, beginning to follow as she gave chase, kicking at him with her powerful hind legs.

I expected as much.

After the fall of the Byronian Kingdom, any Stormriders captured were sent to Stormhold, their previous training ground, where Blagdon had interrogated them for information. The *Kolotor'ix* wanted the Stormriders to defect and serve the Dark Army, but many of them were loyal to a fault and would rather die than serve the man who killed their royals.

Instead, Blagdon turned his questioning to learn better how the bond between a Stormrider and mount was created, for they had such a relationship that the rider could gain aspects of their animal and, in combat, move as one unit. Such an ability would be paramount in improving the *ro'*Shadon cavalry and, with Blagdon being the one to find it, would secure his *Hasta'kan'*s place in society as the *Hon-Hasta'kan* for years to come.

None of the Stormriders knew the intricacies of the bonding ritual, which only deepened Blagdon's fascination with the subject. After reading scrolls found in the library when he'd taken over Stormhold, he had repeatedly performed said ritual precisely as they had described. Yet nothing had ever come from it, leaving him tired, bloodied, and more frustrated. But he was determined not to give up, especially after finding Sir Siral Karog, a human Stormrider who still professed loyalty to the long-deceased Byronian royal family. Blagdon insisted that Siral spend time reading between his duties caring for his mount, hoping that it would trigger lost memories and then he would reveal the secrets that he desperately sought.

Blagdon headed back toward the keep. *Perhaps later I will take Ruin for a ride with Narisa and discuss ideas to help Siral's memories return. The sooner I can bring Stormriders to the ro'Shadon, the better. Having Sir Siral's memories returned, my working toward growing a Stormrider bond with a kelvorvik or kelvorkav would prove advantageous during the kalidesh ik'kolotor.*

If another *Hesta'kan* had made vast improvements while his had not, they might be given the rank of *Hon-Hasta'kan*, something Blagdon found unacceptable. Falling to a lower status meant having fewer privileges: territories, *belvash*, and keeping a smaller portion of taxes. For Blagdon, this meant not being able to properly train and feed his mounts.

Lady Narisa *ik'Blagdon* stood waiting on the steps, wearing her black *Sri'balvash* leathers, the crimson cloth hanging from her left shoulder blew gently in the morning breeze. Though her leather mask covered her lower face, Blagon could tell she was frowning. She held up a missive scroll in her gloved hands, the red and green colors of the wax seal held toward him.

Is Remhold finally sending me an official challenge over the death of Lordson Kerrik-kyr ik'Remhold? Are they declaring a duel against me, or do they hold Mykel responsible when it was I who killed him? He shoved the what-ifs out of his head and looked to his wife instead.

She shook her head, gesturing inside so they could have privacy. "We need to talk."

* * *

"So, it begins." Blagdon frowned, watching the fireplace flames cast shadows around the study, yet felt no peace at its sight. He let the missive fall to the table in the middle of the room, glancing around at the two other occupants, one seated at the desk, the other standing by the bookshelves that lined one wall.

"*Hasta'kan'ix ik'Remhold* blames you for his fifth Lordson-*kyr*'s death and embarrassing his *Hasta'kan*," Gideon said beside the bookshelf.

"I killed Lordson Kerrick-*kyr* in a duel, one he initiated."

"You sent his… parts… to his family in a box." Gideon said, shifting his weight uncomfortably, "and I believe *that* is the issue, not that you killed him, *Hon-Hasta'kan'ix*."

Blagdon felt no such trouble admitting what he'd done. *When one acts with purpose and accordingly, there is no shame to be had.* "His Lordson-

kyr had driven a wedge between the villagers and the soldiers of the territory of Cetra. By overtaxing and taking any useful tools and goods, the villagers could not provide resources for us. His soldiers under him murdered an entire village and burned it to the ground. His death should be made a deterrent to prevent others from doing the same."

"He also raped and abused the women under his direct protection," Lady Narisa spoke up.

Taya, one of the preferred victims of Lordson Kerrik-*kyr*, was now at the Blood Temple, hoping to become a *balvash*.

Blagdon wondered if she'd survive the training; from what little he knew of the Blood Temple, not many initiates did. It was a fitting place for her; *ro'belvash* were quick to bring those wronged into their ranks to punish those who perceived them as the weaker gender.

Weaker in strength, perhaps, but never in mind and spirit.

"Many Shadon would not see his actions as a crime, but a right as a Lordson," Gideon spoke up.

"Attend your tone and words," Lady Narisa snapped from her chair, the *Sri'balvash* taking offense.

"My apologies, my Lady, but I have said nothing untrue. Many *hesta* will take what they want, whenever they want, and damn the consequences because they are law in their territory."

Blagdon wisely said nothing. If Gideon wanted to dig his grave by hand, he'd sit back and watch his wife bury him.

"*Hasta'kan'ix ik'Remhold* may feel slighted by his Lordson-*kyr*'s death," Gideon continued.

"As he should, but more because his Lordson-*kyr* was a *nogut,* and it was his own making." Blagdon sipped his wine and gestured to the missive on the desk, shadows pushing it across the surface to the other man. "But now, he asks for Senka's hand in marriage." His tone was filled with disdain.

Gideon moved forward to take the missive. He read the parchments, his eyes narrowing slightly.

"We knew this day would come, Wilihem." Lady Narisa spoke softer now, aiming to soothe her husband's ire. "Senka has the Sigil of Shadow, the first female to claim it in thousands of years. We knew other *Hesta'kan* would begin to bid for her hand in marriage."

Hasta'kan ik'Remhold is excellent in creating soldiers but lacks what it takes to create proper Lordsons. He did not want them to be the first of the eleven *hesta* to bid for his only daughter's hand. *Why could it not have been another to start this parade of politics?*

"They do not wish for Lady Senka to be their wife. They want her to be her broodmare," Gideon said as he lay the missive back onto the table, the parchment now slightly crinkled.

Lady Narisa nodded. "They want to see if the child born from the union of two Shadon will have a stronger Sigil of Shadow. Even the Blood Temple admits to a curiosity about the subject."

They want to see if that child will be more powerful than our Kolotor'ix, Blagdon remarked silently. Saying such words aloud, even in a room with trusted individuals, was as risky as trying to feed *kelvorvik* a carrot. *Perhaps even more dangerous.*

"I had hoped for a few more years," Blagdon admitted. *I had known this possibility since the Kolosae-ro'ja'aritas had granted her the Sigil of Shadow. However, that doesn't mean I have to like it.*

"We've been getting missives about this for years; I never brought them to you but informed them we were not ready to receive such offers."

Blagdon turned to his wife. "Why did you not inform me of such offers, Narisa? It is not your duty to keep messages of importance away from me but to aid me in dealing with them."

"You cannot duel everyone who sends you a missive you disagree with, Wilihem," Narisa stated flatly, sighing. "Senka was not ready to be a wife, my husband. The Blood Temple taught her how to tend to a male lover and say and do the right things. From your late wife, she was taught to dance, speak, and have manners. You taught her to fight, ride, and lead. She is capable of all these things, yet I did not wish to take her from you for a few more years until *you* were ready. You had lost so much already."

Blagdon turned and looked at her fully. "Until I was ready? My wife, this is not about me, but our *Hasta'kan*, the continuation of its place in society." He tried to be upset, but his wife's concern for him tempered his anger. *Though Senka is not of her womb, she cares for my daughter, and Senka loves her half-brother. Narisa balances me; she is calm when I am quick to anger, and vice versa. The Kolosae-ro'ja'aritas was wise to send her to me when no one else could calm my stampeding heart.*

"Our son is *korrati* of Woodsong; you've seen to that and his career. He is well-protected and has our men loyal to him and his command. Under him, the territory of Cetra will again flourish and provide even more goods and resources. Your Lady Shadon daughter will be a wife and *sesha* someday, and we are in a position where her union does not threaten us."

Blagdon sighed, unable to find an argument suitable enough to present. *Hasta'kan ik'Blagdon* had been the second only to the *Kolotor'ix* for four consecutive cycles and was the envy of all who sought to replace them at the *kalidesh ik'kolotor*. Even when Senka married into a lower *hesta*, it would not move their current position. *That could change when Kolotor'ix meets with Hesta'kan'ix to review our achievements and ranking this year. However, one thing threatens it, and it must be seen immediately.*

Blagdon looked to Gideon. "Your relationship with my daughter ends now."

Gideon looked at him, his face careful not to show any emotion. "My *Hasta'kan'ix*?"

"You and Senka have been having relations for years, in fields on cloudy days or at night in the woods, hoping not to get caught. You are a human; she is my daughter and a Lady Shadon *ik'Hasta'kan*. I allowed it because it would give her the experience to please her new husband, but now it ends. You will find a way to tell her and see your needs elsewhere."

Gideon was quiet for a long moment, his jaw tight.

"Do you have something to say about the matter? If so, spit it out, Gideon, and if not, then do as I ask."

"No, *Hasta'kan'ix*. Excuse me, Lady Narisa." He walked out, shutting the door firmly behind him.

He felt his wife's eyes upon him and looked over. "You have something to say, my Lady?"

"He's held a torch for Senka for quite some time. Some may even have dared to call it love."

"None have dared to do such in my presence; nonetheless, it is useless. Senka must be married to a *Hasta'kan'ix*, or a Lordson; there is no alternative. She is a Lady Shadon, and her children will be the next line of *ro'*Shadon. We must be prepared to defend our station and ally with the other *Hasta'kan* to remain in good standing with their child."

"*Ro'*Shadon husbands have mistresses; some are *belvash*, some human. Why would Senka need to discard Gideon when she could have him as such?"

Blagdon looked at his wife. "Not all of us have mistresses." *If one treated their wife with respect and care, she would give her husband everything he needed, and there would be no need for a mistress who could be a spy, betraying secrets to another.*

Lady Narisa continued writing on parchment, as she had done since the conversation had begun in the study.

I wonder if she is recording this so that her sister knows what is happening, and she finds this as entertaining as gossip.

"You do not think having someone near Senka to report to us what is going on and how her husband treats her is not worth it?"

"Gideon is my foreman and needed here. If Senka is being mistreated, I would expect her to cut off the hand that touches her wrongly."

"What are you going to do about Sir Siral?"

"Are we changing the subject now because I have a point and am winning?"

"Believe what you must. I know there is no changing your mind about Gideon, so why beat a dead *kelvorkav* into a bloody pulp? It only serves to attract more carnivores."

"You are wise, beloved."

She gave a slight *hmmph* sound as she watched the parchment momentarily, then continued writing. "Flattery will get you nowhere."

Blagdon walked to stand behind his wife, running his hands along her shoulders. "Have your scribes at the Temple sent back word about any Stormriders secrets they may have discovered in their archives?" He kissed Narisa's ear gently above her black crimson-trimmed leather mask, sneaking a glance to see what she was writing. Blagdon frowned as the linework seemed similar to his native Shadese but had differences that set the language apart. *I have long thought it was code that the ro'belvash write to each other with, but their sign language is also puzzling. Sometimes, they are more irritating than helpful.*

"If the *Belvash'ix* permits me to speak upon it, I shall. You know better than to peek at my writings," she scolded, and he could hear the smile in her voice.

"If the writing were in Shadese or Common, it would be easier to read, " he said as he straightened, went to the table, and looked the missive over again. "What does my wed-sister say today?" Reddish writing slowly appearing as if scribed by an invisble hand. *I know they write to each other through this means, but I wish I knew more about it. It would be much faster than sending messages by a raven.* Sighing in frustration, for this was one of many secrets his wife would not reveal, he headed toward the door.

"*Sri'balvash* Desira suggests that we speak more about hosting an engagement dinner for the *Hesta'kan* to present their Lordsons to Senka. We can begin discussing possible alliances and start reviewing which would be most beneficial for the *Hasta'kan*. Where are you going now, beloved?" Narisa's amused voice followed him as he began walking quickly toward the door .

"To go riding." As he closed the door, he heard his wife's laughter follow him, ringing in his ears like a sweet honey but bitter at his expense. *She knows I'd rather face a pack of werg than talk about politics.*

Remember where you came from.

Strive to rise above who you once were.

For if not, you will return rather quickly.

— Sir Barriston, Stormrider Commander

RATSBAYNE

Ratsbayne sat in the study that took up the entire third floor of Stormhold's Keep, frowning as he looked over the books and scrolls on the table. Hearing that he had once been a Stormrider had been one thing, but researching and re-learning what that meant was entirely different. Most of the study had been dedicated to the subject— from armor and weapons taken from captured Stormriders to the massive tome that held the name and information of every Stormrider since their creation.

It be all so surreal; how could any o' this be true? Why do Ah not remember anything from before Ah woke in a cave by Thraesh? He'd spent countless hours pouring through scrolls and tomes, trying to find anything that triggered a memory, but so far, the idea he had been a knight with a flying mount seemed as valid as a child's story.

The feeling of someone watching him made him turn, expecting to see the squirrel who had been following him. He opened his mouth to give it a piece of his mind when he noticed it was not the annoying creature but a young woman with brown hair and a light pink dress. "Oh, sorry, Ah thought ya be someone else."

"It's all right," she said, smiling, " I hadn't meant to startle you. I brought you something to drink as well as some food. You've been here for half the day already, and I was unsure if you had eaten." She set down a tray of drinks, sliced apples, jelly, and freshly baked bread before looking over the books and parchments. She tucked her hair behind her pointed ears and began moving books aside.

The sight made him freeze in place as feelings of loss, fear, and hope gripped him, though he could not remember why. "Ya be an elf."

The girl nodded. "Yes, I am."

He took in her pale complexion and the absence of scarification or tattoos. *Ah not sure why Ah be looking fer them.* "Ya be Mun'ari Clan, aren't ya? Same as the Byronian Queen?" The elven clan name tickled at his memory. *Perhaps Ah read it it in a scroll? Ah dun't remember, but dun't want to ask and be rude.*

The elf nodded, though she gave a sad smile. "That is correct. My name is Mari'aida."

"It be sounding similar to the Queen's name."

The girl nodded, smiling softly. "My mother was her best friend and battle-sister during the War of the Turning Leaves. My name combines the late queen's name, Mari'anath, with Haida, one of my blood-father's fellow Stormriders. He and my mother wished to honor them both. Might I have your name, sir?"

The name Haida itched his memory. *Ah think Ah recently read that name in the Stormrider tome.*

"Ratsb-- Siral. Siral Karog." He'd almost given the name he'd given in the village of Thraesh out of habit, though truthfully, he felt more of Ratsbayne and less of Siral as if he were still the stablemaster playing dress-up.

"Well-met, Sir Siral. "It seems you were in the middle of something. Am I interrupting?"

"No, mi'lady, ya not be interrupting, and Ah not be a sir, just Siral."

Mari'aida smiled softly. "I am told that you are a Stormrider, who can only be called as such after they received their training to become a knight and then further trained with flying mounts. So indeed, Sir Siral, you are a sir."

"Ah dun't remember any of the training Ah've supposedly gone through, even after a few o' mah memories returned. Ah have so much to catch up on that Ah dun't know where to start." He picked up an apple, ate it, and then realized how hungry he was. He used the knife to spread some of the jelly on a slice of bread, eating it hungrily.

"I can help with that." The girl pulled out a chair and sat, closing one of the tomes beside her and giving him her attention.

He blinked at that, not used to being taken seriously, to being seen as more than the annoying drunkard, even though he hadn't touched ale in… he frowned. *How long has it been since Ah had to stop drinking?*

"May I first see your amulet?"

Siral looked to Mari'aida, surprised by her question, and took out the pendant he always wore under his tunic. The sunlight from the window catching the relief of a griffin flying over fields and hills with the sun's rays behind it. *Heart of the storm, the strength of the griffin,* the inscription read in elvish. According to a book, the pendants were enchanted to let the wearer fall slower from their mounts while in the air. *It never let meh fall out of mah slingbed any slower or off the roof of that barn Ah helped thatch in Thraesh.*

"Only Stormriders are given them to wear by the king and queen during graduation. Many inns and taverns in Meridiah used to give Stormriders a free night to sleep or a free first drink in appreciation for their service and patronage, but only after seeing the amulet as proof that they were who they claimed to be. The amulets were also shown to prove authority when handling a conflict, should no lawmen be around."

Ah had no idea that they be so important.

Mari'aida turned it over to look at the relief of a leaping stag under a crescent moon taking up the silver back. The Byronian kingdom's standard was long gone after the royal family was overthrown, only seen in tomes and captured banners. Slowly, she ran her fingers over it, her green eyes distant. After a long moment, she blinked and pulled her hand away, almost reluctantly. "Thank you, Sir Siral."

Shrugging, he slipped the pendant back on and under his tunic. "According to these tomes, there hasn't been a Stormrider alive in decades."

The elf's voice was softer than it had been a moment ago, almost sad. "That is correct. Any Stormriders the *ro*'Shadon have encountered have been brought here to be questioned and spoken with about joining the *Kolotor'ix*'s cause. Those who had refused or fought back were killed. You are the only one left that we know of."

"What exactly be the *Kolotorix*'s cause?"

Mari'aida blinked. "What do you mean?"

"Lord Blagdon wants to further his *kelvorvik* and make them Stormrider's mounts. Honestly, the idea of flying murder ponies make meh want to shite in mah pants." He flinched, realizing his language was inappropriate in front of a lady, and muttered an immediate apology. "What be the *Kolotor'ix*'s goal?"

"To see to the safety of the people of both Meridiah and Nar'Shada."

"He rules both kingdoms?"

"The *Kolotor'ix* isn't a king; he's an emperor. The *ro*'Shadon Empire spans across both lands."

Ratsbayne shuffled through the parchments on the table and pulled out a map, setting it down and pointing. "Meridiah be here, Nar'Shada above it, separated by the Shadowgulf Mountains. They be two complete countries. He can't be emperor of both."

"He runs both."

"How?"

"I can't tell you that."

Can't or won't, Ratsbayne wondered, noticing she was still looking at the map and not at him. *Ah feel like a child trying to learn everything all over again.* "Then tell meh something ya do know, like why is it ya be the only elf around. Blagdon had told mah the elves were almost all gone since the *Kolotor'ix* had taken over Meridiah. Yet here ya be."

The elf's eyes widened a touch, and she glanced around. "If you must speak of Leigelord Blagdon, use his title before his name. If someone else hears you speak of the *Hasta'kan'ix* so flippantly, their reactions and your consequences will be dire."

Her concern for him made him change his mind about responding casually and he nodded instead. "Ah try ta remember that, my lady."

"Thank you. To answer your question, the elves hid after the coup, fearing extinction. Our queen and her family, guards, and many loyalists were murdered. We were outnumbered by both the *ro'*Shadon and Scourge, and the elves had already lost thousands in the War of the Turning Leaves. The elves knew they had no chance to fight, so many fled rather than be subjects to *ro'*Shadon rule."

"The tomes say that the Scourge came south, through the Shadowgulf Pass, from Nar'Shada, correct?" When Mari'aida nodded, he continued. "During the war with the Scourge, the *Kolotor'ix* killed the royal family while the armies were distracted. How do we not know he be the one who brought the Scourge?" *If Ah be tryin' to kill someone, Ah'd use a distraction. A war of undead soldiers be a large distraction.*

Mari'aida's eyes widened at the suggestion. "The Scourge outnumbered the Shadon and destroyed many of them in Nar'Shada before breaking through the guard towers of Shadowgulf Pass. Shadon Ambassador Jorrah convinced King Byron to allow them to aid in fighting the Scourge, for they had an experience that the Meridian armies did not. In return, King Byron and Queen Mari'anath would allow the Shadon to start to come south and live among us; at least, that was what my mother believed."

"Ah, think it be sounding awfully convenient. What better way to get yer way than ta 'lend aid' during a crisis ya create?" he said, using his fingers to create air quotations.

Mari'aida frowned at him. "The *Kolotor'ix* nor Ambassador Jorrah created this crisis, Sir Siral. There were sightings of a Sigilbearer of Death who walked among the Scourge, raising the dead of those who fell in battle and adding to her ranks."

Ratsbayne felt an interest in this, though distant. *Slipstream be listening.* "Ah never heard o' a Sigil of Death."

"There are many Sigils, but it was the first we'd ever seen who could raise and control the dead," Mari'aida said quietly.

He waited for her to continue, but when she didn't, he changed the subject. "But ya be here, anyway. Are ya a prisoner?" He stopped, looking over his shoulder at her as if he expected to see a guard standing at the doorway, watching and listening, ready to report back to Blagdon. A bit of hardness slipped into his voice and he found himself protective and willing to go against the Leigelord in defense of the girl he'd just met.

"No, nothing like that," she assured him, waving her hands as if dismissing the whole idea. "Leigelord Wilihem Blagdon is my ward-lord, and Lordson Mykel Blagdon is my betrothed."

"Congratulations?"

She smiled, nodding. "Thank you," she said, but she looked away slightly.

Ratsbayne took notice of the sadness in her eyes. *If that lad hurt her, korrati or not, Ah will kill him.*

She must have seen something on his face because she looked at him worriedly. "I'm safe, I promise."

"Safe and happy be not the same thing, lass."

"I know this, Sir Siral." Mari'aida stood, pushing in her chair. "I should let you get back to your reading. I appreciate your speaking with me." She turned and walked out, letting Ratsbayne think in peace.

He looked back at the window at the capitol city, watching the red banners with a black mask emblem against the white stone of the Temple's tower and palace. *The people be happy, but are they safe?*

Truth unspoken, kept by those who fear it,

Will destroy everything they lie to create.

— Kil'lik'Draven, Bard of the Winds

LENAKA

The air carried the scent of flowers and the Aerukatan Ocean along the eastern coast of Exonesis Mountain. The farmers worked their fields, harvesting fruits and vegetables to be sold in the *helaono*, and fishermen on boats cast their wide nets into the northern part of Ka'epano Lake. Herds of teagot grazed safely in the field, their brown coats contrasting with the green grass.

Lenaka spread her brown and black speckled wings, letting the air currents guide her gently from the Hiena'pei Valley to the capital city of Wan'hela. She flew through the open stone gates, waving to a group of dawnwarrior children playing catch with a ball as they shouted greetings to her. Flaring her wings, she slowed and landed before the *K'hani* temple, touching her hair briefly to ensure her braids hadn't come undone and looked presentable before walking inside.

She felt the temple was one of the most beautiful places in all of Exonesis, and every time she walked past the towering statues that lined the inside corridor, it only served to remind her how small she was in the world and that she was a part of something larger than herself. Each *K'han* statue stood over twelve feet tall, each in a different pose which signified what they had done to shape the world. Soft sunlight shone in from openings in the ceiling, guiding beams onto their forms, highlighting the detailed carvings of their wings and scales, showcasing the care taken to ensure the gems in place of their eyes caught the light, making them seem alive. Each statue had candles and offerings at its base, though some had more than others. Lenaka was quiet as she walked past, trying not to eavesdrop on the others praying, their wings folded behind them so other worshippers could have room to kneel beside them.

At the front of the temple stood the most prominent statue, depicting a *K'han* emerging from raw, unfinished rock, eyes fixed on the sky above as she started to spread her wings and readied to fly to the heavens. This action by *K'hani'Exonia* as she broke through the earth's crust had long ago formed the mountains that surrounded the lands of Exonesis and kept the dawnwarriors safe from outside threats. Lenaka loved this statue the best; her favorite part was the two different colored eyes: a bright yellow citrine, the other a clear diamond, each the size of two of her fists if held together.

Lenaka took a moment and prayed for their protection and wisdom before reaching into her bag, pulling out wax-sealed scrolls, and laying them beside the other offerings.

"I assume those are more writings of your *putri*, Kil'lik'Lenaka?" *O'anu'toki* Rian'Aluu asked warmly, the white painted dots along his cheekbones and line down his chin bright against his light brown skin.

"*Api'koa ma'liko, O'anu'toki.* He asked me to bring them here while he went to the *helaono.*"

He gestured for her to walk with him, nodding to those who smiled in their direction as they passed. "The *K'hani* are honored to have someone like Kil'lik'Draven to write them such works of beauty. When I first read his poetry, I was enchanted by his words and descriptions of the lands of Meridiah and Castet. I had wished to travel to all the places he had, but the *K'hani* had other plans for me." He gestured to sit, joining her on the low-backed bench to make it easier to sit with wings. "How is your *putri* doing?"

Lenaka felt her smile fade slightly. A young *O'anu'tale* walked from a room to the side, carrying a bowl of incense, the mingling scent of spices and flowers following her as she passed them. Lenaka waited until she was out of earshot before continuing, not wishing others to hear their conversation, even though everyone knew about her *putri*. "Kil'lik'Draven is doing well, though some days he forgets to eat or groom his wings and hair."

"It worries you."

She nodded, sighing heavily. "I don't know how to help him, *O'anu'toki*. I try as much as I can, but sometimes I feel as if I am trying to swim up a waterfall."

A male with red wings came rushing in, his sandals making hurried sounds on the stone floor. A few worshippers turned to see what the commotion was about before returning to their prayers, and an *O'anu'tale* tutted at him, shaking her head as she reminded him not to run into the temple.

The male winced and began walking over to the benches. "Kil'lik'Lenaka, there you are!"

Lenaka looked over at her friend, frowning. "Ma'ko'Koani, what's wrong? Is my *putri* all right?" Her mind was already conjuring images of him trapped under a fallen bookshelf in the library or getting stuck while exploring the mines again. *He promised to behave and walk around the garden and helaono. Surely, he has not gotten into any trouble yet.*

"Kil'lik'Draven is speaking before the *Rhani*."

Oh no.

She looked to the *O'anu'toki*, but he held up his hand before she could speak. "Do not apologize; I understand. Go, may the *K'hani* guide you."

"*Haka'nou'u*," she said and walked quickly until she was outside, taking to the air and flying after Koani as fast as she could toward the People's Palace, hoping she could get there before her *putri* created more trouble than she could handle.

"Koani, you couldn't have gotten me *before* he went to speak with the *Rhani*?" she hissed, using his birth name since the crowd below couldn't hear them.

"I only found out when we were rotating shifts." Koani was training to become a *kahena*, a protector of Exonesis' borders. "I figured you were not far behind him."

She gave a frustrated sigh. "He asked me to set some poems at the statue of *K'han'Exonia* while he went to the *helaono* to buy more parchments and fruit. I would have brought him with me if I had known he was planning on heading to the Palace."

The People's Palace had been carved into the side of the largest of the mountains, known as Exonesis Mountain, though the same name referred to all the peaks that surrounded their lands. From there, the *Rhani* ruled and guided the people toward prosperity with the *K'hani*'s blessing.

When Lenaka was younger, she'd even gotten to fly with *Rhan*'Kahan and a group of children her age, including his daughter *Rhan*'Ashana. The *kahena'lo* had cleared the air above the *helaono*, letting the *Rhani* and children have it to themselves while the adults watched from the ground. The children raced around the area as fast as they dared to fly, tossing a ball back and forth for a turn of the hourglass before the *Rhani* landed at the Palace's steps and returned to their days. It was a fond memory that cemented the love of *Rhani* and the people in her heart, and every time Lenaka went to the Palace, she always remembered standing on the steps, watching *Rhan*'Ashana wave to them as if they had all become best friends.

But today, the palace steps were occupied with a crowd of dawnwarriors, some shouting and pointing at each other or at the *kahena'lo* who with hands near their weapons in warning to stay back and not approach the palace doors.

"Why are so many people here?" Lenaka asked, landing and frowning. On one side of the stairs were dawnwarriors wearing bright orange, the color of the Order of the Everlasting Dawn. It made Lenaka's wings itch. *I will never understand how people could turn their backs on the religion of their ancestors to create another with their own rules to fit their desires.*

Koani followed her gaze. "Some of the Order were preaching in the *helaono*'s freed-words zone, and from what I've heard, your *putri* began arguing with one of them. It started to attract quite a crowd. I am sure that the *kahena'lo* brought both parties to speak in a gesture of fairness."

Lenaka scoffed, shaking her head hard enough that her braids flew back and forth, the beads at the ends of her strands clicking against each other. "Fairness? The freed-words zone exists in the first place because the Order began knocking on doors and preaching about the Everlasting Dawn to those who lived inside! How many came to our home and demanded to speak to my *putri*, calling him a hypocrite because of what he'd written about *Uak'hani*? They even say that--"

"He should have been one of the first to convert to the Order of the Everlasting Dawn after they told what had transpired on *Uak'hani*?" Koani finished for her, his lips pulling into a smile that shone brightly against his light brown skin. "You and my family have said it only a *few* times."

Lenaka fought not to cross her arms. "It's not funny."

"No, it isn't. The dawnwarriors had followed the *K'hani* for thousands of years, and when your *putri* came back with stories that they were dead, we no longer believed the old stories and followed their beliefs blindly." At Lenaka's look, he shrugged. "There's been talk about it at least once a month in the Palace on how to better the two groups' cooperation. The freed-words zone was supposed to make it so they could speak their minds in conversation. But the argument grew and began disturbing the peace, so the *lakoni* had to get involved in preventing a fight from breaking out."

"What do you think my *putri* speaks about now?" Changing the subject sounded like a good idea. Even though Koani wasn't as vocal about the Order as the rest of the Ma'ko family and other followers could be, she feared that one day, their differences would cause a rift in their friendship. They often kept their conversations away from turbulent subjects, but attempted to listen and could respectfully agree to disagree. *If only others were so willing to set aside their differences in the spirit of one people.*

"From what Ma'ko'Likoa said, your *putri* wishes to go searching for *K'hani* and prove the dragons are not all dead," Koani answered, taking the subject change in stride quickly, "but that means traveling outside of Exonesis, further than we'd traveled since both the Scourge War ended and the Reign of Shadow began. We both know *Rhan'Kahan* won't allow that; it's too dangerous."

Now I understand why people are so upset, she realized, her heart sinking. *I'd hoped putri had been speaking about something less controversial.* The only dawnwarriors permitted to go outside the protective boundary of the Dawnstone were the *niapa'lo,* the *Rhani's* spies who reported to the palace about events taking place outside Exonesis. Some believed the Shadon were waiting for a chance to torture a dawnwarrior to discover how get into Exonesis and to kill the *Rhani.* At least, that was her *putri's* theory. "Where did he speak of traveling to?"

"South, through Castet to the Shattered Lands."

Lenaka rubbed her temple as she walked toward the palace, feeling a headache coming. *Of course, Putri would want to see the lands where the Ley-line imploded, killing thousands of our brethren and allies during the Scourge War. We don't even know if there are any blightwalkers still out there, waiting for fresh meat to eat.*

A couple of older dawnwarriors spotted Lenaka and rushed over, shouting and arguing, pointing their fingers at her disapprovingly.

"You should be ashamed, allowing him to rant like a madman in public! Keep him at home!" one argued, angrily pointing her walking stick at Lenaka.

Lenaka fought the urge to smack the stick away from her, finding her anger already rising. "I will not keep my *putri* a prisoner in his own home because you feel offended at his words; he has every right to speak as you do. If you don't like what he says, don't listen."

Koani stayed beside her, using his wings to keep people back as he escorted her up the stairs to the *kahena'lo* waiting at the top. "Please let her collect her *putri.*"

"The *pu'uni* bard should stay home!" one of the males behind her shouted, and a few shouted in agreement while others argued with those who spoke.

Lenaka wasn't sure what she would say because from between the palace doors, a grey-and-white-haired dawnwarrior with skin the color of leather exited the palace, leaning on a cane slightly. His other hand was atop a satchel with parchment rolls sticking out of it at various angles, and a heavy book with ribbons in various places was tucked under his arm. He went to her, grinning, even as the people around him shouted.

"I think the *Rhani* listened to me this time."

Apollo,

Nights have passed since we left, terrified that Silene will be destroyed like Andears. Emma, the baker's daughter, is sure that everyone she knows will die soon. I keep telling her to keep her thoughts positive, but I hear her crying when she thinks no one is paying attention.

We don't stop often; our wagons are constantly moving toward Exonesis Mountain. We take turns riding with the children and supplies in the back.

My nights are plagued with dreams of when I woke to discover that you had left Silene, leaving me behind. You cannot go against the Dark Army alone— we are children, and they are soldiers. Play-fighting with sticks and Pa's sword won't save you against them.

All I can do is write on the blank parchments of Ma's notebook and pretend you will read it. I pray to the Light that you are okay. Please, brother, I beg of you… return safely.

Clep

APOLLO

Apollo grunted with effort as he swung the axe at the log before him. He buried the head into the log, but it wasn't quite enough to split it entirely. He set up his swing again, and this time, the log split, his axehead buried in the stump. He let go of the handle and picked up the wood, tossing it onto the garrison woodpile. Even though his scheduled turn to split wood had passed, he volunteered to take another shift, giving him something physical to do besides sparring. He set another log onto the stump and readied himself. The bloodied face of a former soldier appeared atop the stump, milky eyes rolled up to look at him, his mouth still moving as blood leaked out from the corner of his lips.

Gasping, Apollo dropped the axe and he stumbled backward in horror. He looked around to ensure that someone else had seen it, but the soldiers loading the split wood into wagons didn't seem to notice, caught up in their conversations.

Apollo glanced back at the stump where the unsplit log stood on its end. There was no head of the soldier he'd known, no blood spilled on the ground. He could feel the tremor throughout his body; his legs and arms cold as he walked to a bucket of rainwater nearby and splashed it onto his face, trying to gather his senses.

I am safe in Woodsong, and Eratas-kyr is not there, nor the others. Of the nine soldiers who were slain that day, it was only Eratas who haunted him, who Apollo had personally executed. *It's been months; why am I still having these visions?*

After a long moment, he stood and returned to the log, eyeing it as he walked, as if daring it to become the disembodied head once again, but nothing changed. But as he squared himself and readied to swing the axe downward at the log, his ears filled with the sounds of the condemned Eratas-*kyr*'s muffled screaming through his shadow gag.

Apollo backed away, shaking his head as he took a long breath and blew it out shakily. *I am balutrae ik'Blagdon. If I look weak, Mykel looks weak. I have to be stronger than this.* He twisted his hands around the axe and lifted it again.

The axe stopped as Apollo went to bring it down. Glancing up in confusion, Apollo saw dark, whispy tendrils of shadow wrapped around the handle, preventing it from moving. He looked around for the source of the shadow magick.

Kriss'ix Lukras held his hand at his side, gesturing, and the axe shadowed to stick into the stump beside the untouched log. "Your arms are shaking. You should rest in your cabin, Apollo."

"I'm okay," Apollo lied, refusing to acknowledge that he was secretly relieved at the chance to go to the cabin and hide. "I have to cut this wood for the fires."

Kriss'ix Lukras said nothing, moving his hand. Shadows sliced through the nearby stacked logs and the one on the stump, and the cut pieces were deposited in a neat pile on the other side of the area. "Come." He turned and began walking toward the cabins.

If Shadon could do that, why do the kress'ix insist on all of us chopping wood manually? Apollo followed, frowning.

"How is your sleep?" the *kriss'ix* asked, using shadows to speak directly into Apollo's ear.

Apollo appreciated the secrecy. *What would they think if they knew that I was still having nightmares after all this time? Surely, the ones who had slaughtered the people in Andears did not have any visions or disturbing dreams afterward.*

"It is better," Apollo admitted, though he felt ashamed that he had secretly asked a *balvash* for herbs to help him sleep at night. He kept them in a pouch on his belt to avoid someone finding it. He didn't have to use it as often as time had passed since the executions, but sometimes, like now, the ghosts of those he condemned returned to haunt him. "How long will it be until I am normal again?"

Kriss'ix Lukras stopped as if pondering the question. When he looked at Apollo, his eyes were full of dark knowledge. "Taking a life is one of the most life-changing things one can do, no matter the reason. Those who do are never the same again."

"I can't live my life constantly haunted by their visions; there has to be a cure!"

"There is no cure, magick salves, or words to relieve you of this burden, Apollo. There are ways to deal with and try to lessen it, but it will always remain inside you, a part of who you are."

"I don't want it to be," Apollo admitted, "I want to be who I was before."

"That is impossible, I'm afraid."

Why are the Shadon always changing my life for the worse? First Andears, then Clep, and now this? Maybe it isn't the Shadon; is something wrong with me? "How do I deal with this… burden, you call it?"

"There are many ways, some are healthy, others not. Some accept it and use it to ensure others do not suffer by protecting them so they do not go through the same pain. Others run from it, hiding behind their methods of dealing, such as—"

"Drinking?" Apollo interrupted, his mind going to Ratsbayne. *Had he killed someone, and that was what caused him to drink so much? Was the pain and memories too much to bear?* Now that he realized similarities between them, trying to escape visions that haunted them, he felt a pang of guilt over the many times he'd brushed the drunkard off and snapped at him. *I should have been nicer to him.*

"I would suggest not doing that. I suggest finding someone to speak with whenever you have such visions. It will aid greatly."

"Could I speak with you about them?"

The *Kriss'ix* nodded. "You are one of my *kress* and ensuring you are at your peak strength, both mentally and physically, is part of my job. Besides, I will further *Hasta'kan ik'Blagdon* by ensuring you do not fail your duties as *balutrae*. But if you cannot speak with me, I suggest speaking with a *belvash* or the *korrati* himself."

Because if I am strong, that pushes Mykel to be stronger, which helps his Hasta'kan. He was silent for a moment. "Does *korrati* Mykel have problems with what happened, too?"

Kriss'ix Lukras patted him on the shoulder and walked off silently, leaving Apollo to come up with his own answers.

* * *

The following morning, Apollo silently looked from his bed to the empty bed of the soldier on duty. His heart ached. He wished he could see Clep lying in bed next to him, talking about things in Andears outside their shared room's window. He missed hearing him laugh and seeing him feed Memory as she landed on his leather glove. *Where is he now? He was never one to disobey rules or go off on his own; that was always something I would do, and Clep would come to get me before I got into trouble with Pa-kyr. I thought he would have stayed in Silene until I returned. Will Clep still see me as a member of the Dark Army, responsible for destroying our old lives? Would he see me as a murderer when he discovers I had condemned Eratas-kyr and the others?*

"*Balutrae ik'Blagdon,* you are asked to report to the keep," *kriss'ix* Lukras said as he walked into the soldier's cabin, breaking his train of thought.

Apollo quickly began getting changed into his armor and found *kriss'ix* Lukras waiting for him, watching the soldiers perform their morning exercises under the instruction of one of the other *kress'ix.* He followed the Shadon through Woodsong toward the keep, finishing buckling his belt as he did so. Although the armor that Mykel had gifted him was not red and black like the Dark Army's, Apollo started to feel as if he were one of them, and they treated him better than when he'd first come as a farmboy who knew nothing.

Apollo to walk into the keep first, the *kriss'ix* behind him.

"The *korrati* is in the war room. You will find him there." He turned and returned to the garrison, leaving Apollo alone.

Have I done something wrong? Surely, I did nothing as bad as punching Mykel as when I had first arrived. Apollo knocked on the heavy wooden door and waited before being told to enter. He stepped inside, seeing the room's walls were filled with shelves, housing scrolls, tomes, small statues, and trinkets.

Mykel stood over a table, examining a map of Cetra and the surrounding territories. His hair had grown a touch since the last time *Sri'balvash* Desira had cut it and had a slight curl near the ends. He gestured to the wooden figures carved to look like houses gathered together. "These are Meridiah City, Stormhold, and Woodsong. These with walls around them are other garrisons among the territories which border Cetra."

Apollo looked at the carved single homes across the map. "Are these the villages?"

Mykel nodded. "That they are."

Apollo reached over and picked up one of the two white tree figurines, looking it over before replacing it in its place. *Oddly, it means a lot that he even created the Aldarwood for this map, though I can't put it into words.* "You put a village for Andears."

"I told you, I plan to rebuild it so our people have a place to stay as they visit their Aldarwood. Did you think I was lying?" He looked at Apollo quizzingly.

"I'm not sure," Apollo admitted. "People have told me things in the past which were just to get their way."

"What is *Hasta'kan ik'Blagdon*'s words, Apollo?"

"*Scavyr na'kishtu.*" Apollo answered automatically. He had been tested and retested on the history of *Hasta'kan ik'Blagdon*, their lineage, words, colors, and emblem until he knew it as well as his own name. It was his responsibility to know everything there was to know about the *hasta ik'balutrae.*

"*Brak'ha* is known never to have told a lie. If we lie, those we speak to will second-guess our word. We do not honor our *Hasta'kan* by lying, especially on an essential subject."

Apollo nodded, unsure what to say.

"I am planning the best way for you to find your brother so you both can return quickly. There is still much to learn and being away from the garrison hampers this considerably." Mykel picked up one of the pieces on the map, looking it over as he spoke. "Clep would be safer in Woodsong, and you will be more inclined to learn with your mind not occupied with his safety." He set the piece back down in its proper place.

"I appreciate that."

Mykel pointed across the map. "To the east is Exonesis Mountain, the largest mountain on that coast. Since your brother and his company most likely had taken wagons, they will be going slower than if they had just taken horses, and it is not a stretch of the imagination that they have women and children traveling with them. That means more stops, which can work in our favor."

"You can't just look through the shadows and see where he's at?"

Mykel looked at him as if Apollo had asked if the rain was made of gold coins. "If it were so simple, my *balutrae*, do you not think I would have done it already?" Mykel asked, taking a sip of water from the goblet beside him before pointing to the map. "There is where your group will search first. Your brother and those from Silene would have traveled near this town and stopped to get supplies and possibly rest."

"Someone is coming with me?"

"My blood-sister, Lady Shadon Senka *ik'Blagdon*, will accompany you and two others on your search. They will be here in a few days." Mykel looked at the map, frowning slightly. "This part is through Kravast, *Hasta'kan ik'Blackmont*'s territory, but I do not think he will give any trouble to you as my *balutrae* and Senka beside you representing

Hasta'kan ik'Blagdon."

"Why would he give us trouble?" Apollo asked, looking worriedly at the map.

"Hasta'kan'ix ik'Blackmont holds hunting parties at his estate, where he would release a human criminal and allow his Shadon guests to hunt them, without using their shadows, of course, for it would not be a sport then."

Apollo looked at him, horrified. "That's awful! How can anyone allow that?"

Mykel shrugged. "Not every *ro'*Shadon is as civilized as *Hasta'kan ik'Blagdon."*

Apollo looked back to the map. *Clep is somewhere out there and will have to go through a territory where the Shadon hunt humans for sport. I need to find him before it's too late.*

The Shadow and Blood are two pieces of the whole;
Two paths with the same destination.
Without one, there can be no other.
Without the whole, there can be no half.
To the Shadow, we commit our power.
To the Blood, we commit our bodies.
From the Shadow, we rise.

Into the Blood, we fall.

— *ro'*Shadon temple service prayer

BLAGDON

Blagdon leaned against a fence, a piece of parchment rolled in his hand with the silver and purple seal of *Hasta'kan ik'Halidesh* affixed to it. He'd read it twice and already it irritated him.

Hasta'kan'ix ik'Halidesh had traveled twice to Stormhold last season to attempt to get a *kelvorkav* racetrack built in the Stormlands, which, in his words, had "ample land that could be used for entertainment and inns for those traveling to the racetracks." Now the *Hasta'kan'ix* wrote again, offering more of the profits to be split. *Your kelvorvik will not be selling as much, you need to do something for coin,* the letter had said, *There are no uprisings or war to worry about, why not do something else beside train war mounts?*

Even with this new number of profits offered, Blagdon already knew he would turn it down. *The Stormlands were for training soldiers and cavalry, not for sports. It does not matter if there are no war or uprisings, it is better to be a nogut and alive than unprepared and dead.*

He slipped the missive away and watched Senka spur her *kolvorkav, Fyr'ix,* down the archery lane. The sleek black creature made the sharp turns quicker and smoother than any *kelvorvik* rider could imagine. The mounts, bred for speed rather than fighting prowess, were another of Blagdon's achievements for the *ro'Shadon* calvary, who used them for scouts during the Scourge War. In recent decades they were purchased for racing and dressage, for their forms were more pleasing to the eye than the muscular *kelvorvik*.

Senka stood slightly in her saddle, reaching behind her to pull an arrow from her quiver. She aimed at the round yellow targets and loosened her arrows quickly.

Blagdon's eyes turned black as he glanced through the shadows at the targets. Three of the five were in the center, the other two off-center, closer to the outside edges.

Senka used the shadows to retrieve her arrows, and rode to the barn to deposit them into a bucket near the barn where workers would retrieve them, who would take them to be inspected and replaced if needed.

"You were told to be ready to head to Temple."

"I have time to run one more before we leave; the soldiers are almost done."

Gideon chuckled from the fence, leaning against it, arms crossed, a Meridian hat on his head to keep the sun off his face.

Blagdon looked at him for a long moment. *I suppose there are worse choices, and I do not disprove her happiness, but she is a Lady Shadon, and her fate is sealed; she must be paired with another Shadon.*

Gideon spoke again, breaking him out of his thoughts. "There is such a thing as practicing too much, Lady Senka. Your arm is tired, making your anchor point waver. Keep your drawing arm parallel to the ground with your index finger at the corner of your mouth so your arrow is always in the same place, not tilting up or down. You dropping your elbow made the arrows go high."

Blagdon nodded, agreeing with the assessment. He was less versed in archery than in other forms of combat, he knew enough to understand what he was saying was correct. Gideon was often seen on his days off shooting targets, and sometimes he would help Senka improve her aim. *In those moments when you adjusted her arm, standing so close to her, did you whisper into her ear your devotions, knowing it could never be realized?* "You should not have been practicing but getting ready to be presentable for the Temple service."

Senka gestured to her leather vest and breeches over her blue tunic; the sleeves tied down with leather bracers to keep them from interfering with her shooting. "I am ready when you are, *Brak'ha*," she said as she rode through the gate Gideon opened. "I will try again when I return," she said, handing her bow to Gideon, who bowed his head as she passed.

Blagdon observed the pair, but neither made secretive gestures that would have betrayed their relationship nor held any anger or regret of severing it. *I am impressed they have hidden it from everyone else for so long and I feel foolish for not catching it sooner.*

Blagdon walked to Ruin and climbed into the saddle, settling before looking around. Standing side by side, his mount was considerably larger than *Fyr'ix*. A half-dozen soldiers in black and red armor sat ready upon their mounts, the silver emblem of *Hasta'kan ik'Blagdon* upon their pauldrons. Two soldiers would ride in the front on *kelvorkav*, each holding a banner, one of the *ro'*Shadon Empire, the other the colors and adornment of *Hon-Hasta'kan ik'Blagdon*.

There were two guards ahead of himself and Senka, two behind them, and a blue-and-silver painted carriage surrounded by six more guards. The blue carriage had decor painted along its surfaces, which Narisa had commissioned, saying that having actual metal decor, while impressive looking, was impractical and would be more of a target for thieves. The decor was skillfully painted that it looked like metal from a distance, with silvery *kelvorvik* and *kelvorkav* running along its surfaces, the emblem of *Hasta'kan ik'Blagdon* large enough that even from a distance, it was unmistakable of whose carriage it was. Lady Narisa and Princess Mari'aida sat inside comfortably with soft cushions and curtains to maintain privacy and stop dust from coming in. Blagdon had the carriage's walls lined with metal, then covered with wood and painted to however his wife wished, the curtains made of a thin mesh that would slow arrows.

Blagdon watched the carriage quietly as twelve soldiers formed around it, three on either side, his hand flexing on the reins. *They will be safe. I am riding with them and my soldiers are ready to defend the carriage with their lives.*

Ruin snorted and stamped as if feeling his rider's anxiety. Blagdon shook his head to clear his mind of doubts. *Kelvorvik* had a way of turning any negative emotions into a bloody disaster if one was not careful.

Behind the main carriage were other soldiers tasked with guarding an open wagon carrying some of the hired hands; one was Sir Siral this week. Blagdon did not require that they attend the Temple's services since there was a small altar to the *Kolosae-ro'jo'aritas* in the bunkhouse. Still, those who wished to participate were allowed to, alternating weekly to prevent individuals from using it as an excuse not to work.

"*Brak'ha*, is everything all right?" Senka asked once they rode through Stormhold's gates, her voice low. She, too, glanced back at the carriage and then at the area around them, her posture stiffer.

"Once we get to the capitol, I will feel better. When we see our *Kolotor'ix*, Senka, mind your tongue and tone," Blagdon warned his daughter, "I do not wish to have a repeat of what had happened in the past."

"I was a child then, *Brak'ha*," she sighed, "am I never going to live that down?"

"Lessons will be repeated as long as they are pertinent so they may not be forgotten."

"Just as I practice my archery and sword-fighting daily, so we are never caught unprepared again."

Blagdon nodded and fought not to glance back at the carriage carrying the princess and his current wife, knowing that the silent ghosts of the past still followed.

* * *

The capital was too busy for Blagdon's liking, who preferred the solitude of his lands, surrounded by acres of pastures where the mounts' stables could be left in peace. Over a century ago, Stormhold was once considered a part of the Protector's District, but no longer. The Protector's District's barracks were inside the city walls, housing the soldiers who patrolled Meridiah City's streets and manned the watchtowers along the outer walls.

The Market District was always a source of noise and color, with shops lining the various streets, offering many goods from all over Andora. Once the dawnwarriors retreated behind their magickal barrier around Exonesis Mountain and the dwarves bunkered under the Ironfall Mountains, their goods became scarcer. The elves had disappeared and now were all but gone. Finding a good dwarven stout for Gideon and Mun'ari elven wine for Lady Narisa was harder these days. When they did show up in the market, they were often overpriced and snatched up by *Hesta'kan'ix,* who used it as a way to impress someone rather than a way to relax after a hard day's work.

Blagdon never set foot in the Maker's District, whose smoke-filled air was so thick that those who walked inside wore masks to avoid breathing in the fumes. The forges and blacksmith shops inside rang so loudly that the district walls would often echo back, forcing people to shout to be heard. The stone walls were covered in soot and iron, giving the area a dingy look. He'd send someone there if he needed supplies for horseshoes and nails. They made decent enough metal items, but the dwarves who used to work there made better goods that lasted longer.

The elvish palace stood smooth and pale in the Leader's District, with archways and towers creating a flowing silhouette, in stark contrast to the palace in Nar'Shada, which, like the lands around it, was dark and full of jagged structures that jetted out like obsidian from the ground.

The Leader's District also housed the Southern Blood Temple, once a place of worship to the Light. Gifted with the Sigil of the Light, the Truthpriests who had once run the temple were rumored to have the ability to discern truth from lie. Because of this, they were often used as judges and conductors of marriage ceremonies. Since the *Kolotor'ix's* reign began, the Truthpriests were rarely seen, causing rumors that they had been secretly killed off to have complete control over the people.

The crimson banners flowing against the white stone conjured the image that the temple was continuously bleeding. Blagdon thought it was quite the statement that the city's heart still bled.

Blagdon stopped his men beside the stables and waved off the stablehand, who backed off quickly, realizing their mounts were not regular horses when Ruin snapped at his hand. Blagdon patted his mount's neck while two of his Shadon soldiers held their reins as Senka and he dismounted. He took the meat from the enchanted bag on his hip, tossing pieces to *Fyr'ix* and Ruin before walking toward the palace, ignoring the paling stablehand backing up further from the creatures.

Senka took off the bracers, freeing her sleeves from her wrists and untied her hair from its braid, shaking out the white strands to fall around her shoulders, She pulled half of it back and tied a leather cord around it to keep it out of her face. She then looked at her father, gesturing to herself. "Is this better?"

"It is less aggressive, yes."

Sri'balvash Narisa stepped out of the carriage, wearing black leather with crimson trim, silver pauldrons with a long scarf of crimson cloth hanging over her left arm. Her eyes took in the area around them as she turned to face her husband, her lower face covered with a leather mask. The sunlight caught slightly on the embossed images on either side, the rearing *kelvorvik*-head of *Hasta'kan ik'Blagdon*, and a crossed quill and dagger emblem of her branch in the Blood Temple.

Blagdon's breath caught, just watching her walk toward the Temple. This was the woman he woke up next to every morning, slept beside every night, the mother of their Lordson, and sometimes he felt as if it were the first time laying eyes upon her. *Nothing was more alluring than a woman who could handle herself with confidence and grace.* She kept her dagger and whip, the latter wrapped around her waist like a belt, falling behind her like a tail, which Blagdon had to resist the urge to grasp and pull her toward him.

I wonder if she wore it like that to tease me.

Senka sighed, causing Blagdon to come out of his pleasant thoughts. "Why does she get to wear armor to Temple, but I can't?"

"She is a *Sri'balvash*; I cannot dictate what she wears. Conversely, you are the Lady Shadon of *Hasta'kan ik'Blagdon*, and I can say that you don't wear armor to Temple." Blagdon turned, extending his hand to the carriage as the other occupant gave him her hand.

Princess Mari'aida smiled as she stepped down to the stone courtyard, blinking as her eyes adjusted. "Thank you, *Hasta'kan'ix ik'Blagdon*." She smiled, her green eyes sparkling in the light as she looked around, breathing the morning air. *No matter what, Meridiah City will always be her home.*

"Of course, Princess. As long as you are my ward, I will ensure that no harm comes to you to the best of my abilities."

They began walking up the stairs, and the rest of their escort headed toward the ground entrance. Even though they were in the capitol, his storm-grey eyes constantly moved and his gloved hand rested on his rapier pommel under his cloak. *This close to the kalidesh ik'kolotor, every smiling face hides a dagger held behind the back.*

The silence stretched as they walked down the marble hallway toward the Temple's central room, passing the various *ro*'Shadon art pieces that now hung on the walls and stood in alcoves. Blagdon had admired the previous works of art in the Temple, which he had seen shortly more than a century ago when he posed as a messenger to the Ambassador *ik'Nar'Shada* Jorrah-*kyr*. The artwork that had decorated the halls was skillfully done, and he wished he could have seen a few of them again before they were destroyed when the *belvash* took over.

As they neared the main sanctuary, Blagdon nodded to the Princess and Senka, walking down the right hallway while they walked down the left hallway. Males and females were separated at *ro*'Shadon Temples for thousands of years. Even though he asked the reasoning when he was younger, it was never explained enough that he was satisfied with the answer.

Blagdon stopped in the hallway where four curtained booths stood, two on either side of the doorway. He nodded as *Hasta'yo'ix ik'Alixis* came out, holding a cloth to his palm. The *Hasta'yo'ix* bowed his head and walked through the entrance into the sanctuary.

Blagdon stepped into the now-empty booth, looking at the shelf before him, where sat a wooden box, a bowl with a spout beside a dozen glass vials with cork stoppers, a knife, and a pile of cloth bandages. *Ro'Shadon* were expected to blood-swear to the *Kolosae-ro'jo'aritas* before entering the service. The blood symbolized *ro'*Shadon's devotion; they could give as much or as little blood as they wished via the vials, and no one would know the wiser. If your vow was insincere or you did not give enough, your blood would remain in the box as an unaccepted donation, showing the diety's disappointment in either your words or actions.

When Blagdon was a young boy, a *Hasta'kan'*s lordson did not provide enough blood, causing the next Shadon to discover it. Undoubtedly, rumors soon spread that the donator was unworthy, beginning the domino effect of the *Hasta'*s downfall. Blagdon ensured he always gave more than he thought was required so his *Hasta'kan'*s honor would not be questioned.

Blagdon removed his glove and sliced the back of his right hand with the knife. Even though no *ro'*Shadon was supposed to peek into the booth, he refused to risk anyone seeing his maimed left hand. When he taught Mykel about donating blood, Blagdon taught him that slicing the palm causes more pain and makes it difficult for him to grip his sword afterward.

Blood is blood, no matter where you are cut. He closed his eyes, ignoring the sharp pain. "I swear to the *Kolosae-ro'jo'aritas* to put the shadows above all else."

He opened his eyes and looked at the blood in the bowl, silently judging if he had given enough before he took some dust from his pouch and sprinkled it onto the wound to help it clot, ignoring the cloth bandages provided to wrap the wound. *Leave those for those nogut who cut their palms.* He poured the blood into five vials, stoppering them with their corks before setting them into the wooden box and closing the lid. After a moment, he put his glove back on and stepped out, moving the curtain aside to show it was unoccupied.

The next Shadon stepped into the booth, closing the curtain behind him.

Blagdon watched the fabric momentarily as he listened for an indication of his blood being refused. Hearing none, he turned and walked into the Sanctuary.

RATSBAYNE

The Temple sanctuary was large enough to accommodate hundreds of people and tall enough to support many trees end to end. Stained windows cast beams of scattered colors on the whitish stone walls, and seats rose higher and higher on platforms. A heavy bowl of what felt like onyx was passed around the benches, most patrons adding a coin or two into it before passing it to the next person. Ratsbayne handed it to the person beside him, not adding anything. He didn't have any coin to spare, and he wasn't sure that he'd donate it to the temple if he did. *Who knows if they dun't steal all the coins instead of helping others?*

A male in a red robe with a black collar stood behind a pedestal at the front and set down a hefty tome that looked as thick as Blagdon's Stormrider record book but a thousand years older.

It be a miracle it not be falling apart right in front of us all.

The male turned to a page and began reading in Shadese, his voice a dull monotone. The congregation around Ratsbayne began bowing or nodding their heads.

Slightly bored, Ratsbayne looked around at the wooden partition separating the Temple down the middle, wondering if the females on the other side were getting the same dull torture or if their sermon had more life. *Ah wonder if Alandra be there.*

"*Stop thinking with your little brain, Siral.*"

What, it be boring here. Ah dun't even understand anything about what they be saying. Ah dunno why Gideon told meh to come here.

"*Perhaps it is to help you get acquainted with the world around you more. You can learn something, even if you don't understand the language."*

Ratsbayne looked around at the windows to distract himself from falling asleep. The windows were artistic enough, depicting a shadowy figure holding out their arms and tendrils of black bringing what looked like bread to a child. He frowned, wondering if lying in a Shadese Temple was a sin. *Ah ain't ever seen them give bread to children.* His skepticism towards the temple's symbolism was clear, his thoughts filled with uncertainty.

"Stop being dramatic," Slipstream chided gently.

Ratsbayne closed his eyes, bowing his head. *Maybe if Ah look like Ah be praying, Ah can get some sleep in, if Ah dun't snore too loud.* He felt Slipstream sigh heavily and he chuckled to himself.

The bells rang in a sweet melody that reminded him of raindrops hitting in a field of flowers on a half-cloudy day. He stood against the wall, blue and golden light from the stained glass windows falling upon him, making his armor look made of glass rather than metal. Turning slightly, he watched as Mari'aida sat with three elven girls, holding white branches with golden leaves and silver bells in clusters, waiting for their cues from the man standing at the dias, who spoke calmly and confidently.

"The Light lives in each of us, glowing from within our hearts and minds. If we choose to listen, we can hear it, whispering to us like a soft voice on the winds." He moved his hand, and the girls shook their bells, making the soft melody to the man's words.

Around the room, smiles formed on the faces of humans, elves, and dwarves who sat on the benches, listening.

The Truthpriest continued, his face never looking upon only one set of people but slowly taking in all of them. The golden lines of his Sigil of Truth shined on his neck and left cheek, stretching to his long brown hair, which had been pulled back into a neat braid.

"Those who are weak, whose inner glow has dimmed, are not forsaken

by the Light. We are encouraged to go to them, to let our Light aid theirs in rekindling so they can grow and glow, brighter and brighter once more. We need to aid those in need, tend to our ill, defend our weakened so that we may rise together."

The crowd murmured their agreement, many nodding heads.

He looked around the room, scanning for threats or arguments, before his eyes landed on the King and Queen of Meridiah, sitting among the people, their hands held together between them as they watched and listened to the sermon, smiling as their daughters, the princesses, shook their bells.

"Together, we shall live in harmony. Together, we will live forever in the warm embrace of the Light. Let us pray."

The congregation bowed their heads as the Truthspeaker raised his hands, his power brushing them gently.

Siral tried not to sneeze; his tongue tingled with magick, always making his nose itch. He didn't bow his head; his job was to protect those in the sacred place, though he spoke the closing prayer with the congregation.

"Mother, grant us wellness; make our bodies sound.

Father, grant your protection, send us guidance abound.

Brother, see our harvest grow large and long,

Sister, see our animals grow strong.

Grandfather grant us sound leadership to lead,

Grandmother, grant them wisdom, and aid the beginning we heed.

In the Light we pray, in the Light we trust,

Just as the Light shines upon us,

Give us this, now we pray,

And forever more light our days.

So pray we all."

___

"Ratsbayne, wake up," Riky snapped, elbowing Ratsbayne, who startled and looked around.

"Huh?"

"The service is over; move so we can get out. I want to eat."

Ratsbayne muttered his apology and moved to the aisle, standing. He cast one last glance at the Temple interior. There was no large auditorium for a congregation; a wooden partisan split the Temple down the middle, separating male and female templegoers. The windows were different; no shades of blue and gold shone among the stonework, and no Truthspeaker before them at the podium. The feeling of warmth and safety slowly left him cold and shaken, as if the sun had sunk behind heavy rain clouds once again. Ratsbayne headed back outside, feeling more alone than when he'd walked in.

The smells of fresh flowers and warm stone teased at his mind as he descended the temple steps, the sun's brightness against the tower's white walls and nearby palace almost compared to the dimness of where he'd just left.

The sound of the long red banners blowing in the breeze made him look up and his mind began gauging the speed of the wind. He closed his eyes, trying to shut out the intrusive longing to stand at the top of the tower and leap off. *Ah dun't want to mahself, but because the rush of the wind would be exhilarating.* He opened his eyes, looking around as if worried someone would have known what he was thinking and tell Blagdon that he was still crazy. *Maybe Ah am.*

The wall around the immediate area was taller than the others in the city, he knew with a knowledge that he was unsure of that it was meant to keep the Leader's District safe in times of conflict. Red and black armored soldiers of the Dark Army stood vigil along the wall, walked on the paths at the tops, and observed everyone coming and going through the gates. There was a smaller gate nearer the temple for use on Sun's Day and the largest gate before the courtyard in front of the palace in which carriages with visitors would ride through after being searched.

Ratsbayne walked through the smaller gate, watching the crowds of people going to and from the temple, and went to the bridge that crossed the channel of water that created the borders of the districts. He closed his eyes, listening to the sounds of the water hitting the stone sides of the channel and the people talking as they passed by.

"Emir! Emir! Where are you?"

The shouting made him turn on his steed, and he looked at the commander. "Sir Barriston, may I see what's going on?"

The commander nodded, side-stepping his winged horse to stand beside the carriage they were protecting. "Make it quick, Sir Siral, if you can."

He urged Slipstream forward, and the mare lept, quickly taking to the sky and traveling over the people, exclamations of excitement and wonder following them. They landed beside a frantic-looking woman holding a grocery basket. He dismounted quickly. "My lady, are you well?"

"Please, you must help me. My son, Emir, is gone! He's only four seasons old. He let go of my hand as we left Alana's Sticks and Stores." She was trembling so badly that she almost dropped her basket, and Siral took it from her, setting it on a barrel beside a shop and guiding her to sit on a crate.

"We'll find him. What was he wearing?"

The mother frantically wrung her hands together, trying not to cry. "A green tunic, brown breeches. He has brown hair."

He nodded and mounted quickly. "Remain here so I know where to find you."

Siral promptly rode to two nearby silver-and-blue armored guards posted near the intersection of two streets. "A child of four seasons is missing. Brown hair, green tunic, brown breeches. His name is Emir. Spread the word." He rode down the stoned road, shouting. "Child missing! Emir, brown hair, green tunic, brown breeches!"

The guards spoke quietly to each other, and one hurried down the road, shouting while the other stayed at their post but took up the shout to inform others to look for the child. Nearby mothers looked up, immediately checking and holding onto their children to ensure they were all right before shouting Emir's description and walking around the market. Males sitting outside at a table stopped talking, set down their drinks, and cupped their hands around their mouths, calling out for the boy as they walked the street. The citizens began searching together, walking into nearby shops, searching and spreading the word about the missing child.

Siral flicked his reins, Slipstream leaping into the air and running overhead as they looked from a higher vantage point.

Shouting of another sort got Slipstream's attention, their mental connection making him feel her curiosity and knew where to look without a word passed between them.

A man was frantically waving from a wagon, and a group of people was crowding around him. Hands yanked the male from his seat and down into the crowd, the driver disappearing from view.

Siral lept from the saddle, his amulet allowing him to fall slower. He shoved the people back off the driver and Siral stood between the downed male and the people, his shield blocking a rock thrown toward the driver's way. "What is this?" he demanded, shouting to be heard over the crowd.

Slipstream ran lower above the people, keeping them back.

"The child, Emir, he ran him down with his wagon!" a male shouted, pointing angrily at the driver, who had a hand out as if to ward off a blow.

"I didn't see him!" The driver shouted back, tears running down his cheeks.

Three guards began aiding in keeping the crowd back, shields drawn to block fruit and rocks being thrown in the driver's direction.

Siral looked under the wagon, where a boy in a green tunic and brown breeches lay curled in a ball. "Move the crowd back!" he commanded, and the guards began moving forward, pushing the growing crowd further away. Two more guards came up, one grabbing the reins of one of the horses hooked to the wagon and walking them forward while the other helped move the crowd so the horses could be walked forward slowly. The carriage moved, and Siral knelt, using his shield to block the crowd's view of the terrified child. His tone softened. "Are you Emir?"

The child nodded slowly, his face and clothes bloodied, rips on the knees of his breeches. "I fell," he said tearfully, pointing to a loose rock on the street that stuck up from the stone road.

"It is all right, I've got you, lad," Siral answered gently, brushing his gauntleted hand over the boy's hair, the leather palm soft and warm. He gently picked Emir up as he stood, keeping him safe behind the shield to not overwhelm the already scared child.

He turned and spoke to the people gathered around. "Thank you for your assistance in finding Emir. He'd tripped on a loose stone and fell under the wagon. Know that there was no wrongdoing here, simply an accident, and we will look into replacing the loose stone."

One of the guards spoke with the wagon driver off to the side at a table, writing on parchment as he took the driver's account of the events.

The crowd began dispersing, talking amongst themselves, some looking guiltily as if ashamed of their actions of jumping to conclusions.

He gave two whistles, and Slipstream landed, snorting and nodding. He hooked his shield onto his saddle, then set Emir onto the saddle and climbed up after him. With a click of Siral's tongue, Slipstream took off into the air, heading back toward the shop where he'd left Emir's mother, leaving the guards to deal with the crowd and the wagon's driver.

The mother looked up hopefully as Slipstream landed, and Siral dismounted before helping the little lad down. "Mama!" the boy shouted, "I rode a horse!"

"Emir! Thank the Light!"

He breathed out a sigh of relief, seeing the two together again. "He'd tripped on a loose stone and fell. He's got minor cuts and bruises, but I would take him to the Temple of the Light to ensure he doesn't have more serious injuries."

"Thank you," the mother hugged Emir tightly as Siral handed him over. "You are a servant of the Light's work."

"Yes, ma'am." He mounted Slipstream, turning back toward the Leader's District, but noticed his commander and the royal carriage had crossed the bridge into the Market District and were waiting down the street, the royal family watching from their seats.

Siral rode to Sir Barriston and explained the situation.

"I see you have the situation well in hand. Good job handling it quickly and effectively."

"Thank you, Sir. May I suggest we speak to the district managers about allowing wagons on crowded streets? They are wide enough, but accidents like this can still be deadly. We were lucky today. The canals can deliver goods between the districts instead of paid boat rides to transverse the city."

Sir Barriston seemed to think about it and finally nodded. "It would cut down on the safety concerns of unauthorized people in the Defender's District and the Leader's District. I will discuss it with the proper channels. Good looking out for the people."

Siral guided Slipstream to her spot to continue escorting the royal family around the busy city. "We are Stormriders, Sir. It's what we do."

You may speak your mind to your Kolotor'ix.

At least once.

— Shadon proverb

BLAGDON

Blagdon waited outside the Temple, nodding to those who greeted him as they passed and listening to the small talk they initiated, hoping to gain a little more influence with the *Hon-Hasta'kan'ix* before the *kalidesh ik'kolotor*. Blagdon disliked small talk, finding it useless and dull, and looked around, hoping Narisa would save him from any more conversations about things he held no interest in. When he saw one of his soldiers walk past, he gladly excused himself.

"Is my wife and Princess Mari'aida still inside?"

"Lady Narisa *ik'Blagdon* is speaking with the other *belvash*. The Lady Shadon Senka *ik'Blagdon* is over there, waiting for you. Our men have already escorted the Princess to the palace for lunch."

Blagdon nodded. He trusted his men to ensure Mari'aida's safety and stop any assassination attempts upon her. *Besides, I am sure the Kolotor'ix had his people watching her.*

Looking around, he spotted Siral standing off to the side, looking into the garden and walked over. "What did you think of the Temple service?"

"That statue be beautiful."

Blagdon looked to see what he spoke of. "Ah, that one."

The black marble statue depicted an armored male standing upon dragon bones, stabbing upward as his sword sank deep into a dragon's open maw. Rivers of gold were carved into the rock, pouring from its wound, flowing down the blade's edges, the arm of the figure, and pooling on the ground, where carved eggs mingled with the rocks. That piece was one of the first to be commissioned after the *Kolotor'ix* took over Meridiah, replacing the white stone fountain of elves playing with birds.

"Do ya know the story behind it?"

I do, but it is not one to tell publicly or anywhere else. It was one of the few things he regretted of *ro'*Shadon history, and its lesson still haunted those who participated.

"We are not here for stories. You will stay near the others and be ready to leave when I leave my meeting." *I have already spoken to some of my men, who have assured me that you will not stray toward a tavern, even by accident. It would be a shame to waste all this time and effort rehabilitating you to have you spoil my efforts so close to the kalidesh ik'kolotor.*

He turned to see Senka walking out of the Temple and excused himself, glad to use the opportunity to get out of the conversation. He walked over quickly to gather her for their meeting. *The last thing I need is for Siral to ask questions he does not need the answers to.*

* * *

The hall outside the throne room was lined with *hesta'ix* waiting for their turn to meet with the *Kolotor'ix*. Temple days were the most popular days to seek an audience and some used this opportunity to attempt to gain favor by reporting information obtained from their spies. Others tried to reverse a *Hesta'kan* decision they did not like. In the centuries before, the order of audience was first-come, first-serve, making many *hesta'kan* skip Temple services to have a place at the front of the line. The *Kolotor'ix* later changed this, letting the *hesta* speak in the order of their *Hasta'kan*'s ranking. It stopped the misuse of Temple services, but that did not stop *hesta'ix* from occasionally reporting on matters of inconsequence.

Blagdon confidently strode down the hall, walking past the waiting Shadon and stood at the front of the line, as a privilege of *Hon-Hasta'kan'ix*. He glanced back to see a line of annoyed and wondering faces and silently challenged them to say anything. *They undoubtedly wonder what I have to say and if their spies have heard and not reported it.* Blagdon was well aware that other *hesta* had spies in his territory, just as he had spies in theirs. *Sometimes, it was not about finding dirt on your competition but their faces as you appear to have always known their next steps.*

As the herald entered the hall from the throne room, Blagdon stepped forward, nodding to the guards, who opened them for him.

Senka waited for two steps before she followed, as proper for a female.

"Our *Kolotor'ix, Hon-Hasta'kan'ix ik'Blagdon,* and his dau--" the herald inside began announcing, but Blagdon's gloved hand flexed into a fist, and the man choked as shadows gripped his throat.

His eyes grew wide, glancing back at them.

"The Lady Shadon Senka *ik'Blagdon,*" Blagdon corrected before releasing his hand and resting it on the pommel of his rapier pointedly, his elbow moving his cloak back enough for the herald to see the weapon. *Other Hasta'kan can introduce their daughters as simply that, but Senka is the Lady Shadon of Hasta'kan ik'Blagdon and will be introduced as such.*

Blagdon made heavy eye contact with the herald, watching the human debate whether to allow him into the throne room with a sword. *This herald is a new one; I wonder where Bathomere is. He would have never made such a foolish mistake. This new human will certainly not last the day.* He used shadows to move his cloak's collar, the *balutrae* marking of a bluish-black mask upon his neck. "There would be no point in me trying to assassinate him; I am *balutrae ik'Kolotor'ix,* and no one tries to kill him but me in the proper way. Announce us, and let me get on with my morning."

The herald cleared his throat, slightly paler now, and looked back at the throne on the other end of the room. "*Hon-Hasta'kan'ix ik'Blagdon* and the Lady Shadon Senka *ik'Blagdon,*" he corrected and quickly moved away from them as if fearing Blagdon would strike him down for his earlier mistake.

Blagdon began walking, ignoring the herald as if he were furniture.

The marble room was large, lit by full-length windows that lined the right wall, only covered by sheer curtains, casting a reddish tint across the room. A long crimson rug ran the room length to the dias, where a single black throne made of countless bones of different creatures set in obsidian stood. Upon the throne sat a figure dressed in black leather, wearing a red-lined cloak and a black hood. His featureless *koldraka* mask had lines of gold.

Throughout history, the *Kolotor'ix* had always been masked, his hair and skin covered through carefully chosen armor, gloves, and clothing. Blagdon assumed the need for secrecy was to disguise whenever a successor stepped into the role. He told his children that the *Kolotor'ix* unmasked could be anyone they met, so they should treat everyone with the respect they deserve.

When Blagdon reached the bottom step before the throne, he knelt, bowing his head and putting his right fist against his left shoulder. Behind and to the side of him, Senka copied his movement, except she went to both knees. Females and *narshadan* were considered subjects, fulfilling their roles behind society, while Shadon males were protectors, able to rise from one knee quickly to defend their *Kolotor'ix*. She had once made the mistake of bowing on one knee in her youth, arguing that as a Lady Shadon, she should have the same rights as her male counterparts. The *Kolotor'ix* had her remain on her knees for four turns of the hourglass as punishment for speaking out of turn and bowing improperly for her station.

"Rise, *Hon-Hasta'kan'ix ik'Blagdon*," the *Kolotor'ix* said from the throne, his voice overlain softly with whispers.

As Blagdon stood, Senka remained bowed, eyes on the crimson rug that ran the length of the room, contrasting against the grey and white marble of the floor. Since the *Kolotor'ix* did not address her, she would not move or speak until he did.

"What brings you before your *Kolotor'ix*?"

"Lordson Mykel Blagdon's *balutrae*'s brother has gone missing, having left a village of Cetra called Silene."

The *Kolotor'ix* waved his hand dismissively as he descended the stairs to begin walking around Blagdon and Senka as if wishing to see them from all angles. "I have no interest nor time in searching the shadows for a human's missing brother, *balutrae ik'ro'Shadon* or not. Your Lordson should learn to choose his *balutrae* more wisely; a human is hardly a challenge for his bloodline."

"Lordson Mykel will effectively learn and lead *Hasta'kan ik'Blagdon* when appropriate. I do not request that you seek out his brother in the shadows, as that is below your capabilities."

The *Kolotor'ix* stopped in front of Blagdon, his voice low, dangerous."Then I hope you have a good reason for your sake, lest your *Hasta'kan* acknowledge your Lordson as *Hasta'kan'ix* before the sun sets."

"The wayward brother is said to be on his way toward Exonesis Mountain. As *balutrae ik'Blagdon,* he is guaranteed an escort while in my territory and the protection of my *Hasta'kan.* Lady Shadon Senka *ik'Blagdon* will protect and accompany him."

The *Kolotor'ix* turned his body to give Senka his attention. "Stand, Lady Shadon Senka *ik'Blagdon.*"

Blagdon could almost hear Senka's heart pounding as she kept her face looking down at the rug, even as the *Kolotor'ix* moved to stand in front of her. *Stay calm, shira ik'san. Do not do or say anything that will bring dishonor to us.*

"Look upon me."

Senka raised her face slowly and, for a moment, was silent.

Blagdon made a slight sound with his throat.

"Speak, and I obey, our *Kolotor'ix,*" she said.

Hesitation makes one look weak, even in the face of fear. Our Hasta'kan cannot afford this so close to the kalidesh ik'kolotor.

"Do I frighten you?"

Kolosae-ro'jo'aritas, guide her tongue.

"Any *ro'*Shadon or human not frightened by your power and

majesty are *ro'negat*."

"Your Lady Shadon *ik'Blagdon* is wise to say so. You have taught her well, *Hon-Hasta'kan'ix*." The *Kolotor'ix*'s mask never looked away from Senka. "You are accompanying the search for the Lordson's *balutrae*, wherever it will take you?"

"Yes, our *Kolotor'ix*."

"Ensure that you go into Exonesis Mountain. *Ro'*Shadon have never been able to gain access there, and you will be the first. They will not suspect you, for it is common knowledge that *ro'*Shadon cannot be female. You are also trained as a *balvash*, which will be an advantage. You need no Sigil of Blood to perform duties as an assassin or spy. Once there, you will look for any sign of my *kreva ik'Kolotor'ix*. You will also attempt to discover the source of the magick that prevents us from breaching their defenses. If you can disrupt it without being caught, then do so, but do nothing that would not allow you to return to their sacred place."

Blagdon stepped forward. "Our *Kolotor'ix*, she alone will not be able to do all of that without aid, and if she is discovered, she could be lost to us." *I am unsure if I can survive the loss of another of my family.*

The *Kolotor'ix* turned his mask to face Blagdon. "Then I suggest that she be careful."

Blagdon's jaw tightened, and he let out a breath slowly through his nose.

"Do you have something to say?" The tone behind the mask grew lower, almost daring, as he stepped closer to Blagdon, hands slipping under his cloak. "Come, Wilihem, you may speak your mind to your *Kolotor'ix* at least once."

The fact that the *Kolotor'ix* used his first name instead of his title was an insult, but Blagdon would let it go. *There are more significant battles to fight than my wounded pride. He tests me and my restraint because I cannot afford to duel my balutrae yet. There are still too many pieces to set up for Mykel and Senka.*

Blagdon moved on to the last piece of news. "One more minor thing, our *Kolotor'ix*." When the *Kolotor'ix* remained silent, he continued. "I will be hosting a dinner for Lady Senka *ik'Blagdon*'s to choose a suitor. The *Hesta'kan* will be sending their Lordsons, and you wish to be aware of such movements of men of importance. I am already reaching out to *Hasta'heh ik'Carria*t about enhanced security along the roads in my territory."

The *Kolotor'ix* turned and walked back up the stairs to the throne. "No."

"It is our right as the future bride's family to host the dinner of suitors and their *Hasta'kan*."

"It would be within your right if these were normal circumstances. They are not, so it is not within your right to host such an event. The *kalidesh ik'kolotor* approaches and the *Hesta'kan* are preparing to defend their stations and rankings. They will not travel from Nar'Shada to Meridiah to attend dinner, only to return to Nar'Shada. That is wasted time and resources, which I will not allow."

Blagdon glanced at Senka, who glanced at him sideways, eyes slightly wide in confusion, her head still bowed.

"The dinner will be held in Nar'Shada." the *Kolotor'ix* continued, making Blagdon look up at him.

"Our *Kolotor'ix*, you demanded any *Hesta'kan* who left for Meridiah to maintain strongholds there were to forsake their lands and homes in Nar'Shada. I do not have—"

"I am well aware of my laws. You have no land there, so you cannot host the dinner. Instead, the dinner will take place in the palace of Nar'Shada, after the *kalidesh ik'kolotor*. *Hasta'kan ik'Blagdon* will not be burdened with hosting, as it is taken care of, allowing you to focus on your performance in front of the other *Hesta'kan'ix* and myself. With the newest rankings announced, the dinner will be an interesting evening."

How long has he been planning this?

Narisa and he had spent hours figuring out which *Hasta'kan* they wished to speak with first, considering rankings and if they had something Blagdon desired. Changing the rankings directly before the dinner would upset the planned balance, but not allowing *Hon-Hasta'kan ik'Blagdon* to host was a slight that was almost too large to ignore. *If anyone other than the Kolotor'ix demanded such, I would challenge for a duel immediately.*

"Since you have nothing more to say, you may leave. I have other *Hasta'kan* waiting," the *Kolotor'ix* waved his gloved hand dismissively.

Blagdon bowed his head, his fist to his heart, and Senka did the same. "The Shadow's will be done." He began walking toward the door, faintly hearing his daughter following him as they walked past the line of waiting Shadon. He knew a storm would be raging when he returned to Stormhold.

* * *

Blagdon didn't move as the dagger flew across the room at him, barely missing his cheek as the shadows around him deflected it. He kept his eyes on Narisa, hearing the dull *thunk* of the blade and finding the wooden beam on the wall behind him. He had already deflected two other daggers, and there were plenty more where they came from.

"How DARE he!"

"My Narisa, mind your tone and tongue when speaking of our *Kol*—"

She glared at him. "I do not care if he is listening through the shadows right now! He took this from us on purpose! *I had plans!*"

Blagdon made an effort to forget a younger Senka, who used to stamp her foot when upset. If he imagined Narisa doing the same, he would start laughing, an unwise act in the presence of an angry *Sri'balvash*. He went to his raging wife and fought not to smile.

She narrowed her eyes at him. "Don't you dare start smiling, Wilihem! This is not funny!"

He opened his hand, the daggers she'd thrown forming in his

palm, whisps of shadows dancing along the blades before fading.

"Would you like them back?"

Narisa sputtered angrily before snatching her daggers from him, slipping them away in furious motions.

How does she not accidentally cut herself when moving with such fury?

Once they were safely sheathed, Blagdon gently grabbed her chin and tilted her face to look at him. "My beloved, you are beautiful in your fury, magnificent in your anger, yet we must let cooler thoughts prevail so I may have a chance to survive this conversation with either body or clothing intact. I do rather like this tunic."

Narisa's eyes followed his other hand as he ran it over the dark blue tunic with black thread embroideries. When she looked back up at his face, her cheeks were flushed.

Much better.

"How can you, who disarms me with words so easily, claim to hate politics and their games as you do?"

"I cannot lie effectively for long enough to become a player. Why tell lies when the truth, easier to remember, can disarm just as easily?" He ran his gloved left hand over her cheek, watching the anger fade from her face but not the fire in her eyes.

"He's planning something, I know it. He's stripped our control of the dinner's events."

As much control as we would have had during this fiasco, Blagdon thought bitterly, watching the anger flare back in her green eyes like captured flames.

"Wilihem? Have you been listening to a single word I've said?"

Blagdon blinked, realizing he'd been so lost in her eyes that he hadn't heard anything she'd said in the past few minutes. He also realized, at that moment, he didn't care. "No, I haven't."

Narisa opened her mouth to respond, but Blagdon didn't give her a chance, capturing it with his and walking forward as he did so, his hand on her chest, moving upward. As her back hit the far wall, his hand reached her throat, massaging and gripping it with a fierce gentleness that made her cry out.

He pulled back, looking at her, his shadows stopping her from touching him, holding her wrists inches away. "We will remain *Hon-Hasta'kan*. We will be in control."

His eyes ran over her before he leaned in, kissing and biting along her neck.

"Nothing will stop me from taking what is mine."

Shadows wrapped around them as he transported them to their room, where they could find a release for their frustrations.

* * *

Turns of the hourglass later, Blagdon rode Ruin through the paddock gate, careful to keep an eye on the other *kelvorvik*, who followed their alpha and master as they made their way into the fields where they could stretch their legs and truly run. Rotating the packs and herds through the large field was an enormous task, for if two groups who did not get along were trapped in the fields together, it ended quite bloodily. Luckily, the hired hands at Stormhold were experienced and had riders check to ensure no animals were in the fields before allowing the carnivorous ones into it.

Blagdon held Ruin back as the pack ran forward, snorting and kicking their legs in the air. He patted his mount and shadowed himself to the fence line as Ruin raced after the remaining *kelvorvik*.

A hired hand stood with a horse's reins safely behind the fence. "Ya never be thinkin' that a creature that big run so fast," the hired hand spoke up, and Blagdon recognized the speaker immediately.

"How is my lordson's mount faring, Siral?" He asked as he held his hand out for the reins.

Siral shrugged, chewing on a piece of grass sticking out of one side of his mouth. "He be growing. Soon, he'll be as big as Slipstream."

Blagdon looked at the male, whose cavalier attitude irritated his sense of professionalism. *Stormhold was a proud training ground of knights, protectors of kings and queens, and this man held its and my Hasta'kan's future? There must a reason that the Byronian royals had allowed him to be a Stormrider, and I have to trust in their long-dead wisdom.*

"Has Slipstream shown anything of what type of creature she is?"

"She'll show in time, Ah be sure."

He's being evasive on purpose.

"How is your training coming along?" Siral had trained with the Stormhold's soldiers a few days each week. Blagdon did not dare send Siral to the Stormlands to train with their soldiers full-time because Siral would most likely be killed outright for his attitude or mouth. *Having Siral here, where I can monitor him directly, is the best option.* He would train on a regular horse until Slipstream was strong enough to carry a fully armored rider in a few months.

Siral took the piece of grass from his mouth, looked at it, broke a piece off, and continued chewing on it as he spoke. "It be going well. Slipstream says she be strong enough soon but is waiting fer meh to get strong enough, too. But Ah, at least be learning to do better on ground sparring."

"You need it. You were horrible in Woodsong." *Fighting on foot and mounted is entirely different, and the Stormriders had the right idea of training the soldiers in ground combat before putting them on creatures hundreds of pounds heavier than them. At least Siral is beginning to learn something after all.*

"Ah still beat ya in the mounted barrel spar, as well as others."

Blagdon looked at him fully. "Do not be cocky. It does not become someone who is supposed to be a Stormrider. We have trained soldiers in our cavalries to be just as capable, if not more so, than you." *There is a reason we beat your people,* he added silently and mounted the horse, letting Siral walk back alone.

You need not hold a sword to be a warrior.

— Kil'lik'Draven, Bard of the Winds

LENAKA

Lenaka stepped from the library, watching her *putri* attempt to juggle an armful of scrolls and tomes while trying to use his walking stick. She sighed, reaching out to help him by taking the load, but he ignored her, continuing his conversation about correctly classifying some of his stories about the Benstafi elves.

"They are not nautical adventure stories; they are stories about the elven clan that happens to live on the ocean because the Nyfer elves ran them off Andora's shores during the War of the Turning Leaves! That is like classifying the stories of the Fyre elves as a mountain adventure because they live in the Shadowgulf mountains! It is— "

"Kil'lik'Draven! Kil'lik'Lenaka!"

A voice made them turn to see *Rhan'Ashanna* flying toward them, her loyal *lokoni* beside her.

Thank the K'hani, Lenaka thought, taking the opportunity to remove some of the tomes from Draven's arms and tuck them into the bag she kept on one shoulder as he paused in his complaining.

Rhan'Ashana landed, the golden bells woven in her dark brown braids tinkling gently. She was barefoot, but one ankle glistened with golden bracelets as she walked up the stairs, offering a hand to help steady Draven as he came down the last few steps. "Could I have a moment of both of your time before you head back to Hiena'pei Valley?"

Draven bowed, Lenaka following the movement, their left hands held chest-high and their right hands in fists resting on the backs of their opposite hands. "Of course, *Rhan'Ashana*," Draven answered, smiling as he tried to keep his walking stick leaning against his leg so as not to drop it as he bowed. "Have you decided to let me head south to the Shattered Lands?"

Rhan'Ashana shook her head, taking his free hand in both hers as he put his other hand on his walking stick again. "Kil'lik'Draven, for everyone's safety, we cannot allow anyone outside the boundary of the Dawnstone's magick. It is simply too dangerous with the Shadon roaming around Meridiah; we wouldn't be able to protect someone of your importance as much as we wish. We are discussing options, as we said in our meeting." She gave Draven a sympathetic smile and continued. "There are two humans who have just arrived that we'd like you both to meet; as our expert in Meridiah, you would like to hear their stories and record them for us."

Lenaka's heart leaped at the chance to hear new stories and write them down. She glanced at her uncle, who had a similar expression of hope and excitement but was just as quickly replaced with wariness.

"Why have they come here? Who are they?" Draven asked, suddenly sounding suspicious.

Lenaka was used to the sudden mood swings of her *putri;* his paranoia after returning from *Uak'hani* had not lessened over the years, and often, she would catch him shut in his office talking to himself out loud.

"*Putri,* I am sure the *kahena'lo* have searched them for Sigils and made sure they are not Shadon trying to sneak in again," Lenaka spoke up, trying to ease his worries. It was not unheard of the usurpers of the human and elven throne to try such tactics in the past, and it made the position of *kahena* much more dangerous.

"Actually," *Rhan'Ashana* answered, "I was hoping you could tell us. One of them says that she is an acquaintance of yours, a Sigilbearer of Nature named Dulcea."

Lenaka blinked. *A Sigilbearer?* She knew all about Sigils and Sigilbearers, thanks to her *putri's* writing and stories. Still, the only one she knew was *Rhan'Ashana* herself, her golden Sigil of Enchanting taking up a swirling design on her upper arm. *I thought most of the Sigils faded.*

"Dulcea is here?!" Draven's excitement gave way to wariness as his wings puffed, and he looked around quickly, his eyes wide with fear. "Is Ba'hara with her?"

"Who is Ba'hara?" Lenaka asked, looking around for whatever her *putri* seemed to fear.

"I believe he is speaking of her cat," *Rhan'*Ashana answered, her lip twitching, "and yes, she has brought him, along with a human boy who needs a place to stay. We will be getting him a home here, but it will take some time to get everything ready, and he could use some new clothing and a tour. I was hoping that you'd be able to aid in that, Kil'lik'Lenaka."

"Of course, I would be honored, *Rhan'*Ashana," Lenaka smiled. "I am ready to help with anything that they need. Is there anything you can tell me about them?"

Draven frowned, still muttering to himself. "I hope he doesn't remember the time I dropped him in that well by mistake, but he really shouldn't have crawled into that bag."

*Rhan'*Ashana's smile faded a touch. "Sigilbearer Dulcea brought him here because the Shadon army destroyed his home, and the people he was traveling with betrayed him. He may be slow to trust anyone besides her."

Lenaka nodded. She knew about loss and how it tainted one's worldview. However, she was ignorant of how betrayal could affect one's view, only learning of such in fictional stories in the library. *Perhaps I can write about what Clep tells me to further my understanding of the mind.* "I will do what I can to ensure he feels safe."

*Rhan'*Ashana turned, watching two cloaked figures walk over, a giant black cat beside one of them.

The taller of the two lowered her hood, revealing reddish-brown hair that fell in soft curls as if it had come undone from a braid. She smiled and hugged Draven, who picked her up and spun her around, laughing.

"Dulcea! My old friend! I thought you were long gone!"

Dulcea smiled and steadied herself once Draven let her go. "It is good to see ya as well, Kil'lik'Draven. Ya remember Ba'hara, correct?"

Draven gave a small sound as the great cat growled.

Lenaka stepped back nervously, glancing at Dulcea worriedly.

*Rhan'*Ashana's *lokoni* quietly touched his sword as if expecting the cat to attack at any second.

Ba'hara yawned, showing his great teeth, and lay down, watching them with golden eyes that seemed to take in every motion.

"I remember him, aye."

Dulcea smiled and gestured to the cloaked figure beside her.

He lowered his hood, his blue eyes looking tired and haunted from a face paler than she'd ever seen in Exonesis. *I am so used to looking at the different shades of brown and black skin that sometimes I forget that there are those with paler skin outside in Meridiah.*

"Hello, my name is Kil'lik'Lenaka," she offered her familial name, as was customary. One did not give one's birth name to strangers, and only close friends and family could address them with it. It was also considered improper to say one's birth name publicly.

I wonder how Dulcea knows Putri; we have not left Exonesis since he returned from Uak'hani, and I do not remember seeing her before.

The boy looked at her for a long moment as if judging her silently before holding out his gloved hand and giving a whistle.

Lenaka reached forward as if to shake his hand, as she'd read was the custom in Meridiah, when a hawk flew out of the sky, landing on the leather of his glove, which protected his hand from the sharp talons.

"This is Memory. My name is Clep."

Lenaka smiled. It was reassuring to see that the boy was the friend of an ally of the skies. "It is a pleasure to meet you both. Would you like to have a tour around Exonesis?"

Dulcea nodded. "Ah believe that is a good idea. Why don't ya both walk on ahead, and Kil'lk'Draven and Ah will follow at our own pace?" She held her arm out for Draven to put his through so he could steady himself as they walked.

Lenaka watched them for a long moment, frowning. *Just who is she to him? Putri has never spoken of a Sigilbearer of Nature being so close to him.*

*Rhan'*Ashana smiled. "I will leave you in their capable hands." She handed Lenaka a small bag that clinked lightly as Lenaka took it. "Here are skyshards to pay for their clothing and goods they'd wish to purchase."

"You don't have to do that," Clep spoke up, looking embarrassed.

"These are part of the taxes we collect monthly to take care of any repairs as well as care for all those who come into our lands," *Rhan'*Ashana offered gently.

Lenaka knew that there were *hela'ko* who would not like to have goods given away, and this was a compromise to help those refugees they allowed inside the Dawnstone's barrier. She smiled at her *lokoni*, who nodded and followed her as she flew into the sky.

Clep watched them take off, his eyes wide. "Flying and being so free must be incredible."

It is incredible to fly, but we are not as free to do as we'd like as you would believe. As much as it seems we can do as we want, the mountains around us are sometimes less of a border and more of a cage. "So what is Meridiah like?" she asked, changing the subject as Clep tossed his arm upward and let Memory fly around the garden.

Clep looked around as if wondering how his homeland compared to hers. "It is nothing like this. Here, it is so colorful, bright, and happy. Back home, we were surrounded by farmland and woods."

Lenaka laughed. "This is because it is our capital, Wan'hela. The garden also has plenty of brightly colored flowers and sprygts flying around." She smiled, gesturing to the small feathered humanoids darting from flower to flower as they searched for nectar to return to their hives. "Hiea'pei Valley, where *Putri* and I live, has a lot of farmlands surrounded by mountains. There are a lot of greens, but not as many bright colors the further outside Wan'hela you go unless you know where to look."

She gestured to where they could see glimpses of brightly colored cloth over the garden's trees. "The *helaono* over there is full of brightly colored cloths created by crushing the dried flowers and fruits to make dyes."

"The *helaono*? What is that?"

"The market. *Hela* means to sell, and *ono* means place in Dawnese."

"So the *helaono* means the place of selling?"

Lenaka nodded, smiling. "Because we have so many dawnwarriors here, having an open *helaono* with stalls is more accessible than being inside buildings. Each stall has its owner and vendors, known as *hela'ko*. Many goods and services many make themselves or have their families assist in."

Clep looked around as they passed a fountain and walked toward the open area with stalls.

Lenaka glanced over to see a crowd of dawnwarriors standing around, hands in the air as they shouted, standing off to the side of the square.

Clep reached for his satchel, a concerned look on his face, and started to rush over.

Lenaka caught up to him and touched his shoulder. "There is no danger there; I'll show you."

They walked over quickly and maneuvered through the crowd gathered to see two male dawnwarriors standing facing each other on opposite sides of a white square made of painted rocks on the ground. Both males had stripped to loincloths, their wings arched, standing with their bare feet shoulder-width apart. Slowly, they began stomping a rhythm, and the crowd started clapping.

The first male began shouting a steady chant in Dawnese, thumping his chest and making deliberate, sharp gestures with his arms, wooden spear, and wings.

Clep looked at Lenaka, speaking low. "I don't understand. What is going on?"

"Tut'Akai is the younger male," Lenaka said, keeping her voice low, "and he wishes to ask Noa'Powa for his daughter's hand in marriage. This is called the *Maipo o'o K'hani*, the dance of dragons. This part represents the depth of love the suitor has for the father's daughter and shows his prowess and willingness to stand up and defend her."

The younger male returned to his starting position, stamping, and the older male began chanting in Dawnese as he gestured and stomped with purpose.

"What are they saying?"

"Tut'Akai has been declaring his love for Noa'Appai, and Noa'Powa has been saying his demands for his daughter's hand in marriage, what he expects of a future husband."

After Noa'Powa had returned to his position, with his legs apart and spear held horizontally, the males began chanting at each other, their voices mingling as they mirrored each other.

Clep blinked at her. "That's what they are saying? They sound angry — I thought they said they would tear each other's faces off."

Lenaka grinned widely. "The *K'hani* are fierce creatures, and in this dance, the dawnwarriors represent them, fighting for the heart of hearts."

She looked back at the two rivaling males both wanting to protect the heart of the same dawnwarrior maiden. *It really is romantic.*

"Now they pray to the *K'hani* together that their actions be guided and no one gets seriously injured."

Clep frowned. "Seriously injured in what?"

Lenaka didn't have to answer because the two males suddenly rushed at each other, wooden spears meeting each other in sharp sounds as the two men began fighting.

Clep jumped at the sound, looking worried. "Are you sure they're going to be all right?"

Lenaka smiled. "This is common, Clep. One day, a male will challenge my *putri* for my hand in marriage."

"So what happens if Tut'Akai wins?"

"If he wins, he will have earned Noa'Appai's hand in marriage. If he loses, Noa'Powa can give him another chance in the future or refuse his offer. If that happens, Tut'Akai may not ask for her hand again unless he proves to be given another chance or his daughter asks it of her father. Come on, let's get to the *helaono* and get you supplies." Lenaka turned, guiding Clep away from the sound of the two sparring males and the crowd cheering them on.

"Aren't you curious of who will win?" Clep asked, glancing back at the gathered dawnwarriors.

"Word travels fast here, Clep, both good and ill. We will hear about it for a few weeks to come."

Lenaka watched Clep's eyes fill with wonder as they walked through the carved stone gates and into the city. It was nothing of how her *putri* had described human cities with buildings so close together with pointed roofs but open and airy. Light stonework lined the streets, allowing plant life to grow without fear of being trampled. Trees provided shade and filled the air with fragrances of different flowers.

A dawnwarrior child landed near them, her thick, coarse hair so curly and full that the flowers tucked into the coiled strands gave her hair the appearance of a beautiful black bush with orange flowers. She looked Clep over, took a bracelet of woven strands off her wrist, and handed it to him, speaking in Dawnese.

"Um, thank you," Clep stammered, glancing back at Lenaka, unsure what to think or say.

Lenaka stepped up, smiling. *"Haka nou'u."*

The child smiled and excitedly spoke with Lenaka in Dawnese for a moment before flying off, joined by other children who began pointing and finding others to give bracelets to in the garden nearby, laughing.

Lenaka looked at Clep, smiling. "She wanted you to have a bracelet; she and her friends are trying to trade for them."

"I didn't have anything to give them, and what did you trade for it?" Clep looked at his bracelet, his touch careful as if afraid to break it.

"I told him my *putri* is a great bard, and he may have stories of your homeland that she can listen to in exchange for a bracelet."

"Is your uncle's stories that good?"

Lenaka felt her smile slip slightly. "They used to think so."

Clep watched her for a long moment, started to say something, and seemed to change his mind. "So, what did you say to her the first time? Hawka.. Um…"

"Haka nou'u means thanks to you, or more simply, thank you."

"Your language sounds beautiful, like music. Could you teach me some more about your people?"

"Of course, Clep."

Lenaka walked past one of the guards, a sword on his side, a soft smile as he bowed in greeting, keeping his eyes out. "He is one of the guards of Exonesis, called *lokoni,* meaning *longspear.* Their job is to protect the people of Exonesis in our day-to-day lives."

"He's not holding a long spear, though," Clep whispered, and Lenaka laughed.

"They are our traditional weapons from centuries ago, so even now, they have a long spear tattooed on their lower arms," she gestured to the dawnwarrior's lower arm, where a black spear was tattooed under a black band. "It is their way of showing loyalty to each other and capacity as soldiers to all around us. Each line on the spear's shaft means twenty years within the service to our people."

"Do all markings mean something? I've noticed many dawnwarriors have facial paint and tattoos."

"They do. Some mean you are married, others show occupations or how many children you have. It also depends on your family; some have their meanings and symbols." Lenaka gestured to her face. "For example, the dots under the eyes represent family members who have passed on. As our tears pass over them, and they help heal our hurt. A band around the upper arm means you are married because it is where a favor is worn while you are courting. Tattooed bands signify children born of marriage, and where they are located depends on your family, for each has their tradition of where the tattoo is placed. Some tattoos even signify your occupation, education status, and victories. It can be complicated, but they are all beautiful."

"The others believed that dawnwarriors were just stories, but here you are, flying and walking all around, living daily lives. I fear that I am hallucinating, and I am in the woods alone with my book."

How sad and lonely you must have been, Lenaka thought, noticing Clep's hands never strayed far from his satchel as if unconsciously wanting to ensure it was still with him. *He reminds me of Putri, who constantly wants to keep scrolls of parchment and his enchanted quill with him in case something exciting happens that he wants to record.*

They walked through the *helaono* while letting Clep pick out some clothing to purchase with the skyshards that *Rhan'Ashana* had given Lenaka.

Clep sighed heavily. "I don't like feeling like a charity," he complained, "I didn't earn or deserve these."

"Dawnwarriors trade any goods or services with each other if that makes you feel better."

He brightened slightly, and soon, he was bartering healing salves and various potions for his clothing.

After a bit of walking around and trading, they walked back toward the temple, Clep carrying goods that he earned on his own.

"There's no trouble here, no war, no Dark Army soldiers lingering in the shadows, ready to hunt someone or burn down their homes. It's almost too good to be true."

Lenaka frowned slightly. *Is there a lot of that in Meridiah?*

Clep stopped by a fountain, looking up at the depiction of two dawnwarrior children playing with birds, their faces uplifted toward the sky as they held their open hands out for the birds to fly from. "I've never seen any carving that was so lifelike. Do you think that maybe I can ask someone to carve some of the Light's effigies for the Aldarwood back home?" Clep flinched slightly. "If it even still stands. We tried keeping it safe, but for all I know, the Dark Army returned and burned it down. A lot of hardship and evil lives beyond these mountains."

Lenaka blinked in horror. "They'd burn it down?"

Clep nodded sadly. "The Dark Army doesn't worship the Light like we do, so why would they keep it? Life is sacred, and they killed everyone in my village. They do not care what we mere humans think."

"Well, I care what you think." Lenaka walked down the temple's main hall, gesturing to different statues of *K'hani* and explaining their contributions to their society. She smiled up at a sapphire-eyed statue of a dragon with quills tucked behind her horns and a stack of tomes in one hand, her other holding a scroll. "That is *K'han'Kaalei*, patron of stories. She created our writing system and began chronicling our history on scrolls in our library. *Putri* says that she was Hinestra's first bard. She is his favorite *K'hani*, but don't tell the others," she whispered, making Clep smile.

A citrine-eyed statue depicted a dragon with one hand up as if drawing a rune in the air with his claw, his other hand holding a shield. "*K'han'Zaborath*, the youngest K'han, created the ability to enchant goods. My *putri* and I have enchanted quills, so we do not run out of ink when we write. He is also well-known for slaying the tyrant *K'han'Thraxxis*, who enslaved many humans in his territory. Because of this, many *kaheha'lo* and *lakoni'lo* also count him as their patron."

"That's incredible. The Light has different aspects; each has its domain. Are *K'hani* patrons like that?"

Lenaka thought about that. "Perhaps."

"Do you write stories like your uncle?"

Lenaka ducked her head, a little embarrassed. "They aren't as good as *putri*'s. I hope to one day leave Exonesis to write about what is happening outside the mountains, but since we cannot, I try recording what is happening here."

"You can't leave the mountains?"

Lenaka shook her head. "We are forbidden due to the Shadon occupation and the murder of the Byronian royal family. Our leader, *Rhan*'Kahan, was an ally and friend of the elven queen. He took their deaths rather hard; a lot of dawnwarriors did. I was too little to remember it."

"You're over a hundred and fifty seasons old?" Clep blinked in surprise at her.

"Dawnwarriors were once considered an elven clan until we were blessed with flying. We can live to be over four hundred years old."

"That explains why your ears are pointed," Clep said low, almost to himself, before flinching as if realizing he said it aloud. "I'm sorry, that was rude of me."

Lenaka shook her head. "It's okay, Clep. You haven't seen a dawnwarrior before."

"I've never seen anyone with your shade of skin before. Are all dawnwarriors that deeply tanned?"

Lenaka smiled. "Because we fly so high in the sky under *K'hani'Exonia*'s eye, our skins turned darker over time to prevent us from getting burned. Now we are all beautiful shades of brown."

"I wish my brother were here; he'd love to learn about dawnwarriors. Our Nan told us stories about your kind." Clep watched a human walk past them, carrying an armload of scrolls. "I didn't know there were this many humans here."

"We have taken in refugees, though not as much as we used to, for safety reasons. Unfortunately, two cultures can't always get along and sometimes it causes conflict, but we try our best to soothe it over."

Clep stopped, looking at a mosaic on the wall, created with thousands of small pieces of colored material, of a dragon bursting from fire and rock, debris raining around it as its face looked skyward.

Lenaka smiled, looking at the mosaic. "Exonesis was formed when the great dragon *K'han'Exonia* burst from the earth and flew up into the sky, forming the peaks you see around our homeland. They serve as a way to protect us from outside forces and shelter us from severe weather, keeping the lands of Exonesis warm and safe. Because of this, we can also grow crops year-round."

Clep blinked at her. "A single dragon was big enough to make this area?"

"*K'han'Exonia* is the largest of the *K'hani*. Her left eye is seen in the sky as the sun, her right eye, the moon as she flies back and forth over Hinestra, keeping watch on us all. Sometimes, on rare days, you can see her watching us fully with both her eyes seen in the sky at the same time. She guides all dawnwarriors in our everyday lives."

Dulcea came walking up, Ba'hara beside her, followed by *Rhan*'Kahan, whose long braids and golden beads fell down his bare chest and back, folded white wings towering behind him. He wore a loose-fitting garment around his waist, his wrists were covered in bracers of blue and gold, and he wore a thick beaded decorative collar guard that tied in the back. On his hip was a sword, and his dark brown eyes seemed to take in everything but held a caring warmth.

"There ya are, Clep," Dulcea said, smiling, "Ah had wondered where ya'd gone."

Where is Putri?

At Lenaka's worried face, Dulcea continued. "Yer uncle is over there, by the statue of *K'han'Zaborath*." She smiled and gestured to the male with her. "Clep, this is *Rhan*'Kahan, the king of Exonesis."

Clep stammered slightly, unsure of what to do.

Lenaka touched his shoulder gently and held her left hand horizontally in front of her chest, palm down. "This hand represents the ground," she explained as she put her right hand into a fist and placed it on the back of her left hand. "This hand is the sun. Since the sun is rising over the earth, it represents the dawn, which *K'han'Exonia* created when she flew into the sky and looked down upon Exonesis for the first time. Now you bow your head."

Clep copied her movement, blushing slightly as she helped him adjust his hands slightly before bowing his head to the king. "Thank you for having me here. *Haka nou'u*," he added after a moment.

"Greetings, Clep. You are most welcome," *Rhan'Kahan* replied, his voice deep but warm at the same time. "I hope you find our land welcoming and our people friendly."

"I do, sir... Your majesty... um..."

"*Rhan* is the title if you wish to use it, or *Rhan'toki*, which means 'male ruler,'" *Rhan'*Kahan offered gently. "When you become the leader, your people become your family, so *Rhan* is adopted in place of your familial name."

Clep nodded a touch quickly. "Kil'lik'Lenaka told me that, too. I do find your people welcoming and friendly, *Rhan'toki*."

*Rhan'*Kahan smiled, his teeth white against his dark brown skin. "You do not have to be so afraid, Clep; you will find that *Rhan'*Ashana and I are informal when speaking with our subjects unless it comes to important matters. We do not wish to make our people feel as if they could not come to us with concerns, for all share their worries and concerns."

He excused himself, turning as a *lokoni* came up and spoke low to him.

*Rhan'*Kahan laughed, nodding. "It seems that there will be a wedding soon after all. If you will excuse me, I will see to the soon-to-be husband of the Noa family." He nodded and took to the sky, his guards behind him.

Clep looked around, and slowly, his smile faded. "I wish my brother were alive to see this."

The lessons of the past,
Unless read and learned upon,
Become the bane of the future
For they will revisit like ghosts.

— Kil'lik'Draven, Bard of the Winds

RATSBAYNE

Ratsbayne frowned, rubbing his temple. He'd read so much that his eyes felt like they were swimming in their sockets. Hearing a knock at the study door, he shouted for the knocker to come in and give him some relief.

Mari'aida smiled at him as she walked in and sat, glancing at the parchments on the table. "What were you reading about today, Sir Siral?"

She be lot more relaxed around, smiling more. That was a good thing; at least she not being harmed. "Ah studied some about the War o' the Turning Leaves when all the elven clans fought. It sounds like a real *krushku* o' a time." He winced, realizing he shouldn't have sworn before a lady.

Mari'aida smiled, not seeming to take offense. "My mother was an archer and runecarver for the Mun'ari Clan during that war. She and the former queen were battlemates together. She later served as a captain in the former Byronian Army."

"What happened to the king and queen? Ah've read bits and pieces, but not all tomes will tell the truth o' it. Tomes be only as honest as the one who be holding the quill. Ah trust ya to tell meh yer truth."

Her smile slipped slightly, and she forced it back up. "They were slain following the Rule of Conquest."

"Ah've not read about that yet. What is it?"

"It is not an elvish event or time, Sir Siral. In *ro'*Shadon law, if you slay a *hasta'ix* or ruling party, you become the leader in their stead. This law prevents random assassinations and ensures responsibility.

Avoiding taking the mantle after said conquest is frowned upon and often leads to pursuit and death."

"Would that mean whoever killed the assassin is now the leader of whatever they'd had tried to escape?"

Mari'aida smiled. "You catch on quickly."

"Ah blame the lack o' ale. So he uses this law to kill the king and queen, becoming the leader of Meridiah."

"Correct. However, the *Kolotorix* has stated that he did not wish to kill the queen or the princesses. He had only wanted to kill King Byron so he could rule beside Queen Mari'anath, but she had given him no choice and did what he had to do when she attacked Ambassador Jorrah-*kyr*."

Siral frowned. It was unlikely that the *Kolotor'ix* would have announced that he had made a mistake, but he wasn't sure enough to comment on it. *The fact that Mari'aida knows about it when others do not made meh wonder what their relationship is.*

"The queen be a war-general during the War o' the Turning Leaves. He killed her husband, the King. If she hadn't attacked back, Ah be worried."

He stood, leaning against a beam by the window, looking at the capitol in the distance. If an emergency were to happen, they'd be able to ride there within a turn of the hourglass but were far enough away to be left alone by citizens wanting to get close to the mounts. According to the scrolls, as a Stormrider, he could get there faster than any other soldier, making them the first line of defense besides the palace guards within the city proper.

"The princesses? They be de--" he couldn't finish the sentence, for he felt a tightness in his chest that didn't match his emotions. He was talking about those he didn't even know or remember. *Why Ah be worried fer them?*

She looked down sadly. "We were separated during the attack, and I couldn't find them. I ran to the barracks to look for my mother, but she was away leading soldiers, so I hid. I was found and brought before the *Kolotor'ix* by two *belvash*. He'd already removed all the thrones but the largest one by the time I was brought before him. I had no idea what had happened; we didn't know that the King and Queen were dead yet."

Mari'aida played with a strand of her hair, not looking at him. "He turned toward me and demanded where the princesses were. I didn't know how he knew I was their friend."

"Did he know yer name?" His eyes narrowed slightly, and he felt almost a cooperation between himself and Slipstream, wanting to know the same information: *Who is the Kolotor'ix? Who is the man who had killed so many of the people Mari'aida knew and cared for? If they had known her name, it could be someone they had all known, posing as a friend, an ally for so long. But who?*

Mar'aida nodded. "He knew my name. The *Kolotor'ix*'s face is always masked, and his voice is different. I remember he started to walk toward me, and an arrow struck him in the chest." Her lips curved into a proud smile. "I turned to see my mother and her soldiers in the doorway, having fought her way inside. I'd never seen them fight so hard, but the Shadon were fast and easily cut my mother's soldiers down. The *Kolotor'ix* grabbed my arm, holding me so I couldn't run to her. It wasn't until my mother drew her blade and cut a light rune in the air that they lept back, unable to use their shadows."

"Impressive."

"Runecarvers were some of the rarest styles of magick, using specialized blades and movements to cut runes to focus the magick of the world to perform certain things. We've only known of one personally, though there are stories of them from before the War of the Turning Leaves," Slipstream spoke up quietly.

Why ya can remember things Ah cannot, but ya dun't tell meh everything ya know?

The voice in his head was silent.

"The *Kolotor'ix* was so impressed with my mother trying to kill him that he offered her our lives and his hand in marriage. He thought an elf beside him willingly would keep the remaining citizens from rebelling and get the dwarves and dawnwarriors to be part of the greater alliance with the *ro'*Shadon. She accepted to protect me and prevent more innocent people from being slaughtered."

"He thought trying to kill him be impressive? Most people Ah know of would be upset."

"Remember, *ro'*Shadon have a different type of culture," Mari'aida explained, "It took a while for me to understand them as well; they are much different from the Mun'ari and humans."

"So what happened to yer mum?"

"We stayed with the *Kolotor'ix,* and even though they were betrothed, they worked as one to help rebuild the kingdom. Not only did the people lose their royal family, but they were recovering from heavy losses after the Scourge War. It was a very rough time for the people of Meridiah, but the *Kolotor'ix,* with my mother's aid, was beginning to make a difference."

"So yer mum be betrothed to the *Kolotor'ix,* which means ye know who he be, right, lass?" He looked at her, watching her as if he'd be tested on her reactions later.

Mari'aida gave a flat look. "The *Kolotor'ix'*s identity is secret for a reason, Sir Siral. Not even the *ro'*Shadon know the face under the mask."

"Ah not asking about the *ro'*Shadon. Ya can't live with someone that long and not know them. How does he bathe and sleep? He can't keep the mask on all the time."

"I am not with him when he bathes or sleeps. May we talk about something else now? I do not want to be punished because of this conversation, nor should you."

Fine. Fer now. "So where yer mum be now?"

Her smile faded, and such a sadness came to her eyes that Siral had to fight not to comfort her. He didn't think putting an arm around her shoulder when she was betrothed to the Lordson of the Leigelord was intelligent.

He didn't push but waited for her to tell the story at her own pace. *Ah have nowhere Ah have to be right now.*

"My mother went riding to meet a contact who said they knew where some elves were. She wanted to talk to them and see if they would be willing to return."

Ah dun't blame them if they didn't want to.

"During her outing, my mother was ambushed, her guards killed, and she's been missing ever since. We still do not know who is responsible." Mari'aida looked at her hands. "The *Kolotor'ix* went mad, taking his vengeance out on anyone who dared cross him. He'd slain five *hesta'ix* before he received word that I was here in Stormhold, having asked the protection of *Hasta'kan'ix ik'Blagdon*." She pronounced the Shadese words easily but with a slight elvish accent, giving it a unique sound that Siral thought sounded nicer than the native speakers of Shadese.

"Why did ya ask Blagdon's protection?" At her look, he sighed and corrected himself. "Leigelord Blagdon's protection?"

"He's the greatest duelist the *ro*'Shadon have. The medallions on his belt are those he has slain in duels himself. He is not known for leaving an enemy alive; they are more dangerous after they are beaten and still breathing. He'd not take the chance, never again."

"What do ya mean, never again?"

"Assassins slew his first Lady and second Lordson during a carriage ride; no one has ever claimed to have done the deed. Lordson Mykel speculates that the assassin was someone his *brak'ha* had let live in a duel and had carried out the grudge decades or even centuries later."

Even Ah have ta admit, that be impressive.

"With *Hasta'kan'ix ik'Blagdon* protecting me, I'd have a chance at surviving it. The *Kolotor'ix* was furious when he found out, but he calmed his anger. Instead of bringing me back home, he named *Hasta'kan'ix ik'Blagdon* his *balutrae* immediately so no one else could ever kill him. But it made it so the *Kolotor'ix*'s wrath couldn't touch anyone under

Hasta'kan ik'Blagdon, keeping them safe."

"Ah know about *balutrae;* Apollo be one." He was quiet for a long moment, thinking about the conversation. "Talking to ya be helping, lass. It be answering questions Ah didn't know Ah had."

She smiled, nodding. "It's nice to know there are Stormriders again among us. I missed watching them ride across the skies and protect the people. Maybe you can be our protector when my mother is found and weds the *Kolotor'ix.*"

"She never wed him, so there be hope fer her yet."

"He's not that bad."

We will see, lass. We will see.

* * *

The next day, Ratsbayne walked from the wagon, carrying a hay bale using metal hooks instead of having the binding wires cut into his leather gloves. Gideon, Stormhold's foreman, oversaw the operation, and as soon as the wagon was emptied, he had another take its place for them to unload.

"Ah dun't see a fields fer hay around here," Ratsbayne admitted, looking around while he pressed his hands into his lower back, groaning at the dull *pop* from his spine, "where does it come from?"

"We don't grow hay here," Riky replied, grabbing another bale of hay from the back of the wagon, *"Hasta'kan ik'Blagdon* has enough to do with the breeding, training, and maintenance of the mounts for the *ro'Shadon. Montres,* one of the *hesta'heh* under Blagdon, manages the farmlands outside of Stormhold."

Ratsbayne carried his haybale to Slipstream's stable. While the regular horses shared a stable and pasture, Slipstream's was separated, living alone with her colt in a large pasture. Gideon had said it was to keep the Meridian horses safe in case the colt's *kelvorvik*-blood awoke and he began attacking them. *Ah hope they not be lonely, being away from the other animals.*

"Don't worry, I'm not lonely, Siral," the gentle voice of Slipstream came into his head as he set down the haybale.

Ratsbayne walked to the stable door and watched her walk around the paddock large enough for a small herd, but instead held two creatures. Slipstream's coat was no longer grey, but a beautiful bright white, her mane a mixture of white, greys, and blues. Her colt's coat was black but held the same bluish highlights as Slipstream's and his mane was a mixture of black, blue, and grey. Both animals held eyes the shade of Meridian summer skies, making them stand out more among the red-eyed *kelvorvik* and *kelvorkav*.

Leigelord Blagdon had said that *kelvorvik* colts were known for attacking their mothers once they got the taste of blood. Ratsbayne knew better than to argue with the master of the murder ponies and observed the colt whenever it nursed from Slipstream. As far as he knew, both had regular flat teeth for grinding grass, but he hadn't personally checked. The last time he'd seen flesh get close to an animal with *kelvorvik* blood, it was being eaten. *Ah'd rather not attempt that.*

He still didn't remember his past nor any vigorous training or ritual that would bond him to an animal, but was fond of the mare and her colt and would protect them. *"We'd do the same for you, Siral. He does not know you yet, but he will care for you more than just the one who feeds his mother."*

"Have ya thought o' a name for yer colt yet? Since ya named yerself."

"I didn't name myself, Siral; you did, years ago. You were there when I was born, aiding me as we learned and trained together. I may not remember everything, but I do remember you naming me as you brushed me in the stables."

Ah did? He sighed, shaking his head. *There be so much Ah cannot remember.*

Slipstream walked to the window, brushing her head against his shoulder. *"We will remember together, Siral. There are gaps in our memories, and discussing them with each other may help fill in the missing pieces. I still do not remember how I got here before the master found me wandering and brought me to Stormhold to live."*

"The master, huh."

She snorted at him, flicking her tail. *"Do not sound so jealous. I thought I was an average horse, and he my master, but then I saw you and remembered when I touched you as you held your amulet."*

Ratsbayne chuckled before getting the shovel and mucking out the dirty stall. This barn was once used for winged creatures, so their stalls were larger than others. Due to them being the only occupants, Ratsbayne didn't have as much to clean as much as the other stablehands did, which made them act coldly toward him at times. He'd hear them complain in the bunkhouse, saying he was getting a lighter load, was favored by the *Hasta'kan'ix,* and was slacking off constantly by never being around to work. *They dun't understand that the rest o' mah time be filled with studying and training they did not have to participate in. They may think they Ah be the lucky one, but they dun't have the same headaches at the end o' the days.*

"Ah have training later with the cavalry soldiers," he explained to Slipstream aloud because sometimes thinking to her still felt odd. "Ah have a lot to catch up on."

"It will come back to you, Siral. You will catch up to them in no time and soon surpass them. You may not be able to ride me for a while longer, but eventually, you will, so do not get attached to the horse they lend you."

"Ya be jealous of a regular horse?"

Slipstream snorted and flicked her tail, walking off toward their colt, who chased a butterfly around the field. *"Never."*

* * *

Ratsbayne rode a brown mare alongside a wagon, viewing the area around them. The land was open and filled with hues of lighter green, much different than how the lands around Woodsong garrison had been, nestled near the forest. He was surprised by the lack of buildings or fences, even though he could see the tallest buildings of the capitol further in the distance. *Where be everyone? There should be some farmers or villages, but we ain't passed any. How do people live out here?*

Ratsbayne blinked at the sight before him as they rode over a hill. A group of tan-colored tents and temporary shelters stood in a large formation, each with aisles between them and separated into sections. A large tent stood at one end of the camp, tall flagpoles towering over it, their standards too far away for him to tell what they were. Groups of horses were tethered to a large canopy, protecting them from the sun.

There be hardly any trees here. Are we going to really stay out here?

Once they arrived at the tented area, armored soldiers walked over and began unloading the wagon quickly, giving orders in Shadese.

Gideon went to Ratsbayne, handing him a missive with the blue and silver seal of *Hasta'kan ik'Blagdon* pressed upon it. "Dismount and then bring this to the *korrati*'s tent," he said, pointing him toward the largest tent at the opposite end of the camp. He then began walking his and Ratsbayne's horses toward the paddock nearby, not allowing him to question it.

Ratsbayne headed across the grounds, glancing at the folded and sealed parchment in his hand, wondering what it said. *Ah hope it dun't say something similar to 'slay the one who holds this message.' That would be something Kerrik would have and probably had done.*

He glanced around at the soldiers, many of whom were sharpening weapons, sparring either with each other or against straw and wooden training dummies. *Ah dun't see permanent buildings like in Woodsong. Perhaps it is a temporary garrison.*

The smell of stew tickled his nose as he walked past a cooking tent. The cloth sides were rolled up against the wooden support post to keep the cooking fire inside without catching the entire thing ablaze. He saw men in simple clothing cutting meat at a table; another table had vegetables already diced and ready for adding to the stew. Across the way, he saw soldiers hanging up wet clothing on lines of twine attached to poles to dry.

There be no females here?

As he watched a male sitting on a log and working a thread and needle over a pair of breeches, Ratsbayne walked into a male in armor, who immediately began shouting at him to watch where he was walking.

"Damned messengers," the soldier grumbled, pushing past.

Ratsbayne watched him walk off, deciding it was better not to say anything and keep moving. *Maybe Ah am growing more mature, or at least, Ah now know how to pick a fight better.*

Two soldiers stood outside the flaps of the largest tent, looking slightly bored as they waited for whoever was inside.

Finally, an armored male came out and blinked at Ratsbayne. "Who are you?"

"Ah be here to see the *korrati*," Ratsbayne said, looking the male over for some rank, and finally found the signet hanging off the male's pauldron. *A kriss'ix*, he realized, blaming the time at Woodsong with Apollo for this useless knowledge because it had no bearing on him.

The *kriss'ix* looked him up and down before scoffing and walking off, the two other soldiers trailing him like obedient pups.

Siral shrugged and went to the tent's flap, wondering how he would announce himself when there was no door to knock upon. *Do Ah just walk in?*

"Come in," a voice said, and it reminded Siral of how Blagdon always seemed to know when he was about to knock on his door. Pushing aside the thought of asking the man inside about it, for he was sure he wouldn't get an answer, he walked into the tent, looking around.

Fer someone who was supposed to be living like wartime, he sure has a lot o' things that would be hard to move around, Siral thought, taking in the large wooden desk at one side of the tent, the full-sized bed with a straw mattress, and a long table with maps and candles. A dresser with decanters sat against the far cloth wall, and Siral found it challenging to take his eyes from the empty crystal glasses on the metal tray. He finally looked back at the table when the male before him cleared his throat.

"I said, you have a missive for me?" The male, wearing armor with a long crimson cloak down the back, had his hand out for the message. Siral chided himself for being distracted by the decanter, or rather the possible contents it held.

He handed it to him and turned to walk out quickly before the liquid inside started calling his name.

"Hold on," the male spoke up.

Siral sighed and stared at the tent flap, unwilling to turn around as if he feared falling back into the siren's call. *Ah'd been away from it fer so long, ya'd think Ah'd not even look at it. Am Ah still so weak as to be beaten by a liquid?*

"It says here that you are to begin training with my men and for me to see what you are capable of."

Siral nodded. "Aye, ah am supposed to."

"What is your name?"

"Ah be Ra— Siral." He stumbled over the new name; he couldn't see himself as the same Siral in the Stormrider tome, as if it was a case of mistaken identity. The book made 'Sir Siral Karog' important, a Stormrider and queensguard; competent, honorable, a good fighter. *That not be meh.*

The *korrati* nodded, looking over the parchment.

"*Hon-Hasta'kan'ix ik'Blagdon* seems to think that you are something I would be interested in." He rolled the parchment, looking Siral over. "I doubt it; the *Hon-Hasta'kan'ix* may know *kelvorvik* like no *ro'*Shadon, but he does not know soldiers as well as I. You're not soldier material, boy."

"It been a while since anyone called meh a lad." It pricked at him, and he turned to face the *korrati* fully.

"Do not try to fight him; he is trying to bait you into it so he can send you back to Stormhold. He is much more experienced than you, you will not win."

Would it be so bad to go back to Stormhold to be around ya and yer colt?

"You are here to learn from him, hoping that it will jog our memory of our past. We can't do that in Stormhold. Now calm down."

Grumbling, he forced himself to relax his fists and take a breath.

The *korrati* frowned and stepped forward, pointing with an open hand.

Ratsbayne fought the urge to smack his gauntleted hand out of his face.

"I am over three hundred and fifteen seasons old. You and your kind are children to me. It would be wise of you to watch your tone with me, son."

"Ah ain't yer boy, Ah ain't yer son," he snapped.

"You sound just like Apollo did in Woodsong. Are you going to act like that when we need him to help us?"

Krushku. Sighing, he forced his tone to be less insulted. "Ah be Siral Karog."

The *korrati* laughed, but it held no humor as he tossed the missive onto the desk. "So it says. The *Hon-Hasta'kan'ix ik'Blagdon* thinks he can look at any human who can hold a sword and sees a soldier; let the *sae-krushku ik'kelvorvik* leave the soldiering to those who know better."

He bent, writing on a parchment, and handed it to Siral. "Here, go report to *kriss'ix* Krytos; he will know what to do with you."

Siral took the parchment, looking it over. "Er, where is *kriss'ix* Krytos?"

"I don't have time to hold your hand, boy. Go ask around." He gestured, and shadows shoved Ratsbayne out of the tent.

Ah was *asking*, he thought grumpily and opened the parchment, seeing it was written in the flowing style of Shadese. *O' course it would be in a language Ah can't read.*

He signed, heading to find someone to ask where to go, and hoped they were a bit more conversational than their leader.

* * *

Either this be a brilliant idea or one o' the worst Blagdon ever had, Ratsbayne thought as he double-checked his leather armor, eyeing his opponent, who stood in the ring, putting on a black metal helm that matched his metal armor.

Metal rang against metal as swords clashed; the dull thunks of swords hitting swords were the only sounds Ratsbayne had heard in the last hours, his body aching from his helmeted head down to his feet. As many times as he'd tried sparring, he'd gotten beaten easily every time.

Counting Slipstream as a distraction, he'd tuned her out, ignoring her trying to talk to him. *If Blagdon had paid to send meh here to learn to fight, he might as well get his coin back. If Ah really was a Stormrider, Ah'd know how to fight already, and wouldn't this prove it once and fer all?*

"Watch your footing," Slipstream cautioned, able to push through his mental shielding in a moment of tiredness, though she still sounded fainter. *"The dirt can give under you, and it's not like mounted combat."*

Well Ah tried to volunteer for mounted combat, and they won't let meh on a kolvorvik, not that Ah want to be on the back of a murder pony.

His opponent rushed Ratsbayne as soon as he stepped into the center of the sparring pit, without giving him a chance to get his sword up. Ratsbayne backed up quickly to avoid getting hit, tripped on the dirt, and fell backward, much to the laughter of those watching.

"Get up," Slipstream thought to him with a protectiveness.

Don't ya be leaving Stormhold to find mah. Ah be fine.

"Do better, and I won't head out there to kick this idiot for you."

Ratsbayne stood, his opponent holding his arms out to either side, boasting. As Ratsbayne rushed him, the sword and shield came forward, blocking and shoving Ratsbayne to the side, the sword connecting across the back of his leather armor.

Krushku.

"Stop rushing. We don't outrun the wind; we ride it."

Ratsbayne stood, letting out a long breath, holding his shield up.

"Stop fighting and listen to our instincts. We know how to do this."

Stop distracting meh. He swung his blade at his opponent, who ducked and slipped to the side, hitting Ratsbayne across the upper thigh.

"You're weak, go home," the Shadon soldier laughed.

"Stop shutting me out."

Ya be a windrunner, ya dun't know how to fight with a sword and shield.

"Well neither do you, apparently," she snapped. *"Open your mind to me, and let me help. You can't do any worse than you are right now, so you might as well try."*

Ratsbayne sighed angrily, fighting not to rub his stinging leg. He'd not cared for the taste of grass or the feeling of his feet being picked at while he cared for her hooves whenever they were fully open with each other mentally. The feelings were faint, but still, he wasn't used to it in the back of his mind.

He closed his eyes, imagining holding a shield up, keeping Slipstream out. He slowly lowered it, letting her in his mind. He felt refreshed as if the wind had blown across his skin, taking his tiredness and aches.

He sighed, looking at his opponent. "Once more."

"You're crazy, but okay, if you ask for it," the soldier said, laughing. "I'll make it easy for you," he said, tossing his helm to the side and gesturing to his unprotected head. "Here, have a shot."

The other soldiers began laughing, and Ratsbayne saw a few making gestures as if placing bets.

Ratsbayne walked forward, swinging his sword, and the soldier threw up his shield, blocking it with a smirk.

"Too bad, human. My turn."

Ratsbayne ducked behind his borrowed shield as a sword swung at him, letting the wood take the brunt of the blow. Shoving the shield against the sword, he stepped to the side, thrusting with his right hand, aiming at his opponent's armored midsection.

The other soldier saw the strike coming and moved to the side, letting his shield block Ratsbayne's swing.

Ratsbayne was already moving, his shield deflecting the soldier's next blow as it came faster. He then slammed his shield again, hitting his opponent in the face.

"You bloodied my nose!" The opponent dropped his guard, backing up and holding his nose. "You don't strike at the head, you idiot."

Ratsbayne stepped back and rotated his shoulder. "Ya should have worn a helm."

The soldiers watching laughed at their comrade, who glanced around, his eyes narrowed.

"I'll show you how to fight!" Shadows wrapped around the soldier as he rushed toward Ratsbayne, vanishing.

"Behind you, now!"

Ratsbayne spun, his shield already in place when the sword formed from blackness, the rest of the soldier appearing a moment later. Ratsbayne shoved it aside, his blade resting beside the male's neck as he finished forming from darkness.

The male's eyes widened, glancing from Ratsbayne to the steady blade against his skin. "How did you…" he stammered in the growing silence of the soldiers.

"Yield," Ratsbayne demanded, touching the blade harder against the male.

"*Kiv-kyr*," an older voice snapped.

The soldiers stepped back, putting a fist on their shoulders and bowing their heads.

An older male wore a red cloak over his black and red armor, a black and gold sash hanging across his chest. He stood beside *korrati* Krytos, who leered at Ratsbayne. "See to your injury, *kriss*, you are getting blood on my ground." The soldier saluted and rushed off toward the *belvash* tent, ignoring fellow soldiers' small smirks and snickers as he passed.

"A little blood dun't hurt the grass," Ratsbayne spoke up, "it makes the green grass grow."

"There isn't green grass in my sparring pits, and you would mind your tongue and tone before *Korrat'ix* Nicholnor."

Well, Ah can see why ya dun't have green grass, if ya dun't allow yer soldiers actually to train and bleed.

"You are *Hon-Hasta'kan ik'Blagdon*'s newest recruit," the *Korrat'ix* said, looking him over.

Ratsbayne stayed silent.

"How did you know that *kriss* Axion was going to shadow behind you?"

Ain't it be obvious? Ya Shadon always try stabbing in the back. That be yer trick, yer lot in life. Aloud, he changed his wording. "He be telegraphing, sir."

"Well, let us see what you can do against someone who does not telegraph their next movements, shall we?"

The *korrati* began picking up a sword, and the *Korrat'ix* looked at him.

"What are you doing?"

"Getting armed, my *Korrat'ix*, so I can teach this human the lesson."

"That will not be necessary," *Korrat'ix* Nicholnor said, taking off his cloak and folding it. A *balvash* stepped forward, taking it and his sash, bowing her head.

Ah swear she be smiling at meh under that mask; Ah can tell it in her eyes. She's enjoying the idea of meh getting mah arse handed to meh.

"Well, you did draw first blood, insulted the soldiers, and are looking at sparring against their Korrat'ix, who Hasta'kan ik'Blagdon has trained with, and together they made the cavalry something instrumental in taking over

Meridiah and beating the Scourge back with."

How do ya know that?

"Never mind that. Just pay attention, and don't embarrass yourself too badly."

That not be a vote o' confidence. Aren't ya supposed to be on mah side?

"You haven't fought against anyone of his caliber in a long time."

Have Ah ever? Ah dun't remember.

"You are a Stormrider, of course we have."

Ratsbayne glanced at the *Korrat'ix*, noting that the man had a long scar over his left eye from forehead to cheek. *A sword, no doubt.*

The *Korrat'ix* tested the weight of the training sword, tapping his shield a few times to adjust the straps on his arm.

He could feel Slipstream silently watching him, unwilling to distract him as they began testing each other with slower blows, letting each other see the mettle of their opponent and strength. Gradually, the swings became faster, the blocks more solid, until they were locked in a furious exchange of blows and blocks, neither pausing in their motions, each aiming to end the other man. This was not like sparring in Woodsong or among the younger soldiers here, where they would pause, laugh, or make cutting remarks to each other between blows. There were no flashy movements and no showing off.

This was war.

The Korrat'ix is strong, Ratsbayne realized, *stronger than most men Ah be sparring with.*

"He uses shadows to aid his blows, just as Hasta'kan'ix ik'Blagdon uses shadows to aid his defense."

It should bother me how much you know about him.

"He was my master for three years, Siral. You are my bonded rider. Pay attention, and don't be jealous."

A powerful swing landed on Ratsbayne's shield, and he braced himself, struggling to prevent the blade from hitting him as *Korrat'ix* Nicholnor swung down again, trying to make him drop the shield.

Ratsbayne attempted to push upward, but the blade slowly approached him as the *Korrat'ix* used his leverage to start to force Ratsbayne to a knee. He strained, trying to push the shield upward, gritting his teeth as his legs shook.

"He will beat you in brute strength, Siral. Find another way."

Dun't ya think Ah know that? Ratsbayne stopped pushing upward. Instead, he moved behind the shield and turned, twisting so the *Korrat'ix*'s sword slid down his shield, the momentum forcing it toward the ground.

Ratsbayne stepped into the *Korrat'ix*, stabbing at his unarmored inner thigh with his sword, not once, twice, but three times in rapid succession.

The *Korrat'ix* shadowed backward in time to not be seriously injured, cloth torn from where the sword had cut through. "You would have beaten me this day had this been a real battle." He looked to his men. "Protect the spots where your armor is weakest. Your opponent will go for these, and you will die before you know it." He glanced at Ratsbayne once more. "You are faster than I had anticipated; I would have thought you would be exhausted, slow, and sloppy. But you have hardly broken a sweat."

Ratsbayne blinked, feeling his aches fade as his breathing returned to normal. *Ah dun't feel as tired as Ah thought Ah would.*

"That is what it means to be bonded to a windrunner, Siral. We can run on the wind all day and still not tire."

Korrat'ix Nicholnor walked out of the sparring ring, telling the men to keep up their good work, and the *balvash* handed him the cloak and sash so he could put them back on over his armor. He then told the *korrati* to keep up the good work and returned to the command tent.

The *korrati* watched him, then looked to Ratsbayne, anger in his eyes. "You don't fight with honor."

"Honor dun't belong to the soldiers in the midst o' battle."

"You sully the *Hasta'kan* you represent."

Ratsbayne laughed, which, by the *korrati's* expression, he did not expect.

Ratsbayne stepped up to the other male, his voice dropping. "Ah ain't representing a Shadon, lad. Ah be a Stormrider." With that, he turned and walked away.

Apollo,

Our travels have already shown us things we have not seen before. I thought it was a relief when I saw through Memory's eyes that we were nearing a village with a banner different from Leigelord Remhold's. This one was yellow with black arrows in a circle pointing at a human figure. It finally felt like we were getting somewhere, and we'd made it out of Cetra.

We only took one wagon in; the rest of the people kept moving, going down the road to be safer if something happened to us. The village was split into two parts, with a stone wall separating the outside from the inside. The outside houses were wooden homes, with little stone used in their making, unlike the ones in Andears. However, they had a wooden fence around them, probably to keep werg from entering from the woods.

Jacob convinced the guards to let us through the stone wall, saying we had goods to sell. The village was made of stone and had larger buildings inside the stone wall. We went to the store and tried selling, but we couldn't sell or purchase because we didn't have something called a hasta emblem, and we were kicked out after being searched to ensure we didn't steal anything. They said 'our kind' needed to shop outside the stone walls. We soon discovered only Shadon could be within the stone walls and were removed quickly by guards.

Can you imagine being turned away simply because you were human? I'm so glad we do not treat each other like that.

Clep

APOLLO

"Apollo, the *korrati* wants to see you," a soldier spoke up from beside the sparring ring where soldiers were stretching, getting ready for their own spars while others watched the two already in the ring.

Apollo finished his swing with his sword, it deflecting off the shield of his opponent, before taking a step back, a hand up to show he was finished sparring. He held his right fist to his left shoulder and bowed his head, saluting the other soldier to show respect, and stepped out of the sparring ring, putting his training sword into the rack to be sharpened. As much as he loved holding his sword in spars, it was easier to spar with the training swords, especially when he was still learning to fight against opponents with steel shields, cutting down on the wear and tear of his prized possession. He headed toward the keep, curious why he hadn't seen Mykel for their morning spar.

He found the *korrati* standing at the *kelvorvik* paddock, watching them quietly, hands behind his back as he stood safely from the fence. Apollo cleared his throat to let the other male know he was there so as not to startle him. Unlike the other Shadon at Woodsong, Mykel and *Hasta'kan'ix ik'Blagdon* did not appear to constantly rely on the shadows to see all around them and seem all-knowing, but rather only used them when necessary.

I wonder if it is because using shadows tires out ro'Shadon, or because they choose to save their energy for defending themselves. Apollo was sure it was the latter, though he'd recently learned about the former in lessons and was curious to know for sure.

Mykel turned, looking at him with eyes that held more knowledge within them than when Apollo first met him. Sure, Mykel was more educated than him; he was a Lordson and was older, but now it was different. It was as if the reality of the world around him, learning of another culture, and leading soldiers had changed him somewhat, even when not in war.

I may have been a large factor in that change as well.

"You wanted to see me, *korrati?*"

After a moment, Mykel nodded, stepping away from the paddock. "Yes, *balutrae ik'san*, come with me." He began walking toward the keep at a pace that surprised Apollo, who quickly caught up.

The unusual change in routine and the secretive manner raised questions in Apollo's mind. *Was there something Mykel didn't want others to overhear?*

Mykel held no small talk this time with him, walking silently across the grounds until they reached the keep proper and headed inside as soldiers opened the doors for them, saluting.

Apollo followed quietly down the hall until they reached Mykel's office.

After unlocking the door, Mykel went inside and straight to his desk.

Apollo followed, closing the door behind him, assuming that the *korrati* had something he wished to speak about without worrying about anyone listening in. *Even then, I cannot be sure that the Shadon here won't be using shadows to listen in anyway.*

Mykel sat behind his desk, straightening the parchments, not looking at him.

Apollo felt his heart begin to race under his leather tunic. "Have I done something wrong?" he finally asked, unable to keep quiet any longer.

Mykel moved an inkwell to sit upon the top parchment to stop the curling edge from rolling toward him.

Apollo glimpsed flowing Shadese writing upon the parchment, though he couldn't read it upside down, and the turned-up side of the parchment showed hints of a blue and black wax seal. *What did Hasta'kan'ix ik'Blagdon write that has Mykel so bothered?*

"You are not in trouble, currently," Mykel finally said, breaking his silence, his tone deliberate as if attempting to figure out what to say, as if he'd have to report this conversation later on.

But there's no belvash here to record the conversation, so why is he being so careful with his words?

"My *brak'ha* has sent back progress on my future mount, and he has also brought up something that Rat- I mean, Sir Siral- has mentioned about you. Or rather, your family."

My family? Ratsbayne knows nothing about my family except that my parents are dead, and Clep was in Silene at one point.

"What did he say?" Apollo was nervous, though he wasn't sure why. *Maybe it is all the secrecy that Mykel is projecting.*

"Do you know what a Stormrider is?"

Apollo blinked at the change of conversation but answered the question. "I know a little from Nan-*kyr*'s stories. The Stormriders were knights from the past who rode flying mounts to protect the citizens of Meridiah from above."

"Sir Siral was one of these Stormriders."

That can't be right. "Ratsbayne can't even walk a straight line when he's sober. There's no way he'd be able to ride a flying mount and not fall to his death within a turn of a minute glass."

"I remember, but my *brak'ha* says it is accurate, and he never tells a falsehood. Ratsbayne has admitted that his name is Sir Siral Karog, and was found in a Stormrider tome, written over a hundred and fifty years ago."

This sounds too impossible to believe; even if it were true, how would Ratsbayne, a human, live that long?

Mykel looked down at the parchments again, rereading and frowning harder. He set his hands on the desk as if trying not to fidget. "Mykel, what is wrong?"

"Where did your *sesha* get her amulet?"

Apollo blinked. "What?"

"Sir Siral wears the same type of amulet that your *sesha* once had, which, after her death, had passed to your brother. You accused him of stealing it once."

Apollo felt anger and protectiveness grip him, and he forced himself not to lash out. Under the anger flowed the feeling of betrayal, and he wasn't sure if it was aimed at Mykel, *Hasta'kan'ix ik'Blagdon*, or Ratsbayne. *After I had confronted him about the amulet, thinking he had stolen it from Clep, he read the strange writing on the back and said it was his. Did Ratsbayne tell Hasta'kan'ix ik'Blagdon or Mykel about that conversation? Who did they tell? Were they behind where Clep was now?*

He waited for Mykel to continue to figure out where the conversation was going and give himself time to acknowledge his feelings so he did not lash out. *Not long ago, I wouldn't even do that; it says a lot about how far I've come from the farmboy in Andears.*

"Was your *sesha-kyr* a Stormrider, Apollo?"

Apollo blinked at him, stunned by the accusation. "If she was, wouldn't I have known what a Stormrider was then?"

"Not if she didn't tell you."

Apollo frowned. "Why would she not tell anyone if she was a knight? Especially Pa-*kyr*, Clep, and I?"

"Lordson Kerrik-*kyr* was quite adamant about gathering those he felt could aid him in improving his station and *Hasta'kan ik'Remhold*. Perhaps she wished to hide."

Apollo scoffed, shaking his head. "Ma-*kyr* wouldn't have hidden from anyone. She would have fought back, not allowing his soldiers to take anyone away. She would have protected us."

"She would have been captured, and when my *brak'ha* discovered she was a Stormrider, he would have arranged for her and her family to be transported to Stormhold."

"To do what, Mykel? What does *Hasta'kan'ix ik'Blagdon* want with Stormriders?" His stomach clenched slightly, and he wondered what would have happened to his Ma-*kyr* had she been one of these mythical knights Mykel spoke about.

"*Brak'ha* wants to recreate the Stormriders' bond with their mounts so that *ro'*Shadon can be bonded with *ro'kelvorvik* and *ro'kelvorkav*. This will greatly improve the *ro'*Shadon cavalry."

"So where are the Stormriders now? I haven't seen any flying mounts and riders."

Mykel shrugged. "Many of them died in the Scourge War."

The lack of information bothered Apollo, and he wondered if there was more than Mykel was saying. *What if something awful happened to them? What if they were secretly captured or kept in Stormhold until they told all the Leigelord wishes of this mysterious bond?*

Apollo wanted to dismiss this horrible line of thought, but he couldn't. *It would keep Hasta'kan ik'Blagdon as Hon-Hasta'kan, and I have seen korrati Kerrik-kyr take horrible actions to improve his station. Would Leigelord Blagdon do the same to keep his?*

"What would happen after he learned how to create the bond?"

"You'd live in Stormhold with Clep and your family until you joined the Dark Army, then you would train in the Stormlands."

Apollo knew that Clep wouldn't be conscripted; by *ro'*Shadon law, only one per generation was expected to be in the Dark Army, though more could join should they wish to.

He could have stayed with Ma-kyr and Pa-kyr, learning from the belvash about healing herbs while I learned to be a soldier.

"I didn't want to join the Dark Army."

"Yet, here you stand."

Apollo sat in silence, unsure what to say. Finally, he turned the conversation to a more comfortable topic. "What's the Stormrider bond you talked about?"

"A Stormrider bonds with a flying creature, often able to hear each other's thoughts and gain abilities. One Stormrider I read about gained an eagle's vision and could grow eagle's talons when in combat, thanks to his giant eagle mount."

He ducked his head slightly, looking embarrassed. "I'd often sneak into Stormhold Keep's study when I was younger, reading about Stormriders instead of attending my lessons."

"I've never seen Ma-*kyr* bond with a flying creature; she didn't even like the kitten Clep brought home once with a hurt paw, and we had to give it to Thomas to live in the barn. She was busy making salves and potions to sell for coin and help others who were ill. She was a healer, not a fighter."

"Healers can do incredible things, too, Apollo."

* * *

Apollo couldn't get the conversation out of his mind as he returned to the garrison after their talk, his thoughts turning toward Clep and his hawk, Memory. *Clep had Ma-kyr's amulet to remember her, but what if what Mykel said was true, and somehow Clep had unknowingly bonded with Memory?* Nan-*kyr* had told them stories of winged horses and dragons flying with riders who chased hungry creatures from the skies above villages, but he'd never thought these stories had hints of truth. *She said they slowly disappeared, but what if that wasn't true? What if they were in a place they couldn't escape until they gave up their secrets?*

Was Ma-kyr one of these Stormriders and could defend Andears all this time but did nothing? Apollo shook his head, not wanting to believe that the woman who created healing salves for so many visitors would willingly let the Dark Army take her friends if she could help it.

Besides, I'd never seen her with an animal. She hardly let us keep any around.

He thought about the times in the woods when Clep looked through his hawk's eyes, letting him know about things going on in Andears while they were at the lake fishing. To him, it was just a part of Clep, something that made him unique.

Is Clep an average human with an amulet that allows him to do these fantastical things, or did he become something more while I wasn't paying attention?

The thought of *Hasta'kan'ix ik'Blagdon* discovering Clep's connection with Memory and taking him away sent a shiver down Apollo's spine.

Would Clep be safe, or would he become a mere pawn in the dangerous game of a society constantly in flux?

Apollo lay in his cot, staring at the tent wall, listening to the sounds of the soldiers snoring quietly. He knew he should sleep, but his mind was racing with a fear that made his chest tighten.

I wanted to find Clep, see where he'd been since leaving Silene, ensure he was safe, and bring him back to Woodsong to live. But would doing so make me the very danger Clep is running from?

*The hardest truths to learn
are the ones you refuse to see.*

— Kil'lik'Lenaka

LENAKA

Lenaka gently closed the door to her *putri's* room to avoid waking him and sighed a long sigh of relief. She'd spent the last few turns of the hourglass listening to him recount the trip to *Uak'hani,* the creation of the Order of the Everlasting Dawn, and the many arguments he both remembered and recreated in his mind, some of which she suspected did not occur. *Not that I'd ever tell him that,* she thought as she walked to the kitchen and began cleaning up the teacups and plates of fruit and fish that she, Draven, Dulcea, and Clep had shared over the hours of stories told.

Now Draven was in his bedroom, which had previously been her *pari'lo's* bedroom, asleep at long last, snoring comically and muttering as if still telling tales to an unseen audience. Dulcea and Clep slept on borrowed blankets on the floor of the main room; the low-backed couch was moved aside to give them more space room. *Finally, some quiet.*

She loved their home in Hiena'pei Valley with its sagging porch roof and cracked stone wall. Built centuries ago, the house had been created by carving into the very stone of the mountains to develop stacked rows of hovels, allowing for more space on the ground for plant and animal life to flourish. According to Draven, with mere waves of their hands, the Sigilbearers of Stone created thousands of homes throughout the mountainsides, sized explicitly for winged creatures to inhabit. Those few former Sigilbearers still lived in Exonesis, but their Sigils had faded from their skin, leaving them as powerless as the ones without.

A few years ago, Draven had tried fixing a large crack himself while she was out and ended up almost flooding her bedroom in the next rainstorm. She appreciated that her *putri* tried to be as independent as possible but worried that one day, he would get in more trouble than he could handle.

The door to his study held back the plethora of parchments, tomes, drawings, and theories that he had collected over the last two hundred or so years, mainly focused around the continent of Andora. "Let someone else write about Exonesis," he'd say, "Writing about one's people is boring. I want to write about the dragons, elves, dwarves, humans, and all the others outside our mountains."

Lenaka walked around Draven's study, careful not to let her wings brush any of the piles of books or parchments as she began putting some away, trying to leave the ones he was working on currently. She'd had to clean up the room several times a day, especially when he was in a mood and couldn't find the scrolls he was looking for. The walls were filled with compartments for scrolls, separated by subject, each with a tag saying what they contained. Along another wall stood shelves with tomes in various languages, many of which she was forced to learn as a child growing up under her *putri*'s care.

An open wooden case stood on a table by the wall beside many books and parchments containing information about *Uak'hani*. Within it rested an elaborate dagger, cradled on velvet, its hilt twisted in silver bands around a vessel filled with bluish liquid. Her *putri* would get very upset if she cleaned around it, almost protective of it. Lenaka finally made a deal with him; if he kept that desk cleaned, she'd not clean it for him. *Since then, he has maintained the small table as the neatest part of the room.*

A large book sat on a pedestal, with different inkwells beside it where Draven would often sit for hours. He wasn't a bad artist, though Lenaka felt he was a better writer, able to conjure images with words that he could not capture in drawing. She flipped through a few pages once she was sure there were no new ink drawings she'd smudge. The subjects of the drawings had grown darker over the years, ones that would probably make the Order of the Everlasting Dawn thrust them into the faces of every dawnwarrior to convince them to convert. Draven had told her the stories behind the images so often that she could repeat them in her sleep. Sighing, she closed the book and picked up papers strewn across a desk, stacking them neatly and setting them aside.

Her eyes fell upon a framed drawing of his, with four smiling dawnwarriors, one holding an infant in her arms. *Would they understand all that I do for Putri? Would they know the conflict between watching him constantly and wanting my own life? Would they fault me and say I am not doing enough?*

Lenaka closed the study door behind her and walked outside to their garden with a cup of tea. She startled slightly as Ba'hara looked up at her, then lay his head back on his paws, his eyes closing.

Lenaka went to the bench under the flowering Apika tree and sat, looking up at the night sky. *K'han'Exonia*'s left eye shone brightly in the darkness, surrounded by the ancestors of the dawnwarriors in the form of tiny dots of light. *May they see I am doing all I can with what I have to keep my small family together.* She sat silently for a long time, breathing in the calm night air and sipping her tea.

* * *

Draven wasn't in his room when Lenaka went to wake him. She frowned, looking at his bed, its blankets folded and set neatly on the edge. *Putri has good and bad days; it seems today will be one of the good days.* Hearing voices, she headed toward his study. As she reached for the doorknob, she heard her *putri*'s voice and paused, listening.

"The dragons gave the Sigils to the races of Meridiah, starting with the elves and dawnwarriors, then the humans, and lastly the dwarves. Dulcea, I know what I saw in *Uak'hani*— something awful happened— you've read my scrolls, seen the drawings and the dagger in its case. Whatever happened there is the key to why other Sigils have disappeared or grown weaker. Since *Rhan'Ashanna* and you still have your Sigils, and the Shadon still obviously have theirs, one can only surmise that some dragons are still alive. You must help me convince the *Rhani* that we must go to the Shattered Lands to see if the dragons are there. Why else would the white dragons fly south yearly if nothing was there for them?"

"They do not fly anymore, Draven," Dulcea's calm voice contrasted with Draven's frantic tone. "The long summer has taken over the lands of Meridiah; that much is proof of it. If what you say is true, I fear the white dragons may also be dead."

"So you do believe me. Good, at least *someone* does.".

Lenaka flinched, hearing the weight of his desperation and the isolation of his belief. *I try to believe you, Putri, but sometimes your stories are too unbelievable, or I have heard them so many times I can recite them in my sleep. But how do you say that to someone you care about without hurting their feelings?*

"Draven, you've seen and done things most would only dream of. If they do not read your stories or listen to you, that is on them, not you, old friend."

Her *putri*'s voice began dropping, sorrow rising like water in a teacup. "I could have stopped Kiko. I should have stopped her sooner. I looked out onto that broken landscape, with the bodies of the *k'hani* just hanging in the air, and I was so horror-struck that I could not move. I didn't notice that she had clawed out her eyes until it was too late." His voice broke. "I could have stopped her from harming herself."

Lenaka walked away from the door, tears in her eyes as she heard her *putri* begin sobbing and the sounds of Dulcea comforting him. She went to the kitchen, leaning her head against the wall, and let out a shuttering sigh. Draven had someone else to comfort him and hold him. *For once, it didn't have to be me.*

"Kil'lik'Lenaka?"

Lenaka opened her eyes to see Clep looking at her.

"I was wondering if you wanted to go walk around. I thought about seeing what kind of plants you had available in your market, and I was so overwhelmed the first time there that I didn't think to look for the ones listed in my book."

Lenaka nodded, glancing back at the study door, hearing Dulcea speaking with Draven, who let out a small laugh after a moment. "Sure, Clep, I can use some time away." She gathered her pouch of skyshards and headed out with him.

* * *

It was a longer journey to Wan'hela than Lenaka was used to; she'd forgotten what walking for an extended time was like. Clep shared his thoughts about Andears and its people, and it was clear from his tone that he loved his home. *I wish I could stop and write it all down.* The journey took no more than two turns of the hourglass, and by the time they arrived at the stone gates of Wan'hela, the sun was higher in the sky, and the air was filled with the smells of freshly made food for sale.

The *helaono* was full of life, with *hela'ko'lo* shouting as they walked past, trying to attract customers to look at and buy their wares. Lenaka loved it: the sights, smells, and sounds of dawnwarriors and other races coming together for a singular purpose. The stalls held wares from different cultures from all over Hinestra, especially at the beginning of the month, when Benstafi elf traders would come to Cerian harbor in west of Exonesis Mountain. The *niapa'lo* would head out to their ships under cover of night to pay for the trade goods, which were inspected and then brought back into Exonesis for selling.

Lenaka enjoyed learning about the blue-skinned elves who lived on ships and traveled to different lands to make their livelihood, staying far from the trials of living on shore. She loved reading her *putri*'s scrolls of when he sailed with them. He once brought her a stone carving obtained from the Makir dwarves, saying that they were seven feet tall and weighed more than two dawnwarriors combined. Lenaka had never seen a Makir before, and it was not the first time she had pondered the possibility that her *putri* had been again embellishing the truth.

Many stalls held artwork and carvings centered around the Dawnstone, the magickal artifact deep within the mountain that kept the

Shadon at bay. *That is understandable, for without it, we would be overrun and possibly driven to extinction or, worse, slavery, reduced to mere trophies.*

Stories of the shadow-using creatures that now roamed the lands of Meridiah were a common subject in scary tales, where they would pose as humans to capture unsuspecting dawnwarriors who dared to sneak out past the Dawnstone's defenses. She'd once not slept for three nights due to one such tale, and her *putri* had to purchase a small Dawnstone to wear around her neck so she could sleep once more. Now that she was older, she knew the round stone was merely enchanted to create light, but the small lie had helped her at the time.

"You look deep in thought," Koani said, smiling as he landed beside her, careful not to hit anyone as he folded his wings behind him. "You must be Clep."

Clep blinked in surprise. "How did you…"

"Know who you are? You're a new human to Exonesis. It is all the rumor wind has carried about it, and we know everyone else here, so who else could you be?"

Lenaka smiled at the deduction. "I was just thinking about the times my *putri* told me about when the *helaono* had sold more things from Meridiah. You hardly see any of them anymore." Even though there weren't as many Meridian goods, there were still things from other lands, though they took longer to arrive.

Koani shrugged, his wings twitching with the movement. "I don't know what to tell you, Kil'lik'Lenaka." He dropped his voice, his face serious. "What I can tell you is what the rumor wind is spreading today; three *niapa'lo* have returned from beyond Exonesis Mountain."

Her eyes brightened as she looked at her friend excitedly.

Clep looked between the two, frowning. "What are the ni… those?"

"The *niapa'lo* are the bravest dawnwarriors, heading outside their borders to discover what is happening outside the mountain." It was especially risky, considering their physical appearance differed significantly from humans and elves. A dawnwarrior being captured by the humans or Shadon could mean the downfall of Exonesis Mountain and all those within its walls. "What did they say?"

"They are talking with the *Rhani* right now, so I don't know."

Lenaka hit Koani's arm. "Then why did you tease me about it?"

Koani laughed. "What are you two doing today?"

"I needed to get out of the house. Sigilbearer Dulcea is with *putri* at home, so I thought we could use some time away."

Koani nodded. "May I join you?"

Clep nodded, and they began walking toward the *helaono*.

"So what is it that we are looking for, Clep?"

"My ma was an alchemist and healer, making potions using different herbs. She kept a notebook with drawings and notes about what plants to use for various purposes. I want to replenish my stock. When my group betrayed me, they took most of my potions and left me only with a few basic ones."

"Why did they betray you?" Koani asked, frowning, his hand on his sword at his hip.

"They blamed me for some of us dying because I wasn't able to save them and because I wanted to help someone else in trouble. They thought I was leading them into a trap."

"Were you?" Koani asked, observing him carefully.

Lenaka looked at Koani, frowning.

"No. They drugged me and left me in the middle of the night in the woods. I could never betray anyone; I'm not like that."

Koani continued to walk silently.

Changing the subject sounds like a good idea. "Is your mother's book the one you were writing in earlier?"

Clep looked a little embarrassed. "That one is… different. I found it in an alchemist's cave while traveling toward Exonesis."

"What's so different about it?" Koani asked, curious.

Clep shuffled a little, as if debating how much to say.

Lenaka smiled. "It's all right, Clep. We aren't going to take it or anything. We are just curious. I like to read and learn about different kind of books."

Clep shrugged. "Memory and I were taking refuge from the rain and found it. It has a lot of recipes in it, some of which I'd never seen before." He took a moment before continuing. "There were a lot of blank pages, so I began writing in more information. When I next looked at the book, there were more words than I had written, in another's handwriting, as if the book added more stuff on its own."

They stopped to pick up skewered mangoes with honey drizzled on them. Lenaka laughed at Clep as he got honey all over his nose when he took a bite.

"That isn't that uncommon; at least, it wasn't years ago. There used to be a great deal of enchanted goods in Hinestra before. Maybe you found one that will help you heal others. It isn't anything to be ashamed of."

Koani nodded quietly.

Clep let out a breath and nodded, smiling. "Please don't tell anyone, though. I don't want to make trouble."

Lenaka nodded. "Don't worry, Clep. You are safe with us."

They stopped by a stall with weaponry made of golden metal, which sparkled in the sunlight and Lenaka eyed one of the swords. "That is a fine blade," the *hela'ko* said, smiling at her, "made of Dawnsteel mined right out from under us years ago."

"Dawnsteel? What's that?" Clep asked, looking over a dagger carefully before setting it down.

"Dawnsteel is extracted from the mines in Exonesis, which the *Rhani* have prohibited us from accessing in large amounts. The only other place to get it is *Uak'hani*, but it is forbidden to go there. The *K'hani* used to trade it to us, but they are gone. The *Rhani* will have to let us mine more than the restricted amounts they force upon us." The *hela'ko* leaned down to Clep as if giving him a secret.

"Why is Uak...."

"*Uak'hani* used to be called *Uaka o'o K'hani*, the place of the dragons. The name became shorter over time. They are dead, and their dawnsteel is for the taking, and we are forbidden to go there." He spat on the floor. "Dawnsteel protects us from the shadows, cutting like fish through water. You should get one while they still exist because the mines will all be dry, and we won't have anything to protect us from the shadows."

Lenaka frowned at that. "The Dawnstone protects us, *pari*," she said, using the Dawnese word for 'parent' as a sign of respect, "its magick won't allow the Shadon's abilities to work within its reach, and the *kahena'lo* won't allow them to set foot inside our home."

"The Dawnstone is fading; soon, it will just be a rock. No one can protect us but ourselves." He gestured to the *helaono* around them. "If the shadows get in here, we'll all be dead. You should buy a Dawnsteel blade to protect yourself while you still can." He gestured to the swords and daggers behind him and on the counter.

"Come on, Clep, let's see what else there is," Lenaka said, walking Clep away from the weaponry. She walked up to one of the food stalls, smiling as she saw the fresh fish catch. *This will be good for tonight's supper.* "Hello, I want to buy four bluescale fish, please." She opened her pouch and took out the stone currency to purchase it. *It should be fou—*

"That will be six suns," the *hela'ko* said, smiling.

"Six... suns?" Lenaka blinked at the *hela'ko*. *Did I mishear? I've never heard of a currency other than skyshards.* She held said blue stone coins in her hand, each with the engraving of Exonesis Mountain on one side and a dragon on the other.

The *hela'ko* smirked, reaching into her purse and taking out a golden coin with a sun carved onto one side and the symbol of the Order of the Dawn on the other. "Six suns or nothing," she said, slipping the coin away.

A dawnwarrior woman with her child came up, smiling to the *hela'ko*, and picked up five bluscale fish, putting them into a basket and handing them to her child, who had orange beads in his braided hair that clicked as he rocked back and forth excitedly.

The *hela'ko* smiled at the child and greeted the *pari'tale* warmly. "Five fish, that will be four suns."

The *pari'tale* handed over the golden coins and walked off with her purchase.

Clep frowned, watching. "That's not fair; she bought more fish than Kil'lik'Lenaka had picked out, and you charged her less than you're charging her."

The *hela'ko* gave him a flat look. "Respect your elders, child. You must leave if you do not have the suns to pay."

"I thought the currency here was skyshards or trade," remarked Clep, looking at Lenaka as she gazed at the line of stalls, trying to decide where next to buy the fish.

"It is. I don't know what these… suns… are."

"Don't think about going to any of our stalls on this side; we only accept suns here."

As Lenaka looked around, she noticed more stalls along the right side of the *helaono* had orange flags, signifying that they were run by those of the Order of the Dawn.

She frowned, not understanding its purpose. *We all have similar goods and serve those of Exonesis. Why would it matter who worships what in a helaono? Why did religion have a place when she only wanted to buy a piece of fruit from a stall?*

Koani walked over, setting down four golden coins on the counter. "Four suns for four bluescale, *pari*."

The *hela'ko* wrapped the four fish in leaves and handed them over, smirking. Her smirk faded as Koani handed them to Lenaka, who put them into her bag. The *hela'ko* looked as if they had bitten into something sour. Lenaka walked away quickly before the *hela'ko* began yelling at them.

Shouting at the other side of the *helaono* caught their attention. Koani reached back and, grabbing her hand, began pushing his way through the crowd, using his wings to block and move people aside, continuing forward with a purpose. Her heart skipped a beat at the feeling of his fingers on her wrist, tightly holding so they did not get separated but with a gentleness to not bruise her skin. She reached back and grabbed Clep's hand, pulling him along.

Finally, they made it to the crowd's edge where dawnwarriors were shouting, their hands raised toward the sun, orange garments bright in the light.

"What has happened?" Koani looked around for someone to explain, for even though he was a *kahena* trainee, he could still help keep the peace.

"*O'anu'tale* Na'kia'Kiko is gravely ill," one of the followers said, banging a hand drum to get attention from the crowd.

Lenaka met *O'anu'ta'le* Kiko years ago when she came to their home for tea and pie. Even though she had grown up on Draven's stories of what happened at *Uak'hani*, she was still shocked and frightened at the older woman's facial scars and missing eyes that she now covered with a veil.

"We need all to pray to the Everlasting Dawn to heal her! The more light reflected in our hearts, the faster she will heal!" The followers asked of the growing crowd as they moved on, growing louder as more joined in.

I never understood how a request for positive thoughts and prayers to heal an illness works when you genuinely need medicines, rest, and good soups to heal the body. Lenaka turned to Koani and Clep. "I can ask *O'anu'toki* Rian'Aluu to see her," she offered, turning toward the temple to gather the senior *O'anu'toki*. *Even if he were unavailable, any other O'anu'lo would be willing to help.*

Koani touched her arm, shaking his head. "We won't allow anyone from the K'*hani* temple to see her," he said, keeping his voice low as the Everlasting Dawn worshippers continued walking, shouting prayers for their founder's health. He pulled them to the side of a stall for privacy.

"That makes no sense; he can help her," Clep spoke up, frowning, looking from Koani to Lenaka. "Isn't that what priests do?"

"With salves and potions passed on from the *K'hani's* teachings, remedies which the Everlasting Dawn does not believe in. They will not work with her."

Lenaka gave him a flat look. "If I cut you with that Dawnsteel knife and you bleed, I'd use a healing salve to heal you. The salve nor wound care who or what you believe in."

"You'd use a healing salve blessed by your *O'anu'lo*, created from powdered *K'hani* eggshells or scales. They hold no magick, Lenaka."

Lenaka blinked at him, and Clep looked around as if wanting to be anywhere but there. "I'm not going to apologize for believing in what my family taught me, what *our people* taught me." *We are all dawnwarriors; why should we be divided?*

Koani sighed. "I'm not asking you to. I'm asking you to respect our ways and our beliefs. The *K'hani* and magick have been dead for over a hundred years. The Sigils are all but gone. The things that worked with our ancestors no longer work, and we've found another way to live. Perhaps you should stop living in the past with your *putri*." The moment he said it, his eyes widened slightly as if he heard what he said aloud.

Lenaka stepped back from him. "Is that what you think, that I don't look forward to a future? That I'm just as crazy as he is?"

"That's not what I--"he started, but she shook her head, stepping away.

"Come on, Clep. We should be going. After all, *O'anu'tale* Na'Kia'Kiko was my *putri*'s friend; he needs to be told." She left, heading home with Clep as fast as possible, ignoring Koani shouting after them.

* * *

Clep had managed to talk to a human bringing a wagon of goods out of the capital to give Lenaka and him a ride into Hiena'pei Valley, saying it was faster than walking. They rode in silence, Lenaka's throat tight with tears.

"If you need to go fly, you can," Clep said for the fifth time, but she shook her head, unsure what she wanted to do. Some of her didn't want to talk, fearing she'd burst into tears if she started. The other part knew she needed to tell Draven, but she was unsure how to inform him that his friend was dying.

"*Putri*? Are you home?" she called out as she opened the door, looking around to see his empty chair in the main room. *Maybe he is taking a nap. I'm unsure if I am in the mood for a spirited talk after the conversation with Koani.*

"In here, Lenaka," she heard his voice come from behind a door further in the home.

She headed toward the study, where she found Draven looking through scrolls, muttering as Dulcea read a book in a chair. A pile of opened books lay on the table alongside scribbled notes, covering almost all of the wooden surface. This left a small area for Draven to work as he wrote on a piece of parchment, his quill moving quickly across the page.

Sighing, Lenaka moved a pile of books off a chair and sat down. *I'd just cleaned this room last night.*

Draven was the shadow of the dawnwarrior she'd learned about growing up, the bard who traveled around Meridiah on a personal mission to collect stories from the different races. Often, she wondered if the bard everyone spoke highly of and her uncle were not two different dawnwarriors altogether. *Had he not gone to Uak'hani, would he be the way he is today? Would he have still gone from the young bard ready to take on the world, bringing back stories of wonder and awe, to someone telling nightmarish tales that none wanted to hear, full of sadness and death? Would O'anu'tale Kiko still have been injured? Would the Order of the Everlasting Dawn have never been created so Koani and I would not be at odds?*

"Lenaka?"

She blinked, realizing they'd been saying her name for a while. "I'm sorry. I didn't hear you."

Dulcea frowned, setting down her book. "Are ya all right? Ya are pale and look worried."

"Here," Draven said as he pressed a wooden cup of tea into her hands. "Drink and tell me what's on your mind." His dark skin warmed as he smiled at her, patting her hands gently, his fingers leaving her skin lightly covered with ink and dust.

After moving some parchment, she set the cup on a table and forced a smile, changing the subject. "What are you working on?"

"We are rereading my notes about the Shattered Lands, trying to find the best way to go there when the *Rhani* allow it. We do want our people to get there safely and quickly. We could get a boat from the Benstafi elves and sail south, or we could go through Castet, but the desert area there does get rather hot."

Lenaka glanced at some of the parchments, pages of writing, and a drawing of an explosion with purplish inks, with shadows of armored men on the ground and what looked like floating skeletons sketched in black. *That doesn't look like a pleasant place to go.* "I'm not sure the *Rhani* will allow it, *Putri*. It is too dangerous, and we don't know if the blightwalkers are still there."

Draven frowned before adding more notes in the margin. "Even more reason to go. Perhaps the *K'hani* went there to fight or have eggs there. As their allies, we must see if they need our assistance. *K'hani'*Elciath and her white-scaled brethren traveled south often, bringing the white wind in their wake and covering the lands with snow. All things end, Lenaka, and the summer will eventually end when she returns."

He picked up a tome and handed it to her. In this drawing, her *putri* used white ink to create the illusion of snow-covered land, and she found she could almost feel the chill from the image. She'd never seen Eselund herself, but he'd told her stories of how wonderful the world was when covered with a quiet blanket of white and silver. Her favorite part of the story, when she was little, was how it was fun to breathe out and see your breath as if you were a dragon.

She set down the tome carefully and took a breath, shaking out her wings slightly to relieve some of the tension in her shoulders. *I can do this; no one else can break this news.*

"*Putri, O'anu'tale* Na'kia'Kiko has become ill, and she may be dying."

Draven nodded, writing notes in a tome, frowning and muttering before adding more ink lines.

Perhaps he didn't hear me? "*Putri—*"

Draven looked up and grabbed his walking stick from beside the window so quickly that when he turned, he hit a pile of books and knocked them over.

Dulcea bent to pick up the fallen books.

"We must be off; we can take her to *O'anu'toki* — "

Lenaka hurried around the table to beat him to the door, carefully keeping her wings close so as not to make even more of a mess.

"We can't," she said sadly, putting her hand on Draven's, "the Order of the Everlasting Dawn won't allow her to see *O'anu'lo* of the *K'hani.*"

"That's ridiculous! Why would they not wish to see her well? The temple has remedies, salves, and potions, and— " He glanced around, frowning, "Where did I put that list of sicknesses and cures we discovered from the Fyre elves? It is around here somewhere…"

Draven spun, his wing hitting the table, parchments sliding to their feet and almost knocking Dulcea over. He ignored them, going to his shelves, pulled out scrolls, read the tags, and murmured as he discarded some onto the table and began going through tomes.

Lenaka began picking up the parchments, trying to put them somewhere safe until she could put them away.

He finally pulled out a scroll, grabbed his bag, slipped the strap over his head, and shoved the scroll inside while holding his walking stick simultaneously. "I've got it; we can leave now. Come!" He pushed past her through the door, and Lenaka was forced to chase after him once again.

Strength of the Storm,

Heart of the griffin.

— Stormrider motto

RATSBAYNE

Nonstop training kept Ratsbayne on his toes, and his body ached for Alandra to massage his sore muscles. Every morning was different, from sword fighting to archery, then hand-to-hand or shield work in the afternoon. Evenings were spent horseback riding, focusing on speed and combat, alternating to keep soldiers and horses engaged. He was glad for the break in reading over dusty tomes and scrolls and slowly began being able to keep up with the other soldiers, even though they were in better shape. He seemed able to spar longer and was beginning to pick up on some differences between sparring with *narshadan*, humans, and Shadon. Even though he was starting to grow more decent with a sword and shield on the ground, he was most comfortable on the back of a horse.

The *korrati* had Ratsbayne's last week of training be with the cavalry, sending him to where the term Stormlands was coined, a slight basin in the Trogata Plains where the groups would split up and clash against each other until one was deemed the victor.

Ratsbayne pat the horse under him, who snorted and pawed at the grass. He felt uncomfortable in the borrowed armor he wore and wished he could take it off. *Ah dun't like this armor,* he complained for the tenth time since he'd had to put it on. It felt too large for him, and the black and red armor felt... wrong, though he didn't know how to describe the feeling in words.

"I don't like that you're riding a horse and not me in combat."

Funny, that's what Ala—

"If you mention her name after that comment, I'm going to go up there

and kick you in the teeth so hard you will be breathing out of your nose for the next season."

"Siral, what are you laughing about?" Arak looked at him from two horses down, adjusting his grip on his shield as they waited for their *kriss'ix* to give the command to ride forward to meet their foe.

Ratsbayne shook his head. "Nothin', just thinking. We shouldn't be riding down ta meet them, but have some of us stay back to flank them."

Their *kriss'ix* looked at him, frowning. "You want to lead this, human? I didn't think so— "

"Aye, why not? Can't do much worse than ye do. We've been at this all week with no victories," he interrupted the officer.

The *kriss'ix* glared at Ratsbayne. "You think that you are that good?"

There was a *clang* as a soldier threw down his sword. "I refuse to follow a human into battle," he snapped, taking off his helm and tossing it down. The sound was echoed as the rest of the Shadon followed suit.

The *kriss'ix* smirked at Ratsbayne. "I guess you won't be able to lead anyone, after all." He turned to the Shadon. "Get your gear back on and get ready to follow me," he snapped, riding his horse down the line.

"Don't listen to them; they don't know who you are."

* * *

The twilight air erupted with the sound of hooves and metal striking metal so loudly that the shouts of their *kriss'ix* was drowned out. Arrows and shattered lances struck his armor, deflecting those his shield failed to block. It was supposed to be a simple goal of capturing the opponent's flag from the other side of the field, but the game gave way to chaos.

Ratsbayne held onto his rearing mount, leaning forward and using his shield to prevent a lance from striking both of them; he pulled on his reins to keep the mare from slamming down onto a soldier trying to get up from the ground, a blue cloth tied around his pauldron to signify that they were on the same team.

The soldier blinked as the mare's front hooves struck the ground inches from his face. He nodded to Ratsbayne before standing, grabbing his shield, and looking around for his horse. *Whoever had thought to have a cavalry spar in the late hours of the day was a moron*, Ratsbayne decided as he tried to spot not only attacking soldiers but what direction to go in, for he'd gotten turned around amid the battle.

"Look for the sun; it is in the direction of the Capitol city and your opponent's flag."

Why dun't they be using shadows to bring the flag to them?

"Shadon powers are weaker at twilight and during the night when there are no shadows to manipulate. It is mostly more fair during sparring at this time."

He turned in the saddle, barely seeing the red flag at the other end of the field atop the hill, the setting sun making it harder to see against the orange light. Ratsbayne looked at the soldier beside him and held out a hand. "Get on."

The soldier slapped his hand away, sneering. "I don't want your help, human," he snapped and ran toward a *kelvorvik* wandering without a rider.

Ratsbayne shook his head and spurred the mare forward toward the flag. The sight of something racing toward him made him lean far on the horse, and he barely saw the lance pass by him.

"Are you all right?!"

That be close. He shook his head to clear it and turned to see who had thrown it. There were too many soldiers; some locked in swordfights, others trying to swing at each other from horseback as they circled each other, too involved in their smaller combat to realize there was a larger battle around them. He tried to concentrate on his goal rather than his growing frustration.

Ratsbayne adjusted his shield, spurring the mare toward the flag on the other side of the battlefield, and let go of the reins. *Ah be able to use mah sword and shield better, and she be finding the best way to run. Ah need ta keep her in the right direction and keep her safe.*

Arrows pinged off his shield, and he held it higher, tilting it so he could glance under it to ensure he was still going in the right direction. A mounted rider rode toward him, lance aimed at his chest. Ratsbayne tried leaning away but was struck, falling hard onto the ground, dirt hitting his armor as the mare took off running. *Krushku.*

The soldier dismounted and kicked him over onto his back, lance pointed at his throat. "Well, human, I am glad to be the one to take you out of our misery. After all, accidents happen during these spars, and unfortunately, sometimes trainees die."

Ratsbayne realized his right hand was empty; his sword must have been thrown in the fall. As the soldier brought the lance down, Ratsbayne rolled out of the way, his shield tucked against him.

"Stop running!" The soldier yelled, advancing upon him, slamming his lance down on his retreating foe, the blade bouncing off the back of Ratsbayne's borrowed armor and shield.

Ratsbayne rolled to a groaning soldier who was lying on the ground, his breastplate dented as if a horse had either stepped on or kicked him. Ratsbayne grabbed his fallen sword, scrambling to get to his knees.

A blow slammed into his back, once, twice, three times, staggering him, forcing Ratsbayne to stab the sword into the ground to remain upright. Instead of standing fully, he pivoted on his knee toward his left, swinging his shield as he did, his momentum allowing him to take the sword out of the dirt. His shield gave a satisfying sound as it hit the lance aiming for his back, knocking it aside slightly as Ratsbayne stabbed with his borrowed sword toward the soldier's open chest, noting his enemy had no shield of his own.

The soldier stumbled backward and eyed Ratsbayne through his helm. "Stay down, human. You don't know when to quit, do you?"

Ratsbayne shook his head, slowly getting to his feet. "Nope. All Ah got be air and opportunity." He blew out a long breath. "There be the air."

The soldier rushed forward, meeting Ratsbayne repeatedly in furious blows, trying to get through his shield, but Ratsbayne was steadfast in his defense, his shield blocking while his sword parried.

The soldier was slowing and getting tired from his relentless assault, but Ratsbayne felt no aching of muscles, no tiredness gripping him, and the bond he shared with Slipstream kept the fatigue at bay for a little longer. *As long as Ah stay behind mah shield, Ah be all right, and Ah can outlast him. He'll make a mistake first, and Ah can use it to beat him.*

A strike coming from the side knocked the wind out of Ratsbayne.

He stumbled as he blocked the first soldier, turning as he fell to see a second soldier had rushed him, slamming into him with his shield. He fell hard onto the ground, and he felt a dull pain in his ribs. This time, Ratsbayne held onto his sword and started to stand slowly.

The world blurred around him as he was hit from behind, his helm ringing as the world went dark.

"Block! Block! Swing! Forward! Block! Block! Swing! Forward!" The commands came steadily from the male at the front of the group. The burly male shouting the orders began walking around the field, his hand on his sword as he eyed the armored trainees in a large formation, spread enough apart that they would not accidentally impale each other.

Siral blocked with his shield first to the left and right before swinging his sword. He thrust as he stepped forward; his shout echoed by the other young men in armor beside him.

The commander stopped to stand beside one of them, unsheathing his sword and moving beside the trainee in time with his commands. "BLOCK! BLOCK! SWING! FORWARD!" He straightened, watching the trainee for a moment, and once sure the younger male was improving, continued to walk among the others. "Aye, Darious, there ye go. Keep it up, lad."

He stopped, eyeing the stance of one of the elven females. "Kaelith, elbow up when ya swing, lass." He adjusted her arm slightly, watched her do a few swings, and continued down the line.

"Don't ye lose yer counts, keep it steady!" He held up an invisible shield, mimicking his commands. "Block! Block! Swing! Forward!"

The male stopped before Siral, hitting his shield a few times with his sword, forcing him to move the shield higher to block it. "Keep yer shield up, Siral! No one will miss yer head in battle; keep it in place on yer shoulders."

"Aye, Sir Barriston," Siral said, breathless and aching from training already. The day wasn't even half done yet, but he wanted to head to the bathhouse and lie down to stretch his sore muscles. But there were hours of training and studying left, not to mention taking care of his young windrunner mount before the day could be considered over.

"Your enemies will not play fairly or obey the rules you have been taught. What you do will determine how those around you see you, not words! You will be seen as an honorable opponent if you fight with honor. We keep the peace; there is no need for reckless bloodshed."

Sir Barriston's voice darkened. "But if it is life or death, and there is no way around it, honor no longer has a place in the combat. Fight to survive. Fight to protect those you are sworn to protect. Many of you will not make it to graduation and wash out. Some of you will later represent the might of the Meridian skies. The best of you will go on after graduation and defend the royal family. No matter what, you are all knights of Meridiah!"

"HUZZAH!"

"Block! Block! Swing! Forward!"

Ratsbayne slowly opened his eyes, finding himself in a cot, two *belvash* walking past him quietly. He looked around, wondering where he was, and saw he was in an infirmary tent. He started to sit up, groaning when he noticed Leigelord Blagdon speaking with *kriss'ix*

Krytos. *Great, just all Ah be needing is to be chewed out for getting knocked about the head during a mock battle.*

The *kriss'ix* looked over at him as if noticing he was awake, and the leigelord turned and walked toward Ratsbayne's cot, standing beside him. "Siral, you've taken quite a knock to the head. What do you remember?"

"Ah remember who Ah be, if that be what yer asking." He rubbed his head, wincing slightly.

"Slipstream had started bolting toward the side gate at Stormhold, so I knew something was wrong. She's at the stables here now."

Ratsbayne felt protectiveness grip him, and he narrowed his eyes at Blagdon as he started to sit up, hands in fists. *Damn the pain, ya ain't got the right to ride mah her.* "Ya rode mah mount?"

Blagdon gave him a flat look and shoved him back down with shadows. "Slipstream ran beside Ruin, her colt beside her. They both made it here safely, and I am sure they eagerly await your presence."

Ratsbayne started trying to get off the cot and stilled, realizing he couldn't feel his pendant against his chest. He immediately patted his chest, not finding it. "Where be mah pendant?"

Blagdon reached into a pouch, took it out, and handed it over. "I did not want anyone else taking it."

Ratsbayne said nothing as he put the pendant on before standing and looking for his boots, barely noticing that he was in a simple pair of breeches and tunic. He hurried outside, ignoring the *kriss'ix* and *belvash* trying to stop him, faintly paying attention to the leigelord saying it was fine and to let him be.

Ratsbayne hurried outside and headed toward the stables, knowing which way Slipstream was in without thinking about it. *Are ye good, Slipstream?*

The relief he felt on the other end of their bond was like a breath of fresh air washing over him. *"Siral. We are fine, we are here. Master Blagdon came with us to protect us."*

Ratsbayne heard the words, but he didn't care. It wouldn't matter, none of it mattered, until he saw them with his own eyes.

"Siral… Ratsbayne!"

Ratsbayne turned, looking for who had shouted his name, and saw a leather-clad female walking toward him. He found his arms reaching for her, hands running along the leather of her outfit, the mask she wore to protect her lower face from view. He looked down into those eyes that had seen him when so many ignored him. "Alandra… Ah have to see Slipstream first."

"I understand," she quickly made her way with Ratsbayne toward the stables.

Slipstream was licking her colt's back and looked up as soon as they entered the stables, her ears pressing back slightly as she saw Alandra. *"What is she doing here?"*

Stop being jealous. She found meh, not the other way around.

"You don't seem upset about it. Let go of her hand; it's your sword hand. You can't protect me if you can't get your sword out."

Ratsbayne blinked, not realizing he was holding Alandra's hand. *When did Ah grab her hand?*

Slipstream stomped. *"It's the principle of it. Train as you —"*

— would fight in battle, yes Ah know. He let go of Alandra's hand and went to Slipstream, petting her side. *Better?*

"Much."

Ratsbayne chuckled, petting the colt.

Alandra watched them, leaning against a post. "Have you named him yet?"

Ratsbayne shook his head. "Ah be waiting for more of his personality to show. It be how Ah named Slipstream," he replied, remembering a dream that Slipstream would constantly escape the stables and paddock, and he'd spent most of his first years trying to capture her instead of riding. At the time, he'd called her Slippery

Stream, but after a while, the words merged.

"Windrunners be proud creatures who do not allow many to ride them unless they have proven themselves worthy. Slipstream be one of three domestic windrunners Ah read about so far in the Stormrider tome; the rest be in wild herds across Andora." He frowned, thinking. "Ah dun't know how many windrunners are around Meridiah now."

Alandra leaned against a barn post, watching the colt. "When we moved on Meridiah, the orcs and shadow trolls went to Ironfall Mountains to take the lands there. The herds were probably were eaten if they could not be tamed."

Slipstream stamped and started toward her, ears flat, and Ratsbayne quickly moved between the two females, arms out as if to stop a fight. "Ironfall Mountains be where Slipstream's herd was located." He looked to Slipstream, touching her nose to calm her down. *If they are as smart as ya, they be relocated and be safe.*

Slipstream snorted, moving her head away to keep Alandra in sight. *"I don't like her. She's tricky and keeps too close of an eye on you."*

She won't be replacing ye. Yer mah mount, not her.

"You better remember that."

Apollo,

Things are getting worse. The children came back from the woods. We should have been paying better attention. Rebecca, Mary's daughter, went missing while playing hide-and-seeker.

Jacob, Markis, Thomas, Peter, and I went to look for her. It had been growing darker, and we could hear werg in the woods, howling. When the werg attacked, it was too fast for us to see. Markis and Thomas were taken. Peter and Jacob ran forward to help, but I was too scared to go after them.

You would have charged forward and stood beside the others, holding Pa's sword. I'm such a coward.

We found Rebecca's body in the werg den. It cost us Thomas and Markis, and both Peter and Jacob are badly injured.

Mary is beside herself with grief, understandably. Hearing her cries makes me thankful that the mothers in Andears died beside their children instead of suffering so.

Clep

APOLLO

It was early morning when a horn sounded twice, announcing riders were coming through the garrison's front gate. Mykel began walking toward the main road that ran down the middle of Woodsong, his hand resting lightly on his shortsword, Apollo following.

Dark Army soldiers rode through the front gate, stopping their mounts along the road in two lines. Two riders held banners, one of the Dark Army and the other with the emblem of *Hasta'kan ik'Blagdon*. Between them rode two *belvash* in crimson leathers and a third figure wearing black leather armor, contrasting with her white hair pulled into a braid down her shoulder. She rode her mount forward and stopped before Mykel, putting her fist to her shoulder and bowing her head, the soldiers doing the same.

"Lady Shadon Senka *ik'Blagdon*, welcome back to Woodsong," Mykel said, returning the salute, "I take it your journey went well."

Senka nodded and dismounted her *kelvorkav*. "Your welcome is appreciated. The woods shortened the journey, but we had no issues arriving here from Stormhold."

She does not look much older than Mykel, but I know she is the elder of the two.

Senka looked him over, her storm-grey eyes watching as if trying to see through him.

She reminds me a lot of Hasta'kan'ix ik'Blagdon.

Mykel nodded, then gestured toward Apollo. "You should remember Apollo, *balutrae ik'Blagdon*. I know the last time you saw each

169

other was brief."

"*Sholta're.* It is an honor to see you again."

"*Sholta're,*" Senka answered as Mykel dismissed the troops, telling them to get their *kelvorvik* into their proper paddocks and taken care of after the long ride. They each saluted Mykel as they passed, a few eyeing Apollo suspiciously. A soldier stopped to take Senka's reins and guided the *kelvorkav* to the stables.

Mykel began walking toward the keep, Senka staying a few steps behind while Apollo walked beside him.

"*Hasta'kan'ix ik'Blagdon* sends *kelvorkav* riders to bolster Woodsong so you can better respond to threats when shadow teleportation is not as useful. They finished their training two seasons ago, so they aren't new but could use more experience."

Apollo kept trying to glance back at Senka while walking forward, finding it difficult to look at her as she spoke, but Mykel kept walking, head forward, as if her speaking didn't warrant eye contact.

"I understand. It is most appreciated. Wait here." Mykel walked off quickly to assist in a *kolvorvik* giving some of the soldiers a hard time entering the paddock, leaving Apollo with Senka.

Apollo looked at her, noting the ranking on her pauldron. "You are a *kriss'ix?* I thought *ro'*Shadon didn't allow females to lead Hesta or armies."

"Females cannot command Shadon troops, and *Sri'belvash* can command their own. I am in charge of *belvash* and humans." Her eyes were watching Mykel as he worked with the *kolvorvik,* guiding it into the paddock.

"But *korrati* Mykel says that you are not a *bal*—"

Her eyes flicked to him. "I am told to travel with you to find your brother. Mykel is *korrati* and a Lordson; he is too important to go off on mundane errands such as finding a wayward human boy. He has duties to attend to, which need his attention far more."

Apollo sighed at the change in conversation but didn't get angry or insulted at the human comment. "But aren't you a Lady? Don't you have important duties, too?"

Senka gave a slight sound that could have been mistaken for a laugh. "The *Kolotor'ix* has ordered me to help you find your brother, and since I am helping you, you would also aid me in a small errand."

"What kind of errand?" he asked, but Senka remained silent.

He decided to try a safer topic. "I had thought you would have blond hair like *korrati* Mykel."

"I had black hair when I was younger. When I was granted the Sigil of Shadow by the *Kolosae-ro'jo'aritas*, it turned white."

"I understand now why you are called the *shokolar kolotor*."

"*Shokolar* is the opposite of *kokolar*, the color of shadow. It is an insult to say I am not a true Shadon because I am both female and not born with the Sigil. However, I've proven myself to be just as capable as they are, and now I wear the moniker proudly."

I may have insulted balutrae ik'san's blood-kin when I didn't mean to. Shadese doesn't have a word for sorry; what do I say? He decided to change the subject instead. "*Korrati* Mykel said you had studied at the Temple but weren't a *belvash*."

Senka looked at him out of the corner of her eye. "He's spoken a lot about me, has he?"

"I was learning about *Hasta'kan ik'Blagdon*, and he admires you, I think."

"Respects, but not admire. A Shadon would never admire a female, for it could be used as a weakness against him."

It bothered Apollo to hear her speak of females as lower than males, but he knew not to say anything aloud. *Mykel had said it was how ro'Shadon society was, except in the case of belvash, who had proven themselves to be just as dangerous as, if not more, those with the Sigils of Shadow.*

"Anyone who went against you to get to Lordson Mykel would be a fool."

"True, but why do you say that?"

"One, you can take care of yourself. You're the daughter of a great duelist, a *kriss'ix* of females and *belvash,* and I highly doubt that shortsword on your hip is for decoration."

"Flattery will get you nowhere."

Apollo continued, ignoring the comment. "Two, you were training to be a *belvash.* They aren't exactly maidens in distress. Three, they'd have to go through me first."

Senka turned to look at him thoroughly, her gaze so heavy he almost fidgeted under it.

He forced himself to look at her face as he spoke. "I may not be the best fighter, but you're going to be traveling with me, and I can't let anything happen to you. Not because you're *Hasta'kan'ix ik'Blagdon*'s daughter or *Korrati* Mykel's sister, not because I'm *balutrae ik'Blagdon.* You're someone who will be helping and traveling with me. I'd upset my ma-*kyr* and pa-*kyr* if I didn't try my best to defend you."

Senka watched him for a long time as Mykel walked over.

"We can go inside; the matter is attended to." He looked slightly puzzled from Apollo to Senka but didn't ask, turning toward the keep.

Apollo followed, wondering if he'd either passed some unsaid test or made himself look like the most naive human in Woodsong.

* * *

Apollo finished packing his things and looked at his bed, already missing it. *Who knows when I can sleep in a bed again; it could be days or weeks, depending on where we find Clep and if he will even talk to me.* He looked himself over, and although he didn't wear the black and red armor of the Dark Army, he no longer looked like the weak farmboy Clep had known all of his life. He picked up the bag of his few possessions and headed toward the stables to get his horse.

Mykel was speaking to a female and two males petting horses as Apollo walked up.

Apollo blinked at the female, almost not recognizing her except for her unique hair coloration.

Senka had changed out of her leather armor and wore a simple tunic and breeches. Her hair was freed from its braid, making her face appear softer.

The two men wore black armor, cloaks over them to hide the darkened steel, swords on their hips, and one carried a bow, arrows in a quiver on his side.

Mykel turned to look at Apollo. "You may wish to wear a cloak over your armor. It will help you blend in in human villages if they are still wary about soldiers."

I am human, but it may be a good idea since I have long feared those in Dark Army armor.

Apollo glanced at Senka, frowning. "Where is your armor, Lady Senka?" *We are posing as humans in a territory where humans are hunted for sport. If where we are heading is so dangerous, why is she also not protected?*

One of the males snickered, passing a coin to the other.

Senka fed her horse an apple. "If I wear armor, it is obvious that I am not a mere traveler, which will cause questions. Males are expected to wear armor in dangerous areas; females are not. We don't need people to question who we are."

That explains why they are not taking kelvorvik or kelvorkav. "I have a *balutrae* marking on my neck; I thought the idea was whoever saw it wouldn't attack us."

One of the males spoke up. "Sometimes, it may also put a target on you, depending on who *Hasta'kan ik'Blagdon*'s enemies are. If that's the case, we get to defend you." He smiled, and Apollo felt the male may be itching to fight someone.

It will be all right as long as it is not me.

The other male handed over a dark blue scarf. "Put this around your neck; it will keep most questions away and hide your *balutrae* marking."

Apollo took it, nodding as he put it around his neck twice, loose enough that he was comfortable. He looked at the male, who nodded. *It will have to do.*

Senka gestured to the two males. "This is Alax and Tribold, both from *hasta'heh ik'Montres, who fall under Hasta'kan ik'Blagdon.*"

Apollo nodded. *At least they will be loyal to Senka.*

"Two humans traveling alone will be targeted more than if there are four of us."

"It will also be good for your protection, Lady Shadon Senka."

Alax scoffed.

"I will be fine. While we are traveling, you don't need to address me as Lady Shadon. It will give us away. Alax is a sharpshooter with his bow, and Tribold is good with a sword. Plus, you said that you wouldn't let anything happen to me not to disappoint your ma-*kyr* and pa-*kyr*."

I don't know if she is mocking me.

Tribold nodded. "We will train with you on the road at our daily stops. If we travel at night, we will catch up to those camping sooner."

I don't find fault in that logic, Apollo thought, thinking back to when he first left Silene, trying to catch the Dark Army camping at night. *I cannot say that I am unhappy the plan fell apart the way it did.*

"Let us get ready to head out and find your brother," Alax said, heading into the barn to collect his horse, "the sooner we leave, the sooner we can return."

* * *

Apollo looked at Senka across the campfire as the last light of the day left, darkness settling around them in the woods. He had many questions he wanted to ask but did not want to seem rude, so he sat quietly as he listened to Tibold hum tavern tunes and Alax sharpen his sword.

Senka sat on a rock, looking at the woods around them, playing with a twig. "Stop staring and ask already before your head explodes," She snapped a twig in two and tossed the pieces onto the embers, watching them catch aflame.

"I didn't mean to stare, sorry."

"Quit apologizing; it makes you look weak."

Why does she have to be so grumpy all the time? He took a breath and let it out slowly, trying to think of what he wanted to ask, without making her more bothered. "Why don't you wear *belvash* mask and leathers?"

"You've trained as a soldier; why don't you wear their armor?" She responded, picking up another twig and twirling it between her fingers.

Apollo flinched slightly at the question, and Alax tossed Tibold a coin.

She took a moment and looked at him fully. "I am the first Lady Shadon in thousands of years, and *that*'s the question that has been on your mind?"

Apollo blinked in surprise. "What were you expecting me to ask?"

"I expected you to demand that I manipulate shadows or show you my Sigil and let you touch it to make sure it wasn't merely painted on my skin."

"*Korrati* Mykel said you were a Shadon, and so did you. Why would either of you lie about something like that? It seems a dangerous thing to do."

Tribold threw a stick in the fire. "*Ro'*Shadon lie all the time."

"*Hasta'kan ik'Blagdon* doesn't. If she or *korrati* Mykel were going to kill me, they'd just tell me, not lie about it. I would know it was coming and probably where and when."

Tibold's lip twitched. "You have never met the *korrati*'s mother and her sister."

"*Sri'balvash* Desira stays in Woodsong. She protects *korrati* Mykel, sees his injuries, and sends messages for him. Of course, I have met her." He looked at Senka for a long moment before speaking. "Do people often ask you to prove yourself a Shadon?"

"More than you'd think. I usually keep my hair pinned up, and most of my clothing is created with no back to show my Sigil. It is to help reduce the questioning and demands."

"Does it help?"

Senka shrugged in reply.

It seems wrong to be judged by others for what you are instead of being known for who you are. "What else can you do?"

"I can manipulate—"

"No, I don't mean that," Apollo interrupted, making Senka's eyes flick to him in irritation.

Alax looked over, setting his whetstone down and adjusting his grip on his sword.

"Besides being a Shadon, what else can you do? For example, I'm a human but was a farmboy and now a *balutrae*. I used to hunt for food and skins to sell to visitors to Andears to help support my family until my parents died." He gestured to her. "You're a Lady Shadon, a *kriss'ix*, trained as a *balvash*. What else?"

"I'm not a *balvash*; I don't have a Sigil of Blood."

"You trained as one, then. So what else is Senka *ik'Blagdon*?"

Alax looked interested, looking up to listen.

Tribold walked over from where he'd been standing watch and sat on a rock as if waiting for Senka to begin a tale.

Senka looked from them to Apollo after for a long moment. "Why do you care to know who I am?"

From her tone, it was a genuine question.

"You are the sister of *balutrae ik'san* and are important to him. We are traveling together; what else will we talk about?"

Tribold looked between them as if he were a silent observer of a game of catch.

"Why did you leave your brother?"

Apollo flinched but met her eyes. "I'll tell you if you tell me."

Senka raised an eyebrow at him in surprise, then glanced at the two males waiting patiently.

They look just as curious as I am about her. I wonder if they'd ever tried getting to know her.

"I ride *kelvorkav* and am decent at mounted archery. I've trained with the *balvash* in assassination and other skills."

"How good are you at swordfighting?"

"Mykel is better at it, though *Brak'ha* trained us both. When my *khan-kyr* and *sesha-kyr* were assassinated, he sent me to the Temple to become a *balvash*. I returned home to find he was remarried and had a child on the way."

"He sent you away?"

Alax spoke up. "*Hasta'kan ik'Blagdon*'s lordsons and lady were deceased. *Hasta'kan'ix ik'Blagdon* and Lady Shadon Senka *ik'Blagdon* were all left of a once-great H*asta'kan*. If any chose to come against him, the *hesta* could fall and be absorbed easily. He needed to save face with the *ro'*Shadon, so he sent Senka to the Temple to become a *balvash*, which is expected of the eldest daughter of a *hesta*."

Senka didn't look at him, and Apollo wondered if that was because it was the truth. "The Temple was the safest place for me; I didn't realize it then."

"Did any *hesta* try attacking to take them down?"

Tibold's lip twitched. "Three: *Hesta'kan ik'Remhold, ik'Rutherrene,* and *ik'Livingnor. Hasta'kan ik'Blagdon* is a fierce duelist and would not allow his *hasta* to fall into nothingness, fighting with everything he had, making deals and alliances. All three *Hesta'kan* who attacked him suffered and fell in ranking during the next *kalidesh ik'kolotor*."

Alax nodded. *"Hasta'kan ik'Nicholnor* then approached him, having an idea to keep him relevant and protected, training beside him and improving the cavalry. This protected *Hasta'kan ik'Blagdon* from most assassination attempts, for there were always eyes upon the area. After the three months there, he had found a lady to wed, bed, and have an heir with."

Senka kept her eyes on the fire. "I was still at the Temple for three more years before I returned to discover what had happened with the *Hasta'kan.*"

Apollo blinked. "You weren't told what happened?"

"At the Temple, you are instructed to give up your *hesta* connections, that the *balvash* are your only livelihoods and companions. You are never considered to be of your *hesta*, nor use your *hesta*'s title and name again."

"But everyone calls you Lady Shadon Senka *ik'Blagdon.*"

Senka was quiet, and Apollo wondered if she would explain how she could keep her *hasta*'s name, and he leaned in, eager to learn more *belvash* secrets.

"Like you, I am one of two worlds, yet neither of them."

Apollo frowned, disappointed. "Mykel told you how I felt about being a human *balutrae* in a world of *ro'*Shadon."

Senka nodded. "He felt that of all people, I would understand how you feel better than he."

"Is that why you are here with me now?"

"No."

Apollo waited for her to elaborate, but when she didn't, he sighed. "I left Clep in the middle of the night to get revenge on the soldiers who slaughtered the people and burned the village of Andears to the ground."

Tibold began laughing. "You, a child, hoped to beat fully trained and grown men in combat?"

"I'm twelve and six seasons old; I'm not a child."

Alax began laughing harder. "How did you expect to accomplish that?"

Apollo frowned at them and threw a piece of a stick at the fire, his face reddening slightly with embarrassment at the stupidity of his youth. "Slit their throats as they slept."

Alax had to wipe at his tear-filled eyes.

Senka's smile faded when she looked at Apollo's frown. "You're serious."

"I was. Until Ratsbayne caught me before I could and brought me in."

Tibold frowned, looking to Alax, who shook his head. "Who is Ratsbayne?"

"A drunkard who worked in Woodsong. *Hasta'kan ik'Blagdon* took him to Stormhold. He's tall, has long brown hair and a beard, and is obsessed with a squirrel and the grey mare with a foal. He has a strange accent. *Korrati* Mykel says he goes by Siral Karog now, and he was a Stormrider, a type of knight that rode flying creatures. I know *korrati* Mykel doesn't lie, but I still do not believe it."

Senka laughed harshly. "Trust me; he put a blade to *Brak'ha's* throat when he got some memories back, thinking they were tricks he created. If it weren't for *Brak'ha* stopping everyone, we would have killed him."

That certainly sounds like Ratsbayne. I know that Mykel had said he was a Stormrider, but hearing others confirm it makes it sound more authentic.

"So what will you do when we find your brother?" Tibold asked, looking at Apollo.

Apollo blinked and frowned, looking at the fire. "I'm still trying to figure that out."

———————————

He ran through the familiar stone streets of the village, laughing as boys his age ran after him. He turned, leaping onto the side of the fountain in the square as a boy swung a wooden sword at him, laughing, a wooden shield in his other hand.

Apollo grabbed his sword and swung down at the boy, smiling.

The boy's head rolled to the ground, blood pouring over the stone floor. His wide eyes looked up at Apollo, his mouth moving slowly. "Why did you betray us?"

Screaming made Apollo look up to see the village engulfed in flames. He grabbed a bucket off the ground and put it into the fountain, filling it with water to help put it out.

A hand grabbed his, preventing him from moving.

He looked up to see his father, face ashen, black veins up his neck and cheeks, blood coming from his eyes and nose.

"I left you that sword. Look what you do with it! Murderer!"

"No! No, I didn't betray anyone!"

"Lies," his mother shuffled forward from their burning home, hand outstretched, pointing at him. "You left Clep behind and joined our enemies, our murderers!"

"No, I had no choice! It wasn't like that!"

Betrayer. Betrayer. Betrayer.

Murderer. Murderer. Murderer.

The whispers grew louder all around him until Apollo fell to his knees, covering his ears. Please, make it stop!

Those who refuse to build gates
are forced to pick a side
in a place where there never
should have been a fence to begin with.

— Kil'lik'Lenaka

LENAKA

"You cannot enter here," *O'anu'toki* Kowi'Paku said, standing at the gate of Hu'lau Village, blocking their entry. Lenaka could not talk sense into her *putri* and he had taken off as fast as his aging wings could carry him, forcing her to fly after him, leaving the human and the Sigilbearer behind. She felt terrible for it, but she would have felt worse if Draven had gone to confront the *O'anu'toki* alone.

Lenaka looked around the village, wishing she wasn't a part of this conversation.

As the Order's ideals began taking root and spreading, more followers moved from their homes and began migrating there. In less than fifty years, the Order had taken over the entirety of the village, with the idea that their followers could be the first to see the sunrise as it came over the mountain and begin their morning prayers. Their home and furnishings were provided by the *O'anu'tale* free of charge, at least from what she had heard from Koani. *I do not think it is due to caring, but bribery to gather as many followers to the Order as possible.*

She glanced around to see that some villagers had come outside to see what was happening. They stayed far enough back not to intrude upon their conversation but close enough to defend the *O'anu'toki* if things came to blows. Lenaka saw many familiar faces, including those who had traveled to *Uak'hani* with Draven and *Oanu'tale* Kiko on the *Starcaller* many years ago.

There are more non-dawnwarriors here than I saw the last time I went to talk to Koani, she noticed as she glanced among the faces of humans and half-dawnwarriors to see the lone Fyre elf who had been trapped in

Exonesis ever since *Rhan'Kahan* closed the borders. *Had Ikita been turned to the Order as well? Their influence is growing, and it will not be long before it will be more than a fence that divides us.*

"You are not followers of the Everlasting Dawn, and we will not permit you to step inside our land," the *O'anu'toki* spat out, frowning at them.

How would Putri visit his friends if he cannot step onto the grounds?

"Exonesis belongs to all of us," Draven argued, waving his walking stick around as he gestured to the lands around them.

Lenaka ducked to avoid being hit in the head while the *O'anu'toki* was forced to step back.

Her *putri* stepped forward slightly, possibly to catch his balance or even take that piece of land that the *O'anu'toki* had given up.

I sometimes question whether he is genuinely eccentric or if it's all an act.

"This land was given to us by the *Rhani* for our people," the *O'anu'toki* said, trying to step back up, but it was already occupied. He frowned, narrowing his eyes at Draven, who looked innocently at him.

Lenaka spoke up, trying to stop any fighting before it happened. "All we want is to see *O'anu'tale* Na'kia'Kiko."

"He can see her when she is better; she is resting."

"I brought salves and potions to help and made soup," Draven said, reaching into his bag before remembering that Lenaka had brought them so they wouldn't spill. It was meant to be their lunch, but when Draven had hurried outside to head here, she grabbed a bowl and placed it into the box.

Clep had added some potions, telling her to fly after Draven and not worry about him and Dulcea.

Lenaka reached into the box she had set on the ground when they first were confronted, handing her *putri* the covered bowl of soup, a cloth around it to keep him from burning his hands.

Draven took it carefully and held it toward the *O'anu'toki*, who just looked at him.

"We do not want your fake remedies or pity."

"This isn't pity, it's soup. It is quite good if I say so myself; my niece helped me make it for our lunch today."

The *O'anu'toki* swung his hand, knocking the bowl from Draven's hands, and it fell to the stone walk between them.

Lenaka jumped back to avoid being splashed, but Draven's shoes and the lower inches of his robe were now dripping with vegetables and broth. *It is just another thing for me to take care of once we arrive home.*

"Leave here at once, or we will make you leave!" At the *O'anu'toki's* raised voice, the Order's followers started coming closer, some having their hands on weapons. One had a sword on his hip, another had a spear, and Lenaka saw they had long spears tattooed on their lower arms.

I hope this does not come to a fight because they are trained lokoni'lo, and we will lose.

Lenaka tried not to make eye contact with Koani, fearing what she'd see on his face as he watched the scene, still feeling the sting of his earlier words.

"That was uncalled for," Draven said, bending to pick up the broken pottery pieces, "That was one of my favorite bowls."

"*Putri*, let me," she knelt and began picking up the pieces for him, putting them into the box beside the potion and salves. *It's good he didn't start with the more expensive goods.*

She helped Draven straighten and looked *O'anu'toki* Paku in the eyes, leaving the box on the ground beside her foot so as not to risk any more mishaps. "How can you call yourself an *O'anu'po* when you don't care for the people you claim to serve? We are all dawnwarriors, and one of us is sick, so we brought goods to help her heal."

"The Everlasting Dawn will heal her with prayer and light."

"When that doesn't work, then what? You would let her die rather than give her real medicine! The *K'hani* taught the *O'anu'po* how to—"

"How dare you tell me what works and what doesn't! You are a child; you have no idea what you speak about. The adults are talking; leave this conversation."

"My *putri* is her friend! He was with her in *Uak'hani*! If it weren't for her, she wouldn't have even come back to— "

A slap from the *O'anu'toki* cut off her words.

She held her cheek and stepped back as tears stung her eyes. *I deserve that for talking back to an elder, but he is wrong!*

O'anu'toki Paku pointed at them dramatically. "We know the stories. Your *putri* documented them enough times to cover the mountains of Exonesis."

Draven stepped forward, his wings stretching slightly as if they were cramping from staying folded behind him.

The *O'anu'toki* pointed at him, frowning. "You were once a fine bard, but you returned and told tall tales of horrible things that could not have existed. You shook the faith of all those who heard them and were led to the Everlasting Dawn instead. You should be here with us, not refusing to let go of the ideals of dead *K'hani*. If anyone should be the Dawn's brightest ray of light, it is *you*."

Dwarf's dung, Lenaka thought bitterly as Draven's wings flared slightly, blocking the *O'anu'toki*'s view of her, but perhaps also a warning for her to stay silent.

"Then you should let me in as one of the brightest rays of light," Draven spoke up, leaning on his staff. "After all, you did say it yourself."

The motion allowed his wings to drop somewhat, and Lenaka watched as the *O'anu'toki* glared at them for a long moment, then thoughtfully looked at the box the salve and potion were in. *I'm not too fond of the look on his face or the slight twitch of his lip.*

Finally, after a long silence, the *O'anu'toki* spoke low to them. "We will take your salve and potion to *O'anu'tale* Na'kia'Kiko, and she can decide if she wishes to use it."

Draven nodded and carefully took the salve and potion bottles out of the box, his walking stick leaning against his leg. He looked them over, his thumb running over the corked tops wrapped with twine tied in a small bow. After a moment, he looked at the *O'anu'toki*. "I'd like to see her, personally."

"She is resting. I am offering this compromise, and that is it. Take it or leave it."

Draven handed them over, thanked him, and walked away.

Lenaka picked up the box and followed, feeling they'd been tricked.

***

Lenaka stood watching the fishermen on boats in Ka'epano Lake, further outside Hu'lau Village. Angry, hurt, and embarrassed, she flapped her wings behind her in irritation. *Not only did Koani see the conversation and her being slapped, but his family and the other followers did.* She waited for her *putri* to say something, but he stayed silent, sitting and watching the lake down the hill. Finally, she could not handle the silence any longer.

"This isn't right; if I were ill and *O'anu'toki* Kowi'Paku offered to heal me, you'd allow him inside, even if we disagree on certain topics. You wouldn't turn him away because we don't believe in the Everlasting Dawn, and they do. You'd accept any prayers for me, no matter if it was to the Light, the Forgefather," she said, naming a deity she'd remembered in one of her *putri*'s scrolls, "the *K'hani*, or the Dawn. A prayer is a prayer; it should not matter who it is for, as long as it was for my recovery."

Draven nodded silently, watching a fishing boat glide across the lake's surface, sitting on a log.

When he didn't answer, she sighed heavily. "Maybe we can go to the *Rhani* and talk to them?"

"No, it is all right. They've won, and they know it."

His defeated voice made Lenaka forget about her anger. "What do you mean they've won?"

"Why do you think they accepted the potions?" He didn't look at her, but his voice was as if he were a teacher, expecting an answer from a pupil.

"To make us go away quietly," Lenaka admitted grumpily as she plopped onto the grass. She still couldn't get the look of the angry *O'anu'toki* out of her mind.

"*O'anu'toki* Kowi'Paku knew he would not have to use them if he accepted them. He could dump them into the garden and later tell the Order that the *K'hani* potions didn't work."

"He had witnesses who saw us offer it, including Ma'ko'Koani. He couldn't lie like that, even to his followers."

Draven turned his head to look at her. "You are smarter than that, Lenaka. You allowed your anger at his words to cloud your judgment, thus giving him, and the Order, power over you."

Lenaka fought not to shift her weight under her *putri*'s gaze. Her cheek still stung, but the look of disappointment in his eyes hurt worse.

Draven turned to look back at the lake. "Ma'ko'Koani and the others didn't hear what was said between us. You were flippant and needed correction, so he slapped you. He could claim that my weakness made me drop the soup. If we had walked off with the box with the potions, he could say that we changed our minds and argue that those who follow the *K'hani* are selfish toward those who are ill. Either way, he's won the audience of whatever story he tells."

"It's not fair."

"No, it is not; thus, the storyteller's dilemma. You must keep your audience's attention on the tale you wish to spin, or they will put down your work and walk away. It is the same thing with faith. If you do not have people who believe your words, they will leave."

"Is that what happened to *O'anu'tale* Na'kia'Kiko and the others?

They lost faith in the *K'hani*?"

Draven was silent for so long that she thought he wouldn't answer.

Finally, he spoke, his tone softer than usual. "I don't blame her for losing faith after seeing what we had in *Uak'hani*. It's hard to keep it, especially after seeing the remains of hundreds of *K'hani*. We had made it into the forest to a stream to try to wash her face. We put bandages around her eyes by the time Hun'Taboh and Ah'hal'Uk'aka found us and helped me get *O'anu'tale* Na'kia'Kiko back to the *Starcaller*. Still, they didn't go as deep into the island as we had. But what little they had seen and what we told them overwhelmed them so much that it shook their faith badly. They needed to find something else to believe in to survive, hence the creation of the Order of the Everlasting Dawn."

Lenaka thought about that. "Why didn't you lose faith then, *Putri*?"

Draven gave a non-committal shrug. "There has to be other *K'hani* out there. They couldn't all be in *Uak'hani* at the time of the destruction."

That's oddly logical. "What do you think happened?"

Draven was quiet for a moment. He opened his mouth to say something but closed it before beginning again. *I wonder what he stopped himself from saying.* "Possibly the same thing that happened at the Shattered Lands."

Lenaka suddenly had a thought, and she felt foolish for not realizing it before. "That's why you want to go out there; you don't want just to go looking for other *K'hani*. You want to figure out what happened in *Uak'hani* by studying the Shattered Lands."

Draven gave a slight nod, a small smile on his lips and pride in his eyes at her, chasing away the sting of disappointment from earlier. "Whatever happened in *Uak'hani* wasn't natural; the dagger I found on the ground proves that someone else was on those shores before us. Something or someone *caused* this event, something so horrible that it ended with the massacre of the *K'hani* and their kind. Then it happened again in the Shattered Lands, killing thousands of dawnwarriors, elves, humans, and dwarves. The dragons simply did not die out; they were murdered."

Murder. That was a terrifying thought; not only were the great K'hani possibly killed by something stronger than they, but their deaths caused both the loss of sanity of some of the greatest dawnwarriors and a rift between its people so deep that I am unsure it could ever be mended. What could have been that strong to have killed them? Was it still alive? "I've read your articles and saw the drawings you passed out before they were outlawed."

"Is that what you call suppressing the truth?" Draven spat bitterly, his tone returning to sounding more of himself and less of the unsure man she sat with. It partially relieved her to hear it; at least she could deal with this Draven more easily.

"Your descriptions frightened many of us: yours, *O'anu'tale Na'kia'Kiko's,* and the others from the *Starcaller* before a taboo was put on the subject."

It is frightening to know how much history the Rhani and the Order are suppressing. I wonder if Putri had hidden many of his scrolls about what happened. I had never thought about it until now, but would the Rhani have our home searched, looking for them? Are there more truths that we do not know?

"What they said they saw of the island from the ship scared us. Exonesis wished to hear stories of the great *K'hani,* their joy at our handiwork, pride at our worship, and faithfulness. They didn't want to hear— "

"The truth?" Draven snapped, then took a shuttering breath, his wings fluffing slightly. When he spoke again, his voice was lower, like a warning. "Lenaka, I would not wish that sight upon anyone, including our enemies, but we all deserved to know."

"You have said that many times," she admitted. "Some believe a pretty lie is better than seeing the ugly truth."

Draven gave her an offended glare and turned back to look at the water.

She hesitantly placed her hand on his as if afraid he'd pull away.

After a moment, he rested his other hand on hers. "*Putri*, you know I believe you, don't you?"

"The *Rhani* still ask for an audience with me sometimes. Would they do that if they, too, did not believe as well?"

Is he reassuring himself instead or asking a question?

There were rumors that the *Rhani* merely humored her *putri* and requested audiences to censor his stories before he released more lies, but that they, like all of Exonesis, never really believed him.

I wish I knew for sure, but I've never been allowed in the audience chamber, and he is forbidden to speak or write about what transpires during their talks. If he were allowed to, they would all view him differently. Perhaps even I would as well.

Draven finally put his hand on hers, squeezing it gently. "Even if others don't have faith, we will keep believing for them; it is all we can do."

"Kil'lik'Lenaka! Kil'lik'Draven!"

Lenaka turned to see Koani landing nearby, walking over quickly. He glanced around, breathing a little heavily.

"Ma'ko'Koani, what is it?" her *putri* demanded, standing in front of Lenaka, his walking stick held in both hands, perhaps in warning not to get too close.

He took more offense to my being slapped than he let on.

Koani seemed to take the hint, stepping back and holding his hands up to show they were empty. He glanced around her *putri* to look at her. "Are you all right, Kil'lik'Lenaka?"

Before she could answer, Draven spoke, bringing Koani's attention back to him. "She is fine. Her tongue got away with her and was corrected by an elder dawnwarrior who acted accordingly. I would have stepped in her defense if he had crossed a line. What can we do for you, Ma'ko'Koani?" There was a protectiveness in his voice that Lenaka appreciated, a ghost of the man her *putri* indeed was before all of this.

She stepped up to Draven's side and hoped everything was all right.

"*O'anu'tale* Na'kia'Kiko heard that you were outside the village, and she slipped me this to give you." He held out a small pouch, moving forward carefully as if expecting Draven to use his staff on him.

I wouldn't put it past Putri right now; I cannot say what he would or wouldn't do when he has these moments of clarity.

"I can't stay long; *O'anu'toki* Kowi'Paku calls for everyone to come to her bedside for prayers. I will let you know if she improves." He nodded to Lenaka and took off, flying back toward his village.

Lenaka looked at Draven, who waited until Koani was out of sight before turning his attention to the pouch. He poured the contents into his palm, revealing a leather necklace with a pendant of polished claw wrapped in silver.

"I've seen that in your portraits of *Oanu'ta'le* Na'kia'Kiko."

"It was her dragonclaw necklace she'd worn before we went to *Uak'hani*. She must have never gotten rid of it, even after all we'd seen." Draven smiled and put it on over his head, letting the claw hang beside his necklace of a silver dragon curled around a gemstone. "See? Faith."

Red drops create life.

Red eyes watch all.

Red hands hold the quill

That record the rise and fall.

— *Sri'balvash* Inkra'a, Branch of the Quill

BLAGDON

Blagdon looked over the carriages one last time, ensuring that each one had extra supplies in case it was needed. Two dozen soldiers were receiving orders from their *kress'ix*, and Narisa was upstairs making last-minute changes that he was sure to discover after arriving in Nar'Shada. He sighed and walked to the stables, where Ruin was waiting, watching them with dark red eyes.

As Blagdon prepared Ruin, he ran his hand over the creature's thick, short black fur, denser than any animal he had seen in Meridiah. He took care as he affixed the saddle, one of the more dangerous things about riding the carnivorous beasts. A *kolvorvik* may take the opportunity to bite the would-be rider as they were busy with the saddle or kick whoever walked behind them. Blagdon had witnessed the power of a *kelvorvik*'s kick firsthand, watching it crush a werg alpha's chest before the creature could even turn to bite. Walking behind a *kelvorvik* was considered a reckless and often deadly mistake unless one knew how to do it safely, and even then, survival was not guaranteed.

In the past, some *hasta*'s member would forget to keep his hand on the *kelvorvik* while walking behind it and the *hasta* would demand that Blagdon cover the medical expenses. Blagdon would accept the *kolvorvik* back rather than pay the coin, and send the *hasta* on their way. "I am not responsible for your lack of wisdom," he'd tell them.

He used shadows to keep Ruin's head forward as he looked over his mount again before tossing the great steed a piece of meat and letting him walk around the paddock to get used to the saddle, watching to ensure he wouldn't need to adjust anything. Once satisfied, he shadowed out of the paddock and into the keep to speak to his Lady one last time before leaving for the trip north.

Narisa was in the sitting room, talking to some of the servants, pointing as she gave directions. Blagdon watched her momentarily, admiring the woman's ability to step up and take charge easily. He tried to assure himself that there should be no problems while he was gone, but worry still nagged at the back of his mind. His Lordson was in Woodsong, his Shadon daughter out running around with the *balutrae ik'Blagdon*, and he'd be heading to Nar'Shada, thousands of miles away.

If an emergency happens, if Stormhold is attacked by a hasta trying to seize power before the kalidesh ik'kolotor, I will be too far away to lend aid. I may not even be made aware of it until it is over. He suddenly worried if he should stay behind or if he should summon Mykel home with soldiers. *He could say it is a training exercise, a practice of protecting one's village.*

"Beloved? What is it?"

Blagdon blinked and realized the servants were gone. The doors to the room were closed, and Narisa stood before him, a hand on her sword at her hip, concern in her eyes. She wore a blue gown with a black top, the end of a dagger's pommel peeking through the lace between her breasts.

I have never felt more jealous of a weapon than right now.

She reached up and touched his cloak, adjusting it slightly. "There is no need for worry, my Wilihem, and if anything were to happen, the *belvash* in the capitol will aid me. I will have the Stormlands send soldiers to Woodsong, where Mykel will be kept under guard and protected at all costs."

Blagdon blinked at her. He knew he shouldn't be surprised, for his love thought of things he often had not yet done, but still, she caught him off guard daily. "You've already put measures for reinforcements into place," he realized with a slightly relieved breath.

"I may look the part of Lady *ik'Blagdon*, but I am still a *Sri'balvash*, and this is my home. I will defend our people, our mounts, and our lands."

Blagdon stepped to her, running his gloved hand over her face. "Be careful. If anything were to happen to you…"

She held up her hand to stop him. "If an attack happens, I will go to the capitol and send word to the Blood Temple, Nar'Shada palace, Stormlands, and Woodsong. You are *balutrae ik'Kolotor'ix*. I will be treated with respect by any who come to capture me, and if I am not, I am a *Sri'balvash* and will take command of their *belvash* and make them regret thinking of moving against us."

Blagdon held her, wrapping his arms around her and inhaling her scent of leather oil and the freesia flowers that grew beside the keep.

"Know that if the worst happens, my Wilihem, your men and I will have fought to the very last of our lives, your *kelvorvik* and *kelvorkav* will have fed well, and the *belvash* at the Temple will aid your vengeance."

"I do not like leaving you here," Blagdon admitted gently, though her words comforted him, "In the previous *kelidesh ik'kolotor* we had Senka or Mykel here, but this time you will be here without one of us to aid you in your protection."

"I know. But we cannot risk your mounts running wild and making a meal out of all who remain here. I may not be of your blood, but they recognize me as your mate. My duty is here, but my heart goes with you." She turned and walked with him out of the keep, her arm in his as they walked toward Ruin, whose ears turned back and forth, listening to everything around him.

Blagdon looked at the carriages, soldiers, and retainers who would assist him throughout the journey. The first carriage held retainers, a cook, caged ravens for missives, and three *belvash* to tend to injuries. Hired hands, such as Gideon and Siral, would ride horses and ensure the regular mounts were cared for.

The second carriage was for when he wished to be driven instead of riding atop Ruin, or rest when they arrived at their campsites. It had been given extra cushions and blankets for colder nights, and had a lightstone lantern hanging from its interior ceiling, as well as a portable writing desk full of parchment and inkwells.

The third held supplies and provisions needed for the group; baskets of food, barrels of water, pots and pans for the cook, as well as some wood for fires. Tents and bedrolls were already tightly rolled and ready for transport.

Blagdon planned on stopping at one of many *Hasta'kan ik'Carriat* protectorate stations along the way to pay for the services of their soldiers to escort and provide further teleportation services to Nar'Shada. Although he could travel without the extra assistance, it gained more benefits than not. This way, he did not need to remove as many soldiers from Stormhold, his Shadon could rest longer between using their Sigils, and it supported one of his *Hasta'kan*'s alliances. The protectorate stations were located on every major trade and transportation route across Meridiah and Nar'Shada. Carriat *is undoubtedly making their coin this week.*

After a long moment of silence, Blagdon turned to his wife, suddenly making up his mind. "I am not leaving you behind."

"Beloved, I do no—" she began.

Blagdon spoke, his voice carrying through the shadows. "Gideon, to me."

Gideon came over quickly, walking the horse he'd been brushing by the stables, a wide-brimmed Meridian hat on his head to keep the sun out of his face. "Yes, *Hasta'kan'ix*?"

"Give Lady Narisa a horse."

"Wilihem, I do not need to go with you," Narisa protested.

"Get me a saddle!" Gideon shouted, adjusting the reins of the horse he held.

Riky rushed over with a saddle and blanket, laying them over the mare's back, Gideon immediately buckling and adjusting it to ensure it was properly fit.

Gideon turned to her. "Would this suffice, my lady?" When she nodded, he handed the reins to a soldier who tied them to his saddle to have the mare walk beside his horse.

Blagdon mounted Ruin, adjusting himself in the saddle. "You can ride in a carriage until you need to stretch your legs."

Sri'balvash Arika and another *balvash* came from the keep, carrying a chest between them and put it into the carriage.

Blagdon opened his mouth to tell her that Arika that she wouldn't need to bring a chest full of clothes; Narisa would now be standing in for Senka at the engagement dinner instead of her, but she spoke first.

"Your clothing, Lady Narisa." She said, giving Narisa a leather-bound book and quill.

Narisa took them, nodding.

It seems my belvash know my decisions before I know them myself.

A soldier held the carriage door open for Narisa, who stepped in and closed the door behind her before heading to his own horse and mounting it.

Blagdon looked at the hired hand who had been at Stormhold longer than Gideon, but followed his commands and worked as a second-in-command of the hired hands. "Riky, you are in charge of Stormhold and the hired hands until we return. The *kelvorvik* and *kelvorkav* recognize you as one of my people. I trust you will have no problems as long as you pay attention to what you are doing."

"As you command, *Hasta'kan'ix*." He put his fist to his shoulder and stepped back with the gathered hired hands, already giving instructions, pointing to the different paddocks and barns.

My people are among the best in Meridiah and Nar'Shada.

Blagdon took a moment to look at those gathered to travel, Shadon stretching and preparing themselves for the tiring duty of shadowing a great group of people across distances. The trip would be achieved with multiple smaller moves, taking inventory between them to ensure no one was left behind and giving the Sigil users time to rest. There were enough Shadon soldiers to aid in shifts, giving each other time to rest and, at the same time, leaving enough back to aid in the defense in Stormhold.

Blagdon nodded to two Shadon soldiers who rode their *kelvorkav* to the front of the group, each carrying a banner; one of the *ro'Shadon* empire, the other of *Hon-Hasta'kan ik'Blagdon*.

Blagdon looked back to Riky, who had his hand on the pommel of the longsword on his belt. *Stormhold and my family will be safe. Our livelihoods, our way of life, will be safe. I trust in those whom I command.*

He gave the command they began moving through the gates of Stormhold.

* * *

As twilight crept across the land and shadows became scarce, the escort group had already traveled quite the distance, covering hundreds of miles, much faster than they could have on horseback or *kelvorkav*. Blagdon was glad for the protectorate services, using them for as far as their duties allowed, before having his own Shadon use their Sigils to continue after the Carriat soldiers turned back to their station, leaving Blagdon's people to fend for themselves until the next protectorate station.

Feeling someone watching him, Blagdon turned his head to see Narisa had moved aside the heavy curtain, smiling at him as he rode Ruin beside the carriage. "My beloved, is something wrong?"

"You have not eaten." She held out a piece of a sandwich, which he ignored.

"I need to be ready for an attack, Narisa." He kept looking around but glanced at her as she sighed.

"You have soldiers and Ruin to protect and warn you if you falter while chewing. I do not think working your jaw would impede your sword hand."

Blagdon felt Ruin do a few high steps as if he'd heard and understood the compliment, but most likely, it was due to hearing

Narisa saying his name. He patted his mount's neck in appreciation. "I cannot argue with you, my beloved." He held out a hand for the piece of sandwich.

"I have concluded that the protectorate stations are spaced out just enough from each other for travelers to be forced to go alone for a while, so they want more protection at the next station. If I were *Hasta'kan ik'Carriat*, I'd have set up 'bandit' attacks between them when the travelers are between their areas, so purchasing their services seemed more imperative, and they could be charged higher for them."

That was a sound theory, though devious; it skirted the line of honorable intentions too closely for my liking. "Is that what you'd do?" He glanced at his wife, who handed him another small sandwich. He took it without argument.

Narisa gave him a secretive smile. "Many bandits would think twice before trying to attack a caravan with multiple *kelvorvik* and *kelvorkav* guarding it."

"Remind me never to make you my enemy."

Narisa laughed and handed him a waterskin. "I wouldn't need to do all that, Wilihem. I know where you sleep." She smiled and closed the curtain.

I love that woman, but she concerns me.

* * *

Blagdon called for the camp to be made before the sun had set, allowing the last uses of shadow and enough light to see their surroundings. Blagdon tied Ruin to a tree beside the wagon and fed him a few pieces of meat before walking to where the other mounts were already tied; the regular horses separated from the *kelvorvik* and *kelvorkav* for obvious reasons.

It did not surprise him that Siral was already tending to Slipstream and her colt before he had even set up his tent and bedroll.

"Ye be staring, m'lord," Siral spoke up as he brushed Slipstream's coat, not looking at him.

I wonder if his memories are returning more than he has let on. "I came to check on the colt and Slipstream. How are they?"

"Windrunners be resilient, stubborn, and fast as the wind. They both have stamina, which allowed our colt to last longer than a regular horse's would have during this."

Our colt. Interesting. "I've ensured that we've taken more teleports and shorter travels between them to ensure no injuries come to them." *It was also good practice to improve our inventory skills and to make and break down rest sites.*

Slipstream nodded, snorting, and Blagdon went to her with an apple, offering it to her. Slipstream ate it as he ran his hand over her neck. "They are both quite beautiful."

Siral watched him almost protectively. "That she be. That doesn't mean ya get to breed her like a broodmare to make yer Shadon calvary fly."

Blagdon said nothing, looking at Siral with interest and annoyance as Slipstream's ears shot up in surprise. *You are putting things together faster than I had given you credit for.* He turned, walking away to check on the other mounts, ensuring their riders had checked them for injuries, and began brushing and watering them. The last thing he needed was to show up to the *kalidesh ik'kolotor* with dead mounts.

Laughter caught his attention, and Blagdon headed to where the tents were already erected. The scent of stew filled the air as the cook boiled a pot over a firepit. Soldiers were already walking the perimeter in shifts, ensuring no werg or bandits would attack them.

Narisa and *belvash* Alandra sat together, gesturing in their silent sign language and writing, while a third *balvash* was outside a tent, tending to any wounds gained while traveling. A couple of soldiers sparred with each other while others took time to rest in their tents.

He went to the firepit and sat, taking in the sights and smells of a campfire, something he had not done in a while. *I miss this,* he realized.

He used to go camping, sitting on a hill and watching the wild *kelvorvik* herds in Nar'Shada with his Lordsons-*kyr* and daughter, staying out until the moon was high in the sky before riding back toward the manor, Senka half-asleep in the saddle. *The only time I camp now is while traveling toward the kalidesh ik'kolotor.* If he closed his eyes, he could almost hear Eddard-*kyr*'s and Addarys-*kyr*'s laughter and Senka's excited remarks as she pointed out the colts of the pack.

"*Hasta'kan'ix*, your stew, sir," the cook's voice broke through the memory, and Blagdon almost wanted to snap at him for bringing him back. The echoes of laughter and joy faded as more came to the firepit, talking as they sat to eat.

Blagdon nodded as he took the bowl offered and stood, silently heading to his carriage, wishing to be alone in the moment. *No, not alone. I want to be with my children and hear their voices again, but I know I cannot, that the mind plays a cruel jest upon my heart and mind.* Once safely inside the walls of his carriage with the curtains drawn, Blagdon sat and ate with the ghosts of his past.

The door to the carriage opened, and Narisa stepped inside, closing it behind her. One hand held a bowl of stew and a piece of dried bread balanced on it. She sat beside him in silence, taking off her mask and looking concerned. "Are you all right?"

Blagdon took a drink from his waterskin, full of fresh water from the nearby lake. "I miss my boys. We used to camp, to watch the wild *kelvorvik* in the hills of Nar'Shada together." His voice dropped to be heard hardly. "I thought I heard them laughing, and for a moment, my heart lept."

"Memories are cruel sometimes. Men are crueler."

He nodded quietly, looking at his half-empty bowl of soup. "If I had been there in the battle of Calliath, would I have prevented—"

Narisa put her hand on his. "Beloved, do not do that to yourself. You could not have prevented his death any more than you could have prevented the Scourge from overrunning his cavalry company. If Eddard-*kyr* was even half of the man you are, then I know he and his *kelvorvik* fought with every drop of blood in them and made the Scourge pay until the end."

It has been so long, yet why does it hurt so freshly when I travel? It was as if the ghosts of his eldest lordsons waited for him to travel, to be vulnerable, before attacking his mind and heart. "I cannot afford distractions or weaknesses during the *Kalidesh*, Narisa."

"It is not weakness to mourn, beloved, even after so long. We all contend with our ghosts."

He looked at her, wondering whose ghosts she dealt with. *She always seemed so sure of herself; I foolishly never thought she would have her own ghosts haunting her.*

Narisa took his bowl and set it aside before guiding him to lean against her as she gently ran her hand over his hair, her voice soft. "In the Temple, your last test before the graduation ritual is the most difficult. It is to prove yourself loyal to the *ro'belvash*, and to cut all ties with your past life. Initiates often became friends, and some, lovers."

Blagdon glanced at her, raised an eyebrow, and opened his mouth to ask a question, but Narisa put her finger to his lips, a flat look in her eyes.

"There are males who stay at the Temple for such reasons, Wilihem, most of them children born of *belvash* or orphans we bring in from villages. Your mind does not need to entertain the thought of females falling upon each other in lust."

"If it would chase that sadness from your eyes, we can continue that line of conversation."

Her eyes held a trace of humor, her lip twitching slightly, but she cleared her throat and continued, moving the subject onward. "During the last test, the soon-to-be *belvash* is brought into a room with a person tied to a chair and a cloth hood over their head. They are then instructed to kill the bound person, using whatever means they have learned. Most use the methods favored by their particular branch."

Blagdon listened, interested. *It is not often that Narisa talks about the trials in the Temple.* "Do they know who is under the hood?"

"The hood is removed so you can look the person in the eyes. Often, it is a failed initiate you were close to, a family member, or a friend from your past. Before you do the deed, you are instructed to remove your mask to let them see who was about to murder them." Her voice was softer and neutral as if remembering something personal yet unpleasant.

He straightened and touched her face, turning it to look at him. She held a perfect, patient expression with no emotion, but her eyes had the truth; he was not the only one haunted by the past. "Who was it for you?"

"Zakary, my and Desira's brother. He'd been caught on his way to the Temple, seeking to find and sneak us out. I'd not seen him in six years and had no idea he was even in the area, nor his plan."

Blagdon frowned. *How is it that I'd not known she had a brother?* "How did you kill him?"

"I argued not to kill him, but I was told this was the only way to ensure loyalty to the *ro'belvash*, to the *Balsesha*. This was my way to prove that my past, my family, did not hold sway over my heart." She gave a small sigh. "They were never going to let him go; he'd either live at the Temple as one of our servants or die by one of their hands."

Blagdon took her hand in his, gently rubbing a gloved thumb over her hand as she spoke. He had questions but dared not interrupt, fearing she'd stop talking and never speak about it again.

"I didn't have the Sigil of Blood yet, but I had a dagger and writing utensils. He begged me through the gag, shaking his head, trying to talk, but they wouldn't let me loosen it. They wouldn't let me tell him what was happening or even say goodbye. Doing so would be a weakness, and in the Blood Temple, weakness is not tolerated. I slit his throat, making it quick. I watched him bleed out; the light died in his eyes until he just looked at me with empty horror and disbelief." She took a long breath, looking at their hands.

"Doing it quickly was a mercy, Narisa," Blagdon said gently, his other arm wrapping around her shoulders protectively.

"Pretty to think so."

Blagdon frowned, thinking. *I know I will regret asking, but I have to know.* "If Senka had gone through to the final trial, who would they have brought before her to kill?"

She was silent for a long moment, and when she spoke, she didn't look at him. "If you were deemed useless because of your grieving, then yes, most likely, you would have been taken and put before her. Your body would then be taken back, and the story would be spread that you killed yourself in your grief."

Blagdon's eyes narrowed. *It wouldn't be the Kolotor'ix who passes such judgement; he'd challenge me to our scrivik'yo ik'balutrae and be done with it. But if not him, then who? Did the matrons at the Blood Temple have their hands in more affairs than I originally thought? Was Narisa sent to me as a spy of the Blood Temple to kill me if I needed to be removed?*

"Because you were showing promise, another was set up to befriend Senka and take your place instead. But her training never made it that far." She leaned forward to gather the bowls and stood to exit the carriage.

Blagdon put a hand on her arm to stop her. "Who was it, Narisa? Who would be Senka's target had she made it to the graduation to become a *belvash* if not me?"

She gave him a soft smile that told him nothing, raising his hand to kiss his knuckles before putting her mask back on. "It does not matter, beloved. She is here, doing as she is meant to do. Soon, she will be wed. You must rest; a long journey is ahead of us, and you are feeling better." She stepped out and closed the door behind her, leaving Blagdon with his thoughts racing.

Without reason, there is no faith.
Without faith, there is no reason to live.
Therefore— without reason, we die.

— Kil'lik'Draven, Bard of the Winds

LENAKA

"Ah will be leaving Exonesis; Ah have to get back to Meridiah to aid those who still need mah help," Dulcea announced at breakfast. She smiled at Clep. "The *Rhani* have also secured ya a new place to live in Wan'hela, near the *helaono*."

Clep nodded. "I will be heading there later. It will be nice to be within walking distance of things I can trade for. Of course, I'll come visit, Lenaka."

Draven said nothing, poking at his porridge.

"I wish I could go with you, Dulcea; traveling and seeing so many new things must be incredible!" Lenaka said, taking her bowl to the sink to rinse it.

Dulcea gave a soft smile. "It is, but times are not what they used to be, and unfortunately, it has become more dangerous. It makes my work so much more important."

Clep nodded. "You saved my life; I'll never forget that."

"Where are you heading?" Draven asked, frowning as he took a bite of fruit.

"Ah am going to check on a friend and make sure he hasn't done anything more stupid than he already has."

Draven laughed. "He sounds like quite the trouble-maker. I created my trouble when I was younger, and others have had to bail me out more than once!"

From the stories you have told me growing up, I do not doubt that is true.

Dulcea stood, picking her bag up by the door. She paused for a moment and walked over to Lenaka. "Take care, Kil'lik'Lenaka, and watch over Draven. He's still young enough to cause trouble."

"Before you go, I'd like to ask you something." *I may never have the chance if I do not ask her now.*

"Of course, what is it?"

"Did you know my *pari'lo?*" The question hung heavily in the air with the weight of her curiosity. *This is my chance to gain insight into Draven's past and see how long it had been since Dulcea had last been to Exonesis. I would have remembered her, especially her cat, but I had never seen her before, and she is close enough to putri that she does not address him by his familial name. Something is not right.*

Dulcea shook her head. "Ah do not believe Ah had ever met Draven's sister. Ah have only been to Exonesis a handful of times; most of the dawnwarriors Ah had known were those who visited Meridiah."

Lenaka's eyes narrowed. "We've not been allowed to go outside of Exonesis for over a hundred years. How could you have seen those over that long ago?" *I know there is a larger truth than what you are telling us.*

Clep spoke up. "Nan says Sigilbearers live longer than regular humans or elves." His interruption was like a stone thrown into a calm pond, disrupting the growing tension of the conversation.

Draven spoke up excitedly. "Yes, that's true! Humans Sigilbearers have been known to live over a hundred years or two, and scholars believe it is because the innate magick in the air helps their longevity. I know I have a scroll on it somewhere," he turned, hurrying toward his study.

"But magick is fading, isn't it?" Lenaka spoke up, glancing between the two of them. "Isn't that why there are no more than a handful of Sigilbearers now?"

Draven stopped, his wings drooping slightly momentarily, and then he brightened. "We believe it is, but if the *K'hani* are alive, they can give Sigils to others and keep it from fading! We must find them, and I believe we need to go to the Shattered Lands! Where is my map..." he pushed through the study door, muttering about maps.

Clep blinked at Lenaka, looking confused.

She turned to watch her *putri* through the doorway, excitedly going through his scrolls before getting distracted and sitting down to read. *You'll get used to his moments of sorrow followed by extreme joy if you are around long enough.* Most people weren't, however, choosing to leave them to find companionship with the more stable citizens.

"It is not easy taking care of someone and making hard decisions for them that they may or may not know about, not knowing if they would appreciate it if they did. It takes sacrifices that others do not know about and strength to keep going, knowing what it costs. If ya tell him, he may not even understand or get angry with ya for doing what ya had to do to keep him safe. Ya are doing the right thing."

Lenaka glanced over to see Dulcea watching her with sympathy in her eyes. Slowly, she nodded, picked up her bags, and slipped out quietly. Her great cat joined her as they headed toward Wan'hela.

It's best this way so as not to upset Putri.

Dulcea's last words still rang in her ears. *Was there someone Dulcea was caring for and who had been looking over them while she was here?*

* * *

Lenaka was startled as Clep sat up from the bedroll on the floor in the main room, gasping and looking around wildly. She went to him slowly, holding out a cup of water. "Here, this will help. You are safe, Clep. You are in Hinea'pei Valley with my *putri* and me."

He took the drink offered, nodding as he downed the water and rummaged in his bedroll. He seemed relieved as he pulled a book from under his blanket and slipped it back into his satchel.

"Did you have a nightmare?" She sat, carefully ensuring her wings wouldn't knock things off the nearby table.

"I don't know. I was somewhere where the giant rocks stood, leaning against each other slightly, so close they almost touched, but not quite. It was like being inside a mountain. There were great voices that were angry, booming, and echoing all around me. I demanded something they owed me, but they claimed I was unworthy. I could smell the ocean, fire, and grasslands all at once. It was incredible and terrifying at the same time."

Lenaka was quiet, thinking. "I've heard of a place like that; it wasn't mountains. Come, I'll show you." She stood, quickly heading to her *putri's* study after glancing to ensure Draven was still asleep in his room. She began going through scrolls on his desk, frowning. *I know I saw it somewhere.* She pulled a book from under a pile of parchments, flipped through the pages, and walked to the table. "These were some of the reports my *putri* had written when returning on the *Starcaller* from *Ua'k'hani.* It means the place of the dragons," she explained before Clep could ask what the word meant. "It was supposed to be a place where the dragons could live in harmony, and the *K'hani* had as their seat of power, away from any dangers of the world, yet able to participate if need be." She looked through the pages of scribbled writing and drawings, looking for one in particular. "Here! Is this what you saw?" She turned the book, pointing to a drawn image of a deep crater with a broken mountain-like structure near it and skeletons floating above the ground.

"Maybe? I was inside it, but how those two rocks lean against each other with an open top almost resembles the dream."

Lenaka turned the book and looked at the written explanation on the opposite page. She read it aloud, translating the Dawnese to common for Clep.

"I can only imagine what this place looked like before. This area was probably once covered with trees with massive rock structures towering over it, possibly converging to form a cavern or, perhaps, an arena. It is hard to tell for sure, for it is broken like an explosion had occurred within its natural walls, with fragments coming up from the ground like a hand that once was held tightly, but now the fingers are broken apart. I estimate that this place was as tall as

a small mountain and broader than the crater that prevents us from walking to it. The bodies of K'hani, or what is left of them, being skeletons or dried corpses, are floating in midair. I dare not fly closer; I do not wish to disturb the dead nor leave O'anu'tale Na'kia'Kiko.

It is silent, too silent. Exonesis must be told— something horrible has happened here."

"This is an account written by my *putri*. Since then, no one has tried going to *Ua'k'hani*, not even the Benstafi elves. It is considered forbidden."

"Who are the Benstafi elves?"

Lenaka blinked at him. *I keep forgetting that humans are younger than dawnwarriors, and the elves have long been away.* "They are traders, merchants, and sometimes pirates who live and travel the Aerukatan ocean. They come to Cerian harbor sometimes to trade, take passengers, and leave swiftly."

Clep looked back at the description, horrified. "Dragons were not only real but were killed somehow?"

"They were murdered," Draven spoke up, standing in the doorway. His eyes were haunted, hair disheveled by sleep as he stepped into the room, touching the book and pointing at the image he'd drawn so many years ago. "That was nothing natural, I can assure you. Someone killed them, caused this to happen."

"*Putri*, I didn't know you were awake."

"What could do something like that?" Clep spoke up before Lenaka could try to dissuade him from furthering her *putri*'s lengthy storytelling.

"I don't know, but whatever it is, it is still out there, and until we know for sure what it was, it will return and destroy us all."

"I had a dream of it or something like this, but it was taller, whole. It didn't look broken like in the drawing."

"Oh? Do tell!" Draven brightened immediately. His sleepiness seemed to be chased away as he grabbed a quill and parchment and sat at the table, his eyes bright. "Start from the beginning."

Clep looked embarrassed by the sudden full attention but nodded after a moment. "There were many sets of eyes, high above me, looking down from the darkness between the beams of sunlight between the rocks. I was arguing with them, saying that a person who was burning villages was going to continue until they stopped them. They wouldn't believe me and sent me out. But I knew they wouldn't do anything, so it was up to me. I woke up then. I'm sorry I don't remember more."

Draven wrote so quickly that Lenaka was sure the parchment would catch fire. "Tell me about the eyes. What colors were they?"

Lenaka sighed, leaving the room to let them talk about dreams and theories while she started making breakfast. *If it keeps Putri occupied, it should be all right. Besides, what are dreams but our imaginations reaching out to taunt us with realities that do not exist?*

* * *

Lenaka walked into the garden outside their home, picking mango for dinner alongside the fish she'd gotten from the *helaono* earlier. She'd spent the morning cleaning their home and ensuring Draven didn't need anything as he stayed holed in his study, talking to himself aloud as he wrote. *I hope he is not lonely; I try to spend as much time with him as possible, but still, I cannot be there with him every hour of the day and get things done around the house.*

"Can I help?"

Lenaka turned to see Koani with a basket, standing outside the fence, looking a little sheepish. He tilted his basket to show some cloth-wrapped packages. "I brought some sweets from the *helaono*, if you'll allow me to help."

She couldn't help the smile and nodded. "All right, you can help."

Koani smiled and hopped over the fence with a flap of his wings, landing easily and setting the packages down, heading for the next row of plants to begin looking for ripe strawberries. "*O'anu'ta'le* Na'kia'Kiko was given a potion and rubbed with salves to see if it would help her, but you didn't hear it from me."

"Thanks for telling me; I know you didn't have to." *I just hope that it wasn't too late.*

They worked together, laughing and telling stories about less tense subjects, trying to keep their minds off their differences and concentrating on the similarities.

"The Benstafi boats should be arriving in a few days," Koani said as he picked up his full basket of strawberries, "so there will be more goods in the *helaono* soon. I hope that there are more works from the Makir dwarves; they are so rare to find." He smiled, looking at her. "We should go to the edge of the Dawnstone's ward and watch the harbor from the mountainside. We can take a basket and spend the day watching the ships come in."

"I would, but *Putri* is working and needs me to help him."

Koani frowned. "He doesn't need your help to write; he's one of the greatest dawnwarrior bards in history. You don't need to use him as an excuse if you don't want to spend time with me."

"No, no, Koani, it's not that." She shook her head hard enough that her braids whipped around and hit her in the face; she took a moment to rearrange them back to their original positions before continuing, using the time to think about what she wanted to say. "Sometimes, I hear him talking behind the closed door as if someone else is there, but I know he is alone."

"Is there anything I can do?"

"I don't know. I don't know if I should talk to *O'anu'toki* Rian'Aluu about it or tell the *Rhani*." She looked at her friend, and a tear slipped down her cheek. "What if he's actually going crazy?"

Koani set down his basket and went to her, reaching for her hand and taking it gently, wiping away her tears with his other hand. "Kil'lik'Draven isn't going crazy, Lenaka. He's— "

The sounds of rattling and voices made them look toward the

sound to see four dawnwarriors gliding over the trees, trailing long cloths of orange, the ends barely passing over the canopies.

Lenaka watched them pass by silently, heading toward Wan'hela. Trading a look, the two friends hurried to the fence and watched as a line of orange-clad dawnwarriors flew down the road, shaking coconuts filled with beans, the sounds like a dozen angry snakes rattling their tails in warning. Seeing *O'anu'toki* Paku leading the procession, she was a little proud of herself for the analogy.

The *O'anu'toki* landed and stopped beside the fence, head held high as he looked down at her. He finally spoke, shaking a bright orange coconut filled with beans, making it rattle with his words. "*O'anu'ta'le* Na'kia'Kiko has passed into the Dawn's embrace."

The dawnwarriors behind him shook their coconut rattles and shouted prayers for the Everlasting Dawn to take their founder into its gentle light.

"I'm sorry for your loss," she said finally, unsure what else to say.

The *O'anu'toki* gave her a look that she couldn't decipher but began flying again, shouting for all who could hear that their leader had passed away and calling praises to the Dawn, his cries echoed by those behind him.

I wonder if his voice will be out when he gets to the capital.

A few who passed them gave her a look, and she wondered what stories the *O'anu'toki* had spread about the salves and potions. *I'm not sure I want to know.*

Koani adjusted his orange armband slightly. "I should go; they will probably want me to act as security for the funeral service," he said, his voice bland of emotion. He took off without another word toward Wan'hela.

Lenaka frowned, watching him go with a feeling of dread. *Why would there be security at a funeral service? It is a celebration of life, not a place for combat.* However, the rumors that the Order was creating security forces to protect their followers made her wonder if things would get worse before they got better. *Will this mean these religious soldiers and the kahena'lo will be locked in combat in the future? Will there come a day when Koani will have to choose between our friendship and our beliefs?*

Shaking her head to try to clear the thoughts from it, Lenaka gathered the two baskets and headed inside to break the news to Draven.

May you learn from your past,
Protect the future,

But live in the present.

— Elvish toast

RATSBAYNE

Ratsbayne could think of a long list of things he'd rather be doing than traveling on the back of a horse for days on end, even though the journey had been sped up through Sigils of Shadow. Sparring with Gideon and the other soldiers did not feel like being in a sparring ring in the Stormlands; he even found himself missing studying history in the Stormhold study.

Sitting down in the grass with his fresh stew after sparring with one of the other soldiers, Ratsbayne kicked off his boots, the blades of grass tickling his sore feet. He took a deep breath and moved them further away, his nose wrinkling. He breathed, holding his stew under his nose to chase away the stench of body odor and leather. *Ah'll get a bath in the stream in a bit*, he promised himself, eating hungrily.

He'd ensured that Slipstream and her colt were safe before he finally sat down, the young horse hungrily nursing and staying beside his mother in the area closest to the camp, the *kelvorvik* and *kelvorkav* tied up in almost a perimeter around them. *If a werg be wanting to get to the colt, they be having many gnashing teeth to get through.*

Still, even with the extra security of the murder ponies, Ratsbayne tied his slingbed between two trees near his mount, ignoring the tent and bedroll that Blagdon had provided. *Security over comfort*, he told himself. *Ah can get out of a slingbed faster than a tent, and can see what be going on around meh.*

Slipstream agreed wholeheartedly once she realized that *balvash* Alandra had come along on the trip. *"Two people could not fit in the slingbed without tipping them onto the ground."*

Ya be jealous.

"I am not jealous— why would I be jealous of a human female?"

She gets mah attention.

"She gets your affection, not your attention." Slipstream stamped and refused to speak anymore on the subject, much to his amusement.

Ratsbayne removed his clothing and washed them in the nearby pond, watching the water churn with brown as the dirt was freed. After long moments of getting as much of his clothes clean as possible, he hung them on a tree branch to dry and walked back into the water, diving under the surface once he was up to his waist. He came up, shaking his head, his brown hair floating around his shoulders as he ran his hands over his face, wiping at his eyes. From here, he could see the faint firelight of the camp, the tents, and soldiers walking around but could faintly hear them talking. *At least if anything happens, Ah can shout, and Slipstream and the others can hear meh.*

Looking back at the camp made him remember the night he'd met Apollo. *Ah dun't even feel like the same person anymore. Ah wonder how Apollo be doing. Maybe Ah should write him; he may even answer.*

Movement in the water made Ratsbayne open his eyes and look around, but he saw nothing in the pond but himself. He washed himself off and started toward the shore when something brushed his leg, and he jumped, yelling.

A blonde head raised from the water, followed by bare shoulders as Alandra surfaced, laughing.

Ratsbayne splashed her. *"Krushku,* woman, ya scared meh have to death!"* He looked back at the camp, hoping no one heard him yell, and came running. *That would be the thing that would happen, knowing mah luck.*

The *balvash* smiled, wiping water from her face. "If only I could have seen your face..." She leaned in, kissing his chin, which had a neatly trimmed beard, thanks to her teaching him how to care for himself properly. "You are jumpy this evening. Did you have another memory? You tend to seem to go somewhere else and don't realize what is happening around you when you do."

"No, just thinking about Apollo and wondering how he be doing."

"Ah, that's no fun; how about we think about something else?" She teased and took a breath. Before Ratsbayne could ask what she was doing, she sank under the water, and Ratsbayne writhed for an entirely different reason, his hands finding her floating braid of blonde hair and holding it tightly.

Movement to his right made him look up, and Ratsbayne saw Gideon and one of the soldiers heading toward the pond to take their baths. Ratsbayne carefully moved away from them, heading deeper into the water so his upper chest and shoulders were above the surface. *Who knows what Blagdon…er… Leigelord Blagdon be thinking if he hears that one o' his belvash be tending to meh while we travel.* He tilted his head and pretended to look at the moon, his eyelids fluttering slightly.

Alandra's head surfaced slowly and carefully, hidden behind Ratsbayne's form.

"Ya be enjoying yerself, ain't ya?" Ratsbayne asked, his voice low.

"I know you are enjoying it."

Ah can't really argue that.

"I heard about you fighting at the camp, how you beat *korrat'ix* Nicholnor, not a small feat. How did you do it?" She tilted her head curiously, her hand running up his abdomen.

"Ah dunno, it be like when Ah be fighting, Ah become someone else. Ah stop letting mah brain get in mah way."

"Muscle memory from training for years," Alandra said, looking thoughtful. "What else do you remember?"

"Ah be dreaming more, as if Ah be a knight, a protector of a king and queen. Their princesses saw me as one o' their guards they could talk to. The queen had a young human handmaiden who played with the princesses and saw the queen's needs. During an attack, a kitten she held got scared and ran off. She took off after it, and Ah had to chase after her, getting separated from mah charges. Ah woke up after that, Ah dunno what happened next."

"A knight, how strong and brave you must have been. You have no idea how you woke up in a cave still?"

Ratsbayne sighed, shaking his head.

"Mmm. Good knights must get their rewards." She breathed deeply and sank under the water.

He ran his hands over his shoulder as if trying to bathe, the motion half-hearted, as it was all he could not cry out her name and draw attention to them.

Thankfully, Gideon and the soldier left the area, and Alandra surfaced, smiling and gasping for air.

"Ye... be evil..." Ratsbayne managed to get out, his hands finding her and pulling her closer. He picked her up and walked her to the nearest shore, away from the path to the camp. "We be quick and quiet," he whispered, kissing her as he lay her down in the tall grass.

* * *

Slipstream snorted at him as he returned from the pond in fresh clothing, smiling. *"I smell her on you."*

Ratsbayne shrugged; it wasn't as if he would deny it.

"What if the master finds out?"

Ah thought ya suspected that he already knew, he replied mentally, hanging up his wet clothing to dry further and climbing into his slingbed. *Didn't ya suspect that yer... master... sent her to mah bed to find out information about meh?*

Something poked his back, and he sat up, reaching behind him to see what it was. Frowning, he pulled out a rolled piece of parchment tied with a vine. *No, it can't be...*

He looked around, but most of the camp was already asleep, and the soldiers on watch were looking outward, not into the camp. The colt was asleep beside Slipstream, who looked like she was about to fall asleep herself.

Did ya see someone drop this off?

"*Drop what off?*"

A missive… it be here in mah bedroll.

He opened it, frowning, recognizing the elvish handwriting immediately. *Ah thought Ah be rid of ya.*

You are heading into dangerous lands.

Be careful; you are not among friends.

He who took everything will be there— you cannot move against him, or you will lose again.

Do nothing to draw attention to yourself, and survive. You must survive.

It wasn't signed; it never was. Ratsbayne frowned, reviewing it, then looked at the surrounding woods. It had been months since his last message from the squirrel, and he'd hoped it was gone for good. *Ah knew it be too good to be true, but why is it writing to meh now?*

Apollo,

We discovered Mary's body at Rebecca's grave, her knife through her heart. Peter said she must not have been able to live without her daughter. I'd never seen anyone who had taken their own life. We buried her beside Rebecca, Thomas, and Markis.

Everyone's arguing, blaming each other. I've been blamed for not helping save Rebecca, which would have saved Mary, but how could I do that when she was dead when we found her? I cannot bring the dead back to life—if I could, would they not think I would? Ma, Pa, Nan, you and all the others in Andears would be alive with us now.

I've been staying in my tent more, trying to remain out of people's sight. However, Emma came to see me and helped me to remember that not everyone hated me. It's nice. I like how the sunlight makes her freckles darker and her brown eyes turn more amber. I like the way she laughs; it makes my chest tight when she smiles at me. I think you'd like her. I think Ma would, too.

Clep

APOLLO

They rode for the remainder of the morning, stopping for lunch and camp at highsun. Tibold had his turn sparring with him, making Apollo push through his tiredness to get at least a turn of the hourglass in of training. Of the two, he'd rather spar with Tibold than Alax, who always seemed to want to take his head off. *I don't know what I've done to insult him.* He tried asking but never got a response.

Apollo frowned and rubbed his sore arm where he'd taken a blow with a wooden sword, crawling into his tent and bedroll. He fell into an uncomfortable sleep; the hotter air and sunlight through the trees made it hard to find rest, even with his tunic folded and placed over his eyes to help.

He was awoken by someone hitting his foot, and Apollo sat up to see that the tent was much darker and the air cooler. A figure crouched in the doorway of his tent, leaning in to hit his foot, only lit by a lightstone torch. *Is it already night?*

Senka set down the lantern and left the tent, though her voice was easily heard through the canvas. "We should start traveling. Humans should be resting. I can use my Sigil's power now."

Apollo began putting on his tunic and boots, frowning as he stepped outside the tent to see Tibold and Alax folding their tents. "I thought *ro*'Shadon powers were greater during the day when shadows were darker. There are no shadows at night, so isn't there nothing to manipulate?"

Alax raised an eyebrow. "I'm impressed, little one. Most humans believe *ro*'Shadon's power works at night, and they are weaker in daylight."

Tibolt nodded. "Aye, at least that's what the poems say," he said, his lip twitching.

Apollo frowned. "Did the *ro'Shadon* make up those stories and poems about their Sigils working at night and not during the day to make everyone think they were weaker?"

Tibolt clapped his hands to rid them of dust as he finished putting his gear onto his saddle. "It's why the wars *ro'Shadon* won were fought in highsun, when we were thought to be at our weakest. They underestimated us, and we used that against them."

That makes sense; although the shadows are smaller, they are darker.

"My Sigil does not allow me to manipulate shadows— only pure darkness, the absence of light. Shadows share space with light. I can't touch the shadows beside the fire, but I can touch the darkness inside your coin purse and move the coins from yours to mine. The night is thicker in the woods; it gives me more darkness to feel and travel through. I can travel from one darkness to another or reach in and grab things in the darkness. The only other Shadon who can do it is the *Kolotor'ix*, who can manipulate shadows and darkness."

"That is incredible."

Senka mounted her horse, her white hair obscuring her face. "That's one word for it." With that cryptic sentence, she moved her hand, letting the darkness swirl before them, and gestured to him. "After you."

Apollo rode through and looked around, gasping as he almost slammed into a tree, not seeing it at first. Turning in the saddle to look around, he noticed they were in the woods again, but through the trees, he could see a dirt road lit with faint moonlight. *It amazes me how we can be so close to a road, yet the woods are always so dark at night.* He turned as he felt movement behind him, frowning that he could not see anything.

Alax removed a lightstone from his pouch and began riding toward the road. Apollo, Tibold, and Senka followed quietly, heading into the moonlight, where Apollo let out a slight breath of relief. He wasn't afraid of the dark, but it unnerved him. Once, he was hunting, and night had fallen quicker than he'd realized. He'd gotten turned around so many times he finally had to spend the night in a tree until his Pa-*kyr* found him the following day, having sent a search party for him. Since then, Apollo avoided wandering in the woods at night unless he had a lightstone or torch nearby.

The dirt road was well-maintained and traveled, wide enough for two wagons to ride without swerving into the grass. Curious, he looked to Tibold. "What road is this?" he asked, wondering if he could place where they were via the memory of studying lessons with Mykel.

"This is the River's Pass."

I remember seeing it on the map Mykel had shown me. It was the main trade route headed toward Exonesis Mountain, so named because it ran parallel to the Black River, which started near the significant landmark and ended in a lake not too far from there. However, once the River's Pass entered Cetra, the name changed to the Wooded Pass. It continued through the woods outside of Woodsong until it ended in a fork, one heading northwest toward Thraesh and further to Meridiah City, the southern road heading toward Andears and Silene.

As they neared a village with a wooden fence, Apollo noted the yellow banners with black markings in a circle. From his studies with *balvash* Inara, he knew they were arrows pointing toward a humanoid in the middle, the banner of *Hasta'kan ik'Blackmont. Now that I know the Hasta'kan'ix hunts humans for sport, the emblem makes much more sense.* The thought made him shiver. "Where are we?"

"We are at *Et-kivnyta*."

"You're telling me this village is actually named Nowhere?" *That has to be a joke.*

Tibolt shrugged and continued. "We are approximately halfway from Silene to Exonesis; we will go in and see if your brother has arrived. If he hadn't, we'd backtrack by foot toward Silene. If he has already left here, we will go to the base of Exonesis and wait for him."

"That's efficient. I'd thought we'd travel the entire way and look for him through shadows."

Alax nodded, smiling in the darkness. "That would not only take longer, but it would tire us too quickly. Efficiency and energy conservation are important. Think of it as hunting."

"We aren't hunting Clep," Apollo snapped, his voice protective.

"Aren't we?" His lips held a slight twitch in the soft light of the lightstone.

Irritated, Apollo headed toward the wooden gate to see if he could find someone to ask about Clep and take his mind off the fact he couldn't find a reason to argue with Alax's logic. He guided his horse down the village's dirt road behind Tibold's horse, glancing around at the wooden homes and shops. They were simple, modest homes with thatched roofs and signs showing an inn or shops via pictures painted upon them. He could hear cows mooing in a nearby pen, and the air held a mixture of manure, freshly cut wood, and bread baked earlier in the day. Apollo smiled; it vaguely reminded him of Silene, and he half-hoped to hear Clep yelling his name, running out of the inn to greet him.

"Apollo. This way," Senka said, riding past his horse as she headed past the inn, drawing Apollo's eye toward the tall stone wall.

Why are there wooden fences around the front and sides of the village but a larger stone one in the rear? Apollo followed, stopping his horse beside Alax, who was speaking rapid Shadese to a soldier standing at the closed gate. Tibold spoke in the same language, taking out an item from his tunic and showing it, pointing to Apollo and Senka. The soldier finally opened the gate, allowing them to ride through. Tibold nodded and slipped the item away before riding through.

"What is it?" Apollo asked, coming up to ride beside Senka, her expression grim.

"*Ro'*Shadon being *ro'*Shadon."

I am not sure what that means, Apollo thought as he opened his mouth to ask, but the words left him as they passed through the gate.

Gone was the dirt road their horses trod, but now were flat stones tightly packed to create a path between stone buildings with wooden shingled roofs. Lanterns stood every fifty feet, holding lightstones that cast light, creating shadows around them. Signs were written in Shadese, and a fountain stood in the middle of the square, with water pouring from stone pitchers held by vines of stone flowers.

Apollo blinked at the difference in the area and turned back as if to see if the wooden village was still there. *Is this even the same village? Did I bump my head and wake up elsewhere?*

The stone gates behind him shut with a loud *thud* as two soldiers assisted in pushing them together, obscuring the wooden village from sight with wisps of shadow.

"Why is this area so different than the village out front?" Apollo asked as he followed Senka to a shop and began dismounting.

"This is the *ro'*Shadon side," Tibold said, tying his horse to the post out front.

Alax looked around, smiling, and inhaled deeply as if the air within the stone walls was fresher. "A *Halidesh* establishment," he mused, almost wistfully, gesturing to the emblem on the signs of both the shop and the inn, with emblems of an overflowing basket of food and bottles of ale. "Senka, can't we stop and get something proper to drink and a bed to sleep in?"

Senka shook her head, sighing. "We have our duty to do, Alax. The sooner we find Apollo's brother, the sooner we can all return."

"Oh, *Hasta'kan'ix*, you're no fun," Alax complained snidely.

If Senka was insulted, she didn't show it as she walked inside the shop, Tibold behind her as Alax tied his horse to the front and brought up the rear behind Apollo.

"Welcome to my fine store; you are fortunate to be my last customer before I close for the evening. How may I help you?" A clerk came out from behind the counter, smiling as he opened his arms to show off his white and purple tunic fastened with a silver pin of the

Hasta'kan ik'Halidesh emblem. In one hand, he held a parchment pad, and in the other, a quill was almost hidden by his swollen fingers.

So many people back in Cetra are starving, and here, this male is fatter than a pig before slaughter.

"We are searching for this one's brother," Tibold said, nodding toward Apollo, "and stocking up our supplies." He began walking around, looking at the items on the shelves, and started placing items in a basket.

Apollo looked at the rolls of animal skins and fabrics lying along the shelves of one wall with baskets holding spindles of thread and bundles of knitting needles. Bottles of inks of all colors stood beside piles of parchments and leather tomes. *Clep would have been eyeing those had he come here.*

"To which *Hasta* does your brother belong? Let us start there," the clerk answered, a silver-tipped quill poised to write upon the parchment in his hand.

"He isn't *ro'*Shadon."

The clerk gave him a flat look, lowering the parchment. "If he came here, he had to show his *hasta's* emblem to purchase any goods."

"Clep is human."

The clerk's smile faded entirely as he gave a sharp intake of breath, leaving his brown eyes cold. He slipped the quill and parchment away into a pocket. "Then good night to you, and get out. I am closed."

Apollo blinked. "Excuse me?"

"Humans are not allowed here; the stone wall around our village separates us from *them*." The last word was said as if he were discussing dirt on his silk-slippered foot.

"What about *narshadan*?" Apollo asked, trying to contain his resentment of the comment.

"They can only be here with their *Hasta'ix's* permission and sent with a letter or emblem to prove themselves before entering. Being that your brother is human, I cannot fathom how *you* were allowed inside the gate." He looked to the others, his eyes narrowing. "Show me your emblems, or I shall call upon the guards."

Alax shrugged, pulling out a silver emblem of *hasta'heh ik'Montres*, Tribold doing the same.

The clerk nodded, breathing in relief as if the thought of four humans in his establishment was worse than death. "I shall write to the *hasta'heh'ix ik'Montres* and inform him of you sneaking in humans to our village, trying to get around the rules laid by the *Kolotor'ix*. Then I shall demand that *Hasta'kan'ix ik'Blagdon* has a word with you and your *hasta'heh'ix*, though by the time the *kalidesh ik'kolotor* is finished, he may no longer be *Hon-Hasta'kan*."

Apollo blinked in surprise. *I know that a Hasta'kan are above a hasta'heh and a hasta'yo, but I'd never heard of a hasta'heh's members being threatened by going to their Hasta'kan'ix unless it was a matter of importance. It is almost as if he is threatening to tattle to an adult.*

"Please inform me of the words you will send to my *brak'ha* so I may relay them myself," Senka snapped, taking off her cloak and revealing her braided white hair. She turned toward Apollo, undoing her tunic.

Apollo quickly spun around to face the wall. A mirror hanging up allowed him to see the clerk's reflection in a mirror as it went from a dark satisfaction as he stepped toward Senka, who was looking away so Apollo couldn't see her expression.

The clerk reached out and touched Senka's bare back.

Senka gave the slightest of flinches.

Apollo forgot his embarrassment, turning and crossing the area to stand between the clerk and Senka, drawing his sword. "Remove your hand from Lady Shadon *ik'Blagdon*, now."

The clerk blinked and glared at Apollo, pointing a chubby finger at him. "Step back, boy."

"I am *balutrae ik'Blagdon*, and I am not your boy," Apollo snapped, yanking down his scarf with his left hand to show Mykel's emblem. "You will treat Lady Shadon *ik Hon-Hasta'kan ik'Blagdon* respectfully and ask before you touch her, or I will teach you how."

Once the clerk stepped back, Apollo sheathed his sword and picked up Senka's cloak, holding it so she could replace her tunic with some decency. *I shouldn't have lost control like that.*

Alax looked at him as if he'd never seen him before, and Tibold's lip twitched as he gave him a nod.

After a moment, Senka stepped from the cloak and walked to the shelves, her tunic in place again.

I wonder if she's buying herself time not to feel embarrassed.

"Have you seen a group of traders from Cetra move through here?" Tibold asked, his eyes watching Senka.

Apollo folded Senka's cloak and held it over one arm but watched the males in the room, who eyed Senka each with different looks. "One may be selling herbal remedies, like salves or potions," he added, trying to keep the conversation off Senka. *Clep would have made plenty of things to sell.*

"We did, weeks ago. I sent them away and called the guards upon them. They were stealing."

Apollo stepped forward. "Clep wouldn't steal anything!" When he realized his anger was flaring again, he forced himself to take his hand off his sword. *This clerk isn't worth my getting us in trouble.*

The clerk looked at him. "He is human. They always are trying to take advantage of us."

"Let's go," Senka said, her tone giving no room for argument. "*Hon-Hasta'kan ik'Blagdon* will hear about your accommodations and treatment today," Senka snapped to the clerk, walking out the door onto the street.

I don't know if that is a compliment or a threat.

Apollo quickly followed, not wanting her alone. She'd been

embarrassed and touched without permission. It seemed wrong to leave her without protection. They stood outside the shop, Senka adjusting her saddle while Apollo looked around. *The wall isn't keeping humans out; it's keeping the ro'Shadon in. It is going to destroy them one day. The thing that makes humans so resilient is their ability to adapt.* He looked to Senka, holding her cloak up to let her step back into it, letting it go so she could fasten it herself. "Are you all right?"

"Why did you do that?" She asked, turning to look at him with anger and hurt in her grey eyes.

Apollo stepped back, surprised by her reaction. "I thought you'd—"

"That I would be honored that you stepped up for me? I am an abomination, a spectacle to be observed, touched to see if I am real. A human standing up for me only makes me more of one, as if I cannot defend myself."

Apollo's eyes narrowed. "I am not a mere human, and I do not believe the *Kolosae-ro'ja'aritas* ever meant for you to be made a sideshow. It gave you the Sigil for a reason: to be the first Lady Shadon and be treated by your peers as such. You aren't a prize animal to be drooled over, made to strip and be touched without permission. You were trained as a *belvash*, but any *belvash* I know of would have cut off his hand if he tried touching her without permission. I also don't think your *sesha-kyr* would approve of anyone treating you like that. I know Mykel doesn't."

Senka's eyes narrowed, but as she opened her mouth, Alax and Tribold came out of the shop carrying bags.

"Well, you certainly made an impression, *balutrae*," Tribold spoke up as he went to his horse and began transferring things to his horse's saddlebags.

Alex watched Senka and Apollo momentarily, looking between them as if trying to figure out what they'd been discussing. When neither offered information, he spoke, gesturing at the building down the street. "We've been offered a night at the inn, fully paid by *Hasta'kan ik'Halidesh*. He says it is to ensure that *Hon-Hasta'kan ik'Blagdon* knows they are appreciated and that generosity spreads both ways."

Senka frowned, looking at the store, which now had a closed sign in the window. "My *Hasta'kan*'s generosity is that I didn't allow Apollo to kill him." She mounted her horse and rode toward the inn.

* * *

"What a *sae-krushku*," Apollo snapped after they'd sat at a table at *Et-kivnyta*'s tavern, gripping his sword's pommel tightly. "He treated Lady Senka like—"

"A human," Tribold finished.

"No," Apollo argued, "he treated her less than a human. Like an object."

Senka sipped her ale but didn't argue.

Perhaps she already knows it would be pointless to debate how she should be treated with me. Sadly, humans would treat her better than her own society. "If you were a *balvash*, he wouldn't have dared treat you like that."

Senka gave a small, sad smile. "*Ro'belvash* wear leathers and armor for protection and instant recognizability. They are known assassins, spies, and fighters, and their words travel to *Hesta'ix* and the *Kolotor'ix*. I don't look like a *belvash*, and I don't wear their leathers. I can't be *ro'*Shadon because I am female. To the clerk, I was either *narshadan* or human."

"Just because you are human doesn't mean you must be treated less," Apollo replied grumpily. *Just because I understand it doesn't mean I have to like it.*

"Humans rank lower than *ro'narshadan*. Humans are tools to be used," Alax spoke up, tucking away his change in his coinpurse, his cup of ale recently filled. He grabbed another roll off the plate between them, dipping it into his drink before taking a bite, moaning in appreciation.

"*Hasta'kan'ix ik'Blagdon* doesn't think that."

Alax looked at him. "Humans are tools, no matter what *ro'*Shadon you speak with. *Hasta'kan ik'Blagdon* knows that well-maintained tools are the sharpest and most reliable ones. So providing humans and *narshadan* with good tools, needed resources, and enough education to live in the world and not die aimlessly is necessary."

"I am not a tool."

"You are being used to better Lordson Mykel. Every advancement you make only pushes him to further himself. You are very much an instrument of betterment."

Apollo let out a long, frustrated breath. "So why do humans rank lower than *ro'narshadan*? They are just humans who are born in Nar'Shada."

Alax scoffed. "*Ro'narshadan* are suited for servants and working within the keeps because they are born into *ro*'Shadon society. It takes less time to train them than humans."

"Then what are the humans suited for?"

"Slaves and for doing labor that is beneath us."

"*Ro*'Shadon has slavery?" Apollo looked at him, his mouth agape. *I'd thought slavery was something only told in tales.*

"Many *Hesta* own slaves. Slavery has been forbidden in Meridiah by the *Kolotor'ix*, for now, but it still exists in Nar'Shada." Tibolt answered as he came to sit at the table, a bowl of stew in one hand and a tankard in the other. "The *kreva ik'Kolotor'ix* has had a hand in that, I'm sure. The practice may start again when we move into other kingdoms."

Other kingdoms? Is the Kolotor'ix planning on taking over more places like he had with Meridiah? "Where are *ro'belvash* then?" Apollo asked, deciding to change the subject to get them off of the topic of slavery and moving into new lands to take over more people. *I don't want to think about what could happen to them.*

"Below *ro*'Shadon and above *ro'narshadan*."

Apollo rolled his eyes. "Do I even want to ask where *kelvorvik* is?" He asked jokingly.

Senka's lip twitched. "Above *ro'narshadan*, if you ask *Brak'ha*."

Why am I not surprised? "Where do I fall?"

Senka paused, thinking about it. "Other *balutrae* have always been *ro'*Shadon. But you are the first human *balutrae* I know of. I suppose you would fall between *ro'belvash* and *ro'narshadan*."

"What about you?"

Alax looked at him with a very unfriendly look. "I could have your tongue for insinuating that Lady Shadon Senka is less than *ro'*Shadon males."

Apollo returned the look. "You've already said so with your actions. Also, you can't have my tongue; I'm *balutrae ik'Hon-Hasta'kan ik'Blagdon*. Harming me would harm Lordson Mykel, Lady Senka, and *Hasta'kan'ix ik'Blagdon*."

"Is that why you defended me? You knew he wouldn't harm you?"

"I defended you because it was what was right. If he gets his fat *krushku* punished by your *brak'ha*, then I would be pleased."

Tibolt burst into laughter, choking on his drink as he fought to keep it in his mouth, holding the back of his hand to his lips. Alax watched him, laughing harder as Tibolt's face reddened as he could finally breathe.

Senka nodded to Apollo. "Soon enough, you will be more like us than you think."

Every cycle the positions shift,
A never-ending turn of life.
Reminders that nothing is guaranteed —
And our Kolotor'ix commands all.

— Nixus Halidesh, Bard of Eteris

BLAGDON

Blagdon walked into the war room, standing off to the side with the other *Hesta'ix* who had gathered. Some spoke quietly, no doubt trying to make last-minute deals and empty promises, while others listened, pretending to look at the tapestries on the wall or the table that dominated the room. The table was made of wood from Nar'Shada, so grey in places that it was almost black, and the map of Andora was carved intricately. Inlays of gold formed names of permanent landmarks such as the oceans or mountain ranges. A carved figurine of low walls around a castle and tower marked Meridiah City, and another made of obsidian created the Nar'Shada palace and Northern Blood Temple. More miniature carvings of banners with the *Hesta'kan* emblems marked the territories that could be moved, added, and removed as rankings changed.

Along the map's border were twelve octagons carved into the wooden top in front of each of the seats along the long side, six on either side of the table. Today, the *Hesta'kan* emblems would be in their respective slots, the *Hon-Hasta'kan'ix* on the right side of the *Kolotor'ix*, the *Kon-Hasta'kan'ix* on his left, and alternating down the table, with the last *Hasta'kan'ix* sitting at the far left side.

Around the octagons embedded in the table were round gems, each color representing something important. These gems were smaller than the *Hesta'kan* emblem slots but still noticeable from other seats, constantly reminding everyone of what they stood to gain or lose.

Emeralds showed the number of total territories a *Hasta'kan* could claim if they could hold them. *Hasta'kan ik'Blackmont* had been skirting inside the rules by chipping away at his border territories for years, slowly increasing the size of his single territory until it now stretched from Cetra to Exonesis Mountain.

Rubies represented five *belvash* and corresponded to the number of emeralds. The top five rankings could obtain more than one territory, and with that, more *belvash* to help control them. Losing rank meant losing *belvash*, who were either taken by the victor or replaced by the Temple.

Citrines indicated the percentage of taxes the *Hasta'kan* could keep for themselves. Every seat had at least one citrine, showing they could keep one percent of the taxes. In the top five ranks, the number of citrines indicated different percentages: two citrines meant three percent, three citrines meant five percent, and four citrines meant ten percent.

Finally, the top two rankings had an onyx, showing they had priority in seeing the *Kolotor'ix*. Their words supposedly had more influence with the leader of the *ro'*Shadon and the other *Hesta'kan'ix*.

During the *kalidesh ik'kolotor*, it wasn't just status in flux but territory, aid, money — and secrets. Tonight marked the final night of fixed ranks, as the emblems were to be pried from their places, leaving the slots vacant. The *Hesta'kan'ix*, ordered by rank, would recount their achievements and victories of the past cycle. On the third day, the emblems would find new homes, and the twelve-year cycle would commence afresh with the *Kolotor'ix* unveiling the goals for the *ro'*Shadon for the upcoming cycle.

At the head of the table, of course, was the *Kolotor'ix*'s seat, and at the other end sat a now-empty chair. For fifty-seven years, it had belonged to the *kreva ik'Kolotor'ix* Liana, the first of the station to be invited into the war room. Whispers held that the *Kolotor'ix* was becoming weak for allowing a non-Shadon to sit and listen to matters far beyond their understanding. Since her disappearance, the *Kolotor'ix* had not taken another *kreve ik'Kolotor'ix* to carry his heir, and the seat had remained empty.

Blagdon watched as other *Hesta'kan'ix* came into the war room, some alone, others talking amongst themselves, trying to gain last-minute favors and deals. He said nothing, observing who spoke to who, who stood silently, and pondered what deals would be made in the future that would harm his *Hasta*. It was never a matter of whether *if* such harm would happen, but *when*.

The doors to the far side of the room opened, and the soft talking stopped immediately as if cut by a blade. The *Kolotor'ix* walked in, his cloak barely brushing the floor behind his boots, his hood raised. The mask he wore gleamed slightly in the torchlight, the gold lines down the front of it contrasting against the *koldraka* from which it was made.

The Kolotor'ix's true identity birthed almost as many interesting theories as the whereabouts of Liana.

All present immediately knelt, their right fists to their left shoulders, heads bowed.

"We have endured another cycle," the *Kolotor'ix* began, his voice carrying the weight of his authority. He gestured toward the table with his gloved hand. "Attend your places." His words were a command, a reminder of the hierarchy that governed their society.

Blagdon stood first, going to stand behind his chair, looking down at the emblem of *Hasta'kan ik'Blagdon* in its slot. Five emeralds and rubies, four citrines, and an onyx surrounded his emblem, each flush with the tabletop.

I cannot ignore the possibility that my emblem may be in another slot when I return to Stormhold.

The other *Hesta'kan'ix* rose and walked to their spaces in the order of ranking, each silently looking at the table, either at their emblems or glancing at the gems of another ranking's spot.

Once all the *Hesta'kan* were behind their chairs, the *Kolotor'ix* told them to take a seat. He stayed standing behind his chair for the moment, watching them. He raised his hand, and *belvash* walked into the room with trays of goblets for the *Hesta'kan'ix* to pick from as another came forward, pouring watered wine. During the fifth *kalidesh ik'kolotor*, a

Hasta'kan'ix had gotten so drunk that he'd thrown up while presenting his *Hasta'kan*'s worth. It was not a mistake repeated.

The *Kolotor'ix* began walking around the room after the last *Hasta'kan'ix* was served. "My reports have shown that some of you have done well in providing resources valuable for the *ro'Shadon*, while others…" he paused, allowing speculation of who he glanced at behind his featureless mask before continuing, "have not been as forthcoming in their support. This will be remedied, of course."

He then gestured to *Sri'balvash*, who stood behind a desk along the wall, piles of parchments in front of her.

Blagdon saw that her mask had an embossed emblem of a crossed dagger and quill—the same branch as *Sri'belvash* Narisa and Desira.

"*Sri'balvash* Caristha, you may inform us of the overall health of our lands."

Blagdon sat back in his chair, sipping his water, having refused the watered wine. This was an unnerving time of the *kalidesh ik'kolotor*, in which the *Kolotor'ix* let everyone know what he knew. Many, like he, believed the *ro'belvash* reported back with information, serving as spies throughout the lands. Others thought he was all-knowing, using the shadows to listen in on everyone and everything at once. Blagdon believed the more realistic choice between the two. As nerve-wracking as this report could be, it significantly reduced time spent at the *kalidesh*, for it would be useless to report things that the *Kolotor'ix* had already been aware of.

Sri'balvash Caristha began, looking over her parchments. "The overall yields in all the territories are down an average of twenty-four and six percent due to stunted growth of plants, attributed to less water in lakes and rivers, which have surface levels lower than at the last *kalidesh*. *Hasta'kan 'ik Armtomb* has created more irrigation systems, which has greatly aided in preventing the loss of crops."

Armtomb sipped from his goblet, smiling and nodding.

"The wildlife has grown smaller, leaner, and more active during the night when it is cooler, which has begun changing the migration of predators such as werg. This puts livestock and populations located in safer areas now in danger."

That is not good. A pack of werg could easily take down a young or pregnant kelvorvik. I will have to increase patrols around my land, as well as around the villages.

"What is making these changes happen?" *Hasta'kan'ix ik'Halidesh* asked, concern in his eyes.

"The long summer," *Hasta'kan ik'Carriat* answered, looking at the map on the table. "The humans believe the white dragons bring winter to the lands; without them, the hot days continue year-round."

The longer-serving *Hesta'kan* glanced at each other quietly but did not voice their thoughts.

No words need be said when we know what transpired.

The *Sri'balvash* continued. "The humans and *ro'narshadan* work less during the hottest hours, now earlier or later in the day. Infant mortality is rising, and older people are dying due to heat-related illnesses."

Shealbri frowned. "Less people mean fewer taxes to collect, fewer workers to farm our resources. I thought the changes to the twelve-day workweek were to prevent this." During the last *kalidesh*, the *Kolotor'ix* introduced a twelve-day workweek to help the humans with their labor. The schedule was set so that people worked for three days, then had one day off, and then worked another three days. This created a cycle of thirty-six days in a month and twelve months in a year. *Although this new system is somewhat helpful, it didn't solve the problems as we had hoped.*

"In the southern Meridian territories of Cetra and Krevast, there are reports of a woman named Dulcea and a large cat attacking Dark Army convoys at night and sabotaging their missions. This has led to a twelve-and-one percent drop in effectiveness, with supplies meant for garrisons going missing and thought to be in the hands of those planning rebellions against your rule. New laws have been passed, warning against such actions."

Blagdon frowned, remembering reading the name in Apollo's account of what happened in Andears. *I will have to have Mykel watch for her. Perhaps I can sway her to my side and discover what she knows and who she is.*

"According to their spies, there have been more reports of this Dulcea entering villages and aiding the people, but they have been unable to see or capture her. The people refuse to turn her in, revering her as a folk hero, a figure of resistance to the *ro'*Shadon rule. Multiple checkpoints are set up on some roads to look for her under the guise of keeping the people safe from bandits, to no avail."

Blackmont scoffed. "Let them come to Krevast; I will make a new cloak out of that cat."

Caristha paused a moment before reading down the list. "In the area of the Ironfall Mountains, the shadow orcs and trolls have been fighting for territory, but it has not come down from the mountains into the other territories."

The *Kolotor'ix* turned to Blackmont. "Send word to your wayward brethren and tell them not to spill their squabble onto *ro'*Shadon lands. We gave them those mountains in exchange for their aid but no other lands. If they cannot control their population and fighting, *I will.*"

The shadow orc narrowed his eyes. "That is not my territory, our *Kolotor'ix*; I have no say in what they do there. However, if it were given--"

"You are currently not of a high enough ranking to have more than one territory, and the Ironfall Mountains fall outside the territories, specifically for the trolls and orcs to thrive in, as requested by both warchiefs."

Blagdon was silent, watching the interaction. He did not particularly care for Blackmont, his rules, and his way of running his territory, but he understood the *ro'*Shadon needed the orcs to beat back the Scourge and gave them land to call their own in exchange. *I only hope that no flying creatures living in the mountains have been hunted to extinction.*

"Regarding army readiness, *Hesta'kan ik'Nicholnor* and *ik'Blagdon* have diligently trained *ro'*Shadon cavalry. *Hasta'kan ik'Carriat* has been patrolling the roads and setting up escort stations for people to hire soldiers during travel. This has been a great way to produce income and keep an eye out for bandits, which has decreased significantly."

The *Kolotor'ix* began walking around the table silently as the *Sri'balvash* continued.

"In border defense, the dwarves are holed up well inside Ironfall Mountain, unable to enter Meridiah without the troll and shadow orcs seeing them. The border around Exonesis Mountain is still impenetrable, with Shadon unable to use their shadows after getting too close to it. *Hasta'kan ik'Blackmont* has had Shadon try flying wrightwings over the mountain to drop onto its surface, but the shadows seem to fail, with the Shadon falling to their death."

A few of the *Hesta'kan* suddenly looked concerned that the *Sri'balvash* would announce more failures for all to hear.

"*Hasta'kan ik'Blackmont* has increased patrols around the area, but they still find signs of camps along the borders. However, they do not see any new humans in the area, leading them to suspect the dawnwarriors are still taking humans into Exonesis. Whenever they have had a Shadon pose as a human with the group being brought into the mountain, their broken body is later found in the woods, as if dropped from a great height."

Sri'balvash Caristha continued with her reports, but Blagdon was no longer paying attention; his thoughts were on his only daughter. *Has Senka successfully posed as a human, or have the dawnwarriors discovered her identity, and now she lay in the woods, unclaimed by all but nature? Has Blackmont discovered her and is waiting to expose her today to make me look incompetent? Is Mykel's balutrae with her still?* He shook his head slightly as if stretching his neck to clear his racing thoughts. *I cannot change any outcome in Exonesis, but I can change the fate of my Hasta'kan, for good and ill.* He closed his eyes and whispered a prayer that Senka would return safely.

Finally, the *Kolotor'ix* stopped behind his chair, nodding to the *Sri'balvash*, who bowed her head and sat behind the desk. "Tomorrow, you will make your case for your *Hesta'kan* to move upward in rank. I will know if you tell falsehoods."

Blagdon glanced around the table at those gathered eagerly expecting to sit where he did now. *Tomorrow, everything will change. Let the kalidesh ik'kolotor begin.*

Stormriders are met with hardship,
both mental and physical requirements that come with great sacrifice.
We must provide them with the best we have;
not only armor, weaponry, and shields.
But also security and aid for mental and physical health;
for their hearts and minds are among the greatest among us.
Without it, they cannot be whole again.

Without them, we all fail.

— Sir Barriston, Stormrider Commander

RATSBAYNE

Ratsbayne glanced at Blagdon as they rode in the carriage, the tension tangible as the Shadon Leigelord looked out the window stoically at the night sky. Blagdon had approached him while he was grooming Slipstream and told him to accompany him, but he had remained silent since they had gotten in the carriage. Finally, Ratsbayne couldn't take it any longer. "Ah dun't understand; why don't we just ride there, or ya shadow us to wherever it be we are heading?"

Blagdon glanced at him for a long moment as if debating whether to answer before looking back out the window. "It is considered rude to show up unannounced to another *Hasta*."

"But ya be the First Leigelord, or so ya keep reminding everyone."

"*Hon-Hasta'kan*," he corrected.

"So can't ya just show up?"

"I could. But I would rather arrive quietly."

Wouldn't that be arriving quietly, with no one knowing you are there until you arrive? "So that be why we not taking yer usual carriage with the markings of *Hasta'kan ik'Blagdon* on the side?"

"Quite."

"Won't we be at risk of bandits? That be why carriages have markings, so everyone knows not to touch it."

"One would only think so."

It almost sounds like he wants someone to try to take this carriage. Maybe he needs to kill something. As long as it not be meh, Ah be okay with that.

There was a knock on the front wall of the carriage as it came to a stop, and a voice filled the shadows inside. "*Hasta'kan'ix*, we are at the first stop."

Blagdon took a long breath and let it out slowly. "Very well." Those two words carried a weight Ratsbayne did not expect.

We shall see where we are soon enough.

Blagdon silently glanced at Ratsbayne before stepping out of the carriage, the door opening for him.

Curious, Ratsbayne followed, looking at the woods around them. The trees were just as tall as the ones in Meridiah. He wouldn't have known he was in Nar'Shada if it weren't for the dullness as if the land had been painted with a mix of grey, muting the usual vibrant colors of the world. Looking up, Ratsbayne noticed that the cloud cover was still blocking out most of the starlight, furthering the dreary atmosphere.

Turning from his thoughts on the deary sky above, Ratsbayne watched Blagdon walk toward two stone formations stuck into the earth. Curious, he stepped closer, recognizing that Shadese was carved into the rocks, but couldn't read it. *What these be?*

Blagdon reached forward, the glove of his right hand slowly tracing down the inscribed language. His movement held a heaviness, one that came only from the thing that all creatures run from but never can beat.

These be graves. Why are they not magnificent things with carvings and Hesta emblems? They be simple, almost overlooked. That dun't sound like the Hasta'kan'ix, who reminds all who see him who he is, and is proud of it.

Blagdon turned to the other grave marker, putting his hand on the curved top of the stone as if it were the shoulder of another male. Even though he had no idea what Blagdon was saying in low Shadese, Ratsbayne suddenly felt as if he were interrupting something private. He quickly walked back toward the carriage, looking around the woods quietly as he kept his back toward Blagdon.

The guards posted silently around them in a perimeter, hands on their swords, looking everywhere but toward the mourning male. *Ah can't tell if it be out of respect, or if they be expecting an attack. Only a Shadon would attack a man at a gravesite.*

Feeling eyes watching him, Ratsbayne glanced over to see Ruin, who had walked beside the carriage during their journey, eyeing him steadily, ears turned toward Blagdon.

He ain't even tied to the carriage; what be stopping him from running off and terrorizing the world?

Ruin turned his head slightly as if sensing his thoughts, and Ratsbayne stepped back, turning slightly so as not to give his full back to the giant *kolvorvik.*

Blagdon walked past him, returning to the carriage silently.

Ratsbayne glanced back at the stones, noticing flowers lying at their bases. He quickly turned and climbed into the carriage before it took off without him and left him with the giant murder pony that looked like it wanted an excuse to eat something.

Blagdon and the guards were silent; the only sounds were the creaking of the carriage's wheels on the dirt road and the hooves of *kelvorvik.*

Ah miss Slipstream's voice in mah head.

The further they were from the capitol, the less he felt her presence unless he concentrated. It was odd since he would have done anything to have his head to himself before, but now, he felt as if a piece of him wasn't entirely there. He knew she was safe, alive in the stables, and protected by Gideon and the guards Blagdon put on her and her colt, but the further she was, the fainter her voice was. But something told him she'd run across the land to find him if he called to her. *The feeling be mutual.*

Finally, the carriage slowed down, and footsteps toward the carriage followed the sound of hushed talking. Ruin's form filled the window beside the door, protecting the occupants.

"Hon-Hasta'kan ik'Blagdon?"

Blagdon clicked his tongue, and the great *kolvorvik* stepped back, letting a guard look into the window at the two men.

Ratsbayne gave a small wave of his hand in greeting, which the male dismissed, looking to Blagdon instead. He stepped back from the window, and the carriage began moving again. He saw a stone wall and gates to either side as they headed into a large area with a massive keep in the middle.

"Where we be?"

"This was once the home of *Hasta'kan ik'Blagdon*, but now the territory of *Hasta'kan ik'Nicholnor*. This is where you will train. You have only a few days before you must be ready."

Ready fer what?

* * *

Ah dun't even recognize mahself, Ratsbayne thought as he ran a hand over his jawline, which now sported a much shorter, trimmed beard that made him look younger. He had lost track of how much time the *belvash* had scrubbed, poked, prodded, healed, and trimmed, his fingernails trimmed and cleaned, his hair now even and pulled back from his face.

"*You look good,*" he heard Slipstream say softly, her approval a comforting reassurance, though her voice sounded so far away it made his heart ache.

How do ye even know Ah look good? Ah could look like an ogre fer all ye know.

"*Fine, you look awful and should wear a cloth sack over your head at the dinner. Do you feel better now?*"

Ratsbayne began laughing, and he could feel pride and happiness echoed by his mare. *You be pretty spirited, Slipstream.*

"*What does the armor look like? I cannot wait to see it on you.*"

Ratsbayne let his laughter die out and walked from the bathhouse toward the dressing room, where Alandra waited to assist him in his armor after their bath. She'd arrived on horseback in the late hours of the night, hood on her closed cloak raised to prevent her from being identified as a *belvash.*

Ah remember when Ah dreamed that Ah be a squire, helping ah knight don his armor. Now it be meh.

"You'll never leave that room if she helps you."

She shaved mah beard and hair, and helped ensure Ah look good. If Ah dun't look good, it will reflect on Leigelord Blagdon. However, he couldn't help but wonder why he should care what a Shadon thinks of him. Ratsbayne shook his head, trying to think about the dinner ahead of him. *This isn't the time to reflect upon the past. Ah may not like where Ah be now, but at least Ah be alive, and so be Slipstream.*

He stopped when he saw the armor on the stand waiting for him: a magnificent suit of silvery metal polished so brightly that he could pick food from his teeth using the reflection as a mirror. A long dark blue cloak hung from its back from under the pauldrons, which had golden relief on either side, a homage to the emblem of *Hasta'kan ik'Blagdon,* but modified to be a windruner's rearing head inside the circle of twisted lines. On the chest in gold was the symbol of the Stormriders, the griffin flying over the hills before a sunset. He touched the cloak, feeling its weight. *It be heavy enough to use to help capture or deflect a sword in combat, yet light enough to move with.*

"The Byronian cloak was lighter in color; this dark blue reminds me of the ocean at night."

Ratsbayne blinked. *We've seen the ocean?*

"Of course we have; Stormriders rode all over Meridiah to keep the peace. We saw the Aerukatan Ocean when we went to protect the queen and princesses while they met with the ambassador at Cerian harbor."

"Are you going to keep fondling it, or will you let me put it on you?" Alandra said, taking Ratsbayne from his thoughts. She had put on a robe but left it gaping open, and Ratsbayne began imagining her wearing nothing but the dark blue cloak.

"Don't make me come in there."

"Oy, sorry, sorry." Ratsbayne began drying off so he could put the underclothes on to prevent his armor from chafing.

* * *

"Again."

Ratsbayne grunted and swung his sword at Blagdon, who blocked it. He moved quickly, his sword slashing out at him. Ratsbayne danced backward, keeping his sword up, deflecting the steel. It had been many turns of the hourglass, and Ratsbayne was becoming more used to his new armor. He still was not as fast as Blagdon, who wore lighter leather, but the fact that he was blocking more of the duelist's blows said he was improving.

Blagdon stepped back, taking a moment to sip from his waterskin, a sheen of sweat on his brow that Ratsbayne watched a shadow wipe away. *If Ah ain't watching, Ah wouldn't have noticed it.*

"Your bond with Slipstream has been aiding you greatly. A lesser man would have given up long ago, not used to the armor."

"Ah take the compliment, milord."

"*Ro'*Shadon do not use that title."

"Ah ain't Shadon."

Blagdon took another sip of his waterskin. "You will remain here for the rest of the day, training. I need you to be able to move comfortably in the armor."

"Ah dun't feel uncomfortable now. At first, Ah felt like Ah was playing pretend, and now —"

Blagdon held up his hand. "A simple yes or no would have sufficed. How does the sword feel in your hand? Is the balance correct?"

Ratsbayne looked at the sword Blagdon had given him to use. It was a beautiful piece, the pommel ending in a metal point perfect for striking, with a crossguard of two griffins standing facing each other, their wings outstretched to protect his hand. A blood groove ran down a third of the blade. "Aye, it be perfect, as if it be an extension o' mah hand." He sheathed it and held the sheathed blade to Blagdon.

"Keep it; it was specially made for you."

Ratsbayne blinked at him.

Blagdon sheathed his sword and picked up his cloak, putting it on. "I reviewed the old scrolls and found the blacksmith's book. Brightstar, the sword of Sir Siral Karog, was three-twelves and six inches long and weighed six pounds and two ounces. The blade is folded steel and *koldraka* to ensure it would last longer. Other than the blade's material, the sword is recreated faithfully."

Ratsbayne blinked at him, then at the blade. "Ah be told *koldraka* be expensive and rare."

"It is."

"Ah can't accept this; it be too much."

Blagdon looked at him. "I spent too much on it for you to refuse it. The only time that leaves your possession is when you are dead, and then it will be put behind glass in my study. Until then, it is yours. Get your armor and sword cleaned before supper so we can return to the capital. You still need to tend your mount and colt." He turned and left the barn, leaving Ratsbayne blinking.

The deepest truths
You can hold in your hand
live in the scrolls
which others have banned.

Those must be brought to light
To let everyone see
What truths kept hidden
That others don't want free.

— Kil'lik'Lenaka

LENAKA

Lenaka's breath shook as she looked at her reflection in the mirror, her multiple braids now intertwined and pinned to wrap around her head like a crown with white, red, green, and gold beads. *It wasn't as smoothly done as if I had paid the hair-maidens to do my hair last week, but I am sure they were busy. O'anu'toki Paku may not appreciate the colors of the K'hani, but the Order of the Everlasting Dawn are not the only ones celebrating the life of O'anu'tale Kiko.*

The memories from the last time she'd worn white crept into her mind, and she forced herself to take an even breath. *I am not a hatchling anymore, heading to my pari'lo funerals.* The flowers were strung as a bracelet but the fragrance made her stomach twist, and she began second-guessing her breakfast.

"Putri?" She entered his office and frowned, seeing his dinner from the previous night untouched on the table. She set down her white garments and began picking up the forgotten food.

Draven sat at his desk and looked up at Lenaka as she touched his shoulder gently, eyes shining quietly with unshed tears. It took him three times to speak, and his voice was hoarse and cracked as if it hadn't been used in days. "I've tried writing all night but can't find the words. I'm a bard and can't write how I feel."

Her heart broke for him, and she hugged him tightly as his shoulders shook. "It's all right, *Putri*. *O'anu'tale* Na'kia'Kiko knows how much you cared for her. She knows."

He stood as if not realizing she still held him, turning as he went to a shelf. He placed a wide wooden box on the table. He picked up the parchment he'd been writing, laid it in the box, and sprinkled sand over it to dry the ink, obscuring it. Draven then took his mourning garments from the table and walked out.

Lenaka could not remember the last time her *putri* was so silent, and a part of her was relieved at the change, though she immediately felt guilty for her selfishness.

Draven reentered the study, and his garments fit looser on him as if, over the last week, he'd lost more weight than she'd realized.

At least he'd gotten a comb through his hair and feathers.

Draven went to the table and reached into the box, taking the parchment by the corners and gently lifting it, tapping it gently to shake the loose sand back into the box.

She looked at the final product that had captured his attention for days. An image of *O'anu'tale* Kiko dominated the parchment, but instead of lineart, the drawing was made of written words in various thicknesses. Lenaka knew her *putri* had a talent for writing and sketching, but this was unlike anything she'd ever seen him create.

Draven carefully rolled the parchment, sealing it with a wax seal, and slipped it into his belt before putting on a hat. "I'm ready."

* * *

She took her *putri* to the Temple, where Draven could talk with *O'anu'toki* Aluu. She would have usually asked Koani to sit with him, but she hadn't seen him in the last few days and was sure the Order was keeping him busy.

In the outskirts of Wan'hela, homes with ladders and lifts began making it easier for non-dawnwarriors who stayed there. The *Rhani* were becoming more involved with the outside world, allowing refugees inside to live here peacefully, a hot debate topic in recent years. It was one refugee she was searching for, and she flew to the landing outside the door of a small home and knocked, waiting.

Clep opened the door, looking at her, frowning as he smoothed his white linen tunic.

"You look better," she said, noting that dark circles under his eyes were lessening. *Perhaps in a few days, they will be gone completely.* "Did you get some good sleep? How was the first night in your new home?"

"I did," he answered, stifling a yawn slightly, "and Memory has been asleep all morning as well. I think she's tired from flying so much." He glanced back at the small home he'd been given. "It's noisier than Andears or Silene were."

Lenaka smiled. "Well, at least you are near the *helaono,* and wagons can take you to the villages outside Wan'hela. As for Memory, you did say that she's spent most of her time in a cage recently, so being out where she can fly safely is wonderful, though I cannot say the same about the sprygts," she replied, laughing, as Clep blushed.

"She didn't know they weren't food," he explained as they walked down the dirt road toward the *helaono.* Clep looked at the white cloth streamers on poles and hanging on the stalls, blowing gently in the morning wind. "We never had a color for mourning," he commented quietly. We just wore our least dirty and worn clothing for our funerals—except for the last one."

"When my *pari'lo* died, I was given my first white clothing. I had never even noticed we didn't wear the color until then. I still feel the itching around my neck of the linen sometimes, as if I never really took it off, even after we burned it."

"You burn the clothing?"

"To not burn your funeral garb afterward is to keep the spirit of *K'han'Natsulith* around, inviting him to take more people for his horde."

"Who is *K'han'Natsulith*?"

"He is the mate of *K'han'Exonia.* While she lives in the skies, he lives deep in the earth. She is our giver of life, and he is the taker of it. They love each other very much but can never touch again."

"That's so beautiful and sad at the same time."

Lenaka nodded. "It is why we used to bury our dead, to keep

them safe."

"Used to?"

She sighed sadly. "*K'han'Natsulith* brought his undead to the surface to prove to his beloved that he was strong enough to stand at her side and beg her to return. But *K'han'Exonia* saw the pain it was causing the living, which hurt her heart deeply. Tears of liquid fire fell to the ground as she wept, where they are said to remain suspended in the Shattered Lands." She paused, looking at a stall with candles for sale, and ran her hand over one absently. "The *Rhani* had an idea and spoke to *K'han'Natsulith,* telling him they had a way to send his beloved gifts which would soothe her troubled heart."

Clep seemed entranced by the story, so she continued telling the tale that her *putri* had taught her. "We would burn our dead, their ashes rising high into the skies, to *K'han'Exonia,* who could put them in the stars. So we began doing so, and this soothed both *K'hani*'s hearts. Since then, no firey tears have fallen, and no horde has risen."

Clep was quiet, thinking. "I don't think I could ever go to a dragon and talk to them. I'm not that strong."

"Being strong has nothing to do with it; it is standing up for what is right. That is the bravest thing anyone can do. The *Rhani* are our leaders because they do what they must for the people. However, some disagree with their actions and wish things to return to how they were before."

"What do you mean?"

"The Order of the Everlasting Dawn do not like us burning our dead. They feel we dishonor them by denying their living families their bodies to visit and commune with. It has been a long argument with no end in sight."

"But what if *K'han'Natsulith* decides to raise his horde again?"

"It is a worry many of us have. My *putri* had told stories about what happened in the land of Meridiah when the horde walked, adding so many to their numbers. Some of us fear if it were to happen here…"

she trailed off, looking at the surrounding mountains, rubbing her arms as if cold.

"You'd be trapped with them."

What do you do when the very thing that protects you from the monsters outside traps you with the monsters within?

* * *

Drums beat upbeat music as they walked toward the Village of the Stars. The men remained silent as the women and children danced, their singing and smiling punctuated by tears.

Lenaka sang with them, although she frowned at the altered lyrics of familiar tunes she'd known since childhood. The *K'hani* were erased from the songs, replaced by praises to the Everlasting Dawn. These songs were sung more softly, with only half as many dawnwarriors joining in, as not everyone felt compelled to change tradition for a deity they didn't believe in. *But the important part is we walk together as one, even if we no longer share beliefs. Grief touches us all, no matter who you worship.*

Clep followed behind Lenaka and Koani, who rubbed his shoulder with a pained look after switching with the next team of coffin bearers.

Lenaka handed him a waterskin, which he accepted with a silent nod. She glanced ahead for her *putri*, able to spot him easier by his hat sitting upon his greying hair as he helped carry the wooden base of the coffin on his shoulder with five other dawnwarrior males, a folded fabric on his shoulder to ease the weight.

*Rhan'*Kahan had carried the *O'anu'tale* in the first team with *O'anu'toki* Paku across from him. The teams of coffin bearers were male and separated by height, so there was no fear of the coffin tipping or falling during the travel. By tradition, females were not allowed to carry the coffin, and the males could not speak while the procession walked.

The funeral procession started with a steady walk but gradually became slower as the sun grew higher in the sky, not due to the dread of lying to rest a beloved member of society but because many dawnwarriors were not used to walking for long periods.

Our wings spoil us, and death reminds us to take nothing for granted.

According to tradition, no one could be higher than the deceased during the journey from Wan'hela to the Village of the Stars, which her *putri* had described as "a living recreation of the deceased's journey from birth to death." All dawnwarriors, from the children to the *Rhani*, walked, though *pari'lo* sometimes took turns carrying the youngest, and the eldest sat in carts pushed by others.

As they passed the villages, some joined the procession while others stepped outside to observe it, their doorframes adorned with flowers in respect and observance. The only Iryn dwarf couple in Exonesis joined the crowd, white ribbons woven in their beards, and a few humans stepped forward, holding fabric stretched between poles to help keep the sun off the elderly.

There may be more holding the people of Exonesis together than that which tears them apart.

At highsun, the funeral procession paused and the coffin was set onto the shoulders of new bearers. Many dawnwarriors left the procession, walked to the grass, and removed their sandals. They laid out small woven straw mats and sat on their knees, Koani and his family among them. Guided by *O'anu'toki* Paku, the dawnwarriors repeatedly began raising their arms toward the sun and earth. The males started mouthing quietly as the females chanted in Dawnese, praising the Everlasting Dawn.

She glanced at Koani, who was on his mat beside his sister, praying as well. Lenaka looked away, not because she was ashamed, but because she felt it was rude to watch someone while praying, as if she were interrupting something private. *I had not realized so many were of the Order of the Dawn in Exonesis, including hakena'lo and lakoni'lo.* She even spotted a few *niapa'lo* among them — the select few she recognized, as not every member openly disclosed their role as a spy for the *Rhani*.

After the prayer session, Koani returned to the procession and took another turn carrying the coffin while the other dawnwarriors began moving onward.

Draven used Clep's back to lay a parchment against it, writing furiously and drawing small diagrams quickly sketched in the margins. He quickly tried blowing on the parchment to dry the ink before they began walking.

Lenaka frowned as she realized most of the Order of the Dawn were walking in the front of the procession near the coffin and not as dispersed among them as she'd originally thought. *How long until the differences between the K'hani and Everlasting Dawn were too large to ignore?*

* * *

When they had finally stopped to rest and eat, Lenaka sat on a rock, rubbing balm onto her aching feet and wincing as she found multiple blisters. She glanced at her *putri*, who sat hunched over a parchment, writing. *How he has the energy to write is beyond me. I want to lie in the grass and sleep for a month.*

"Why can't you fly there? It would be faster," Clep asked once they had found a place to sit together. Now that the procession had stopped for the evening, the males were vocal about their aches and pains. Even though many had taken the time to stretch their wings while standing, none dared to take to the sky.

"*K'han'Natsulith* takes soul to the heavens to live among the skies under the watchful eye of *K'han'Exonia* as stars. If anyone else is higher than the deceased, they risk their soul being taken instead of the *O'anu'tale*'s. That is why the coffin is raised on our shoulders as we walk and why it is placed on a portable wooden stand while we rest."

"Or," Koani said, sitting and tossing two apples to Clep and Lenaka, "it is just an old tradition. The *K'hani* are de—"

"We are not going to get into it tonight," Lenaka snapped, irritated and tired. *This is not the time nor place to debate the K'hani's current state of life.*

Koani glanced at Clep, then at the other dawnwarriors, some

glancing over. Like the other members of the Order of the Everlasting Dawn, he wore a splash of orange somewhere, though it was a single ribbon tied around his upper arm this time.

I hadn't noticed the Order sitting away from the rest of us until now. How sad it is that even in mourning someone we all cared for, we are still divided.

"You're right, Kil'lik'Lenaka; we can let this debate go during the funeral. I didn't mean to upset you. I'll let you get some sleep, all right?" He gave her a hopeful smile and seemed relieved when she gave him a nod and a small smile. He then walked off to his family, glancing back once at her before sitting beside his *pari'tale* and sister.

Clep smiled sadly. "He likes you. He looks at you like Apollo looked at Alexis."

"Who is Alexis?"

Clep's smile faltered slightly. "She gave Apollo his first kiss in the woods in Andears. He was embarrassed but smiled whenever he talked about her." He shuffled somewhat as he bit into a peach as if to shake off the memory of his brother.

"That reminds me, I have something for you, Clep," She said, reaching into her bag for a small wrapped item and handing it to him.

He unwrapped the cloth and discovered a small wooden figurine of a boy with yellow painted hair holding a sword. Puzzled, he looked at her.

"It's supposed to be Apollo, from your description of him. I had it painted in the city by one of our craftswomen. I thought that you'd like have it with you today, and tomorrow we can find a place and burn it since we cannot give him a real funeral. That way, you and he could know peace. That is if you wish to. I know you don't believe in the *K'hani*, but if it would help both your souls ease their burdens, I'll stand beside you."

Lenaka bit her lip, unsure how to continue. *The explanation sounded better in my head than aloud. Perhaps I am too much like Putri and must write things down before speaking.*

Clep blinked rapidly, holding the figurine tightly. "Thank you. I'd… I'd like that."

Apollo,

We've traveled a day since that village and decided to camp in the woods. I looked through Memory's eyes and saw a girl running through the woods as if in danger. I tried convincing Markis, Edmont, and Jacob to go with me to help her, but no one wanted to listen. "We have our own problems; we don't need theirs," they said. So I went on my own.

She was hiding in the woods, frightened. I discovered Leigelord Blackmont, hunts humans like prey! The girl, Anara, was running for her life, and soon, they'd find our camp. Soldiers grabbed her, putting her over their shoulders, saying she was to be the Leigelord's bride and bear him many sons, and if she didn't, her family would be hunted next.

I ran back to camp and tried telling them, but Jacob refused to listen, telling us to pack and leave quickly. I hated leaving her behind. You would have convinced Jacob and the others to rescue her.
I wish you were here.

Clep

APOLLO

As soon as Senka created it, Apollo walked through the darkness portal, ready to leave *Et-kivnyta* behind him. When he stepped into the woods on the other side, the dark shape on the other side of the clearing before them was so massive that Apollo thought it had swallowed the stars in the sky. The clouds parted enough to let the moonlight hit the face of the largest mountain Apollo had ever seen.

I knew that Exonesis Mountain was large, but Nan-kyr's stories never said it was this big.

"Close your mouth before you catch bugs to eat for dinner," Senka remarked, adjusting her cloak over her armor. Before raising her hood, Senka wrapped a cloth over her white hair, hiding it.

Alax looked around at the clearing. "There is a fire up ahead, and we can ask them if they've seen your brother. If they haven't, then he may not have made it this far, and we can backtrack or even wait here for him to show up."

"Sounds like a plan," Apollo agreed and began walking toward the campfire.

Tibold grabbed his arm. "Alax and I will wait here with the horses; that way, they won't try to steal them or make your stay there. You can say the rest of your people are here if you need an excuse to leave."

Senka handed Alax something, nodding to him before walking with Apollo through the clearing.

There were at least two dozen people near the small camp, and one of the men seemed injured, a female wrapping a cloth around his bleeding arm, chiding him for not holding still. "It's healing slower without potions."

The male frowned. "Get me a potion to put on it then; it's been weeks; it should be more healed than this."

"You are the idiot who got cut by werg, and we're almost out." The girl frowned, rummaging in a bag momentarily before pulling out a bottle of red-orange liquid sealed with twine and wax.

Apollo blinked, noticing the twine was tied with a bow at the top. *That's Clep's potion; he always tied his twine in a bow to help people remember where they got it so they would return and buy more from him later.* He hurried forward excitedly. "Where did you get that potion? Is the healer who made it here?"

The group was startled, looking at him suddenly, some reaching for weaponry in his excited tone.

Senka touched Apollo's arm over the cloak, stopping him from moving forward. "Excuse my companion, he's a bit rattled. We ran out of healing potions and saw a pack of werg in the woods. We'd been hoping to speak with the healer who had made our potions before; they looked like that."

Apollo blinked at Senka. *I thought Hasta'kan ik'Blagdon didn't lie.*

"No," the injured male said, "we don't have a healer with us." He spat on the ground.

"Is the healer in a village nearby?" Apollo asked.

The male's voice became irritated as he spoke. "He's not here, all right? He's gone."

"What do you mean, gone?"

"Thank you," interrupted Senka, who turned Apollo and walked him back to the woods where Alax and Tibold waited, frowning. "Calm yourself, or you will get us found out."

"Those were Clep's potions."

"They may have bought them before. Scaring them won't get us answers."

Tibold closed her eyes; they were black as night when he opened them. "I don't see anyone matching his description nearby, nor a cage for a hawk." He blinked, his eyes becoming normal again.

Apollo frowned at Senka. "*Ro'*Shadon don't apologize, and *Hasta'kan ik'Blagdon* tells the truth and never lies."

Senka gave him a look. "I left our healing potions with Alax and saw we werg yesterday. I manipulated the truth to fit what I had said."

Alax looked at Apollo, his irises fading from black. "That is the group from Silene; the female just asked if they thought we were asking about Clep. What do you want to do?" he asked, hand going to the pommel of his sword, a slightly eager tone in his voice.

"I want to find my brother."

"Even if it means becoming the very thing you ran from in the first place, as you threaten innocent humans to get answers?" he asked, making Apollo glare at him.

"No, not that."

"You are the most frustrating human I've ever met."

As Tibold and the others began setting up their campfire, Apollo watched the group from Silene quietly, wondering if the line he didn't want to cross was getting blurrier by the day.

* * *

In the early morning, Apollo offered to hunt teagot for breakfast after another night of rough sleep. The morning dew chilled the air, making it easier for him to walk over the fallen leaves. By the time he'd come across a small creek, the morning light had begun warming the surface, and frogs had begun croaking. A bird whistled, and Apollo caught himself smiling. Finally, he sat on a fallen log, breathing in the cool air. The sounds and smells of the woods around him soothed his nerves, and he took deeper breaths. *I haven't hunted alone in so long; I'd almost forgotten that the hunt wasn't the only reason I went into the woods so often.*

Seeing a heard of teagot ahead, he climbed off the log and moved carefully so as not to scare them, an arrow nocked but not drawn. According to Pa-*kyr*, the deerlike creatures had grown smaller over the years but still had good meat and skins. He followed a teagot buck quietly, waiting for it to begin grazing. When it stopped moving and started eating what Apollo hoped was clover, he crouched and pulled his arrow back.

The snapping of a twig to his left made the buck look up, ears turning, and it took off, bounding through the trees as they ran further away. Apollo spun, pulling the arrow back toward the noise, his heart pounding. *Please don't be a werg.*

A female stepped out, her hands at her side to show they were empty, but Apollo didn't lower the bow. He'd seen plenty of dangerous people, even with nothing in their hands.

She spoke quietly as if afraid to spook him or be heard. "You're Apollo, aren't you?" She stopped moving forward when she realized he wasn't lowering the bow. "I didn't recognize you at first."

"Who are you?" His voice sounded a little harsher than he'd meant, but she'd spooked him. *She was the one wrapping the injured boy's arm the previous night.*

"I'm Emma, the baker's daughter from Silene. Do you remember me?"

"Not really," Apollo admitted. *I'd been so focused on revenge then that I didn't pay attention to anyone around me, especially Clep.*

Emma flinched. "We traveled with Clep from Silene; he always spoke about you."

Apollo concentrated on keeping his grip. Holding the stance for an extended amount of time wasn't easy.

"He was worried about you."

"Where is he?" Shorter sentences seemed easier right now. "Why wasn't he with you last night?"

Emma flinched. "We thought you'd left Silene to report to the

Dark Army. Some of us feared that Clep was also a spy for the Leigelord and his son, and they would burn Silene as they did Andears. When he went with us toward Exonesis Mountain, we thought it was to lead us into a trap."

"Where. Is. He?" Apollo asked through gritted teeth, his arms beginning to burn and shake.

"We left him. We— I," she corrected herself, "put herbs in his tea to knock him out and left him in the woods after taking his potions. We left him a few for himself," she added quickly as if trying to convince him not to be angry. "I'd hoped he'd returned to a village we'd passed." A tear ran down her cheek, and she looked at him. "I am so sorry."

Apollo said nothing as he loosed the arrow.

* * *

Senka looked up as Apollo stalked past her, taking off his cloak. "Where's the teagot?"

He kept walking, ignoring her, his eyes fixed on the group across the clearing. The male with the bandaged arm pointed and laughed with the others beside a cooking pot tended by a female. He barely heard the others saying his name as if they were far away.

Someone grabbed his arm.

Apollo turned, swinging, but Senka seemed to have anticipated this, ducking under his arm and grabbing his wrist, twisting it behind his back as she tripped him, riding him face-first into the ground.

"Let me up!" He shouted as hot tears ran down his cheeks. "They betrayed my brother; they drugged him and left him to fend for himself in the woods!"

Tibold hurried over, pulling Apollo up by the collar as Senka stepped back, marching him toward their camp. Once they were near their firepit, he shoved Apollo away. "You certainly got their attention," he said, nodding toward the Silene group, who were standing, talking to each other, some with weapons in hand.

Alax leaned against a tree. "You shot the tree beside the baker's daughter from less than three feet away. Was that on purpose, or are you that bad of a shot? Should I hunt next time?"

Apollo glared at him. "You were watching."

"You are *balutrae ik'Blagdon*. Of course, we're watching. Do you think we are *negut* and allow someone other than *korrati* Mykel to kill you?"

Apollo sighed, more frustrated at himself at the moment. "I couldn't do it, not even after all she's done." *I'm not sure I can take another life.*

"Do you want me to do it?" Senka asked from behind him.

The question was so casually toned that it startled him out of anger. "What did you say?"

"You heard me. Your enemies are *Hasta'kan ik'Blagdon*'s enemies."

Apollo looked across the clearing at the group from Silene. Emma had returned and talked quickly to the others, who glanced around as if searching the woods for an angry archer.

Alax spoke up, his voice eager. "If you want them all dead, we could do it."

Apollo blinked at him and Tibold, who was watching the group as if he were a werg debating which teagot to pick off from the herd first.

Apollo shook his head, looking back at the group. "There are children; I don't want them to see me as a monster."

"We can use shadows; the children wouldn't even see the attack, just the aftermath."

Apollo glared at Alax.

Senka walked to stand between them, looking at Apollo. "Is that how you saw us, as monsters?"

"Yes."

"And now?"

Apollo thought for a long time before answering. "I'm realizing that monsters wear all sorts of faces." He looked back at the group who had betrayed his little brother, leaving him alone in the woods to live or die on his own. *Clep is out there, somewhere. I can only hope that he is still alive when I find him.* "The worst monsters are the ones you see in your reflection." He sighed, picking up his cloak and putting it over his armor. "Let them realize that for themselves." Apollo turned, heading back toward *Et-kivnyta.*

Tibold stepped in front of him, but spoke to Alax. "So what did she say, the girl from the group?"

"They left Clep a while ago, in the middle of the night before the rainstorm so that he couldn't follow their footprints. They took his healing potions and his salves for injuries. They robbed him and left him for dead."

Tibold raised an eyebrow but didn't respond, much to Apollo's surprise.

"When I shot the arrow at the tree beside her, she got scared and ran off before telling me anything else. Now I don't know where he is." Apollo sighed, frustrated. *I shouldn't have lost control of my anger.*

Senka looked at Alax and Tibold. "You two can look for him; I'll stay here with Apollo."

Apollo blinked at her. "Are we splitting up? I'm not going to look for my brother?"

Senka glanced back at Exonesis Mountain. "You can't shadow teleport, and I'm useless until nightfall. They can search for him, provided your brother hasn't gotten turned around in the woods and has walked back toward Cetra instead of Exonesis Mountain."

Apollo frowned. *He wouldn't have; he has the Memory to see through and find the Mountain.* But he would not reveal that secret, not if there were plots involving Stormriders and *Hasta'kan ik'Blagdon* already asking questions about Clep and their ma-*kyr*'s amulet.

Senka turned back to Apollo. "You and I will remain here and wait if Clep finds his way here. That way, you can get some rest."

"I've slept enough, Lady Shadon Senka."

Senka stepped to him, speaking low. "You've been having nightmares this entire trip. You mutter the name Eratas-*kyr* often and fight off something in your sleep. Waiting here will allow you to stop looking and your brother to come to you."

Have I been having nightmares again? There are times I wake up and don't remember them at all.

He turned to look at Alax and Tibold to see what they thought, expecting Alax to give him a witty remark about only children having nightmares. He blinked, realizing the two Shadon were gone.

When shadows gather,

None survive intact.

— Shadon proverb

BLAGDON

Blagdon had never been one for the political arena, and sitting through the other eleven *Hasta'kan'ix* to speak of their achievements gave him a slight headache. Unlike most things in *ro'*Shadon society, the lower-ranking *Hesta'kan'ix* spoke first, going higher in rank. He kept his face passive as he sipped from his goblet, his left hand in his lap as he half-listened to *Hesta'kan'ix ik'Rutherrene* speak about opening another temple in the territory of Kalkora. *Narisa will be ineterested in learning about it, if she does not already know.*

"*Hasta'kan ik'Nicholnor* has been diligently training the next batch of *ro'*Shadon cavalry," *Hasta'kan'ix* Errok *ik'Nicholnor* said, giving a slight nod to Blagdon, which he returned. "The *Hesta'kan* have set two-hundreds, four-twelves and one recruits to be trained as soldiers this past year. Currently, five-twelves of them are being considered for cavalry training. In the last cycle, two-hundreds and five soldiers graduated from their program and became fully trained cavalry. They will be sent back to their *Hesta'kan* to report and, from there, be sent to wherever they are needed within the realm."

"What was the failure rate of this training?"

"Seventy percent, our *Kolotor'ix*, though it has been greatly improved by the presence of *Hasta'kan'ix ik'Blagdon*, who, according to *Korrat'ix* Gravis *ik'Nicholnor*, has improved relationships between mounts and their riders. Since our arrangement with him, there has been a greater failure rate, but that is because we accept and train the very best to protect our people. Soldiers who graduate now are stronger, faster, and better than those who came before the Scourge War."

"What becomes of those who fail?"

"They are trained soldiers, and if they wish, may try again to reenter the cavalry in two years."

Of all the Hasta'kan, I would accept if Nicholnor was named Hon-Hasta'kan.

Hasta'kan ik'Blackmont claimed yet another productive cycle, if one could call it that, with several hunts conducted in which others were invited to participate after dinner. Blagdon always ensured he was too busy to attend.

How one could hunt down the ones who maintain your territory, grow your food, attend your land, is beyond my understanding.

Hasta'kan ik'Remhold began speaking of his *Hasta'kan's* achievements, to which Blagdon gave the man beside him little attention.

"It was then when *Hasta'kan ik'Blagdon* stole the territory of Cetra and slew my Lordson-*kyr*. Because of this, I could not count its harvests, lumber, and goods among my contributions."

Blagdon looked at his goblet before taking a sip of watered wine, unbothered by the claim. "He did not explain why. The reasoning behind actions is almost, if not more, important than the action itself."

The *Hesta'kan'ix* traded looks; some interested, some bored, but all interested in the growing tension.

Blackmont gave a slight sound of disapproval.

Of course, you would be less interested in knowing why someone did something, as long as they could be hunted afterward.

The *Kolotor'ix's* mask turned toward Remhold, silently waiting.

It was now the other man who looked less sure of himself. "Our *Kolotor'ix, Hasta'kan'ix ik'Blagdon* replaced my Lordson-*kyr* and inserted his own as *korrati* of Woodsong garrison, a child who has taken a human as his *balutrae*, making a mockery out of one of our most sacred traditions and rites."

The other *Hesta'kan* glanced at Blagdon, some whispering low to each other or trading looks.

Nicholnor looked digusted; Halidesh sat back and sipped his wine as if watching a play unfold on one of his tavern stages.

So this is how it is going to be.

"Yet," the *Kolotor'ix* spoke quietly, "you've not answered why Cetra was taken from you and your Lordson-*kyr* replaced." His mask turned toward Blagdon. "Explain why I had sent you to investigate, *Hasta'kan'ix.*"

"Yes, our *Kolotor'ix*. Former *korrati* Kerrik-*kyr* ik'*Remhold* abused the people of Cetra. He raped women, overtaxed the villages, and stole the best tools and materials, leaving them with broken items and spirits. I received first-hand reports and statements from witnesses, an account from a survivor whose village was burned to the ground after the soldiers murdered all other inhabitants. Fortunately, the whitewood tree did not catch fire."

Shealbri frowned. "Why is that fortunate? Those damned trees are cursed."

"The tree is poisonous, not cursed. Their fruit is only good to eat once it falls from the branches when most fruit is considered rotten. The toxic fumes would have spread to the surrounding woods and lake, contaminating the animals, water, and crops. The land would have been unusable for at least four-twelve and two years."

He took a moment and continued. "As the previous *Hon-Hasta'kan'ix*, I am permitted to hold up to five territories as long as I can defend them. I have two— Stormhold and the Stormlands— used to train and maintain our cavalry mounts. I wagered Cetra as a condition for winning the duel your Lordson-*kyr* foolishly challenged me to. He agreed on behalf of his *Hasta'kan*. He lost."

Blackmont looked interested, leaning forward and looking at the map where Cetra and Krevast bordered each other.

I will need to speak to Mykel about bolstering his borders sooner rather than later.

"You sent back his… his…" Remhold began, hesitating as if trying to find a word.

"I sent back his head and penis in a box to you and your lady. After the duel, which I offered to return him to you alive, the young human female he took advantage of was allowed to castrate him. After he threatened me and mine, I ended the duel and his life."

"You allowed a human to interfere with a duel? Or any Shadon matters, including your Lordson's *balutrae*," Rutherrene spoke up, "you are growing soft with affection for the chattel."

The *Kolotor'ix* said nothing, watching the interaction.

"Any male who takes advantage of a female does not deserve to be called a male. It would do no good to castrate a corpse, and his screams of agony served as a deterrent for others who may have thought to follow in his stead. The females who cook and tend the soldier's clothing are safer; the men are not preoccupied with bedding females but are training and protecting the territory. They've become more focused and productive, improving the *ro'*Shadon."

Blackmont began laughing, hitting the table open-handedly. "The *ro'*Shadon are improved by your Lordson-*kyr* losing his cock!"

The *Kolotor'ix* tilted his head in interest. "*Hasta'kan ik'Blagdon* did not steal the territory but won it rightfully. Words of your Lordson-*kyr*'s misdeeds had reached my ears far before your own. Or," he asked, looking at Remhold fully, "did you know about them and simply do nothing?"

The silence grew heavy as eyes turned to Remhold, whose face contorted with anger and embarrassment. He started to stand, looking at Blagdon.

"It is forbidden to duel during the *kalidesh ik'kolotor*," the *Kolotor'ix* reminded them, his voice soft yet dangerous.

I will have my turn to do so soon enough.

"Of course, our *Kolotor'ix*," Remhold said, sitting as if he were merely adjusting his chair.

"I noticed you had done nothing to correct your Lordson-*kyr's* actions and sent *Hasta'kan'ix ik'Blagdon* since Stormhold is on Cetra's northern border and can hold it." The *Kolotor'ix* watched him. "Do you have anything else to say before we move on to *Hasta'kan'ix ik'Branial?*"

"I do, in fact, our *Kolotor'ix,* have one more item to address before those gathered today."

"Then continue, and be wary of any more accusations you throw."

Remhold nodded, gesturing to his territory on the map, the northeastern part of Meridiah. "My people have been attempting to push into the land of D'Lcee for years and have successfully blocked off most trade to the land to weaken them."

Blackmont snorted as he set down his goblet. "Attempting? Most trade? Is this not the land of a ten-season-old human leader?"

Blagdon looked at the map. *It is possible that Remhold has stopped all land trade into the small country since his territory is their western border, and their northern border is the Shadowgulf Mountains, but their eastern shore is open to trade with the Benstafi elves.*

"I am awaiting the significance of this matter," the *Kolotor'ix* spoke flatly. "My patience is thinning rapidly."

Remhold did not look dismayed by this. "We have lost many of those we had sent into D'Lcee to attack their leader."

Blagdon waited patiently. *Remhold may be a nogut regarding some matters, but bringing a subject up, especially with one's failures, without reason was to invite downfall.*

"I have reports of a soldier protecting the young leader and her lands, wearing black-scaled armor with wings like a dragon's, their face within the helm of a dragon's open maw."

The others turned, looking at Remhold, their faces holding a mixture of emotion, Blagdon among them.

"Are you certain of your claim?"

"I do not doubt the words of my soldiers. He described the armor to me. He said the knight wielded a greenish-blade in one hand and a scaled shield in the other, cutting through his company and leaving burning corpses in his wake."

"Did the burns have green along the edges, like poison or acid?" Carriat spoke up, his face worried as he leaned forward in his chair.

"My soldier did not get that good of a look at the wounds. He ran for his life."

"Good," Blackmont spoke up, "he has brought word of a bigger prey to hunt and kill!" He turned to the *Kolotor'ix*. "Allow my men to—"

"No," came the answer behind the mask.

Nicholnor looked at D'Lcee's location on the map, frowning. "How long ago was this encounter, *Hasta'kan'ix ik'Remhold*?"

"At least fifty-seven seasons."

"Why was I not made aware of this before?" the *Kolotor'ix*'s angry voice made everyone look at him.

"I did not dare interrupt your wrath with tales of a single knight. To do so would court certain death, especially so soon after the *kreva ik'Kolotor'ix*'s disappearance."

I wonder if there is a connection between Liana going missing and this new threat.

"Has the knight come south, or have they remained in D'Lcee the entire time?"

"I am unsure, but every time we have tried a campaign to push into the land, the knight shows up and beats us back. The Shadowgulf Mountains prevent us from attacking from the north. The people of D'Lcee have discovered that attacking us at night without torches has been more effective."

Nicholnor leaned back in his seat, his face deep in thought, as Carriat frowned deeply and looked at the map.

They are undoubtedly mulling over military strategies, as am I. Why did he not ask for aid?

"The knight will not be slain but brought to me alive," the *Kolotor'ix* announced, and Blagdon breathed a sigh of relief.

At least there is a hope that the past mistakes will not be repeated.

"The knight will have to go through your territory of Montak if they want to attack us, which is far enough from my lands. Surely, you can stop one little knight," Shealbri spoke up as he sipped his watered wine.

"*Negut,*" snapped Nicholnor, "it sounds like a dragonsoul knight. Some of you do not remember what it is like fighting them. If you did, you would not rush to meet them in battle."

Silence spread around the table.

The *Kolotor'ix* leaned forward, steepling his fingers before his mask as if in thought. Finally, he spoke. "A dragonsoul may be among us again after the destruction of the dragons. This is quite the turn of events."

I could not agree more, but is this a turn for or against us?

Remhold smiled. "Of course, since my *Hasta'kan* is the one who brings this news to you, I hope our *Kolotor'ix* will see we have a proper reward."

The mask turned to regard him. "What are you expecting for such a reward, *Hasta'kan'ix ik'Remhold*?"

"Our *Kolotor'ix*, one-hundred, four-twelve and four years ago, we walked on the Dragonland after you had asked them for a dragon's soul to become the very knight we speak of now. The arrogant lizards denied you and, in doing so, doomed their raced to our blades and shadows unless they gave their souls to you and those you deemed worthy. We walked away empty-handed."

Oh yes, remind the Kolotor'ix of the ro'Shadon's most significant failure. Perhaps I may not have to worry about him at the dinner if he kills you first.

"This dragonsoul knight proves there may be others alive out there. This proves there is hope for you to become what you've longed for, to lead the *ro*'Shadon into a new era with more power than we'd dreamed. You will not walk away empty-handed this time."

"A fine speech, but you do not answer my question."

When Remhold spoke, his eyes passed over Blagdon just a moment before looking at the *Kolotor'ix*, speaking louder for the room to hear. "I wish your claimed daughter, Mari'aida, to be betrothed to one of my Lordsons."

Blagdon choked on his drink and set down the goblet.

The other *Hesta'kan'ix* looked between them, some looking eager for the inevitable fight to occur.

Nicholnor spoke up in the shocked silence. "The girl is betrothed to Lordson Mykel *ik'Blagdon*."

"Should such a bounty not go to someone who brings our *Kolotor'ix* the dragonsoul knight and not just someone who speaks of what may or may not exist? I see no parchments or proof. Why should only *Hasta'kan'ix ik'Remhold* get this opportunity when any one of us could bring him in?" Carriat added.

"D'Lcee borders my territory, and my people will capture him," Remhold snapped.

"Your men have proved incompetent now; you have said it yourself. Let someone with real experience do the deed," Blackmont snapped, pounding his fist on the table. "Let me and mine bring the knight and take your elf's hand in marriage."

"You'd split her in half in the mating bed," Armtomb snapped, shaking his head, "you shadow orcs are large, brutish creatures who have no business being wed to the *Kolotor'ix*'s claimed daughter."

Blackmont laughed. "We know how to bed humans; I have already gotten a new human wife. She will be bearing my sons later this year. Elves are heartier and can take—"

"Finish that sentence, and I will meet you outside the moment the *kalidesh* is over and you will never have claim over anything again," Blagdon stated quietly, but his tone caused the others to stop talking momentarily.

"So it is settled, whoever brings back the dragonsoul knight alive gets wed to our *Kolotor'ix*'s claimed daughter."

Blagdon's hand played along the stem of his goblet, half listening to the others argue. He looked at Remhold, who smiled at him coldly. *I would applaud your cleverness if you were not messing with my plans for my family and Hasta'kan.*

He turned, glancing at the *Kolotor'ix*, who did not seem to pay the arguing *Hesta'kan'ix* any mind, his mask fixed on the land of D'Lcee on the map. For the first time, Blagdon wondered if Remhold may have maneuvered in a way he could not counter.

* * *

They were allowed a break to relieve themselves and regain their composure and had fruit to snack upon, but lunch was pushed back until after the meeting was concluded. It was thought to motivate getting to the point in conversations, but it was proving challenging this *kalidesh ik'kolotor*.

"*Hasta'kan ik'Blagdon*, you may begin telling of this cycle's achievements."

Blagdon looked from the others to the *Kolotor'ix*, who had begun walking around the table as the last two *Hesta'kan* spoke. *Perhaps his legs were falling asleep after sitting for hours. I know mine have.*

"When I took over Cetra, I aimed to use it better than *Hasta'kan ik'Remhold*. The humans and *narshadan* in our territories are essential; depriving them of good tools, food, and supplies weakens us. They cannot harvest without proper tools; without the harvest, we cannot feed our people. Without our people, we do not have soldiers, farmers, or those who work for us. Without them, the *ro'*Shadon return to what we were before Nar'Shada."

The *Hesta'kan* looked at each other silently.

Blagdon removed a folded parchment from his vest and opened it, reading off the list Narisa had prepared for him. "Under the leadership of *korrati* Mykel *ik'Blagdon*, the relations between *ro'*Shadon and humans in Cetra are beginning to flourish and will yield more resources whenever the Dark Army travels south into the lands beyond. The productivity of my territories is as follows: food production is up over two-twelves and six percent. The lumber collection is up by four-twelves and one percent. Reports of criminal acts between *ro'*Shadon and citizens are down to twelve percent. Reports of rape and abuse toward women are down one hundred percent." Blagdon fought not to look at Remhold at that.

Sri'balvash Caristha glanced over, pausing in her writing, and slightly nodded before continuing.

I would not have noticed if I had not been looking in that direction.

"*Belvash* have started visiting the villages to teach the basics of living under *ro'*Shadon law, which the villagers lacked. Under *Hasta'kan ik'Remhold*, the villages were raised quarterly for goods and able-bodied males to send to the overpopulated Woodsong. Those who fought back were slain, and one village burned to the ground with all but two murdered. There are small remnants of *Hasta'kan ik'Remhold's* poor territory, such as the woman with her cat, but it is nothing my Lordson cannot handle."

Remhold turned toward him to say something, but the *Kolotor'ix* spoke first.

"Do you have a rebuttal to this claim that you wish to speak, *Hasta'kan'ix ik'Remhold?*"

Blagdon spoke before the other man could. "If it pleases you, our *Kolotor'ix*, I have written testimony of a survivor of the burned village, written by *Sri'balvash* Desira, for he never was permitted to learn to read and write until my Lordson became *korrati*. There are also statements from the remaining six villages of Cetra addressing *Hasta'kan ik'Remhold's* mistreatment." Blagdon set down a thick stack of folded parchment on the table.

The *Kolotor'ix* moved his hand and the shadows deposited the parchments at his end of the table, out of the reach of the *Hesta'kan'ix*.

"Korrati Mykel *ik'Blagdon* has begun to allow any soldiers who wish to return to their villages to do so, to protect and improve them. They will begin educating their families. This means more taxes and resources from those working and less to idle soldiers."

Caulmer and Shealbri traded looks, the latter nodding in agreement.

Shealbri is responsible for general taxes, treasury, and coin; his finding merit in Mykel's actions is a good sign.

"Have you anything else to offer, *Hasta'kan'ix ik'Blagdon*?" The *Kolotor'ix* looked at him, continuing his walk around the table.

"I have one more piece of news, and then I will leave you for other matters of attention." When the *Kolotor'ix* gestured for him to continue, he looked around the table. "At Woodsong, a human drunkard has been serving under *korrati* Lordson Mykel ik'Blagdon—"

Remhold groaned.

Good, you remember him. "He has no memories from before three years ago. I believe he was dosed with Ny'fer hunting potion, which put him to sleep and is the cause behind his memory loss."

"That is what you have, a drunkard with no memory?" Halidesh laughed, ringing a bell on the table. A *balvash* came in with a fresh pitcher of watered wine and set it down before leaving quickly.

"Perhaps you have been around your mounts so long you have forgotten the value sober people have. I hope he doesn't work around your *kelvorvik*, or he won't last long," Caulmer spoke up, amusement in his voice.

Blagdon took mental note of everyone who snickered or smirked. *I will remember this when you ask for my daughter's hand later.*

The soft footfalls of the *Kolotor'ix* were the only sound from their leader as he moved patiently around the table, arms hidden behind his back. No one brought up trivial matters at a *kalidesh ik'kolotor* without reasoning. "What use does a drunkard hold of your territory and my empire?"

Now you will see why mine will be Hon-Hasta'kan. He raised his voice to ensure all around the room heard his words. "He has regained his memory; he is a Stormrider of old, claiming loyalty to the Byronian ruling family by name."

The *Kolotor'ix* stopped moving.

Suddenly, the room was silent, whispers and snickering dying in the throats of those who would have uttered them. Eyes flicked from the *Kolotor'ix* to Blagdon.

"How is that possible?" The *Kolotor'ix*'s voice was softer, deadlier.

"Stormriders, like Sigilbearers, can live longer than their counterparts due to their bonds with their mounts, a well-known fact."

Other *Hesta'kan'ix* paused and nodded as if they did not wish to appear ignorant. *Liars, the lot of you.*

"What did you say his name was?" Carriat asked, ready to write down on a piece of parchment. *Of course, the Hasta'kan'ix of security will look for any mention of him in their records room.*

"He is Sir Siral Karog, and his portrait is within the pages of the Stormrider records. I have a *balvash* questioning him, and she has confirmed that what he has spoken is what he believes to be true."

"Just because he believes it does not make it true," Blackmont said.

Nicholnor spoke up. "What of his mount? Does it live?"

You are interested in training soldiers who may one day ride upon flying kelvorvik, or even have the Stormrider bond if I can reproduce it. But what would you be willing to give me?

"His mare was disguised as a regular horse but is nursing a colt, sired by the *kelvorvik* Kruger. She has not shown what type of animal she is yet, but I suspect she is a windrunner. It is possible the magick stripped her of her ability to run upon the air, but her colt may retain it. If it is true, we can have *kelvorvik*-blooded mounts that run on the air, literally and figuratively heightening our cavalry."

Whispers began across the table, no doubt in surprise and longing to see this speculation come to life. *I am sure I will soon be getting offers to purchase said mounts.*

The *Kolotor'ix* kept walking, looking ahead once more. *"Hasta'kan ik'Blagdon,* is there anything else you have to offer?"

"No, our *Kolotor'ix.*" Blagdon sat back in his chair, watching the reactions of those around him and knew he would be the subject of many talks long after the *kalidesh ik'kolotor* was over.

Done is the day
the light fades away
no more tears
no more sadness or fear
gone is the pain
of yesterday
all that is left
is tomorrow.

— Dawnese funeral song

LENAKA

Clep's gaze was fixed on the vast expanse of the night sky by the Ka'epano Lake. "Your parents, they reside up there among the stars with your *K'hani*?"

Lenaka glanced up from her stacking sticks into a small pyre and looked toward the stars peeking between the clouds. "Yes, I believe they are."

"Do you think Apollo and the others are up there, too?"

Lenaka nodded. "I do. What does the Light believe? Where does it say that we go after we pass on?"

"The Light from one fades and ignites into another, like candles sharing flames. A piece of their light goes into us after they die. I carry a piece of Nan, Ma, Pa, and Apollo with me because I knew their light."

"You also knew Andears' light, so do you carry pieces of each of those villagers within you as well?"

Clep nodded quietly, swallowing hard.

A familiar voice spoke up, making Lenaka turn quickly in surprise. "You must have a very bright soul, and they are lucky to have someone like you to carry all that light into the world." Draven smiled, placing a hand on Clep's shoulder gently.

I thought he'd be sleeping; what is he doing here? She glanced down at her *putri's* wrapped and bloodied feet and frowned, knowing he was hurting but glad he was there.

"Through you, Clep, we will know them and keep their light

within us so they will never fade."

Clep looked like he would burst into tears, and Lenaka gave her *putri* a thankful look.

Draven nodded and walked to the small pyre, fiddling with the sticks and slipping a folded leaf into the pyre's open center. He then straightened, groaning softly as he stood. "Do you need a moment more?"

Clep shook his head, his eyes shining with unshed tears. "I think I'm ready."

"Here, it is bad luck not to wear a white garment that you can burn afterward," a soft voice said, and Lenaka turned to see *Rhan'*Ashanna with Koani beside her, acting as her *lokoni*.

*Rhan'*Ashanna held out strips of white cloth, tying them around each of their left wrists. "We will burn these after the funeral so that any lingering effects of *K'han'Natsulith'*s soul gathering do not stay with us."

"We are honored by your presence, *Rhan'*Ashanna," Draven said, bowing his head over his hands.

The *Rhan* nodded as she handed Clep a thin reed. "Are you ready to begin?"

He took it, his hand shaking slightly, but nodded silently as he carefully placed the cloth-wrapped figurine of Apollo onto the pyre, his fingers lingering before slowly pulling away.

*Rhan'*Ashanna took out a box with flint and steel and struck it near the reed, igniting the pitch shoved into the hollow end. She replaced the materials into the box, closed it quietly, and stood, handing the reed to Clep.

After a long moment, he slowly lit the straw stuffed into the bottom. The flames began spreading through the straw, going into the gaps in the pyre to the bark shavings. As the fire grew, it caught the leaf package Draven had tucked into the pyre beginning to burn, and with it came the soft smell of incense.

*Rhan'*Ashanna began a dance with almost playful movements, and

Koani, Draven, and Lenaka joined in, moving together as the gestures became less innocent and more purposeful as the dance continued. Each movement in the Dance of Life held significance, with the fluid, expressive motions telling a story that showed the chapters of life: the innocence of childhood, the challenges and trials of adulthood, and the wisdom of old age. As they danced, they began singing.

Ikanu noko'alo

nela kōnu

Un'nui'lo noko'alo

aila i ukanu noko'alo

Nopu hepa

paikanu

wan'na'a

nuikanu

Clep watched quietly, his eyes fixed on the fire and the sparks flying high into the night sky, carrying the sweet smell of flowers and spices. Tears slipped down his cheeks as he mouthed quietly, saying something too low to hear.

Had he been saying goodbye to each person from Andears by name?

The silence let him hear his last two words.

"Good-bye, Apollo."

Apollo,

We had no fire tonight because it was raining and remained inside our tents. I heard whispering about us, accusing us of being spies. Their reasoning is we were the only survivors of Andears and you ran off to join the Dark Army. They also believe that my trying to save Anara is a trap, that I would deliver them to Leigelord Blackmont and get paid for capturing them.

I wish you were here. I know that you probably died fighting the soldiers and I am writing for no reason, but I need to pretend still that you will one day read these and that I am not truly alone.

Emma has brought tea to my tent. I will write more later.

I pray the Light treats your spirit well.

Clep

APOLLO

After night fell, Apollo sat beside the fire, but he wasn't enjoying it. Sharpening his sword, he kept his eyes on the campfire where the group from Silene had adjusted their tents to be closer together, the children and women in the wagons instead of in bedrolls. *Some of the tents are empty*, Apollo observed silently, mentally noting which ones. It reminded him of the first time he'd tried going into the Dark Army camp and tried slitting throats of soldiers as they slept. *Look where it got me.*

Senka sewed a hole in her cloak, casually glancing around now and again. "You hardly ate your rabbit," she observed. It was the first she'd spoken since twilight, making Apollo startle.

I'd forgotten she was there. "I'm not hungry."

"You don't eat, you don't sleep. When your brother finds you, you will be nothing but a skeleton. Then you will be useless to him and Mykel both."

Apollo sighed with irritation. "I'm not worried about Mykel, Lady Senka. He's back at Woodsong. I'm worried about Clep, who isn't surrounded by soldiers and *belvash* sworn to protect him."

"Worrying does nothing," Senka replied flatly. "All it does is occupy your mind when you should be relaxing or training. Alax and Tibold will find him if he doesn't come here first."

"Well, I can't help but wonder if—" Apollo started, but he spun, sword in hand, feeling someone watching them.

A cloaked figure stepped carefully from the darkness of the woods, the firelight casting soft orange light upon its features, and the darkness making it larger than anyone Apollo had ever seen.

Whoever, whatever this is, it is not Clep, he realized, standing slowly.

Senka turned quickly, gasping, keeping her dagger by her leg where only Apollo could see it.

The figure slowly held their hands out to their sides to show they were unarmed before reaching up to lower their hood, fire firelight reflecting softly on a dark face with white markings down their nose and across their cheeks. "Greetings," he said in a voice deeper than Apollo imagined it would be, "I hear you are looking for a healer named Clep."

Apollo's eyes narrowed, and he tightened his grip on his sword. *I don't know who this is. Is this someone from Silene? I want to think that I'd remember someone so tall and broader than I am, but I was almost blind with anger back then.*

"Who is asking?"

"My name is inconsequential to this conversation," the male said, keeping his eyes on Apollo. The firelight almost made the brown hues reflect golden flecks, and his hair was pulled into multiple thick twists, hanging around his shoulders.

"Are you of *Hasta'kan ik'Blackmont*?" Senka demanded.

Apollo froze. *I'd been so wrapped up in finding Clep and being angry with the people from Silene, I'd forgotten whose territory we are in.*

"I am not," said the stranger.

"Do you know where my brother is?" Apollo asked, trying not to demand Clep's location.

"I may tell you if you can tell me the name of his owl." The stranger's tone was patient as if he had all the time in the world.

"He doesn't have an owl. Clep has a hawk named Memory."

The stranger nodded once. "Where are you from?"

Senka gave a long sigh. "We aren't answering questions until you answer his. Where is Clep?"

"Safe," the stranger answered.

Apollo waited, but he didn't elaborate. "We're from Andears, in Cetra. It was burned to the ground, and he and I were the only survivors."

The stranger was silent, watching Apollo for a long moment before giving another nod. "Come with me." He turned and walked toward the clearing.

Apollo kicked dirt onto their small fire to put it out and gathered his bag, sword in his hand. He glanced at Senka who gave him a look that clearly said *he'd better not be leading us into a trap.* Apollo shrugged and walked after the male, Senka behind him.

The male stepped into the moonlight, looking at the mountain as if watching something.

Apollo looked as well, blinking as he saw a creature in the darkness, wings outstretched, coming in for a landing. *Is it a dragon, like in Nan-kyr's stories?*

As it grew closer, Apollo could see it was a winged humanoid. The figure landed; she wore a black sleeveless tunic, breeches, leather slippers, and a belt with a sword fastened around her waist. Her skin was a dark brown and her head was bare of hair, with black tattoos running over her scalp.

Apollo blinked, never having seen a bald female before.

Senka gasped beside him, and Apollo turned to see that the stranger had shed his cloak, black wings stretching from his back as he turned toward them.

I thought dawnwarriors were made up.

A movement made Apollo look over to see the group from Silene heading their way quickly, pointing at the dawnwarriors, the male with his arm in a sling running to catch up to them. Apollo slowly sheathed his sword in an attempt not to give in to his anger.

The female dawnwarrior spoke in a language that Apollo did not understand. The words sounded airy and beautiful but contrasted with an undertone of warning and anger. The male stepped forward, his wings snapping out to their full width, each wing as long as Apollo was tall. The group from Silene stopped abruptly, and the children collided with the adults.

"Please," the injured male from Silene pleaded, "you have to let us into Exon—"

"You are those who had traveled from the village of Silene with the healer Clep." The male interrupted in Common, gesturing with his hand. "You know his decision to have you remain outside our borders. Return to where you came from, unwelcome traitors of one's kind."

Apollo blinked. *Clep decided to leave these people outside Exonesis? Though I cannot blame him, if they abandoned me, I'd also leave them to their fates.*

The female spoke softly to Apollo. "We will take you into Exonesis, where you will find your brother."

Senka sighed. "Finally."

* * *

The dawnwarriors picked up Apollo and Senka, effortlessly taking to the night air, their wings powerfully moving them higher and higher. As the wind rushed past Apollo, he glanced down and immediately regretted it. The ground grew further away, and the group from Silene became like ants; too small to ever notice or worry about. He slowly took his eyes off them and looked around at the larger world, gasping at the dark trees and silvery lakes. *If it were daytime, could I see Woodsong from here?*

The female dawnwarrior set down Senka on a ledge on the side of the mountain. She glanced over as the male landed, putting Apollo down.

"This way." He pointed to a tree before walking Apollo toward it, staying behind him as if to stop him from fleeing.

Where would I go, down the mountain? Between the tree and a brush was a small opening, and it made him hesitate and start to pull his sword, but the dawnwarrior stopped him with a large hand on his lower arm, preventing Apollo from drawing it. *He's so much stronger than I am,* Apollo realized, and he worried that he would not be able to save Senka if the female dawnwarrior attacked her.

The dawnwarrior walked Apollo into the small cave, taking out a lightstone that dimly lit the area, which was only small enough that only two people could lay comfortably inside. He stood in the doorway, his wings arched slightly to fill the opening, preventing anyone from entering or exiting the cave. "Strip."

"What?!"

"You must be checked for a Sigil of Shadow before you enter Exonesis Mountain."

"I don't have a Sigil of Shadow."

The male dawnwarrior gave him a flat look.

Sighing, Apollo lay his sword against the stone wall and began stripping out of his armor. Apollo undid the scarf from around his neck, and the dawnwarrior stepped forward and grabbed him, putting a knife against his throat. "You dare attempt to enter Exonesis, Shadon!"

"I'm not a Shadon! I'm not a Shadon! I'm a *balutrae.*"

The dawnwarrior's eyes narrowed. "I do not know this word."

"I am a human marked as a rival for a Shadon Lordson."

"Why would a Shadon do such a thing?"

"I punched the *korrati* in front of his soldiers. A *korrati* is the commander," he added before the dawnwarrior could ask what it meant. "Because I embarrassed and challenged him, he named me his *balutrae,* which means I am his rival and cannot be killed by any other Shadon but him."

The dawnwarrior let him go and stepped back. "Finish stripping so I can ensure you have no other Sigils." He lowered his knife but kept it in his hand.

After Apollo was nude, the dawnwarrior searched him, making

him stand with his arms out and turn slowly. Finally, Apollo was allowed to redress as the dawnwarrior male walked away, going to the female companion and speaking quietly in their language. The female broke out into laughter as Apollo exited the cave.

Apollo looked at Senka, who had a smirk on her lips. *She didn't peek through the cave's darkness at me, did she?*

The dawnwarrior female waited for Apollo to join them.

"Hold out your weapons."

Apollo carefully held out his sheathed sword and dagger, Senka holding out hers.

As they did so, the female dawnwarrior tied a white cloth around their weapons' crossguards and sheaths. She also unstrung Senka's bow, handing the string to her. "You may put your weaponry away."

After they did, the male dawnwarrior then held out cloth bags. "Place these on your heads."

Apollo held his bag and looked at Senka, who gave him a glare that he took to mean *if I die, I am coming back to haunt you.* He slipped the bag over his head. After a moment, he felt himself lifted again, air rushing over him. "Senka?!"

"I am here," he heard her voice say from somewhere in front of him.

After twisting and turning, they landed and were carried further before being set down. When the bags were pulled off their heads, Apollo blinked; the only light was from the lightstone the female held, and the area around them was covered in rock. He turned, but there wasn't enough room to see past the male behind him to make out where they were. He looked up to see they were inside, surrounded. *There's no escape if something goes wrong.* "Are we underground?"

"Come," said the female, walking away, "this way to Exonesis."

* * *

Apollo had no idea how long it had been but felt embarrassed, tired, and slightly claustrophobic in the dark tunnel that never seemed to end. Sparkling veins of metal glinted from the walls around them, and the passage was just wide enough for the dawnwarriors to walk single file, their wings trailing behind them. Apollo stopped to look at the veins of metal, but the male dawnwarrior told them to keep moving.

My legs and feet hurt, and I can hear Senka's small sounds of pain behind me. "How much longer?" Apollo looked at her over his shoulder to see Senka limping slightly in the dimness of the lightstone.

They stopped, and Apollo was about to ask why when he noticed a couple of carts sitting on a metal rail in front of them. "Get in; this will take us through the mountains."

Apollo climbed in after the female dawnwarrior, and Senka climbed into the second cart with the male dawnwarrior. The carts were not that large, and the dawnwarriors had to keep their wings tucked against their backs. After a moment, the carts began moving down the rails much faster than it would have been to walk.

"Are these mining carts?" Senka asked, saying the first words she'd spoken since they'd entered the tunnel.

The female dawnwarrior nodded. "They were, though now they are used for moving refugees. The tunnels are too long to travel by foot in one day."

Apollo frowned, looking around at the widening and narrowing tunnel system around them, seeing other tunnels branching off to the side of larger areas. *I'd get lost in these tunnels if I were alone. Maybe that's the point?* "You don't mine here anymore?"

"We do not mine dawnsteel from our mountain; it is forbidden."

Apollo thought about it. He'd never seen dawnsteel before but had heard of it during his lessons with Mykel. It was a rare metal, similar to *koldraka*, and only mined in a few places in Andora. According to his lessons, dawnsteel could hinder the Sigil of Shadow, able to cut through shadows created by *ro'Shadon*. *I wonder if it was the golden veins he saw in the rock earlier.*

"What is your family name?" The female dawnwarrior asked, glancing over her shoulder at him.

"Farmer."

She frowned. "I didn't ask your occupation, young man. What is your family name?"

"In Andears, we didn't have family names. Your name was what you did. Our village had Bakers, Woodsmen, Goodwives, and Thatchers. We were Farmers. I am the son of Ford Farmer."

The female dawnwarrior looked past Apollo to Senka.

"Where I was held, I had to relinquish my family name."

Apollo blinked at her. *It wasn't quite a lie, but it skirted the truth.*

The male dawnwarrior behind her spoke up. "Where were you held?"

That is the problem with lies; once you started one, you added more until it was harder to remember them.

"We were in a territory where the *Hasta'kan* hunts humans as prey. Prey do not have family names."

I admit, I'm impressed and slightly scared of how easily she can lie.

"Do you know who the leader of the Shadon is?"

"The *Kolotor'ix.*"

The female made a sound that was between a sigh and a scoff. "Who is the *Kolotor'ix*?"

Apollo shook his head. "No one knows who he is."

"You've lived under Shadon's rule for your entire life, and you don't know who your leader is?"

"I lived on a farm far from the capital. So no, I don't know who he is. No one does; he's masked, gloved, and has a hood over his hair. No *ro'*Shadon has ever seen his face."

The dawnwarriors looked at Senka, who shook her head in agreement.

The cart ride was gentle enough that the sounds of the wheels on the rails made Apollo close his eyes and lose himself in thought. When the cart finally stopped, Apollo startled, realizing he'd fallen asleep. He climbed out slowly, checking his chin, hoping he didn't drool.

The dawnwarrior female ahead of him said nothing, holding her lightstone as she walked down the tunnel; most of the light was blocked by her body so Apollo could not see much ahead of them. But the air moved a bit more, and he could see more rocks around them as the light grew brighter. Finally, the dawnwarrior moved out of the way as she exited the tunnel.

Apollo first saw the stars, the sky high above them, and the mountains around them. The air smelled fresh, with a touch of saltiness that he found odd on his tongue.

"Welcome to Exonesis," the male dawnwarrior said, guiding Senka out of the tunnel.

Apollo glanced at her to see by the torchlight that she was frowning, her eyes wide as she flexed her hands quietly at her side. He opened his mouth to ask if she was all right, but she shook her head once, meeting his eyes. *I'll have to ask her later what's wrong.*

Two armored dawnwarriors stood on either side of the tunnel entrance, a third closing a heavily barred door before stepping forward to walk with the male who had escorted them, each carrying torches.

"This way," the female dawnwarrior said and began walking toward a building carved into the rock of the mountain, towering high above them, the moonlight accenting statues of armed dawnwarriors standing on pillars , looking as if they were going to launch at them at any moment.

Apollo glanced to see four more dawnwarriors with swords walking behind them. *I did not expect an armed escort everywhere. Is everyone treated like this?*

The dawnwarriors took them down the hall past a mosaic of a dragon breaking through rock and statues of dawnwarriors before finally taking them to an open door, gesturing for them to walk through first. As soon as Senka followed Apollo into the room, the door closed behind them.

Apollo went to the door and tried to open it, but it wouldn't move. He looked at Senka, his eyes wide. He reached for his sword but found the white rope tied around it wouldn't allow his weapon to be drawn from its sheath. Taking off his belt, he began examining it. *It is like one continuous piece of white rope with no beginning or end, but I can't find a knot in it.* "I can't get my sword out. Can you get your dagger or sword from their sheaths?"

He glanced up to see Senka was struggling to draw her sword, frowning harder now. "They are peace-bound; I've read about it in the libraries at the Temple, where weaponry are bound with enchanted rope so they cannot be drawn to attack the place you are visiting. They can only be removed by dispelling the enchantment or if the wielder is in mortal danger."

"What determines if we are in enough danger to break the enchantment?"

Senka shrugged.

Not liking that answer, Apollo tried a different question. "The door's locked. Can you open it by moving the pieces inside the lock?"

Senka gave up fighting with her weapon and went to the door, holding her hand over the keyhole to prevent light from getting in. "I can't feel the shadows or the darkness since we'd walked into that tunnel." She began walking around the room, hands running over the sandstone as if looking for a hidden door.

Apollo frowned. "Why didn't they search you like they did me?"

Senka made a sound, and Apollo blushed, embarrassment rushing back over him again. *I hope she didn't see me naked; it would be akward, especially since I am her brother's balutrae.*

"I am a female; I can't be a Shadon." She sat on her knees beside the door and closed her eyes.

"What are you doing?"

"Resting. You may as well save your strength for fighting if we must." He glanced out the windows, too narrow to fit through, even if they tried sliding sideways. Frustrated, he finally sat against the wall, closing his eyes.

* * *

The door unlocked, prompting Apollo to jerk awake. He quickly looked around, trying to remember where he was, and saw Senka still meditating on her knees. She opened them and slowly stood as if stiff.

How long had we been in here?

A dawnwarrior opened the door and smiled at them. "'*Apikoa maliko.* You have been permitted to walk outside the restricted areas where only our *Rhani* can go. We will walk you out of the palace and into the *helaono,* our marketplace. From there, you may explore your new surroundings. *Lokoni'lo,* the guards, will tell you if you are somewhere restricted."

Apollo looked at Senka, who smiled and followed the dawnwarrior down the hall. *Why do I feel like the hens just allowed a fox into the coop?*

Once outside, Apollo looked around the morning air, surprised by the emptiness of the air above the garden and the quietness of the marketplace. "You would think that everyone would be flying around. I hardly see anyone." He looked around at the stalls with wooden shutters closed and others with their wares put in locked chests on shelves behind the empty counters. "I expected it to be more..." he waved his hand, trying to find a word.

"More?" Senka finished for him, her grey eyes looking around as they walked down the steps and through the garden. She frowned, watching colorful creatures fly from one tree to another.

I've never seen so many colors of flowers before, Apollo mused, looking at the trees with multiple fruits hanging from their branches.

As they walked into the market, they found it just as quiet, just as empty.

"This doesn't seem right; there should be more people. Where are the children?"

Apollo looked at Senka confused. *Why would she want to know where the children are?* "Maybe they are afraid of us," Apollo answered, remembering the fear that ran through Andears whenever the Dark Army was announced nearby.

"Ya not be who dey fear this day," a voice came from a stall to Apollo's right, where a woman sat on a stool behind the counter, an inked brush in her hand dipping and moving over a piece of parchment. She paused in her writing, looking over the inked lines before adding more dots and flourishes.

Apollo walked over, drawn to her familiar-sounding accent. *She almost sounds like Ratsbayne, er, Sir Siral, yet different at the same time.* "Hello, I'm Apollo."

"Ah know who ye be," the woman said, stopping her work to look at him fully, her orange eyes taking him in. Strange bronze markings decorated her dark brown skin, seeming to glow in the sunlight that came through the opening in her canopy. It reminded Apollo faintly of the warm strength of embers when dirt was kicked over them, trying to cling to life before being snuffed out.

The woman looked back at her parchment, looking over her work. "Ye be the human alchemist's brother, no?" She picked up the parchment and set it into a shallow box, reaching into a bag and sprinkling sand carefully onto the writing, the movement making the many golden earrings along her pointed ears twinkle as the hoops and chains hit each other.

Senka's voice held slight awe. "You're a Fyre elf."

Apollo was intrigued; he had only ever known of the Mun'ari clan when it came to elves. *I shouldn't be surprised there are different ones, but what is an elf doing here? Were they in hiding from the ro'Shadon? Were there other elves here, too?*

"So what do the people here fear if not us?" Senka asked, seemingly recovering from her shock.

"The *K'han'Natsulith* flies dis day."

Apollo blinked at her.

The elf chuckled, continuing. "Ya be new here. The dawnwarriors believe that the *K'han'Natsulith* ferries the souls of the dead to the heavens. Dey believe that until the body of the dead is burned, the *K'hani* will take the soul of whoever is above the corpse instead. So no one flies until the funeral. It will be a day or two before they come back." She shook the box with the parchment and sand, ensuring the sand covered the parchment, and let it set a little longer.

"Who died?" Senka asked, and Apollo swore he saw a bit of excitement in her eyes.

I hope it is due to hearing about dragons and not because someone's life is gone.

"An important religious figure from the Order o' the Dawn, deir founder. Ah try to avoid deir religious disputes as much as Ah can, and Ah refuse to leave mah home due to them. Their beliefs mean nothing to meh."

Apollo couldn't stop the question. "Dragons are real?"

The elf looked at him, amusement in her fire-colored eyes. "O' course dey are, human. Ya be too young to remember dem. But if you ask the dawnwarriors, depending on who dey are a part o'— de Order o' de Dawn or de *K'hani*— dey will tell you differing answers."

"What are the *K'hani*?" Apollo asked.

"The Elders o' de dragons, de most important o' dem who did great things fer the world."

"Oh."

"Why would they give different answers?" Senka asked, looking over the rows of scrolls, reading the tags attached along their rolled edges.

"The dawnwarriors split beliefs when de bard and his band of adventurers returned from de Dragonlands, saying de dragons were all dead. Most of the group created deir religion, naming it de Order o' the Dawn to have some semblance of peace. It is all quite foolish if you ask me."

"Why is it foolish?"

Apollo was glad Senka was asking questions because his mind was buzzing. *If the dragons were truly dead, would it mean that winter and cooler weather would never come?*

"It's divided de people more than unite them. De funeral has been de most solidarity Ah'd seen from the dawnwarriors in de fifty or so years Ah have been here."

The elf turned and looked over some scrolls before taking two and setting them down before Apollo. "Here, one on de *K'hani* and one on de Order o' the Dawn. Ya will be wanting to read them before they all return and try to force ya to choose."

She picked up the parchment she'd been working on from the box, shaking it to get the remaining sand off it before carefully rolling it and tying it with twine. "If ya want more information, de *K'hani* temple is over dere, by de People's Palace," she gestured across the garden to the doorway between the large pillars carved into the mountain. "De Order o' de Dawn members have deir services in Hu'lau Village, three times a day; sunrise, highsun, and sunset. Ya can't miss it; it has orange cloth and streamers all over deir trees and doors."

Senka moved, adjusting her cloak and taking the offered scrolls from the counter. "We will go over these." She turned, walking toward the garden.

Apollo smiled at the elf. "Sorry, she's like that. We appreciate your help. Do you know where my brother is?"

"Aye, he is in Hinea'pei Valley, staying with de bard Kil'lik'Draven. Out de east gate dere, den half a day's walk. It is a little place on the bottom row with a garden and fruit tree behind a fence."

"Thanks," Apollo said and raced after Senka, who was walking steadily toward the temple. Noting the determined look on her face, he frowned. "What is it?"

"Nothing."

He grabbed her arm. "Don't lie to me," he snapped.

Senka stopped walking and looked at his hand until he removed it. Her grey eyes moved up to look at him.

"I am *bal--*" he began, but Senka cut him off by stepping in and stomping on his foot.

"Ow!"

"Shh," she hissed, glancing around, dropping her voice. "Do you want to live long enough to see your brother?"

"Of course I do."

"Then don't try pulling the '*I'm balutrae' krushku* with me. I know exactly who and what you are. We know where he is, and that's all we need. Now, we leave and return to Woodsong."

Apollo blinked at her. "You can't mean that."

"We were told to find him. We found him. He's here. Mission accomplished. I need to get to my *Brak'ha* immediately with this information."

"With what? Two religions that don't see eye-to-eye? That hardly sounds like something important enough to bother the *Hasta'kan'ix* with. What aren't you telling me?"

She rolled her eyes at him. "The amount of things I don't tell you can fill the Traxxian Crater."

"Stop *belvashing* me, Senka."

Senka blinked at the misuse of the word.

I'm sure it's not a real word, but from what I know of belvash they like to skirt the truth with half-omissions, which is still lying, something I can't stand.

"What is it that you have to leave so quickly? Is there someone following us? Are we in danger? There's hardly anyone here, Senka, so tell me." He gave her steady eye contact. *It makes me uncomfortable; maybe it will do the same to her.*

"You heard the elf. Your brother is in Hinea'Pei Valley, through that gate." She pointed at the large gate by the marketplace. She glanced around before dropping her voice. "I need to get information to *brak'ha ik'san* immediately. Our status in the *kalidesh ik'kolotor* depends upon it. You are *Balutrae ik'Blagdon* and must continue to improve our *Hasta'kan*. That requires this information to get out of that gate," she turned, gesturing to the gate beside the temple they used when they entered Exonesis. "You need to decide who you are loyal to."

"You want me to choose between duty and family? That's *krushku*, coming from you of all people."

"Clep is here, safe. Leave a letter with the elf for him if you must, but we have to leave. It is the only way." When he just looked at her silently, she sighed. "If *Hasta'kan ik'Blagdon* does not remain *Hon-Hasta'kan*, then may lose Cetra. Mykel will lose his garrison and his position. Another *Hasta'kan* will oversee Andears' Aldarwood, Silene, and the other villages. The new *Hasta'kan'ix* won't be as forgiving. Would you sleep at night knowing *Hasta'kan ik'Blackmont* will be hunting the people from Silene, the soldiers you trained with? Or if *Hasta'kan ik'Remhold* regains the territory when you could have prevented it with this information?" Her cloak moved slightly, Apollo glimpsing a scroll held tightly in her hand hidden under it.

Did she steal that scroll from the stall? Apollo narrowed his eyes. "You are trained like a *balvash* and are a silver-tongued serpent when you want to be."

"I know my duty. Do you know yours?"

They stared at each other for a long moment.

"I'll meet you at the gate." He turned and walked toward the marketplace, not giving Senka a look back to see if she was following.

One Hasta'kan's fall
Is another's rise.

— Nixus Halidesh, Bard of Eteris

BLAGDON

The *Hesta'kan'ix* gathered in a side room before the meeting, murmuring in small groups, trying to get last-minute deals and guessing who would be in what ranking. As Blagdon closed the door behind him, he was given a few looks, some supportive, many not. He ignored them as he went to the table against the far wall and picked up a plate. The palace cooks had made breakfast for them, and the scent of hot bean juice and tea filled the air, making the morning a tiny bit better. *At least this is the last night; we will return home after this.*

Halidesh walked over to stand beside Blagdon, getting a plate. "We will support *Hasta'kan ik'Blagdon* if you fall in ranking, Wilihem. If you lose the Stormlands and we build the racetrack there, we will still need *kelvorkav* to race."

"That requires you to have the Stormlands as your own," Carriat spoke up, stepping beside the table with a cup of hot tea.

Blagdon set a few pieces of fruit onto his place beside boiled eggs and went to get a glass of fresh goat's milk. "The Stormlands are used to train soldiers. Carriat trains their escort soldiers, Remhold their border soldiers, and Nicholnor the main cavalry. The archers, spearmen, and others train there as well. Where else is there that much land for soldiers and their mounts to train if you were to build a racetrack?"

Halidesh smiled. "Stormhold, of course."

Blagdon stepped toward him, and Nicholnor walked over quickly as if trying to stop a fight before it started.

"There is no need to move our training grounds from the

Stormlands. Even if the *Hon-Hasta'kan* is not Blagdon, he will have enough territory to hold it, and if not, I will, and I won't allow you to take the training grounds from my soldiers."

Halidesh frowned at the three *Hesta'kan*. "One day, you won't be as important as you think. We don't need this many *Hesta'kan* who specialize in troops. We all have soldiers, but you make it your identity, except you, Wilihem. You are all about your damned mounts."

"They are the mounts you are begging me to purchase so you can make more coin. They are the mounts used to haul goods and farm resources for your inns and taverns. They are the mounts used to carry the cavalry that allowed us to take Meridiah. You would still be in Nar'Shada without my *damned mounts*." He walked off to a table, ignoring the *Hesta'kan'ix* watching them.

Halidesh gave a shake of his head and stormed off.

Nicholnor laughed with Carriat as they approached the small table and sat across from Blagdon. "You may hate politics, but you have a razored tongue when you wish it."

"I blame Lady *Sri'balvash* Narisa."

Carriat nodded. "Aye, our ladies bring out the best or worst in us, depending on the situation. Speaking of ladies, how is Lady S—"

"Lady Shadon Senka is on a mission from the *Kolotor'ix* and cannot attend tonight. Lady Narisa will stand in her stead. That is all I will say upon that subject."

Nicholnor nodded. "If you lose the Stormlands and I am in charge of it, I will allow Mykel to train among the soldiers there. He may not be a *korrati*, but he will be trained well."

Blagdon nodded. *It is not the ideal picture of the future, but I will accept it.*

They ate quietly, finishing their meals and discussing training regiments for the soldiers for the upcoming cycle, a safe topic no matter what ranking they became today.

Carriat bowed and walked off, speaking low to Shealbri and

Caulmer, who looked at Blagdon as they spoke low.

Let them say what they wish. I will deal with one crisis at a time, and right now, it is not my daughter's hand in marriage. We must survive the next few hours first.

* * *

The conversations died as they were led into the war room. The unease was thick in the air, as if the room collectively held their breath, holding onto the last bits of hope that they would at least exit with the same rank or better than they had entered with. As they crossed the threshold, the shadows that thrived inside them faded, leaving emptiness within each Shadon who entered. The windows cast long shadows across the marble floor and on the table and chairs, yet the *Hesta'kan'ix* could not reach to touch them. The greatest of the *ro'*Shadon beneath the *Kolotor'ix* were now powerless, reduced to mere humans. It was a grim reminder that all power given could be taken.

The table in the middle of the room was now covered by a long crimson banner with a black mask, the fabric raised in some places and lowered in others as it followed the map's contours. Without the shadows, none could peek underneath to see whose emblem would be where, nor plot secretly with whispers spoken into each other's ears.

Blackmont finally began speaking of his next dinner's schedule, his rough voice louder than the silence he tried to break. A few lower *Hesta'kan'ix* gave short responses, but the higher ones were silent. Blackmont frowned and finally let the conversation die at their disinterest.

We have bigger things to worry about than a barbaric dinner.

The far doors opened, and the *Kolotor'ix* entered, his featureless mask with a thin red line down one side, bisecting where his left eye would be. There were variants of this mask, the most common with golden dawnsteel that contrasted the bluish tones of the *koldraka*. The crimson was dark against the metal, almost like blood. His black hood covered his hair and neck, tucked into a red tunic with black leather over it, the cape black with glimpses of its crimson lining as he padded into the room like a shadow incarnate.

Sri'balvash Caristha followed, heading to the desk at the side of the room, setting her tome upon it, and taking out a box that contained a quill made of a vulture's feather.

"The third day is upon us," the *Kolotor'ix* spoke into the silent room, "and your slates have been wiped clean for the next cycle."

With a movement of his hand, the banner of the *ro'*Shadon empire slid away from the table, slowly revealing the table's map. The slots around the border were filled with golden carved emblems, too far away for the *Hesta'kan'ix* to tell whose was where, though some tried craning their necks to see.

"Let us see where your successes and failures have cast you."

Blagdon stayed still, his hand on the pommel of his rapier under his dark blue cloak, squeezing it slightly.

Some of the *Hesta'kan* shuffled slightly as they adjusted, ready to move toward the table when called.

Blagdon caught a few mouthing quietly under their breaths. *It is too late for the Kolosae-ro'jo'aritas to hear prayers to grant success of your Hasta'kan. If you wanted its aid, you should initially do the work.*

"Remhold, take your seat."

There was a sound of a collective intake of shocked breath, the *Hesta'kan'ix* glancing at each other both in shock and fear. Remhold stood waiting for someone else to step forward, as if the *Kolotor'ix* did not just announce that his *Hasta'kan* had fallen from *Ero-Hasta'kan* to *Tribya-Hasta'kan*. Such a drop was not unheard of but hardly ever transpired. The realization that no one was safe and nothing was guaranteed passed over to everyone, but under that was a cold satisfaction. Someone new would become one of the top ranks, gaining the trappings and benefits with it.

"Remhold," the *Kolotor'ix*'s voice darkened as he suddenly appeared via shadows inches before the *Hasta'kan'ix*, wisps of darkness fading around him.

Blagdon and the other *Hesta'kan'ix* quickly stepped back and dropped to a knee, leaving Remhold alone before their leader.

Remhold, startled, slowly walked toward the table, stopping and looking down upon the emblem at the last seat to ensure the *Kolotor'ix* wasn't jesting.

"I do not understand, our *Kolotor'ix*... why?"

The question was louder than the voice that spoke it. It was not a rule that the *Hesta'kan'ix* could not ask why they dropped in ranking, though Blagdon couldn't remember right away the last time it transpired.

Blackmont made a slight sound as if clearing his throat, or possibly to hide a scoff.

Nicholnor looked at the marble floor, shaking his head.

The *Kolotor'ix* looked at Remhold, walking toward him slowly. "First, you overtaxed the territory of Cetra, weakening the people who were meant to maintain our farming, carpentry, and fishing resources. Without the proper tools, they could not harvest as well and could not build the needed equipment. Your greed led to the territory failing in their responsibilities."

"That was my Lor—"

The *Kolotor'ix* pointed at him with a gloved hand. "Your Lordson-_kyr_'s failings are *your* failings. If you want to remain a *Hasta'kan'ix*, do not interrupt me again. You've had yesterday to speak; today, you *listen*. Secondly, the compounding of your first failure made the people resent my *ro'*Shadon. This led to the fostering of rebellion, not just in Cetra but in other territories. This is intolerable, and now the other *Hesta'kan* must also deal with it instead of seeing to their duties."

"Third, your Lordson was foolish enough to challenge the *balutrae' ik'Kolotor'ix* with such risk that it cost you territory and his life. Poor management and critical thinking skills can only be birthed from a poor leader."

Blagdon watched the verbal pummeling as if committing every

blow to memory.

"Fourth, there is the matter of the deaths of numerous *ro'Shadon* soldiers and their *belvash* in the attempts to capture D'Lcee over months of fighting. The Blood Temple did not hear from the *belvash-kyr* sent with your soldiers, for they have died among those they were sent to heal. I was told nothing of this! You have every right to try to take a territory beside yours, move onto its borders, and press your advantage, but the instant there were whispers of a dragonsoul knight, I SHOULD HAVE BEEN INFORMED! I would have gone personally to see the truth; I would have had an army ready to meet them in battle or win them over. You took it upon yourself in an attempt to steal what is RIGHTFULLY MINE!"

The room echoed with the *Kolotor'ix's* angry words, the shadows seeming to growl with unworldly anger. Even *Sri'balvash* Caristha looked up from her writing, eyes wider.

Remhold dropped to a knee quickly.

I wonder if we are about to again watch our Kolotor'ix's wrath sweep across the lands and, if so, whose hesta would suffer the most after Remhold's?

The *Kolotor'ix* was silent for a long moment, his chest moving as if he'd run a great distance. He turned and walked toward the table. Finally, the *Kolotor'ix* spoke, his voice calmer. "You've cost the Blood Temple and the *ro'Shadon* valuable resources. It takes years to cultivate properly trained *belvash*, and you throw their lives away. Your Lordson-*kyr* went through villages, taking whatever females he wished. If I hear of this happening again from *any* territory, the *hesta'ix* will be brought to me, and I will send back their penis stuffed and mounted to be adorned on the wall of your *Hasta'kan's* keep for generations to come."

Remhold was paler, a hand on the floor to keep him from swaying.

The *Kolotor'ix* looked at Remhold. "Does that answer your question, or shall I continue?"

"N-no, our *Kolotor'ix*, I understand now."

"We shall see." The *Kolotor'ix* looked at the gathered *Hesta'kan'ix* who were still on their knee, many with heads bowed. "Livingnor, take your seat."

* * *

The rest of the seating of the *Hasta'kan* went smoother, with none asking the reasoning of the rising or falling of rankings, not wanting a repeat of the embarrassment that befell Remhold.

"Blagdon, take your seat."

Blagdon walked to the table past Remhold, who hadn't looked up from the table since he sat at his place. Nicholnor and Shealbri nodded to him as he sat at his place at the right of the *Kolotor'ix* for the fourth cycle in a row. Looking down upon his emblem embossed in gold in the table slot, he breathed a breath of relief.

The *Kolotor'ix* stood behind his chair at the head of the table, gloved hands resting on the wooden back.

"Each cycle will bring new goals, incentives, and glory to the *ro'*Shadon. You know your places and will now use them to bring us higher than before. To do this, we must better enlist the loyalties and resources of those who fled while we took over during the Scourge War. This means we must locate *kreva ik'Kolotor'ix* Liana."

Many *Hesta'kan'ix* looked up at that, their expressions speaking for them. Not everyone thought the *kreve ik'Kolotor'ix* should be granted special privileges, for before Liana, it was just a term for any female who carried the child of the *Kolotor'ix*.

Blackmont grumbled but said nothing, looking at his emblem on the table, its place unchanged from the last *kalidesh*. His *Hasta'kan* had slaughtered many elves during the Scourge War, and his feelings about the *Kolotor'ix* having an elf rule beside him was a poorly kept secret.

Hasta'kan'ix Nicholnor nodded. "I agree; her knowledge of the elven people, their ways of society and warfare, is crucial in gaining a foothold in cooperation. The elves have ways of the land that will aid us during this long summer so we do not have the losses of resources we have had on our own."

Remhold said nothing, not looking up from the table since he'd sat.

The *Kolotor'ix* nodded, continuing. "I have someone trying to enter Exonesis as we speak to see if *kreva ik'Kolotor'ix* Liana is there. If she is successful, we will have more information on how to possibly beat their defenses to gain control of their lands and Akima Bay. This will open a great deal of trade with the Benstafi elves."

Blackmont looked up, eyes narrowing slightly. "Our *Kolotor'ix*, if a scout has been sent through my territory toward Exonesis, why was I not informed? I would have had my soldiers accompany them."

"Perhaps this was a test to see how much is happening in your territory you are aware of."

Blackmont seemed to deflate slightly and looked at his emblem on the table, letting out a frustrated breath.

At least I know Senka can get through his territory without his knowledge. It is a relief, especially when she is posing as a human.

"I also want to send scouts to look into the lands of Castet to the south and Inknaras to the west of the Ironfall Mountains to see if they, too, suffer from the long summer. This will determine our next courses of action in the upcoming cycles."

Nicholnor and Carriat glanced at Blagdon, and he knew they thought the same thing he did. *He is preparing to invade and take lands and resources needed if they do not suffer the hardships Meridiah faces.*

"Our *Kolotor'ix*, we cannot afford to stretch our resources and soldiers too thinly. We will not be able to defend and feed both Nar'Shada and Meridiah if we are invading as well, nor will we have the *Hesta'kan* to take over more territories while soldiers also are fighting for D'Lcee," Carriat spoke up.

"I will amend the rankings and their benefits of the number of territories and *belvash* appropriately. I am more than aware of our current limitations."

There were many nods and sounds of affirmation around the

table. However, some of the more military-oriented *Hesta'kan'ix* were frowning and looking at the map as if already planning and trying to decide how to allocate troops and supplies accordingly.

"As for D'Lcee, it should not be that hard to take a land led by a human child of ten seasons. We will bring it into the *ro'Shadon* lands as part of Meridiah and take its fertile crops for our use."

Remhold at the far side of the table flinched slightly, still looking at the table as if studying the map.

"The dragonsoul knight will be dealt with accordingly, either bending the knee to me or dying. It cannot be left alive to rally more insurrection to its cause, nor let the people believe there is cause to create rebellion. Every loss suffered under its sword only bolsters its resolve and legend. Such things must be dealt with swiftly and completely. It will be brought to me, alive if possible."

"Our *Kolotor'ix*, what will we do with the land of Atermir?" Rutherrene spoke up, gesturing to the north-westernmost lands of Meridiah that butted up against the Shadowgulf Mountains.

The *Kolotor'ix*'s mask turned to look at said land. "There are woods and elven ruins, but the rest of the land is poisoned swampland and useless to us."

Blagdon frowned, thinking. "Our *Kolotor'ix*, *Tribya-Hasta'kan'ix ik'Remhold* said that the knight he'd encountered had black-scaled armor and a greenish blade."

Remhold gave Blagdon an unfriendly look.

Blagdon ignored it and continued. "Do you think this knight, if it is indeed a dragonsoul, and the lands of Atermir may be related somehow? Were not black dragons known for poison breath?"

The *Kolotor'ix* quietly drummed his gloved fingers on his chair.

Blackmont shook his head. "There is no reasoning why a creature from Atermir would travel all those miles out of its territory to be in D'Lcee. It would be too risky, leaving one's land with no defenses."

"The humans believed the white dragons flew from Eselund to

the lands south yearly before the long summer. The distance between Atermir and D'Lcee is not even half that. It is not a stretch of the imagination that the dragonsoul knight could be from Atermir."

"If it even exists," Rutherrene spoke up, sipping watered wine. "We still have no proof other than Remhold's account, as shaky as it is."

Remhold glared at them but remained silent.

"I can send a scouting party to see what they can discover," Carriat said, "My territory is closest to Atermir, and our *belvash* have various potions to aid in counteracting poisoning."

"I can send troops to defend your scouting party if you'd like," Nicholnor spoke up, looking at him. "That way, you are not stretching your people too thin, and my soldiers are specialized more in larger combat than escort services."

Carriat nodded. "I will take that partnership into consideration, Nicholnor."

"Perhaps this is the perfect time to test your Stormrider, Blagdon, in D'Lcee against the dragonsoul knight."

Blagdon set down his wine glass. "No."

"No? After waxing so eloquently about it, do you now doubt your precious Stormrider's abilities?"

Blagdon looked at Branial. "I do not doubt his abilities, but as he is still regaining his memories, throwing him into combat against a dragonsoul knight guarantees his demise. He is more useful to us alive than dead."

The *Kolotor'ix* nodded. "I agree, the Stormrider should not be tested so. If it comes to the dragonsoul knight being unable to be taken alive, I will come personally to D'Lcee and end his life."

The table was silent. It was known that once the *Kolotor'ix* stepped onto the battlefield, no enemies of theirs would be unscathed. Blagdon looked across the map at the dragonlands, the island furthest northeast, knowing that those there had suffered that dark truth worst of all.

Leaving home
means leaving a piece of us behind
that we don't notice is gone
until it is too late.

— Kil'lik'Draven, Bard of the Winds

LENAKA

The funeral procession finally entered the Valley of the Stars as the sun grew lower in the sky on the third day, casting long shadows that fell onto the various openings of tombs that dotted the tan, rocky mountains. Few plants grew here, the air drier and less humid, leaving the ground sandy and easy to dig.

A wagon carrying wood and incense headed to a large flat rock in the middle of the valley, where the funeral pyre would be created. The dawnwarriors carrying the coffin took it to a nearby flat rock and carefully placed it onto it. They would keep an eye on those making the pyre, to prevent them from accidentally standing over the height of the coffin. Four *lokoni'lo* stood around the coffin, ceremonial spears in hand, guarding the deceased, while others walked with *Rhan'Kahan*, who checked on his people.

The females immediately began heading to the right, where a special area with earthen ovens carved into the rock would be cleaned and prepped for creating the last supper.

The males headed to the left, finding places to stretch and sit, rubbing their sore muscles, and complaining about their aches. They found relief in having to have been silent while walking, but now that the sun was setting, they could speak.

Those of the Order of the Dawn stopped what they were doing and headed to the side to begin their prayers, led by *Oanu'toki* Paku. They kneeled and bent forward in waves, hands open, as the last light rays entered the valley.

Lenaka, torn between her duty and concern for her *putri*, frequently paused in her task of kneading the bread dough to look for Draven. She found him often talking animatedly to someone while trying to write simultaneously, once almost hitting someone with his wings as they moved expressively. Lenaka looked back at her work, ducking her head as she realized the disapproving glances and slight throat clearing from the other dawnwarrior females being directed her way. She attempted to explain, to make them understand the depth of her worry, but her words fell on deaf ears.

"Your role is to assist in this important feast, not to coddle your *putri*."

Lenaka walked over to the small wagon that held barrels of water that the women had hauled from Ka'epo Lake and dipped a ladle in, pouring water into the wooden bowl to take back to her station, and saw *Rhan'Ashanna* unwrapping cloth from the flat rocks which would be used to cook upon. They had been washed on the first day and dried in the sun to prevent cracking when putting them over the fires. A *lokoni* stood beside her, nodding his head to Lenaka to let her know she was seen. Deciding it would be better not to disturb her, Lenaka returned to her station and dough.

To her surprise, Clep was waiting for her.

"Is something wrong?" She asked, looking for her *putri*, and found him still talking with some of the younger males, who seemed to be eagerly listening to his words. Lenaka looked at Clep, wondering why he was there if nothing was wrong.

"Can I help?" he asked, his walking staff leaning against the rock beside him, "I used to help Ma cook."

"I'm sorry, Clep," Lenaka said, relieved, "by tradition, the females have to cook the last supper."

"Can I stay and watch?"

"As long as he doesn't touch anything," one of the females answered, dicing mango and putting the pieces into a wooden bowl.

Clep nodded and watched Lenaka as she began creating dough

from crushed wheat, spices, and water. Finally, it was the right consistency, and she started pinching off and rolling the dough into palm-sized balls, carefully setting them into a large bowl. Once one layer was done, she headed to where *Rhan'*Ashanna stood near the ovens.

*Rhan'*Ashanna went to Lenaka and began helping her use stone rods to roll the dough balls into flat discs, which they handed to the older females to set on the stones to cook.

"Why do females cook the supper and not the males?"

*Rhan'*Ashana smiled as she flattened out more dough. "This meal is very traditional, from the roles to what we eat to the tools used to prepare the food. We females carry the gift of *K'han'Exonia* within us, so when we make it, we bless it with her influence."

"What gift is that?" Clep looked confused.

"Life," a dawnwarrior female said from where she sat on a rock, removing a fruit's reddish-purple skin and dropping it into a bowl to the right while placing fruit into a separate bowl. "*K'han'Exonia* gives life, and her mate, *K'han'Natsulith,* takes it. So for a male to prepare the final supper is to invite death onto all who eat it."

Clep folded his hands on his lap as he sat on a rock, as if suddenly aware of their power. "I've never heard of a tradition like that. It is very unique."

Lenaka smiled. "It goes back to when the dawnwarriors were first hatched with wings, separating us from our elven kin."

Clep blinked at them, eyes wide. "Did you say *hatched?!*"

Ka'ae'Mamani laughed beside the firepit, using wooden utensils to carefully pull off the dough once it bubbled, flipping it over so it cooked on the other side. Her black and grey hair, twisted into long strands, was pulled back to keep it out of her face as she cooked. Her brown wings, speckled with stripes of grey and black, fanned slowly behind her as if ensuring the temperature of the air around the cooking bread was consistent. "Yes, human, we are hatched. Dawnwarriors grow in the female's bellies until it is time to be born; then, they pass with a soft sack around them, much like a snake's eggs, that prevents injuries to the *pari'tale'lo* and hatchling. A wing caught under the pelvic bone can be catastrophic."

Clep looked horrified, and Lenaka smiled. "Ka'ae'Mamani has been a midwife for many births, including *Rhan'Ashana's*."

The older dawnwarrior smiled, the motion accentuating the white and black dots along her cheekbones that signified not only family members who had died but those lost in childbirth.

No matter how skilled someone was at medicine, not everyone could be saved from the simplest procedures.

"After birth, the membrane around the hatchling hardens as the sun dries it, and the dawnwarrior's wing hook breaks the shell to begin hatching. In the months following, the wing hook harmlessly falls off as feathers grow to replace the pin feathers." Mamani laughed at Clep's expression as she set the baked bread on a plate with many already stacked and began setting more flattened dough on the stone after rubbing it with plant oil to prevent it from sticking. "I still think I have my son's winghook in a box at home."

Clep shook his head, his cheeks reddening with embarrassment. "I had no idea that births could differ among species that seem so similar."

Mamani chuckled, smiling widely. "Oh yes, the first time I tended a human's birth, I was shocked by how messy it was."

Lenaka headed back toward her station to get more dough and smiled as she listened to the women laughing at Clep's words. *At least there is some laughter to help spice the food we create, and hopefully, that spirit of happiness and peace will spread among those who partake in it. We could use a little more peace these days.*

* * *

Lenaka sat beside Draven, food spread on long pieces of fabric, everyone sitting on the sand. At the end of the cloth was *Rhan'Kahan*, and past him at the other end of the cloth stood the funeral pyre with the coffin bearing *O'anu'tale*. It was a tradition that the dawnwarriors spend one last feast with their dearly departed before they were sent to be with the great *K'hani*. It was a final show of respect, which was supposed to bring the group of mourners together.

Amidst the lively chatter, Lenaka was captivated by her *putri's* tales of his travels with *O'anu'tale* Kiko.

"When we turned down the road, five Nyfer elves glared us down. They began chanting, stomping, and making faces while they made gestures like stabbing and slashing at the air, which I could only surmise were threats of what they'd do to us if we continued forward. They moved in perfect unison like it was a dance they had rehearsed many times. I looked back at *O'anu'tale* Kiko and found she was shaking and pale; she had never seen anything like it before— well, neither of us had, really— and then I noticed more Nyfer elves in the woods around us. We were surrounded. It was an ambush!" Draven added, using his wings and arms dramatically as if to paint the image before him.

"Come on, Draven, you can't expect us to swallow that. An ambush is when the enemy has you surrounded without your knowledge; they won't reveal themselves. Nyfers are one of the most feared elven clans in history, and they wouldn't make such a rookie mistake. You're just making it up." A dawnwarrior male chuckled, his laughter echoed by a few others who nodded in agreement.

"I am telling you, it is a Nyfer ambush!" Draven said, but the dawnwarriors were too busy laughing and talking to listen. Sighing, his shoulders slumped slightly, making Lenaka frown and lean toward him.

"Don't worry, I believe you."

Draven straightened, smiled at her, and continued talking, bolstered by her words. "We were then captured and brought before their chieftain, who demanded to know why we were in their territory. We told him that we were on the way to Meridiah City to celebrate the name day of the newest princess, and they scoffed. They didn't believe the dawnwarriors would want anything to do with the elven clans, especially when we didn't participate in the War of the Turning Leaves."

"Why didn't the dawnwarriors participate in the war?" Clep asked, taking a drink of water from his wooden cup.

He reminds me of Putri, curious about everything around him and willing to learn about it.

Draven smiled at him. "*Rhan'*Kahan had sent emissaries to speak with the elven clans before, asking them to stop the fighting; there was more than enough land in Meridiah to live peacefully. They sent back either bodies or answers of no."

"If Andears had sent back a body, Leigelord Kerrick would have killed us all. He had my village slaughtered and burned to the ground just because someone threw a rock at a soldier."

Some of the dawnwarriors reacted to that, blinking in surprise, and one of them started to ask a question, but Lenaka cut him off to draw attention away from Clep's village.

He already feels bad about it; we do not need to question him. "We felt it wasn't our place to shove our way into the war and would remain neutral until forced to take a side. The war was about the lands of Meridiah, and we had secured our place in Exonesis long before that. We did not need to gain more land, and stepping into the war and picking a side could cause us to lose what we had."

Draven smiled at her as if he were proud that she remembered his stories.

How can I forget when you tell them constantly?

"Why are they called Nyfers?"

Lenaka thought about that, frowning as she realized she didn't know the answer. She glanced at Draven, as did the others at the table, who looked eager to see the old *pu'uni* bard stumped.

Draven smiled, spreading fruit paste on his piece of bread. "It used to be an insult given by the humans. "Knife-ear," they'd call elves, referring to their ear shape. After a while, the clan took the name proudly. Still, many elves consider the term an insult, even today."

The dawnwarriors listening grumbled, and Lenaka spotted some skyshards changing hands quietly. Her lip twitched at that.

"So, what stopped the war?" Clep leaned in, seeming entirely enthralled by the stories.

"The marriage of Mun'ari elf queen Mari'anath and human noble Byron, who became king. You see, the humans were caught in the land wars between the seven elven clans when all they wanted to do was live in peace."

"So, who won the war? The Mun'ari clan, I assume, because the queen was of them?"

Draven sipped his tea thoughtfully and set his cup down before answering. "Who wins at war? There are no winners, only losers. No one walks away from the war unscathed; there are memories, scars both inside and out, and lost friends and family. No one is ever the same."

There was silence for a bit as the veterans of the War of the Turning Leaves nodded, muttering their acknowledgment of the truth that was spoken.

Clep seemed to sense the change in mood. "So you said there were seven elven clans?"

Draven's eyes lit up. "Oh yes! There used to be eight elven clans, but then we grew wings and were no longer counted among them. But the Sin Dh'arin clan was completely run off Andora during the War of the Turning Leaves. Rumor is they are now across the Aerukatan Ocean; what I'd give to travel there!"

As Draven began speaking more about where else he'd love to travel, Lenaka looked at Clep, continuing to answer the question.

"The Fyre elves went into the Shadowgulf Mountains, where the toxic fumes from the lava pools make it nearly impossible to survive there. Because of this, the other clans couldn't attack them easily, though if they were still there, it would be a mystery how they had survived the climate. The then-war general Marianath created a treaty with the Munari and Nyfer clans, but the particulars of it are unknown—"

"Because I wasn't there to record it," Draven added grumpily.

Clep chuckled, hiding his smile as Lenaka rolled her eyes and continued.

"The Benstafi elves took to the oceans, sailing around the continents and making their homes on the open waters, using trade and travel to make their way in life."

"And pirating, which is why the Shadon haven't left Andora. I don't think they have a navy," Draven spoke up thoughtfully

"Yes, *Putri*."

Clep frowned. "If the Nyfers were so powerful, why would they let the Mun'ari win?"

"Well, the Mun'ari were adept magick-users, with runecarvers and sigilbearers; in addition, they had the blessings of Stormriders after the human noble Byron became involved involuntarily," *Rhan'*Ashana spoke up, eating a piece of bread she folded around some fruit.

"Involuntarily?"

Draven smiled. "Oh, Byron was captured by the Nyfers and later rescued by the Mun'ari when their camp was attacked. Instead of letting him go, they took them to their war-general to get information. But she fell in love with him and married him years later."

Clep frowned. "The world is more complicated than I ever would have imagined."

Draven laughed. "Oh yes, and it makes a wonderful story to tell."

* * *

Voices woke Lenaka up from where she'd fallen asleep against a tree; the calmer tones of *Rhan'*Kahan contrasted with the heated ones from *O'anu'toki* Paku and others. Sitting slowly, she realized that she was not the only one who had been woken; many were beginning to look around to see the disturbance's cause. Lenaka glanced over to Draven, who was writing in his notebook while lying down instead of sitting up to watch. *Of course, he'd be recording everything.*

"She deserves to be buried with her family, her people, not have her body treated like refuse!" *Oanu'toki* Paku snapped, gesturing to the body of *O'anu'tale* Kiko, her coffin resting on the wooden pyre that kept her elevated above the rest of the dawnwarriors.

*Rhan'*Kahan shook his head, the firelight of torches making the light play along his features, his braided hair gathered and covered with a white cloth held by dawnsteel pins, a gesture of mourning and respect for the dead. "All due respect, *O'anu'toki*, but we have not permitted the burial of our deceased in over a hundred and fifty years, not since the Scourge War. You know this; all of Exonesis know this. We will not risk the possibility of our loved ones rising as blightwalkers."

"The blightwalkers are gone; the Scourge War has been long over! Yet you hold fast to this unfounded fear of years past! You refuse to honor our dead by lying them to rest in their family's tombs! You refuse to honor our living by keeping us prisoner inside the walls of Exonesis!" The *O'anu'toki* threw up his arms, gesturing to the mountains around them, his voice rising.

Movement beside Lenaka made her glance over to see Clep and others beginning to sit up on their blankets, looking confused and whispering to each other.

"What's going on? Why are they arguing?" Clep asked, rubbing his eyes and glancing to see Memory still asleep in her cage, head tucked under her wing.

Lenaka kept her voice low, leaning over to Clep to not wake those still asleep around her, glancing toward the arguing dawnwarriors. "They are arguing against burning the *O'anu'tale*'s body because—" she started, but Draven interrupted her.

Clep's eyes were horror-filled as he glanced at Lenaka. "You mean that all the people in Andears could rise again because we buried them and didn't burn them?"

Lenaka wasn't sure what to say.

Draven muttered absently, still writing. "The first dawnwarriors were entombed as sacrifice and honor to provide the first meal of the hatchlings of *K'hani'Exonia*, whose eggs were left here when she ascended to the skies. Many of those hatchlings later became *K'hani*. Since then, none have hatched, but the tradition remained until the Scourge War forced changes."

"Wait, not all dragons are *K'hani*?"

"That is correct." Draven answered, his voice monotone as he concentrated on his writing instead of what he said. He paused in his writing, crossed out something, and continued, his enchanted quill never stopping in its movement as ink flowed, creating words quickly.

"So what makes the difference between—"

"You will not burn her, turn her into a pile of ashes so the Dawn can no longer recognize her! It is forbidden!" Ma'ko'Taka shouted, standing beside *Oanu'toki Paku*. The distraction caused them to turn back to the argument, and more dawnwarriors were also beginning to pay attention.

"If the Everlasting Dawn was so omnipotent, would it not be able to tell who she was, even if she were burned to ash?" Draven muttered, turning over a piece of parchment to continue recording on the back. "It sounds contradictory if you ask me."

"I am *Rhan*, and you would do your best to remember that." *Rhan*'Kahan's voice dropped in a warning.

The *lokoni'lo* began coming closer to create a barrier between them and the growing crowd.

Lenaka glanced around to see *Rhan*'Ashanna standing to the side, four *lokoni'lo* beside her, hands on their weapons. *Koani looks torn as if having to decide who to protect if this goes badly: his O'anu'toki or his Rhan. For once, I am unsure which side he'd choose.*

"You are only *Rhan* because the *K'hani* supposedly chose your bloodline to lead the dawnwarriors— but where are they now?" *O'anu'toki* Paku gestured to the skies and the rocks around them. "I see no *K'hani* nor hear their cries! They do not live in the skies; they no longer fly among us! *O'anu'tale* Na'kia'Kiko witnessed their bodies in *Ua'k'hani*, as did Kil'lik'Draven! They know the truth— your *K'hani* are dead, and you forbade them from telling everyone!" The *O'anu'toki* stepped closer to *Rhan'*Kahan, pointing at him dramatically, making those watching tense.

O'anu'toki Aluu stepped forward, trying to calm the emotions of those around them, his hands open to show there was nothing in them. "Perhaps if we all calm down, we can discu—"

O'anu'toki Paku ignored him. "Perhaps you sequester the truth because you know that without your *K'hani*, you are no longer fit to be *Rhan*. *They* are the reason you sit on the throne. They are the reason your daughter will be the *Rhan* after you pass, that a child she bears will lead after her death. But without the *K'hani*, without your precious sacred bloodline, what are you then, *Rhan'*Kahan? You have no family name and nothing of your own other than what we, the dawnwarriors, have given you! Without the *K'hani*, you would not rule Exonesis, and our people would be free!"

His voice rose in tone until he shouted to be heard and pointed at those watching. "We would be out in the skies of Meridiah, freely soaring under the sun once more, flying as far as we wished! We could see the valleys, the hills, the mountains, the oceans! We have survived the Scourge War and still live as prisoners because of you!" He jabbed a pointed hand toward the coffin angrily. "You rule us in life; you rule us in death! When are our lives ever our own?"

Dawnwarriors began shouting, some arguing in agreement, others against what was being said. *Lokoni'lo* moved through the crowd, hands on weapons, unease on their faces. *Rhan'*Ashanna looked around worriedly, her own *lokoni'lo* standing around her as others began shouting and walking toward her. When she backed up against a boulder, Lenaka saw a flash of fear on her face.

She cannot crawl onto it to escape, for risking being higher than O'anu'tale Nakia's corpse.

Clep was tapping Lenaka's wing repeatedly, and she looked at him. "What is it?"

He pointed to the other side of her.

Lenaka turned and saw the parchment and quill lying on the blanket, but her *putri* wasn't there. *Oh no.* She turned, looking around frantically for him in the crowd, but it was hard to see when everyone was standing, wings moving, and people not staying still. Lenaka began pushing through the crowd, trying to find him before he got too close to the arguing dawnwarriors. *Where is he?*

"What would you have me do, *O'anu'toki?*" *Rhan'*Kahan was saying, his own voice raised in frustration. "Allow the blightwalkers to rise here in Exonesis, where those without wings would have nowhere to run? What if our dawnwarriors return from the dead and be able to fly? Then what will you do? We hardly knew how to fight them before, and we do not now have the soldiers to fight back the number of blightwalkers who would rise from the Valley of the Stars. Burning our dead is a practicality born of necessity."

"You will not—" the *O'anu'toki* began, but a woman screamed from the crowd, and both he and *Rhan'*Kahan turned toward the sound, seeing a dawnwarrior woman pointing toward the rocks.

Lenaka turned, wondering what had caused the commotion, and gasped.

Draven stood with his head bowed as flames licked along the wood of the pyre, growing higher as the kindling between the larger pieces of wood caught fire.

Where were the lokoni'lo who were guarding the pyre?

The *O'anu'toki* rushed toward him, shouting. "What have you done? What have you done!"

Lenaka ran toward her uncle, and the dawnwarriors around her seemed to have the same idea. Everyone seemed to be moving quickly, some toward the *O'anu'toki* and others past him toward the pyre. Chaos broke out, with insults and shouts thrown at one another, dawnwarriors and humans grabbing each other and trying to get closer. Followers of the Order of the Dawn began grabbing anything they could to dump onto the pyre to prevent their founder's corpse from burning. Someone began climbing the pyre, trying to get to the body before the flames, before a hand grabbed her leg, pulling her down as she kicked at them.

"Stop this!" *Rhan'*Kahan shouted unsuccessfully, his voice drowned out by the commotion. He hurried forward to prevent people from hurting themselves, his *lokoni'lo* and *O'anu'toki* Aluu trying to stay with him.

O'anu'toki Paku had tackled Draven onto the ground and was punching down on the older dawnwarrior when Lenaka finally spotted her *putri.*

"You were supposed to be on our side! How can you abandon your people? *O'anu'tale* Na'Kia'Kiko believed in you, and you betrayed her!"

Draven curled to his side, his wing crumpled under him as he tried blocking the blows with his arms.

"*Putri!*" Lenaka fell to the ground as two fighting dawnwarriors shoved into her from the side. Swearing, she quickly scrambled to her feet, glancing around to re-orient herself. She couldn't see her *putri* or the *O'anu'toki* as *lokoni'lo* moved forward and tried to separate the two groups in the crowd, their wings flared and shields up. She ran toward the pyre's flames reaching higher into the night sky, using it as a beacon.

As she broke through the crowd, she saw the figures of her *putri* and another dawnwarrior still fighting on the ground, backlit by the glowing firelight. A flash of metal caught her eye in the firelight. Before she could think of the word *knife,* the other figure plunged the blade home.

"*PUTRI!*" Lenaka rushed forward, sliding to her knees beside him, and grabbing for anything to stop the bleeding, pressing her hands over Draven's. "Keep your hands here," she said as she looked around for something to pack the wound with but found nothing nearby. "Someone help me!"

A hand pressed a cloth into her palm, and she saw Clep reaching into his satchel as he searched for something. He set down his tome beside him, giving himself more room to search his bag, moving things. "I have to have more salves here; I didn't think I had traded them all in the *helaono*..."

A bloodied hand reached up, touching Lenaka's shoulder.

Lenaka looked at her *putri,* his pained face still smiling.

"I helped her..." he coughed, blood spilling out between his teeth, looking black in the light of the pyre. "I helped free Kiko from her torment."

"You did, *putri.* Now, hold on." She looked at Clep, who held out a bottle, unstoppering it quickly. Lenaka held the potion to Draven's lips, tilting it into his mouth as he swallowed but began coughing and choking. "Slowly, *putri.*" She paused and tried again. Once he had taken a few swallows, she looked at Clep. "I need *O'anu'toki* Rian'Aluu. He may still be with *Rhan'*Kahan. Hurry, please!"

Clep nodded and quickly rushed off, leaving Memory's cage beside Lenaka as if to keep her company.

"There are so many stories in the stars."

She looked at Draven, whose eyes were fixed at the sky above them, watching the pyre embers float higher as if to join them. "It's okay, *putri*; there are plenty of stories to tell here too. Tonight will be one to write about when we get home."

"Yes. It will be," he said, wincing in pain, and Lenaka pressed the cloth against his wound harder, the cloth and her hand coated with warm liquid.

"SOMEONE HELP ME!" She screamed, trying to get anyone to hear her over the sounds of shouting.

"Lenaka..." Draven was looking at the tome Clep had laid beside his satchel, trying to reach it with his hand but couldn't.

"*Putri,* what is it? Do you want this book? It's Clep's. Don't touch it, you're bloodied."

"Blood is the key," he mumbled, reaching for his ever-present satchel. He pulled out a cloth-wrapped item, and Lenaka grabbed it, taking the cloth and pressing it against his wound, ignoring the object that fell to the sand.

"*Putri*, stop moving your arms. You need to lie still. You are still bleeding greatly." She put Draven's hands on the cloth to keep them close to his wound while she looked through Clep's bag for another potion.

"Blood is the key… You must go south, Lenaka, and become part of the story that will change our world."

Lenaka ignored his ramblings as she read the labels by the dying firelight, found a healing potion, and pressed it against his lips. "Drink, *Putri*."

He slowly drank, touching her braids that fell around her shoulders. "You look like Miha'a."

Lenaka swallowed hard; he seldom spoke of his deceased sister. "I know, *putri*."

"Kil'lik'Lenaka!" Clep ran from the crowd, stumbling, *O'anu'toki'* Aluu beside him, hurrying over once he saw the situation.

"I tried giving him another healing potion, Clep. I don't know what else to do; you weren't here to ask if it was—"

"It's okay." Clep shook out a blanket he'd grabbed and pressed it against Draven's wound over the blood-soaked cloth.

O'anu'toki Aluu began taking things out of the pouch on his belt and opened a bottle, moving the bloodied cloths and pouring it into the wound. Draven hissed in pain, and the *O'anu'toki* muttered an apology. "It is made of eggshells, and it will—"

"Not work," a voice interrupted, and Lenaka turned, seeing *O'anu'toki* Paku holding a bottle in his hand. "This real healing potion will work, not one of the *K'hani*'s useless liquids."

You cannot be seriously arguing religion right now.

Lenaka started to open her mouth to retort, but Clep beat her to it, saying something different. "Thank you for your help. If you can save Kil'lik'Draven, then please do so. We will take whoever's help we can."

O'anu'toki Paku knelt on the opposite side of *O'anu'toki* Aluu, the two trading sharp looks before he put the potion to Draven's lips and helped him drink.

As Draven coughed, the two *O'anu'toki'lo* began praying, each to their deities, their voices overlapping. Clep closed his eyes, his mouth moving wordlessly.

Lenaka glanced at Draven, looking to the side with wide eyes as if listening to something. She looked around but saw nothing other than more dawnwarriors, noticing something was happening and starting to head over. *Lokoni'lo* stepped in their way, keeping the crowd back.

"He's coming… He will bring the winter again, white winds on dragon wings, coming from the south to blanket the lands. He's coming, Lenaka!" Draven said excitedly, squeezing her hand with his bloodied one.

I have no idea who or what he is talking about. "Calm down, *putri*, and you can tell me about it later."

"I knew it. I knew I was right. She is south and will be coming to make the world right again. You must be there to write about it for me."

A loud cracking of wood sounded, and the pyre behind them collapsed, making them jump. Even *O'anu'toki* Paku was startled, and he looked up at the embers flying into the air, frowning heavily.

Lenaka glanced from the falling pyre to Draven, noting he had a dagger in one of his bloodied hands beside him in the sand, his skin clean where his fingers curled around the blade. *Was that the dagger he'd found on Uak'hani? I didn't know he'd brought it with him.*

"*Putri*, did you bring—"

She stopped as she saw Draven's eyes were fixated on the stars above, a smile on his face, but the light in his brown eyes was dimming to nothingness. She glanced at his chest and saw no rising, no falling.

"*Putri?*" She shook his shoulder and tried again, her voice shaking slightly. "*Putri?* Please, say something. *Putri!*"

O'anu'toki Paku placed his hand on Draven's forehead and ran down it, closing Draven's eyes. "His light has faded from this world; may he—"

Lenaka slapped his hand away. "He isn't dead! He's unconscious, he isn't...." Her voice failed her as she looked at *O'anu'toki* Aluu, who said nothing but slowly placed Draven's arms across his chest, the dagger falling from his grip.

"I'm so sorry, Kil'lik'Lenaka." Clep touched her shoulder, and she jerked away from him, scrambling to her feet, her breath heavy as if she'd been running.

"It's not true! He's not dead!" She shook Draven hard enough to lift him. "You can't leave me here alone! Come back, *Putri!*"

Koani walked over; he glanced from Draven to Lenaka, his face ashen slightly as the blood drained from it, realizing what had happened. "Kil'lik'Lenaka..." he started, stepping closer.

Lenaka covered her ears, shaking her head, her wings thrashing with the emotions that warred in her head. "Stop talking! It's not true, he can't be.... He's all I have...." Lenaka stood and turned to fly off, fly far away from the talk of death, the lies and pain that remained here.

Koani grabbed her arm, pulling her to him and holding her tightly against his chest. "You can't fly; if you do, *K'han'Notsulith* will claim you too."

"I DON'T CARE!" Lenaka shouted, fighting his hold upon her. "Let me go! Let me fly! Let him take me!" She raised her chin, screaming at the silent skies. "Take me! Take me instead...." Her voice broke, giving way to sobs as she sank to her knees, Koani following her, wings arched around her to give her privacy. She screamed wordlessly, her arms hugging herself as she fell to the sand and prayed for the *K'hani* to trade her life for the one she loved most in this world.

For the first time, the *K'hani* were silent.

Our duty dictates our actions,
not our hearts.
Hearts can be led astray.

Hearts can deceive.

— Nixus Halidesh, Bard of Eteris

APOLLO

The guards around the tunnel entrance of Exonesis let them out without a problem, much to Apollo's surprise, after Senka explained that they'd received a message that something had happened with her father and that they had to return immediately.

They are more worried about people coming in than out. But who would want to leave such a beautiful, open place? It seemed as if they had no real worries; the shops were plentiful in the marketplace, and the people came together to mourn someone who had died. It seems like a giant village.

Senka hardly spoke as they went through the tunnels to the carts and sat behind Apollo in the first cart. He could feel her bouncing her leg slightly as they sat, as if nervous or excited. *I doubt she'd tell me if I asked.*

He glanced back down the dark tunnel behind them, knowing he'd been so close to finding Clep and now was leaving him again. He closed his eyes, imagining his brother's face when the Fyre elf gave him the note, saying he was alive, safe, and would return when he could. *I couldn't tell where I had been, but I had a long story to tell him the next time we saw each other. I hope he understands.*

Apollo closed his eyes, falling asleep, the soft clicking of the wheels soothing him.

"What do you want?" Clep snapped, shouting at him from the stall in the marketplace in Exonesis. "Look at you! Look at what you've become!"

Apollo looked to the side, seeing a mirror leaning against the stall across the walkway, and blinked at himself. He wore black and red armor of the Dark Army, a korrati's insignia hanging from his pauldron, which still had the Aldarwood in relief. I'm a korrati? Where's Mykel?

"Are you even listening to me? You joined the enemy, our enemy! What are you going to do now? Look at yourself!" Clep shouted, pointing at him.

Apollo looked at Clep slowly. "I'm not your enemy, Clep. I never have been."

Clep gestured at the frightened dawnwarriors around them running and cowering behind stalls, children hiding behind mothers. You want to take me back to Hasta'kan'ix ik'Blagdon. You want to let them question me about Ma!"

"Ma-kyr," Apollo corrected, without meaning to, and reached out to his brother.

He blinked, realizing his hands were full. He looked down to see he held his bloodied sword in one hand and a lit torch in the other. Startled, he dropped the torch.

The marketplace went up in flames.

Senka climbed out of the cart, jarring Apollo awake. He glanced around, realizing that they had stopped. *I swear the journey from Exonesis was quicker than the one into it.*

Senka began walking quickly down the tunnel after the dawnwarrior carrying a lightstone lantern. He scrambled after her, and they fast-walked through the tunnels. *I wish the dawnwarrior weren't with us so we could talk, but I still am unsure why we are hurrying.* Apollo began to doubt that he could keep up much longer when the air grew cooler and he saw the tunnel entrance ahead.

Stepping out of the tunnel, Apollo gasped, seeing the world bathed in moonlight, the trees and lakes below shining as if made of silver. Immediately, he began looking his armor over, breathing out a sigh of relief as he saw it was the leathers Mykel had given him, not the Dark Army metal armor. He glanced at Senka, who seemed to be breathing a bit harder as if she'd pushed herself to get through the tunnel as fast as she could, her hands flexing slightly.

The dawnwarriors carried them toward the mountain's base. Apollo closed his eyes, the feeling of his blood rushing through his body making him smile. It was a shock when his feet touched the ground again, and he opened his eyes, feeling slightly disappointed to be back on the earth.

Once on the ground, the dawnwarriors moved a golden stick over the peace bindings, the cloths dropping off harmlessly. *How did they do that? Was it magick?*

The dawnwarriors gathered the white ropes and took off into the sky, returning to the mountain.

Apollo tested to ensure he could draw his sword now and was relieved to find he could again. *That's good. The last thing I need is a sword I can't draw.* Sighing, he looked around and noticed that the group from Silene was still there, a firepit illuminating their faces as they watched them with a mixture of sadness and anger.

Senka paid them no mind as she quickly walked toward the woods as if on a mission.

Apollo rushed after her, surprised at her speed and having to work to stay beside her. "Lady Shadon Senka, we can slow down," he said once he was close enough not to have his voice carry.

"It is the third night of the full moon, which means the *kalidesh ik'kolotor* is almost over."

"I don't understand; just wait a minute and slow down, won't you?" Apollo pushed after her as she walked deeper into the woods, wincing as leaves and branches struck his face and limbs, unable to see them in the growing darkness the further they got from the forest's edge.

He walked into Senka's back, not realizing that she'd stopped.

The feeling of his blood rushing swept over him, and he found himself unsteadily reaching out to the large tree trunk beside him to remain upright.

Senka looked at him. "Tell Mykel that you are here, but I must go."

Apollo blinked. "Mykel? But he isn't near here..." he blinked, realizing the tree he leaned on had white bark. He looked around, seeing the shape of the keep in the darkness, the *kelvorvik* paddock beyond that. *Are we back at Woodsong already? I didn't even realize she had created a darkness portal. Can she even teleport us that far?*

Senka stepped into the moonlight, her voice clear. "Our *Kolotor'ix*, hear my voice. I must speak to you of the utmost importance, for I have found a lead about what you seek."

Whispers filled the shadows around her and gathered, forming two hands. They wrapped around Senka, closing in around her. As Mykel stepped out of the keep, the shadows faded, taking Senka with them.

* * *

Mykel sat in the *korrati*'s office of the keep, listening to Apollo recount everything that had happened. A *Sri'balvash* checked him for injuries and declared him healthy before having a second *balvash* bring him food and water.

Sri'balvash Desira sat at a desk in the corner, writing nonstop on parchment. *Has she truly been writing everything that I have been saying?*

Mykel had said nothing the entire time, which did not help Apollo's nerves.

"That was when she called our *Kolotor'ix*, saying she had information on a lead about something, and she was shadowed away, as you saw." Apollo finished, taking another drink of water flavored with local fruit. *I feel exhausted, even though I have done nothing but talk for the last two turns of the hourglass.*

Mykel frowned. "I do not know what my blood-sister has to offer our *Kolotor'ix*, so I will not speculate." He leaned forward slightly. "Are you better now knowing where Clep is located, even if you did not see him yourself?"

"Better?" Apollo thought about that. *Everything happened so quickly that I haven't had time to process anything.* "I suppose I do feel better, especially knowing he's safe and not in *Hasta'kan ik'Blackmont's* territory being hunted."

Mykel nodded understandably. "I am also relieved you are not being hunted either. I've had much to attend to in your absence; *kriss'ix* Lukras felt it was because you were not a distraction to me, and I could fully focus on being *korrati*."

Am I a distraction?

Mykel walked to the map on the table and looked it over. "We are readjusting the Hydehall garrison by the southern village of Mytel. It is a farming village, and the garrison nearby keeps the area safe from bandits and wolves. You are to go there and learn under *kriss'ix* Lukras, who will be acting as *korrati*. You will shadow him, learning to tend to those under you, defend others, and lead."

Apollo blinked at him, unsure how to feel about this turn of events. *I've just arrived, and already I am being sent away.* "I've hardly had over a full season to learn how to fight properly and learn *ro'*Shadon culture, and now you want me to learn to lead?"

Mykel shrugged. "It will not be as difficult as you think, for *kriss'ix* Lukras will do most of the work while you observe and learn. You will continue your sparring and your studies with *Sri'balvash* Inara, as well as learn to ride. I will still be in charge of Cetra and will visit when I come around to collect taxes quarterly. This separation may be what we both need to grow and when we meet again, we shall be stronger than ever."

Apollo nodded and left the keep, feeling numb. He tended his armor silently in the soldiers' cabin, listening to the others laugh and talk around him. *I've never been a part of them, yet I feel sad that I will leave here.*

Eratas' cot had a new soldier on it, as did the cots of the other eight soldiers responsible for the attack on Andears. The soldiers tended their black and red armor, sharpening swords and resting on their cots as they waited for their assignments. *Will my spot always be here, or will I be replaced with another fresh soldier eager to join the Dark Army under Hasta'kan ik'Blagdon? Is that all we are, those who are replaced at a moment's notice?*

Apollo looked at his armor, running his hand over the raised Aldarwood on his pauldron, his thoughts going to Clep. *At least he is safe and knows what the future holds for him. He'll be making salves and selling them in a marketplace in Exonesis, just as he'd always dreamed of doing. Meanwhile, I am the balutrae ik'Blagdon and becoming a swordsman, just like I'd always pretended to be with sticks and wooden swords in Andears. But now I am training to become a korrati if something happens to Mykel.*

He lay on his cot and wished he could return to the day before he knew what real fighting was and the true cost of peace.

The most difficult dance is not the one on the dancefloor,

but of those on the sidelines waiting their turns.

Watch them, for they are the most enertaining.

— Nixus Halidesh, Bard of Eteris

BLAGDON

He looked at himself in the mirror for a moment before readjusting his leather vest over his tunic. The dark blue trim contrasted nicely with the cream color of the linen tunic, the sleeves held down by black bracers to keep his sleeves from being loose around his wrists.

"That is a welcome change from your usual attire," Narisa teased gently as she sat, wearing a simple dark green gown. She'd come from the Blood Temple that afternoon to ensure that Blagdon was adequately attired for the evening. She had been a most welcome sight, and he had insisted on time together in the bedroom before Blagdon allowed her to aid him in dressing. Now that they had both sated their frustrations and celebrations, they were ready for the next crisis.

"I see the potions I gave you have masked almost all the scent of working with *kelvorvik*." Her hands touched the bracers on his wrists, her fingers running over the carvings of *Hasta'kan ik'Blagdon*'s emblem. Watching her face in the mirror, he saw her frown slightly.

"Do they bother you, beloved?" He asked quietly. They were gifts from Alyssa-*kyr*, his first wife, and he treasured them. He never could think of her passing as her 'death,' no matter how others may have spoken about the event. *It was an assassination.*

"It is not that, my husband. Do you expect a duel tonight?"

The question made him blink, for it was not his reasoning that the bracers would bother his current wife. "Why do you ask?"

"You wore them so your sleeves would not catch while you pulled your rapier."

His lip twitched. *She is as practical as she is deadly.* "I always expect a duel; I am the *balutrae ik'Kolotor'ix*."

"You and I both know it would not be a mere duel but a slaughter with the *Kolotor'ix* taking personal insult to anyone who harms you." She paused momentarily, glancing into the mirror to ensure no lip paint was on her teeth. "I am not so insecure as to be insulted that you are wearing gifts from your previous wife. They are precious to you, and I do not feel I must compete with a ghost for your affection."

Blagdon checked his hair in the mirror, frowning when a strand refused to stay where he wanted it. "My wife is wise, cunning, and too smart for one such as myself."

She laughed a happy sound that tugged at his heart. "You just want me beside you tonight to deal with the political side and ensure you do not duel everyone there."

I cannot debate her wisdom. "If I could breed creatures worthy of the *belvash*, in a show of appreciation for their duties to my *Hasta'kan*, I would."

"We don't like to compete with animals for blood," She half-joked, turning and pouring some oil into her hand and reaching for his hair.

Usually, I would have never allowed a balvash to touch me with oil on their hands, but alas, the spell my wife has upon me has superseded my common sense and survival instincts. If she truly wished to kill me, she could do so quickly and repeatedly.

Narisa ran the oil through his hair, ensuring it would stay in place for the most part. "If we can get through this dinner without an incident, that would be enough for me."

"There are no guarantees this night."

* * *

As expected, the other *Hesta'kan'ix* and their Lordsons wore their finest clothing, making Blagdon look plain beside them. Those intelligent enough to realize that he could duel them at a moment's notice were wise enough to keep their remarks of his attire to themselves. Though some gave judging looks, he said nothing, for he had on bracers, a rapier, and his wife upon his arm. *That is all that I require.*

Narisa remained at his side, smiling and making small talk while greeting each *Hasta'kan'ix* warmly. The *Sri'balvash* showcased her skills wonderfully as she maneuvered conversations into ones Blagdon could listen to without growing irritable and ensured to include the few ladies who attended, much to the irritation of the *Hasta'kan'ix* who tried taking over the conversation to turn it toward why they were worthy of Senka's hand in marriage.

While the women spoke, Blagdon took a few moments to play 'find the disguised *belvash*,' in which he was rewarded for discovering at least two among the crowd, not counting the women playing music. As Narisa reached for her glass of wine, she made small gestures with her other hand at her side. He felt himself clever for even seeing it himself.

Nicholnor walked over with a glass of wine and turned so his back was to the wall, like Blagdon's, so no one could walk up from behind them. He took a sip, glancing at the man beside him. "You look ready to be done with this entire thing."

"I do not care for much of the night's conversations thus far." He sighed slightly. "Before you ask, I am not talking about offers for Lady Shadon Senka's hand until after dinner." He'd had to repeat that at least three times so far, for *Hesta'kan'ix* had already tried bartering for his daughter. *Let me have a little more time this evening before I speak of giving her away.*

Nicholnor gave a short laugh. "I came over because you looked like someone had slipped a lemon into your wine." He took a sip of his wine, sighing. "Speaking of uncomfortable things, Blagdon, look at what just walked in."

Blagdon followed his gaze to see a male in blue and silver armor, with a dark blue cape down his back, sword on his side. The man's brown hair was trimmed to his shoulders, curling at the ends, and his beard was trimmed and neat. The man stood straighter, his chest forward slightly, not with effort, but with a confidence that had not been there before.

For a moment, Blagdon almost did not recognize him. "Ah yes, excuse me." He walked across the room, examining the male before stopping beside him, noting a few guests were also looking. *Good.*

"Sir Siral, you look better than I had expected. I take it you are used to the armor by now?"

Siral looked at him. "It fits better than Ah thought it would and feels familiar."

"Memories have a strange way of making the unfamiliar familiar again," Blagdon said, remembering the first time he'd danced with Narisa after his wife's assassination. It had felt both familiar and strange, right and wrong, simultaneously. "Feel free to walk around and mingle. You are a guest here, Sir Siral, my new Lord Commander of the future Shadon Stormriders."

Siral blinked at him. "Sir?"

"Someone must command the future Stormriders. *Hasta'kan ik'Nicholnor* will aid you until you can do this independently at Stormhold. You have seen the Stormrider training firsthand, which I have only had glimpses of. You and Slipstream will be leading a new generation of the Stormriders. Be honored."

Before Siral could answer, Blagdon walked off, noticing Mari'aida speaking with two Lordsons who smiled at her too warmly for his taste.

"Lady Mari'aida, how is your evening thus far?"

"Hello *Hasta'kan'ix ik'Blagdon*. My evening is going well, is yours?" she asked, smiling.

"My apologies; your betrothed, my Lordson, cannot be here tonight." He handed her a glass of wine, holding his arm a touch higher to ensure the Lordsons saw his bracer and the rapier on his hip.

The lordsons seemed to take the hint and bowed, excusing themselves quickly.

Mari'aida gave him an amused look as she took the glass. "I thought you did not like politics."

"That was not politics. That was protecting my Lordson and his beloved."

"We only discussed the long summer and its implications on the land in Meridiah. Crops are suffering due to the extended heat. They thought that by speaking with me, they could gain the *Kolotor'ix*'s attention. I have no doubt their *Hesta'kan'ix* sent them to do so."

"Be that as it may, I do not wish to have them believe that Lady Shadon Senka is not the only one available for marriage. You will be wed to my son, should you wish it." He added the last because without it, it sounded like an order, and the last thing he needed tonight was the *Kolotor'ix* taking offense where none was offered.

Mari'aida smiled at that, dropping her voice slightly. "You did save me from a rather dull conversation; Lordson Edia was beginning to speak upon soil differences between Nar'Shada and Meridiah, an argument I have found quite boring."

Blagdon chuckled. "I have found myself to have dull conversations as well. Perhaps we should have both rushed back toward Stormhold before dinner."

Mari'aida laughed. "We could not do that, but I appreciate the sentiment."

The music changed, and Blagdon saw the double doors at the far end of the room open, the doors tall enough to be seen through the crowded room.

The *Kolotor'ix* stepped into the room, wearing black leather pants, a black velvet vest over a white shirt, and a black cape that billowed as he walked down the floor, hardly making a sound. His mask was affixed to his face, and a hood covered his hair. Those in the room stepped back, putting their right fists to their left shoulders, going to either a single or both knees, depending on their gender.

Blagdon went to a knee and moved his hand, shadows forcing

Ratsbayne to a knee across the room.

The only one who remained standing was Mari'aida, who, once the *Kolotor'ix* stopped in front of her, curtseyed, keeping her back straight as she lowered herself.

I don't know how she does it; Lady Narisa had tried learning how to bow in that manner but could not make it look as easy as she does.

The *Kolotor'ix* silently held out a gloved hand to her.

She put her hand in his, and the *Kolotor'ix* walked to the open floor with her before leading her into a dance, holding her right hand in his left. Instead of having his other hand on Mari'aida's waist, he held her upper arm. It subtly spoke of dominance; his partner was not his lover but someone under him. She would be unable to end the dance, to escape his grasp, unless he allowed it.

The music started quietly, growing darker as the two dancing figures moved across the floor slowly in time with the instruments. The music slowly sped up, and the two dancers, one in black and one in light yellow, moved faster.

Mari'aida had no choice but to meet the pace and direction of the *Kolotor'ix*, her skirt's layers moving like water around her, her hair spilling across her back, whipping with the motions of turning quickly. If she struggled, her face did now show it; she was looking into the mask of her partner with unwavering faith that he would lead her safely.

Suddenly, the music and dancers both stopped; the momentum of his dark cloak enveloped the petite woman, concealing her almost completely before slowly falling back to lie behind the *Kolotor'ix* again.

The *Kolotor'ix* removed his hand from her upper arm, stepping back from Mari'aida, her other hand still in his.

She went into a curtsey, dropping lower and keeping her upper half still until she was as low as she could get, almost sitting on the floor, her eyes staying on his mask, tilting her head up as she descended.

The *Kolotor'ix* let go of her hand, turned, and walked away as the final notes of the music played, leaving the room in shocked silence.

Clapping started quietly, slowly building, as the *ro'Shadon* stood from their bow to show their appreciation for the visual representation of the darkness conquering the light.

Blagdon did not clap, even though he found it artistic and impressive. Instead, he went to Mari'aida and held out a hand to help her stand, which she took with a smile, breathing harder. He offered her a glass of water in his other hand, walking her back to where he'd been standing earlier. He carefully used shadows to help Mari'aida regain her balance.

"That was breathtaking," he said after she'd drank some.

Mari'aida gave a small smile in appreciation, and Blagdon looked at his *balutrae*, the man sitting upon the throne above them, who used dance to remind everyone that he conquered all.

* * *

Blagdon sat at the long dinner table, listening to the other *Hesta'kan'ix* and their guests laugh and talk, conversing about subjects he didn't care about. He ate the roast duck and pig, missing his home, his family, and the sounds and smells of Stormhold.

A few *Hesta'kan'ix* tried to hide their disappointments as they spoke to those beside them, trying to get into deals and settle debts now that the newest rankings were announced. He did not miss *Hasta'kan'ix ik'Remhold*'s soured expression as two other guests laughed about something, glancing at Blagdon.

Let them laugh, let them plot. I am Hon-Hasta'kan'ix for another cycle.

Mari'aida ate her baked fish quietly, smiling a thin smile as if listening to the conversations, but Blagdon could not help but wonder if she was bored. *I do not doubt that she remembers when this room did not have black and crimson colors but blue and gold and when the laughter was less of plot and more of joy.*

The *Kolotor'ix* sat at the head of the table, his plate and goblet empty, his mask giving no expression away as he listened, though now and then speaking to Mari'aida. The *Kolotor'ix* never removed his mask; something as small as dinner would not change that. It was thought that he had the shadows sustain him, or he could feed through the *ro'*Shadon under him.

Blagdon felt it was much simpler; he'd eat in a private room after all had left.

The *Kolotor'ix* straightened from speaking low to the *balvash* pouring more wine into Mari'aida's goblet and turned his head as if listening to something.

Blagdon watched the movement, interested in what had gotten his attention. Narisa had stopped speaking, noting that he was not paying attention to her and watching around the room quietly.

The *Kolotor'ix* raised his gloved hand, and the conversations around the table died slowly. He stood and looked to Blagdon. "Wilihem, with me."

All eyes looked from the *Kolotor'ix* to him, but Blagdon stood and nodded. Shadows wrapped around them, and when they parted, they stood in a small reading room with bookshelves and a standing closet in the corner.

The *Kolotor'ix* quickly walked to the closet, opened it to show it was empty, and put his hand into it, whispers filling the air. He stepped back, his gloved hand holding another's hand, as Senka stepped from the closet, blinking in surprise.

Blagdon schooled his expression, trusting himself not to show the relief he felt or the nervousness that took him.

Senka immediately went to her knees, bowing her head. *"Our Kolotor'ix, Hasta'kan'ix ik'san."*

The *Kolotor'ix* took her hand and helped her stand, guiding her to a chair. He then held out his hand, a goblet appearing in it, which he held to Senka, who turned her head to cough, using the motion to take out a small vial and drip a liquid into the goblet as she took it from him.

She glanced at the liquid carefully before drinking.

I approve of her caution, though I doubt we could do anything if the Kolotor'ix poisoned the goblet's contents. Blagdon stood where he had appeared, waiting, his hands crossed in front of his waist.

"Drink and organize your thoughts. Then speak. Carefully." The *Kolotor'ix* sat across from Senka, his mask giving nothing away, leaning slightly toward her like a predator ready to pounce. "You said you have a lead on information I had asked for."

Blagdon now walked to Senka's chair, standing behind her, a hand on the back of it, barely touching her shoulder in a reminder to think before speaking and that he was there; she was protected.

Senka set the goblet down carefully upon the table between her and the *Kolotor'ix*, taking a long breath and letting it out before speaking, her voice a little shaky. "I may have a lead on where the *kreva ik'Kolotor'ix* Liana is."

Blagdon felt the weight of the *Kolotor'ix*'s gaze settle upon his daughter, and he said a silent prayer that whatever Senka spoke would not make things worse.

"Is that so? Do tell me, what do you believe you know?"

"The *balutrae ik'Blagdon* Apollo and I were able to enter Exonesis—"

The *Kolotor'ix* gave a sharp, eager sound.

Senka continued after a moment. "He was made to strip in a cave and thoroughly searched for Sigils. My belongings were searched, and our weapons were peace-bound by an enchanted rope we could not cut."

"Did they search you?" The *Kolotor'ix* asked, his voice soft.

Senka shook her head.

"What happened when they saw his *balutrae* mark, *shira ik'san*?" Blagdon spoke up, curious and concerned yet relieved that they had not made Senka strip and discover her Sigil. *They did not believe a female could be ro'Shadon. That will work in our favor if the Kolotor'ix ever chooses to invade.*

"Apollo told them that we had lived among *ro*'Shadon, and he was marked by one of the Lordsons as a rival, which meant only the Lordson was allowed to kill him in *ro'*Shadon law. They did not seem upset or worried about this information."

"Perhaps they already knew, for human refugees have undoubtedly told them information of the *ro'*Shadon in the past."

Senka nodded and continued. "I could not use my powers nor feel the darkness. We were taken through a tunnel and mining cart system, and when we came through, we were in a large city with open spaces where a temple, palace, and marketplace stood with gardens. We were taken to a room and left for a while before they let us out."

"They let you freely walk around?" The *Kolotor'ix* sounded eager about this new information, his gloved hands hidden by his cloak.

"Drink, *shira ik'san*," Blagdon reminded her, to give her a break and to let her have a moment to choose her words carefully.

Senka took her father's hint and sipped her water before answering. "We walked around the garden and marketplace; it was vibrant with many colors, but hardly anyone was there. One of the vendors said that an important leader of one of the religious orders died. But she did know Apollo's brother's name and said he was there in Exonesis, but at the funeral, days away."

The *Kolotor'ix* nodded. "Dawnwarriors do not fly during their funerals. You believe you have a lead on Liana."

"The vendor we spoke to was a Fyre elf, and among her wares was a scroll with a Mun'ari elf seal that looked newer than most of her other scrolls. She said two religious groups split the dawnwarriors, giving us scrolls of each to learn about since we'd be staying there. When she gave us the scrolls, I stole the Mun'ari's scroll from her back table."

Senka pulled out two scrolls, setting them down on the table. One was already opened with a dragon head seal, and the other was tightly rolled with an unbroken blue Mun'ari seal holding it closed.

The *Kolotor'ix* reached forward, his gloved hand caressing the Mun'ari seal gently. "Where is the third scroll you spoke of?"

"I told Apollo that we had to leave, but he argued. I told him he had to decide between duty as a *balutrae* or duty to his brother when he knew he was safe and could visit him later. He was angry but went to leave a note for his brother with the vendor."

My Lordson may have chosen a good balutrae after all.

"While Apollo was away, I snuck into the nearby *K'hani* temple and left the Order of the Dawn's scroll on their altar. If they are fighting as much as the Fyre elf implied, it may be enough to cause discord among the dawnwarriors and possibly give us an opening into Exonesis."

Blagdon fought not to frown. *I do not see how leaving a scroll would cause discord between the dawnwarriors, but if someone left a scroll of the Light's prayers on the altar of the Temple, it may cause upset among the ro'Shadon.*

Senka took another drink. "I couldn't think of why a Fyre elf would have an unopened Munari scroll, especially when they were enemies during the War of the Turning Leaves. No other Fyre elf has been spotted south of the Shadowgulf Mountains except this one. I believe it is possible that the *kreva ik'Kolotor'ix* Liana, or if not her, someone from her clan, is hidden in the Shadowgulf Mountains."

The *Kolotor'ix* was silent for a long moment.

If it were true that Liana was in the Shadowgulf Mountains this entire time, and we could not get to her, this would not be taken lightly. The volcanic mountains were full of sulfuric air, preventing the *ro'Shadon* from taking it over, who counted it as inhospitable. *If somehow the Mun'ari elves survived there, so close to Nar'Shada, without notice, what other things have been happening that we have no idea of?*

The *Kolotor'ix* finally stood, taking the Mun'ari scroll in his gloved hands. "I will have the *ro'Balvash'ix* look over these scrolls. You have given me what I requested you to deliver and have done well. Go and prepare for your engagement dinner."

Senka bowed her head, her fist on her shoulder, before standing. "As you command, our *Kolotor'ix*."

Blagdon spoke up. "Our *Kolotor'ix*, we need my wife. She has everything Senka needs for the evening. We had not expected her to be here tonight and was supposed to stand in her stead."

The *Kolotor'ix* moved his hand. Shadows wrapped around Senka, and she was gone once more. "She will be back in a turn of the hourglass. I have already informed your *Sri'balvash* wife." He walked out of the room and down the hall toward the dining room, Blagdon following.

What will this mean for the ro'Shadon? Will we invade the Shadowgulf Mountains now? How will we survive its toxic environment? He shook his head to clear it of doubts. *I must not imagine how I would survive in that environment until I survive tonight's.* He stopped at the doorway and steeled himself for the political minefield awaiting him.

RATSBAYNE

He watched the Leigelord throughout the evening, feeling as if he were at a game where he knew none of the rules. He felt overdressed, even though the Dark Army soldiers guarding the room wore fancier red and black armor, making him look plain beside them. *Aren't soldiers supposed to blend in, not stand out?*

"You aren't a soldier; you are now a Lord Commander of Stormriders," Slipstream chided him gently, a touch of pride in her voice. *"I believe you will do a good job."*

If yer the only Windrunner we know of, they will be breeding ya like crazy, and Ah don't like that. How am Ah supposed to train and ride ya if yer pregnant all the time and can't wear a saddle? He sighed, shaking his head, and decided to change the subject. *Ah not seen the squirrel since he left that missive, ya wonder where it be?*

"You probably scared it the last time you saw it," came the mental reply. *"Now stop talking to me and enjoy yourself."*

Ratsbayne sighed, watching three females walking through the crowd, wearing form-fitting gowns with masks adorned with gems and feathers framing their eyes. He followed them with his eyes, his gaze dropping lower as they walked past him, watching the shapely—

"Ahem."

Ratsbayne snapped his eyes back up at Slipstream's annoyance. *Ah was just looking.*

"Mmm-hmm. I can hear your thoughts. I know what you were thinking."

He glanced around the massive room, observing the crowd as he stayed by a wall, out of the way as much as he could. Couples danced on the dance floor while small groups of well-dressed people mingled and laughed. He recognized a few individuals from Stormhold and the Stormlands, but other than that, he knew no one else. He felt out of place, especially wearing armor while everyone else wore fine clothing. *Ah dunno what to do, or where to stand; Ah ain't a guard here, protecting people, but a guest.* At the far end of the room, on a dais, stood a single throne occupied by a dark-masked figure who oversaw it all. A sense of foreboding ran through his body like ice in his veins. *Danger*, his instincts screamed at him, and for once, he was inclined to listen.

"Relax and enjoy yourself, but stop looking at the belvash; those are tricky ones."

A few Lordsons and Leigelords walked past him, stopping to gaze at him, point at his armor, and speak in Shadese. Ratsbayne felt the urge to fidget slightly. *Ah feel like a horse at an auction for everyone to look at.*

Sighing, he headed to a table with rows of goblets filled with refreshments, a *belvash* standing behind it and handing out the drinks to those who stopped by, smiling. She turned to him, her eyes sparkling behind her black leather mask with silver accents. She held out a goblet from the row of drinks before her.

"Would you like a drink?"

"Aye, thank you, lass," Ratsbayne said as he held his hand out for it.

She handed him a small goblet and turned to the next couple, smiling as she passed them drinks.

He walked away from the table to the windows on the long wall, standing with his back to the wall between them. From here, he could see the entire dancefloor and exits. *This is as far away from the crowd as Ah will get.* He sighed and raised the goblet, hoping the apple juice would not be as tart as his last glass in the Stormlands. *Whoever thought making juice out of all green apples was an idiot.*

The scent of a golden wheat ale tickled his nose.

Ratsbayne froze, his body trembling slightly as it recognized what his brain had not: that the liquid in the goblets at the *belvash*'s table was not fruit juice but ale. His lips went dry, and his breathing quickened in anticipation of the feeling of refreshment and warmth that beckoned him to partake. Nothing else mattered, the room around him fading as he stared into the goblet, the liquid trembling in its metal confines, begging to be freed. *Ah be an adult, perfectly capable of stopping mahself. One drink won't hurt.*

He raised the goblet.

"Take your hand from your sword, Sir Siral; you are at a dinner, not a sparring ring." Lady Narisa's voice suddenly came from beside him, making him jump, his hand squeezing the pommel of his sword. The liquid in the goblet held in his other hand sloshed, and he mentally swore, trying to keep it steady.

When did she get here? When did Ah put mah hand on mah sword? Slowly, Ratsbayne released it and breathed a breath that shook slightly.

"Try this one. It will be better to your liking." Lady Narisa said as she held a goblet to him. "Let me have that one." Her quiet voice held no room for argument or debate.

Ratsbayne traded goblets with her carefully.

She took a small sip from the goblet, her eyes watching him. "Very good," she smiled as if commenting on the taste of the ale.
Ratsbayne was quiet, unsure what to say.

Lady Narisa gestured toward the dancefloor. "The dance is harder than it looks, and even after years, one may be unable to master it completely. It is not as simple as breaking a Meridian horse but like riding a *kelvorvik*. It will always be dangerous, threatening to take you under. But one day, you can take all the necessary steps to keep moving forward. Until then, you will stumble frequently. Do not be ashamed of it." She smiled at Ratsbayne. "Do you understand?"

Ratsbayne nodded quietly, his throat tight. He smelled the new goblet's contents before taking a sip, finding it fresh apple juice with a hint of citrus. His body wanted to recoil at the taste, as if it had been craving the wheat ale and balked at being given a poor substitute. He felt tricked, betrayed, and relieved.

"Walk with me," Lady Narisa slipped her arm into his and began walking, giving him no choice but to follow. As they passed a table, she set the goblet of ale upon it without missing a step and led him toward the other side of the room. Smiling, she greeted those who started his way. "Ah, I would stop and speak, but we are looking for *Hasta'k*—there he is, if you will excuse us," the *Sri'balvash* said, pretending to see someone in the crowd, keeping them moving.

Ratsbayne frowned, looking at Leigelord Blagdon, who gave a raised eyebrow as they walked past him. "Mi'lady, your lord husband is back there."

"I am aware. The non-alcoholic table is over there, ahead of you. Remain on this side of the room." Lady Narisa turned and walked to her husband, speaking low.

Blagdon nodded at Ratsbayne before slipping his arm around his wife and walking into the crowd with her.

"I am proud of you," Slipstream spoke up softly.

Ah dun't know how Ah feel right now. Ah want to both cry in relief and scream in agony. Why did she stop meh? How did she know?

He felt her at a loss for words, but her care for him came through their bond like a warm blanket he wanted to wrap around him tightly.

"You are not alone, not anymore."

* * *

Ratsbayne stayed near the wall on the safer side of the room, occasionally answering questions from the Leigelords who stopped to look at him. It was slightly annoying that they would speak about him, not to him as if he were a set of armor in Stormhold's display case.

Leigelord Remhold walked to him, looking him over with narrowed eyes as he stepped closer to Ratsbayne. "You are not fit to be in any armor, not even in the armor of those we slaughtered all those years ago. You are useless, a drunkard, and you will remain that and only that."

He kept talking, but Ratsbayne ignored him, his eyes watching a Lordson talking with Lady Mari'aida. He was larger than most of the other Shadon and wore black and yellow, like the orc seen towering over the other Shadon in the room. He glanced at the orc, who had a quiet, almost fearful female human at his side, then the Lordson. *They must be kin.* Mari'aida was laughing, but Ratsbayne could tell it was to be polite, not that something humorous had been said.

Ignoring the still-talking Leigelord, Ratsbayne began moving along the outskirts of the room, trying to get closer enough to hear what was being said.

"Please excuse me, Lordson Rigus. I should also talk to some others in the room," Mari'aida said, turning to walk away from the Lordson, who grabbed her arm.

"But I am not done talking with you. Perhaps you'd like to come to Kravast where we can play a game," the Lordson laughed at his joke as he leaned in toward her, dropping his voice. "After all, I've heard elves are quicker than humans, and I like sport when I hunt."

"He is drunk," Slipstream realized, and Ratsbayne felt her disappointment.

Ah dun't care. Ratsbayne waited for a female in a large gown to move past before he walked forward.

Mari'aida was speaking softly, trying not to make a scene, but Ratsbayne's eyes were watching her lips, trying to decipher what was being said.

"Unhand me; I have others who wish to speak to me."

"I demand an audience with you." The Lordson looked her up and down, stepping into her to whisper in her ear before he licked it from lobe to point.

Mari'aida gasped and slapped him as he straightened, making those around her glance. Her voice wasn't as soft now. "Don't *ever* touch me again."

The Lordson glared at her but then laughed when he saw others staring. "Now I see why your kind lost your war; you can't even take a joke. Get away from me, knife-ear," he said, shoving Mari'aida roughly.

She stumbled backward, her heel catching on the hem of her gown, and she fell to the floor, her blonde hair and wine spilling around her.

It was dark; the only light sources were the lightstones set in the wall at equal distances, illuminating the hallway dimly, just enough for him to find his way. His armored footfalls echoed slightly as he knelt, touching the body at the bottom of the ladder. The human's skin was pale, the eyes long empty of light. The man's white and black hair was unadorned with the crown that usually sat upon it, and it took him a moment to realize that what he thought was a cloak on the ground around the male was, in fact, blood. He touched it with a gauntlet, finding it tacky to the touch.

Someone had slain the king hours ago.

He stood, moving down the hall carefully but quickly, his shield on his arm. There's not enough room to draw my longsword here, he realized and drew his dagger instead. He tried not to think of what had transpired, what could have happened, or who could have done such a thing to a man who had taught him so much.

Keep moving, he told himself, and find the queen and princesses before it is too late. Worry about yourself later.

"It is quiet outside, but still hurry, Siral," Slipstream said in his mind, sounding slightly worried.

He did not blame her; if she were injured, he'd also be hurt, and vice-versa. Bonded forever as rider and mount, they would share each other's thoughts, stamina, and lifespan. They'd live longer than the unbonded counterparts of their species, but a life-threatening injury was still a concern.

"Slipstream, stay hidden as best as possible until I can call for you."

"Of course," came her reply, but they knew they wouldn't be able to get

to each other quickly if something happened.

A figure lay on the ground up ahead, long blonde hair obscuring her face.

Siral quickly started to get to her when black and red armored figures stepped from the shadows, followed by more behind him, blocking his path forward and any retreat he had planned.

He didn't stop moving forward as he adjusted his shield's straps on his arm, then slammed its edge into the throat of the first figure, catching him off guard. A hand grabbed his shoulder, and Siral turned, stabbing with the dagger in the opposite hand, hitting flesh between leather pieces. He fought, with more adversaries coming into the area via shadows, preventing him from reaching his goal. His mind focused on one goal: getting to the one lying on the ground, no matter the cost.

Either the enemies fled or were rendered a non-threat; he wasn't sure which in the rush of battle, but he stepped over a groaning body as he made his way to the form on the ground. He fell to a knee and transferred his dagger to his shield hand, not wanting to sheathe it while bloodied.

He reached out, turning her gently to face him, and moved aside strands of hair from her face to see it better. Blood splatter was dark against her pale skin; her throat slit from one side to the other, the light blue gown stained purple with blood. Her eyes, which once sparkled like the sunlight on the lake outside, were dim and void of laughter and joy. Her face held a look of shock, no, horror, instead of the regalness of a woman who knew how to remain calm in a crisis. This wasn't the look of the war-general, the wife and mother he knew she was. She'd been frightened, and it tore at his heart that he wasn't there to protect her, to keep her safe as he always swore he would.

He ran the back of his hand over her cheek, watching those red lips that would never say his name again, never smile as she watched him training and make his heart race, even if she never knew it.

He cradled her to his armored chest, his shield between her and whoever dared take her away. No words, no tears came to him, his body shaking with grief and anger as he clung to her.

After so long in silence, he took a cloth and wiped his dagger, sheathing it before standing with her body in both arms. If someone attacked him now, he would have no way to defend himself.

Let them come.

He blinked as he heard something clatter to the ground and glanced to see it was her beautiful silver crown, with dozens of crystals that twinkled in the dim light. He tried but could not retrieve it, unwilling to set down the beloved queen to retrieve her symbol of power. Slowly, he straightened, carrying his fallen queen down the dark hall.

"She died quickly," Slipstream said helplessly, keeping her emotions from her rider.

Perhaps she'd meant it as a comfort, but it was instead a reminder that he'd failed. He was a Stormrider, assigned as a Queensguard, tasked with protecting the queen and the princesses.

He'd failed.

He failed his duty, his kingdom. He failed to protect that which was most important.

He failed to protect the woman he loved.

"I failed."

The shattering of glass echoed the sound of the crown falling to the floor in his mind, and a female voice urgently cut through it.

"Sir Siral, Slipstream! *Ai luri cala'on!*"

He came to himself with the elven maiden in his arms, held behind his shield protectively. Glass lay shattered around them, and Slipstream circled them, ears forward, daring anyone to get closer to her rider or the elf. He looked down to see green eyes looking back at him, not the blue his queen had, but with the same shape, the same pale skin, and pointed ears adorned with golden jewelry.

She repeated the words, slower this time, less frantic. "*Ai luri cala'on*, Sir Siral."

It's not Queen Mari'anath, he realized, but still, the protectiveness gripped him, and he looked from her to the orc Lordson, who was shoving at armored guards who were trying to help him stand, his leg crumpled under him, blood down his face and tunic.

"I'll kill you!" he was shouting, pointing at Siral with furious motions as he started to get free.

Other soldiers were groaning on the floor, one of them holding their throat.

The guests stayed back, their faces holding mixed emotions but mostly curiosity.

Not what Ah'd expect from watching a fight.

Siral clicked his tongue once, and Slipstream went to him, turning so he could put Lady Mari'aida onto her bare back. He stepped away from his mount, drawing his longsword and standing protectively between them and everyone else in the room. *No one will get to them without going through meh.*

"I'll see her to safety." Slipstream turned and headed out the balcony, moving quickly through the air as if she were running on the ground below.

"I say again, the first Shadon to use shadows against him forfeits their *Hasta'kan's* claim to my daughter's hand," Blagdon's voice came from every shadow in the room as he stepped forward within Siral's sight but wisely out of reach. His rapier was still sheathed, hands folded in front of him.

"He attacked my Lordson!" A second, more furious voice came from the crowd somewhere to their left.

Siral didn't care to see the orc who spoke, still watching the Lordson, who was using a soldier's arm to stay upright.

"If you wish to challenge him without using shadows, be my guest," Blagdon replied, "after all, he fought without a weapon."

"How dare you allow this man to attack my Lordson and deny us the means to protect ourselves!"

"I never said not to defend yourself. I said no use of shadows unless you wish to forfeit your claim for Lady Shadon Senka *ik'Blagdon*'s hand. It is not my fault you cannot see beyond shadow-usage as a means to protect oneself."

The larger orc shoved his way out of the crowd and pointed at Siral. "I demand that man's head!"

"I've already told you how you may attempt to retrieve it."

"How dare you—"

Narisa stepped forward with a smile that didn't reach her eyes, a dagger in her hand hidden by the folds of her gown. "Lady Mari'aida is the claimed daughter of our *Kolotor'ix*, my husband's *balutrae*, and the betrothed of my Lordson. We will not stand to have anyone insult her, and honestly, neither should any of you." She looked around the room accusingly.

"A human stepped in before you; you are growing slow in your old age, Wilihem," Liegelord Remhold said, his voice full of contempt.

"*Hon-Hasta'kan ik'Blagdon* did not fail to move; he chose not to, for he knew he had it covered," the masked man spoke as he pushed off the throne, standing.

Many in the room fell to their knees, a fist on their chests.

Siral remained where he was, watching the offending Lordson, who glanced around and went to a knee slowly, pain on his face.

Good. Ah hope it hurts.

Shadows pushed Siral to a knee, and he saw Leigelord Blagdon looking flatly at him. He turned so everyone could see the bruise-colored marking of a mask on the side of his neck.

After a moment, Siral blinked, his thoughts drifting, and he realized he had missed most of the conversation.

Leigelord Blagdon was glaring at Leigelord Remhold, pointing at Siral. "That *human* is the Lord Commander of the future arial *ro'Shadon* cavalry, starting with the windrunner-and-*kolvorkav*-born colt, my

Lordson's mount." He stopped, looking at the room around them. "My people are loyal and will die before anyone harms those who are under our protection. *Hasta'kan ik'Blagdon* protects Lord Commander Siral Karog, his mount Slipstream, and her colt. Challenge us at your peril."

Korrat'ix Nicholnor stepped up, his uniform unmistakable among the gowns and tunics of the civilian lords and ladies. "*Hasta'kan ik'Nicholnor* defends the Lord Commander Siral Karog and his mount as well."

Another Leigelord stepped forward, nodding to Leigelord Blagdon. "As does *Hasta'kan ik'Carriat*."

Lady Narisa carefully stepped to Siral, giving him a small nod and speaking softly. "You may lower your longsword; the danger has passed."

Siral did so carefully.

"We are safe among the hired hands in the stables, my rider. Lady Mari'aida is shaken, and my colt is beside me. Gideon and I will not allow anyone to come to them in harm."

Good, ya keep it that way. Did any glass cut ya? He felt bad that he couldn't remember if he saw her bleeding or not when she came to him.

"Not that I know of, but you may check me after this dinner."

The *Kolotor'ix* pointed at the orc Leigelord and his Lordson, who held a cloth to his broken nose. "You've forfeited your claim to Lady Shadon *ik'Blagdon*'s hand. Leave at once."

"You cannot—" the Lordson began, and shadows went over his mouth.

"Our *Kolotor'ix* has spoken. I suggest you leave now," a Leigelord spoke up, putting down the wine goblet to rest his hand on his shortsword.

A few of the Leigelords began quietly putting their hands on weaponry.

"This is not over, human," the orc Leigelord said as he glared at

Siral.

Siral thought about staying silent, but hells, he couldn't. "O' course not. But for tonight, it be. Ya be free to leave on yer own accord, or would ya care for assistance?"

"*Krushku*," the Lordson snapped, spitting on the floor before storming toward the doors. The others moved quickly out of their way to let them pass.

BLAGDON

The room was silent, and once Blagdon was sure he could take his eyes off Siral, he looked through the shadows for other injuries. Three soldiers were slowly gathering themselves off the floor, having tried stopping Siral and failing.

I wonder if he even noticed them.

Narisa moved her hand, the blood from clothing and on surfaces flowing into a bowl she'd taken from the table. "Well, that was entertaining; nothing is better than a dinner and a show. With your permission, our *Kolotor'ix*, shall we return to tonight's arranged festivities?"

He gave a silent nod, and the *belvash* in the corner began playing their instruments again, helping lower the tension in the room. The *Kolotor'ix* sat back on the throne and moved his hand, shadows sweeping away the shards of glass across the floor until it was clean again.

The other guests began making their way to the dancefloor, though Blagdon could see those standing on the outskirts whispering to each other, some glancing over at them. He took a moment to glance around the room, taking in who was speaking with whom and watching for possible future alliances or troubles.

The side doors opened and closed quickly as Siral quickly walked out.

This is proving to be an interesting evening indeed.

We protect the land of Meridiah,
but we follow the leader's orders.
Until such a time the leader is deemed unworthy of such
and is taking the kingdom to ruin.
Then, we defend Meridiah and her people.
The people first,
Meridiah always.

— Sir Barriston, Stormrider Commander

SIRAL

Air. Ah need air.

He didn't remember making it down the hallways, but as soon as he rushed down the steps outside, he grabbed onto the railing for support, gasping for air as if he'd been suffocated. His entire body trembled under his armor, making his breath shake slightly.

"Breathe, Siral, or you will pass out," Slipstream gently spoke in his mind.

Ah remember. Light above, Ah remember it as if it be yesterday: finding King Byron, fighting those who were there in the tunnels— were they of the Dark Army, or were they others who betrayed us? Ah didn't notice their armor at the time, Ah'm not sure Ah remember it clearly enough to know. The Queen… our beloved Queen Mari'anath…

"Siral?"

He spun, drawing his longsword, ready to defend himself.

Gideon slowly walked up the stairs, arms out to show he was unarmed, his voice softer, as if talking to a spooked horse.

That may not be a bad analogy.

"Lady Mari'aida told me what happened in there," he said, gesturing toward the castle, "she asked me to check on you."

"If Ah be in trouble, she'd be breaking in the window to get mah."

"I heard she did that already." Gideon lowered his arms. "I checked her over; she's got minor cuts but nothing serious. You may want to tell her that horses aren't meant to go through windows."

"She ain't a horse. Slipstream be a windrunner."

Gideon nodded, taking out a waterskin and handing it over to Siral, who took a long drink after sheathing his sword. "Come, let's get you away from the castle and to the stables so you can walk off the adrenaline."

Siral nodded, glancing back at the castle, and walked with Gideon silently, looking around. The black walls were filled with spikes and sharp edges, unlike the smooth-flowing structure of the palace in Meridiah. *It's like the palace here be part of the mountains or jagged chunks of obsidian.*

Patrols on *kelvorvik*-back rode through the stone and ash street, banners of red and black held high. The sight of them now made Siral's stomach clench.

This be the land of the people who killed everyone Ah cared about, and Ah now beginning to understand Apollo's point of view.

He suddenly remembered the missive the squirrel had brought and left on his slingbed. *'He who took everything will be there— you cannot move against him, or you will lose again.' Who was it that the missive spoke of? There was every Leigelord there; who was the one who orchestrated the attack on the Byronian royal family? Was it their leader? Who was writing these missives, and what did they know?*

"You know," Gideon said, breaking his train of thought, "now that they know you are a Stormrider and what you are capable of, they aren't going to let you not swear fealty to the *Kolotor'ix*," Gideon opened the barn door, letting Siral walk in first. "Not that you had a choice to begin with."

Siral ignored him, looking to Lady Mari'aida, who nodded from where she stood, brushing the colt. "Are ya all right, m'lady?"

"I'm safe now, Lord Commander, thanks to you."

Siral blinked, not used to the term being used with his name. *Ah still ain't even used to Sir before mah name; now Ah got a new title, one Ah dun't deserve just because Ah be the only Stormrider alive.*

Slipstream snorted at him as Siral checked on her, taking off his gauntlets to run his hands over her coat, feeling for stray pieces of glass that Gideon may have missed.

If she has any glass on her and be ridden, or her colt suckles from her and ingests it, it can be fatal. Ah be responsible not only for her, but also for our colt. Once he'd removed a few slivers from her coat, he picked up a brush to go through her mane and tail.

Slipstream waited patiently, and once he was done, she turned and pressed her forehead against him.

Siral closed his eyes, resting his head against hers. He could feel his heartbeat slowing, and his breathing began to match Slipstream's. *Being with her feels safe, whole, like home.*

"I thought you didn't know how to fight that well," Gideon said, breaking the moment between rider and mount.

Slipstream snorted and began eating hay beside her colt, more relaxed now that he was there and safe.

"From what Lady Mari'aida says, you beat up several well-trained Dark Army palace guards and Lordson *ik'Blackmont* with no issues. If it weren't for her saying it, I'd think someone was spreading tall tales about you because you don't fight like that from what I'd heard."

Ah didn't think Ah did either, at least, not that well, Siral admitted silently. "Ah guess it be a good thing ya not bet on mah, huh?"

Mari'aida smiled a small smile. "I saw little, but from what I had heard, I am glad it was in my defense. I am quite sure that *ro'*Shadon will be thinking twice before ever harming me."

"Lordson *ik'Blackmont* should have known better than to touch you at all. You're the claimed daughter of the *Kolotor'ix*. He's lucky he didn't kill him outright."

"I am also the ward *ik'Hasta'kan ik'Blagdon*. Either one is within their rights to ask for a duel or even the Lordson *ik'Blackmont*'s hand as punishment. Though rarely done, he could even ask for the Lordson's life."

Siral blinked at her. "Why would that be rare? Ya would think it would force the Leigelords to teach their Lordsons to obey the laws. After all, Leigelord Blagdon killed Lordson Kerrik-*kyr*."

"The Lordson challenged *Hasta'kan'ix ik'Blagdon* to a duel and lost. Because he was in charge of Cetra and died, Cetra fell to *Hasta'kan ik'Blagdon* since they could hold that territory. Duels are different from outright fighting or assassinations."

Siral shrugged. "Can an assassin challenge someone to a duel and make it look like the target is legitimately killed so the assassination is hidden?"

Gideon raised an eyebrow in surprise but nodded. "It's been known to have happened."

Siral shrugged, glancing out the window at the palace. "There still be time."

* * *

"Are ya all right, m'lady?" Siral finally asked, once Gideon had left to continue his chores and check to ensure that the orc Leigelord and Lordson had indeed left the area. He pulled himself onto a haybale to sit, his legs shaking now that the danger had passed.

"I am," Mari'aida said, petting Slipstream, who was watching him closely, "that was quite a display, even by *ro'*Shadon standards."

"Ah be surprised no one stopped meh," Siral admitted.

"They tried."

"Oh." *Ah dun't remember anything.*

"You wear the emblem of *Hasta'kan ik'Blagdon* upon your armor; to touch you with intent to harm you is courting death." She was quiet for a moment. "That, and you frightened us."

He cringed inwardly and started to reach for and comfort her but stepped back. He didn't want someone to get the wrong impression. "Ah never would harm ya, M'lady, know that."

"I believe you."

"That *krushku* never shoulda talked to ya that way. Or touched ya. No one should, ever."

She nodded quietly. "Lordson Mykel will be pleased with how you stood up for me tonight."

"Ah didn't do it fer him," Siral said as he walked to Mari'aida, looking her over for injuries. Her hair had fallen out of its updo, leaving it loose around her shoulders and back, but she looked unharmed.

Siral was quiet, looking out the window before looking at her. "Ah be turning down the position of Lord Commander. Ah cannot follow Leigelord Blagdon while another path calls fer meh."

Before Mari'aida could react, he took her hand and went to a knee.

"We, Siral Karog and Slipstream, bonded rider and mount, swear upon the Light to follow ya, Lady Mari'aida, to defend Meridiah and her people from all threats until the time o' our deaths. May the Light guide ya and keep ya upon the Lighted Path for all of yer days."

Siral looked up at her, a tear running down his cheek. "We be yers to command."

How cruel the world is

to continue

when your own has

stopped.

— Kil'lik'Lenaka

LENAKA

"Kil'lik'Lenaka?"

Lenaka moved her eyes slowly, lying on a blanket on the ground. Koani had kept everyone from going to her, but she heard the whispering and the looks from the dawnwarriors, some with pity and others with satisfaction. She hadn't moved from where Koani had carried her, further from both the pyre and Draven's body as the *Rhani* had walked over to find out what had happened, *lokoni'lo* taking up posts to ensure no one defiled the fallen bard.

"Kil'lik'Lenaka?" Clep asked again, and she blinked numbly at him, seeing he held Draven's dagger and had been writing on parchment with the enchanted quill. "You should drink something." He held out a wooden cup.

Lenaka sat up, took it slowly, and sipped, finding tea in it. She held it close, looking at the dawnwarriors talking amongst themselves, some working at creating another pyre. There were not as many trees here, and the group had only planned for one pyre to be built for the funeral, not two. *Finding wood will be difficult unless someone goes back to find some.* "One of them did this," she said, her hoarse voice almost monotone, as if it was as numb as the rest of her.

"One of them did what?"

"One of the dawnwarriors stabbed *Putri*, but I couldn't tell who. He wouldn't have died if he hadn't been stabbed. One of them killed him, and I don't know who!" Her voice finally warmed with anger; no, not anger, something deeper and more primal. She watched some dawnwarriors who sat off to the side, speaking with *O'anu'toki* Paku.

Was it one of you?

Lenaka looked at the *hela'ko*, who had demanded that she pay in suns instead of skyshards in the *helaono*.

Was it you who stabbed Putri?

A part of her wanted to stand up and shout for the one who did the deed to step forward so she didn't live the rest of her life wondering if anyone who smiled at her was the one who took away her only family.

Clep took the cup and held her hands, shaking them. "Look at me, please," he pleaded.

She turned her eyes to him, tears hot and painfully sliding down her cheeks.

"Apollo was full of rage after what happened in Andears. I lost him to it. Please don't make us lose you too. Mako'Koani and Kil'lik'Draven wouldn't want that. Your *pari'lo* wouldn't have wanted that."

*Rhan'*Ashana walked over, kneeling beside them, her *lokoni'lo* standing to the side, watching.

Lenaka could not help the little voice in her head from speaking, hissing suspicion into her mind. *Was it one of you?*

The *Rhan* held out Draven's silver dragon pendant and *O'anu'tale* Kiko's dragonclaw pendant. "I thought you would want these," she said softly.

"I want my *putri* back, not necklaces." Lenaka snapped.

*Rhan'*Ashana winced, handing them to Clep, who silently held his hand out for them. "We cannot do that, but we can bring him peace."

Lenaka stood angrily. "You could have given him peace long ago by listening to him! He died knowing no one believed him, that the people he served as a bard, those he loved with all his heart, thought he was crazy! He told wonderful stories, he was harmless, and *someone* out there—" she gestured angrily at the others "— killed him! If you want him to have peace, find his murderer." She walked off, away from those gathered, from those who betrayed her. Until she knew who had done it, she'd never be able to trust any of them again.

She was left alone as others worked to create Draven's pyre over the ashes of *O'anu'tale* Kiko's, with only Clep coming over to check on her with another cup of tea and her bag of a few belongings she'd taken with her.

He set Memory's cage down beside her. "Keep an eye on her, please," he asked before walking off again, leaving Lenaka wondering if Clep had been talking to her or the hawk.

She glanced at the parchments that Clep had left beside her things and picked one up, looking it over to see her *putri*'s handwriting, a recording of the argument they'd heard before he'd been killed. *Should I continue writing it so everyone knows that one of the dawnwarriors murdered the greatest bard we'd ever known?* She picked up his enchanted quill and began writing. *I'll take these to Putri's study to keep until the time is right to release them to the public. It is what he would have wanted.*

She glanced at the sky for a long time, wondering where her *putri* would be after his spirit joined *K'han'Exonia*'s left eye.

"Lenaka? We're ready."

Lenaka blinked, looking at Koani, who had tear streaks on his cheeks.

Draven's body had been moved from where he died, and a small pyre was built on a boulder instead of the ground to keep it higher than everyone else. His form lay covered by his blanket upon the top, and his wings outstretched as if ready to fly to the heavens to join his ancestors.

Koani held his hand out for her, taking it gently and walking her to where *O'anu'toki'lo* Aluu and Paku stood; they looked at her expectantly, eager to see which she chose to perform the final ceremony.

Rhan'Kahan gently touched her shoulder as if he were in deeper mourning than he'd let anyone see. "We have had dinner with him earlier, but do you wish another last supper or drink?"

Lenaka's throat tightened so much she was afraid she wouldn't be able to breathe, and she shook her head rapidly, tears threatening her eyes once more. *How can I do this? How do I go forward?*

"Would you wish me to speak in your stead?"

Lenaka's voice squeezed out of her throat as the tears slipped down her cheeks. "Please."

"I would be honored." He hugged her gently, a hand running over her hair as if he were soothing his own daughter's fears and sorrow. "If you need anything, you just let me know. You need not to do this alone."

* * *

Lenaka sat beside a boulder, keeping it between the others and her so she could mourn in peace without being looked upon. *Someone watching here tonight killed him and is pretending to be sad that he's dead when in reality, they are laughing at my tears, joyful that he is gone from this world.* She watched *Rhan'*Kahan speak to the crowd as if she were in a dream. She felt odd, all of her numb and unfeeling, the tears steadily falling down her cheeks. *I'll have to have another tattooed dot for putri under my eye,* she realized absently, though trusting someone to do it would take a while.

*Rhan'*Kahan lowered a torch onto the pyre, both *O'anu'toki'lo* watching, one with reverence, the other with disgust. The flames caught and began to hide Draven's body from view as the embers floated higher and higher into the night sky until they faded from view among the stars. *Which stars will be his? Will he be with my pari'lo, his family?*

*Rhan'*Ashana went to her, helping her stand as the dawnwarriors began their dance, retelling the story of life to death through fluid motions of their bodies, moving as one. As she followed the dance, Lenaka felt she was merely going through the movements instead of feeling the emotions it invoked. She stumbled and trembled so hard that she couldn't continue the dance. *Is there something wrong with me? Why do I feel so numb when I should be feeling more than anyone else?*

*Rhan'*Ashana gently helped her to sit on the ground and held her hand as the voices of the dawnwarriors began singing, united.

Ikanu noko'alo

nela kōnu

Un'nui'lo noko'alo

aila i ukanu noko'alo

Nopu hepa

paikanu

wan'na'a

nuikanu

As their song ended, Lenaka looked at the pyre, seeing its remains still burning and rising into the sky. She slowly moved her right hand and held it horizontally to the ground, her left hand making a fist and resting upon its back, opposite of bowing to the *Rhani*, signifying the sun's setting, the ending of a life.

Tears fell onto her hands as she bowed low, her braided hair falling like a veil around her face.

"Goodbye, *Putri*, I love you."

* * *

She turned, slipping away toward the mountains, using the darkness to conceal her while everyone was asleep. The funeral pyre had died down, with embers still glowing in the darkness, guards watching it to ensure none blew onto those who slept on bedrolls and blankets. Lenaka quietly headed away from the group, Draven's satchel over her shoulder. *Putri had said to go south. I'll honor his final wish and meet the white dragon he asked me to write about; after that, I do not care what happens.*

She stopped, glancing around before slipping into one of the many tombs and taking out her dawnstone pendant, using it to light the way as she carefully walked down the tunnels and past the sealed stone doors of tombs. Inside one with a broken stone seal, she continued around the sarcophagi of dawnwarriors long past, the dust thick enough to make her cough, making her wish she had a cloth to tie over her mouth and nose. The hallway gave way to many rooms dedicated to families linked together by blood. Each room held the entombed bodies of the dawnwarriors, as well as their most precious belongings. Now that the bodies had been burned instead of buried, fewer rooms were being dug and used, with urns being created out of clay and belongings being passed down to members of the family. *I wish I had some of putri's parchments with me; I know one of them had the location of a tunnel hidden here.* She headed deeper, her breathing the only sound for hours.

As she entered a room with a statue of a dawnwarrior holding a quill, she fell to her knees, sobbing, the sounds of grief echoing in the stone room. *Why were the K'hani so cruel that they could not protect the one voice among so many who sang their praises and fought to tell the stories of what had happened to their homes? To their own families and kin? Was the Order of the Dawn correct, and they no longer live, and this was proof that they could not protect them anymore?*

She clutched the pendants around her neck. *No, I must have faith; if I can do anything for putri now, it is to have faith.*

After a long time, she finally willed herself to stand again.

Draven had once told her a story of a dawnwarrior maiden who had fallen in love with a human, and they used secret tunnels to meet each other. She had thought it was romantic then but a silly tale. Now, Lenaka clung to the hope that there was a bit of truth to the story and searched the carved stone names for the tomb of the girl's family. *They were supposed to be buried in this part of the Valley.*

Finally finding it, Lenaka stepped into the room, careful not to stir up any more dust than she had, for inches of the stuff coated everything. She began moving things carefully, trying to find anything that could indicate a tunnel, but she did not see anything but spiders and more dust.

Lenaka sighed heavily, stepping back to look around the room in the limited light of the necklace. Armor stood on stands, and fabric bolts lay covered in dust on shelves. There were decorations on the wall, covered in spider webs, and two sarcophagi, one with a male carved onto it, the other with a female. *The girl and her brother.* She had a horrible idea, and before she could talk herself out of it, she walked to the sarcophagus and pushed the lid with all her might. The heavy stone slid aside a few inches, and Lenaka put her lightstone necklace inside it, leaning in, hoping to see a secret tunnel.

A skeleton looked up at her, arms crossed over its chest, tattered clothing barely clinging to its frame. Lenaka stumbled backward in horror and hit an armor stand with *kahena* armor. The armor fell and clattered loudly in the small room.

A hand clamped around her mouth and stifled her scream.

"Shh! Do you want to wake the dead?" Koani's voice hissed in her ear.

Lenaka almost passed out from relief. Once he removed his hand, she rounded on him. "What are you doing here!"

Clep stepped into the room, holding his lightstone in one hand, Memory's cage in the other, his eyes wide as he looked around. "You left! What are you thinking?"

Lenaka stumbled on her words, unsure how to explain the situation.

"We need to go south," Clep said with a certainty that didn't match his slightly scared expression.

If I were in my right mind, I would be afraid, too.

Koani looked between them as if they shared a secret he knew nothing about. "Why are we going south?"

"*Putri* said I need to go to be there to write down when the white dragon comes to change the world."

"You are a decent bard, Lenaka. You don't need to prove— "

"I was told to go south by the person who has been writing to me in my tome," Clep spoke up, "They said the cure to the Lingering Rot was there. I *have* to go. I owe it to Ma and Pa."

"*Putri*'s stories told of a dawnwarrior and human couple who used to meet in a tunnel in the tombs. This is her family's tomb; I thought we could find the entrance here." She began moving through the room carefully, looking for signs of a tunnel or door.

Koani sighed, beginning to help. He held his lightstone and blew the dust off surfaces to look at the carved rock surfaces for clues.

Lenaka blinked, noticing some spiderwebs in the light were moving, and walked to the wall, feeling it. "There's a draft here," she pondered aloud, searching for an opening with her hands.

Clep went to her, holding the lightstone to help her.

"You're going just to believe something that someone has written, even though you have no idea who it is?" Koani asked, his voice letting Lenaka know that he was frowning deeply.

"Yes," Clep and Lenaka said in unison, and they glanced at each other.

"Let me see your dagger. I may be able to pry open this door," she said, holding her hand for it. Clep placed it in her palm, and she began using it to try to fit the blade into the crack in the wall.

"You two are insane."

Lenaka felt the dagger catch something and heard a *click* before the wall slid open, revealing a tunnel that smelled of old air and dust. *There was truth to the tale, after all!*

Coughing, she looked back at Koani. "We are heading south. Are you coming with us or not?"

Koani sighed, ensuring his sword was on his hip, his bag on one shoulder. "I'm going to regret this, aren't I?"

Clep walked into the tunnel a few feet, the lightstone guiding him as he looked around at the walls, the light reflecting off the small veins of dawnsteel embedded in the rock.

Lenaka looked at Koani and picked up a dagger and sword from on top of a shield, whispering apologies to the dead before stepping into the tunnel. *At least I am armed.*

Koani swore and followed quickly. "You do know the stories say the tunnels collapsed, and the lovers died inside it, forever buried, right? Who is to say that these tunnels are not destroyed?"

Behind them, the wall slid shut.

They looked at each other wide-eyed and quickly rushed to it, frantically pushing against the stone door. After several minutes, Koani swore, punching the wall and shaking out his fist, wincing. "We're locked out of Exonesis. There goes the idea of watching the Benstafi elves in the harbor after this." He gave her a flat look and looked away as if not wanting to voice his current thoughts.

It may be best.

The three of them glanced at each other, then at the darkness of the tunnel and the unknown ahead of them. *Don't think about the walls caving around them, the air running out, or the lack of food or water. This was a horrible idea.*

Clep looked at them quietly. "Surely someone will know we're missing and look for us."

"There's so many tombs no one would know where to find us. Shouting for help wouldn't work either; we're too deep underground for our voices to carry."

Lenaka hung her head. "What was I thinking? Now you two are going to die with me, and no one knows where we are to rescue us. I'm so foolish."

"We are in this together, Lenaka. We will find a way. I have faith in us." Clep stepped forward, the lightstone shining in the darkness. "There is only one way to go now."

Together, the three began walking.

Too often the enemies are the ones we do not expect,
the ones in the darkness who lie in wait
for the opportunity to strike.
Too often we think we are ready,
that we know what will happen
and prepare.

Too often we are wrong.

— Nixus Halidesh, Bard of Eteris

BLAGDON

Blagdon stood with *Hasta'kan'ix ik'Carriat*, talking about obtaining more *kelvorkav* for his scouts for the protectorate stations, when Narisa approached him and touched his arm. "If you will excuse me, *Hasta'kan'ix*."

"Of course, Wilihem." Carriat nodded and headed to his Lordson to speak with him.

Blagdon walked with Narisa to the hallway where Senka waited, wearing a blue gown with black lace. If one looked carefully, they'd see *kelvorvik* created in the black threads running along the gown. Her hair was pulled up, and she wore an onyx necklace with matching earrings. As she turned so he could see the entire gown, Blagdon noted that it was backless, letting her Sigil be seen clearly. As she stopped and looked up at him, he found himself at a loss for words.

"She looks beautiful," Narisa spoke up for him, smiling as she moved forward and slipped a dagger into a slit on the side.

Blagdon blinked slowly. "She will not need a dagger in the *Kolotor'ix*'s presence, Narisa."

His wife made a dismissive sound. "We do not go unarmed, and it is a slit she can reach through to get to her thigh hilt."

Of course, it would.

Senka smiled and took her father's arm as he walked her into the ballroom, Narisa opening the doors for them. A few attendees turned to see who had entered, and when they realized who it was, Blagdon watched as *Hesta'kan'ix* whispered to their Lordsons to get their attention. He ignored those who began heading their way, watching as Narisa went to speak with them instead. *She has done more than her share this evening. I will have to get her something to show my appreciation. I wonder if she'd like a vacation home in the foothills of the Ironfall Mountains on the edge of Cetra.*

Leading Senka to the dance floor, he turned to face his daughter and held her right hand, his left hand resting on her hip. *I am her brak'ha, and none will dance with her before I.* As they began dancing, his left hand rested on her hip. He pushed from his mind what the other *Hesta'kan'ix* and their Lordsons were thinking, focusing on his *shira. She is more important than them.*

"You look so much like your mother. I do not tell you often enough."

Senka smiled, blushing slightly. "I miss her."

"You always will." He moved with her to the music, his voice low so only they could hear each other, though he had no idea if any Shadon were listening via shadows. "Lady Narisa has told you what to expect, yes?"

Senka nodded. "After our dance, I walk to the least favored *Hasta'kan*'s Lordson and invite them to dance. Once our dance is over, they leave for the evening, and I move to the next Lordson, and up until our most favorable is the one I am dancing with last."

Blagdon's lip twitched, and he squeezed her hand to stop her eyes from wandering around the room. "Do not look at certain ones too hard already, Senka. I would suggest counting to three and looking to someone else; that way, there is no set way to tell who you will dance with next, though we already know who we would choose as least and most favorable."

"Lady Narisa reminded me who is strongly suggested for the good of the *Hasta'kan* as she did my hair and helped me with my dress."

"She is wise to do so. Remember not to make any promises or give them false hope while you speak to your dancing partners."

Senka nodded. "What happens to those who leave after I choose the next Lordson to dance with?"

"Many will have *belvash* or members of their servants to remain outside and report back who has left, and in what order, to use in negotiations. Let me worry about that, *shira ik'san*."

"What else am I going to do, *Brak'ha*, besides worry about them stepping on my feet?"

Blagdon laughed and allowed himself to enjoy this time with her, dancing to the soft music as they made their way around the dancefloor so that all could view the potential bride from various angles.

Senka made eye contact with those watching now and then, but never too much, mouthing quietly to the count of three for each Lordson she spotted. She spent more time speaking low to him about archery or asking about *Fyr'ix*, as if to keep both of their minds off worrying about the task at hand.

Alyssa-kyr would be so proud of you.

As the music ended, Blagdon felt his heart ache. He wanted to tell the bards to continue playing and let her remain his little girl, safe in his arms, for as long as he could.

Senka reached up, touching his cheek. "It's okay, *Brak'ha*," she whispered.

Blagdon nodded and kissed her forehead before stepping back, slowly letting her go.

Narisa went to his side immediately and handed him a goblet of wine, which he took absently. She slipped her arm in his and leaned over, speaking softly. "She'll be okay, my husband."

I wish I could guarantee that.

Senka waited a moment, looking around at the crowd gathered around the dancefloor, their faces holding different emotions ranging from curiosity to eagerness. It reminded Blagdon of a pack of *kelvorvik* watching a lone calf that walked accidentally into their paddock and now had nowhere to escape.

His daughter walked to Lordson Haskel *ik'Remhold* and bowed at the waist, asking him to dance.

Lady Narisa coughed gently to hide the smirk behind her hand.

Hasta'kan'ix ik'Remhold glared at him across the room, and Blagdon toasted him with his goblet.

Shira ik'san has a good head on her shoulders, and I am Hon-Hasta'kan'ix. We will be fine.

* * *

It felt like hours, watching Senka move across the dancefloor, each time with a different Lordson partner. Narisa remained beside him, her hands folded in front of her. Now and then, Blagdon felt movement and looked to see Narisa playing with a beaded bracelet on her wrist. He took her hand, kissing her knuckles to give him a closer view of the beads, each with decorative markings in raised paint. *What is this? It is not one that I have made for her.*

She pulled a bead, broke the thread holding it, and slipped it into her pocket.

"What, my love, are you keeping track of?" he asked quietly, leaning in as if to kiss her cheek while whispering in her ear.

"Which of the Lordsons have their hands on Senka's Sigil, rather than her hip as they dance."

Blagdon straightened, nodding. He'd also been watching, seeing who valued what power Senka could give them over who she was. He, however, had been committing the list to memory while his wife had the more intelligent idea. *At least we have thought the same and can discuss it later.*

Out of the corner of his eye, he saw Shealbri heading toward him and sighed slightly.

Narisa immediately intercepted the incoming *Hasta'kan'ix* with an almost empty goblet of wine. "*Hasta'kan'ix*, I do not believe I have seen your beautiful lady in a long time. Hello, Lady Karolinda; you are looking stunning this evening. I was about to get something more to drink. Would you escort us to the table, *Hasta'kan'ix*?" She moved with them through the crowd, far from Blagdon's view, talking low.

Shadows and blood bless my wife.

One by one, Senka walked and chose Lordsons to dance with, and one by one, the *Hesta'kan'ix* and their Lordsons left afterward, some looking disappointed, others understanding.

Halidesh watched as Lordson Harkin bowed to Senka and walked to the dancefloor. Smiling, he went to Blagdon and stood beside him, watching. "At least I know where I stand in things," he said as he gestured to the last *Hasta'kan'ix*, who stood across the room speaking with one of the soldiers and nodding quietly. "Your lovely wife has spoken with me about our possible arrangement of the racetrack."

Not this again.

"Why did you not tell me you were working toward a new type of racing mount faster than *kelvorkav*, bred just for racing? I certainly cannot wait to see them, and yes, Lady Narisa has said it is a delicate process, but the fact that you are working toward it certainly makes my blood rush!"

Blagdon had no idea what Narisa had told him but nodded as if he'd planned it. *I will accept if it buys me time to have you stop fluttering about my ears.*

Halidesh laughed, patting his shoulder. "This news and to be the second choice for Lady Shadon Senka's hand, you honor my *Hasta'kan*. If you ever stop by one of my establishments, you will have the best treatment."

"Of course. You are too kind."

Lordson Harkin walked over, bowing his head to Blagdon. "It was a good game. I am honored to have been a player for so long, *Hon-Hasta'kan'ix*."

Blagdon nodded. "You were worthy of it."

Halidesh sighed. "I wish you and your wife a good evening and will take my leave. I hope to talk with you later about these new mounts to purchase." He bowed his head to Blagdon, then turned and saluted the throne before walking out with his Lordson.

Why cannot every Hasta'kan'ix take losing so gracefully?

Lordson Artis Nicholnor smiled as Senka stopped before him, speaking softly before nodding and extending his hand toward her, leading her to the dancefloor. As they danced, they spoke quietly, Senka laughing about something said between them.

At least Artis has his hand on her hip and not her Sigil.

Blagdon went to the beverage table to stretch his legs and get more wine. With the other *Hesta'kan'ix* and Lordsons gone, the room was much quieter now. He let out a long breath and felt someone step beside him.

"It seems we will be family now," Nicholnor spoke up, smiling.

Blagdon took a sip of wine. "As long as my daughter is treated properly, yes."

Nicholnor raised an eyebrow at the implied threat.

Blagdon smiled. "Senka has been trained at the Blood Temple; do you think she would allow herself to be mistreated? Do you think *I* would?"

"You have no worries about that, Wilihem," Nicholnor said, shaking his head. "It would be much different if I were Remhold, and I would not have been here as long as I have."

Blagdon scoffed, shaking his head. "He was the first to leave."

"Technically, it was Blackmont, but I agree with that choice wholeheartedly. He is not right for your daughter or your bloodline. Do not fear for her safety; I will not allow harm to her if I can help it."

Blagdon nodded, looking out the window above the table at the ground below. Retainers and *belvash* waited outside the palace, observing who left and when they could report back to their respective places. A few of the *Hesta'kan'ix* were smart enough to shadow home, so it appeared they were still inside, waiting to dance. This would only throw off the rumors for a bit, for the *belvash* who played tonight would set the records straight.

"I can hear the rumors spreading already," Nicholnor spoke up.

"Those who feel slighted will already find ways to make me pay for Lady Shadon Senka's choice." He closed his eyes to listen to those outside, wondering what was being said, when another voice, closer, darker, caught his attention instead.

"I will take this dance. You can leave."

Blagdon and Nicholnor turned quickly, each settling a hand on their weapons at their hips. Blagdon blinked, not believing his eyes, and looked at Narisa, who stood beside Lady Nicholnor, both women paler. Even the music died out as he looked back at the dancefloor as if the *belvash* playing had faltered in their evening duties.

The *Kolotor'ix* stood beside Senka, his cloak removed, a velvet hood blending into the red and black vest fastened over a black tunic. His masked face looked at the Lordson, who glanced at his father helplessly, wondering what to do.

I am wondering the same thing.

Hasta'kan'ix ik'Nicholnor nodded once, taking his hand from his sword pommel.

His Lordson stepped back from Senka, bowing to the *Kolotor'ix* and leaving the dancefloor to stand with his brothers, who were whispering amongst themselves.

Nicholnor gently set down his drink on the table. "Another night, *Hon-Hasta'kan'ix*," he said simply before saluting the *Kolotor'ix* and walking toward the exit, his Lordsons and wife quickly following him, the doors closing behind them.

The silence left behind was deafening.

The *Kolotor'ix* held out his gloved hand to Senka, who looked to Blagdon as if wondering what to do.

I wish I knew.

Senka slowly put her hand in his, and the *Kolotor'ix* put his other hand on her hip before leading her into a waltz. The *belvash* slowly began playing again, matching the dancers' movements. It was slower and darker than the other dances, but perhaps that was Blagdon projecting.

Narisa walked to Blagdon quickly, as if afraid if he were the first to move, he would head straight for the *Kolotor'ix* and demand a duel. She dropped her voice, having to rise onto her toes to speak into his ear. "The other *belvash* have no idea what is going on."

Blagdon's eyes didn't move from the dancers. "I do not doubt that, beloved."

The two moved fluidly across the dancefloor, the *Kolotor'ix*'s mask looking down upon his partner. As he moved with Senka back toward Blagdon, he spoke, not using shadows to project his voice or be heard over the soft music. The few *belvash* remaining in the room paid close attention to every movement and sound as if they would be tested later. "You are mine, Lady Shadon Senka. I will defend you as long as you reside under my roof."

Blagdon's hand instinctively moved toward his rapier, not to draw it but to find something to grip other than the other man's throat. *Those are the exact words I had spoken when I had taken in Lady Mari'aida as my ward to protect her from his wrath. His attention may be on Senka, but those words were meant for me. I have his shira; now he has mine, but to what end?*

As they turned and danced across the dancefloor, Blagdon was listened to the couple via shadows, for any misunderstanding now would be fatal.

Senka's voice was careful. "Forgive me, our *Kolotor'ix*, I do not understand."

The *Kolotor'ix* spoke softly as he moved her around the empty dance floor. "What part of you are mine, Lady Shadon Senka, is hard to understand?"

"The *ro'*Shadon are yours already; we all belong to you. We are yours to command."

There was a touch of amusement in the voice behind the *Kolotor'ix's* mask. "You have such a silvered tongue, a gift from your *Sesha-kyr* and *Brak'ha.*"

Blagdon's hand tightened on his pommel enough that the leather glove creaked softly.

"Once Liana is returned to me, she will keep the peace in the land and coax the other races back into the fold. Then I will make her the elven queen of Merdiah. I will need a *roje ik'ro'Shadon* here in Nar'Shada to rule beside me, and I choose you."

Narisa was signing frantically with one hand at her side, her other now holding Blagdon's wrist as if to keep him from drawing his rapier. Her grip tightened slightly at the *Kolotor'ix's* words, and she gave him a questioning look.

Blagdon shook his head, at a loss for what to say. The *Kolotor'ix* had never had a queen, and no *kreve ik'Kolotor'ix* had been given ruling authority. Liana had been the closest he'd had to a queen, but she was never his equal. *Was the Kolotor'ix planning on changing how he ruled the ro'Shadon, creating a new position to do so? What would this mean for our future?*

"I am honored, our *Kolotor'ix,* but I would not be a good fit for such a position simply because I am a Lady Shadon. I do not have—"

"Training to lead? Knowing how to fit in with all of the people she rules? You are a bridge to the *ro'*Shadon, *ro'belvash, ro'narshadan,* and the humans."

"I don't belong to any of their worlds, our *Kolotor'ix.*"

The *Kolotor'ix* moved his hand from her hip to touch her face. "I want you, my *roje ik'ro'Shadon.*"

Blagdon's eyes narrowed, and Narisa's grip tightened on his wrist.

"You do not belong to their worlds because you belong to them all. You are meant for more than a single caste could offer. Ever since you have gained your Sigil, you have been apart from the society you were born into. Your destiny has been waiting to join your life to mine and stand with me. To command them, one and all. Our union will create a legacy that will span generations. Our children will become legends."

Blagdon's eyes widened, and he forgot to breathe. *A child of the Kolotor'ix, the result of a union of the most powerful of us and a Lady Shadon. I cannot fault him for doing this, but it does not mean I like it.*

He glanced at Narisa, who was paler, her eyes narrowed as she signed, her movements pointed as she glanced at one of the *belvash* in the room who signed back beside the refreshment table. *She is no doubt asking herself the same things I am: why did we not see this as a possibility? How did we miss something so obvious?*

As the dance finished, the *Kolotor'ix* stepped back and raised her hand to his mask as if kissing her knuckles. Then he gently let her go, turning to Blagdon and Narisa. His mask moved as if he looked at Blagdon's hand on his pommel, then up to his face. "Are you going to duel me over this, my *balutrae*? Did you not want your *shira* to have a match worthy of her heart and womb? Is this small thing where you draw the line?"

Narisa spoke low to Blagdon, her voice urgent as if fearing he'd strike quicker than she could talk. "You have been named *Hon-Hasta'kan'ix*, and we cannot afford to lose you, not with Mykel in charge of a garrison away from Stormhold, and now this. Please, beloved, do not doom what we've worked so hard for."

Blagdon slowly removed his hand from his rapier with effort.

"You mistake my intention; it is not anger you see, merely surprise, our *Kolotor'ix*."

"As I took our engagement into my own hands, it is only fair I allow the Lady Blagdon to arrange the wedding as she desires."

Narisa made a small sound beside her husband.

A wedding. He wants to wed my daughter and have a child, the most potent Shadon in history, with her. He wants to make her his roje ik'ro'Shadon, a new position that will put her in the sights of every ro'Shadon as a potential target. I should be overjoyed, but all I can feel is suspicion. How long has he planned this? Was this his goal when he sent Senka away to Exonesis? Was it a test, and if so, for which of us?

"Our *Kolotor'ix*, are you certain it is me who deserves this honor?" Senka spoke up softly, and Blagdon was torn between chiding her for being self-conscious and proud that she was not so arrogant that she felt she was the only one worthy of this just because of her Sigil.

"Why would I take you, who is singular to all others, and treat you like any other? You will be my *roje ik'ro'Shadon* and our children; I have high hopes for them."

Blagdon put his arm around his wife's waist, forcing his other hand to stay loose at his side. "We have much to prepare. You honor us, our *Kolotor'ix*." The words were more difficult to get out than usual.

The *Kolotor'ix* stepped away from Senka as if permitting Blagdon to go to her now. "An honor well earned."

"You hone my edge and make me strive for greater heights, my *balutrae*."

There was little humor in the *Kolotor'ix*'s voice at that. "I feel the same, Wilihem."

He turned, watching Senka walk to Narisa quickly, the two females grasping hands as they looked back at him. "I look forward to seeing what you plan for this event next year, Lady Narisa. Good evening, Lady Shadon Senka, my *roje ik'ro'Shadon*."

With that, the *Kolotor'ix* shadowed away.

End of Book II